A silencer would do the trick, though he loathed guns. It made killing so impersonal.

That was for later.

First, Rowan needed to be broken. He wanted her to melt, to burn. He needed her emotion, her temper. Mostly, he wanted her fear. Then—only then—would he confront her.

Until that time, he had many things to do. He'd marked the chosen for death. Nothing could now alter their fate. He was a god; fate would run its course. Then he and Rowan would meet again. She would know him and know fear.

And beg for her life before she died.

Allison BRENNAN

THE PREY

A Novel

BALLANTINE BOOKS • NEW YORK

Copyright © 2006 by Allison Brennan

Excerpt from *The Hunt* copyright © 2006 by Allison Brennan

Published in the United States by Ballantine Books, an imprint of The Random House Publishing Group, a division of Random House, Inc., New York.

BALLANTINE and colophon are registered trademarks of Random House, Inc.

This book contains an excerpt from the forthcoming mass market edition of *The Hunt* by Allison Brennan. This excerpt has been set for this edition only and may not reflect the final content of the forthcoming edition.

ISBN 0-7394-6227-X

Cover illustration and design: Tony Greco & Associates

Printed in the United States of America

To my mom
You always had faith in me

ACKNOWLEDGMENTS

I never really understood all that went into producing a book. I thought a writer wrote it, an editor edited it, and a publisher published it. There are multiple editors, copyeditors, cover designers, marketing professionals—dozens of hard-working people who all deserve to be acknowledged for their fine work.

Everyone who had a hand in producing this book at Ballantine, thank you for making this process as easy as possible. Especially, Gina Centrello and Linda Marrow for being so enthusiastic; Charlotte Herscher for encouraging me to dig deeper; and Dana Isaacson for great advice on villains.

Wally Lind and Rick Litts from crimescenewriters were invaluable, sharing their experience, expertise, and time, especially about the prison system. If I've made any technical errors, it was certainly not because of them.

Trisha, you believed in me from the very beginning. Thank you for being a true friend.

Jan, Sharon and Amy, thanks for being my first readers—I'd never have finished this book without you.

Karin, Edie, Barbara, Michelle, Kathia & Michele for your constant support and encouragement.

I'd never have realized my dream without my fabulous agent Kimberly Whalen, who really worked above and beyond the call to make everything come together . . . thank you for taking a chance on me.

And of course my husband, Dan, and our kids need to be acknowledged for putting up with my late-night writing binges, quickie dinners, and messy house. You are my motivation. I love you.

PROLOGUE

He studied her from afar. Objectively, as a scientist might contemplate an interesting germ. Even at this distance, she was a beautiful woman.

Long blonde hair pulled tightly back in a braid; aristocratic profile; small, sharp point for her nose. Her facial bones might be considered regal, though he thought them too angular. Her athletic body lean, quietly muscular. No one feature was soft.

Except her eyes.

They were covered behind dark John Lennon glasses, but he remembered they were the color of the sea, the blue-gray hue of the Atlantic Ocean on a clear day. Yes, her eyes were soft because they showed emotion, so she kept them hidden behind those hideous glasses. She wanted to be as hard as she appeared, but inside she was soft. Weak. Female.

He'd see those eyes again one last time in the moments before he killed her. They would fill with fear; she would know the truth. Heart pounding hard in his chest, he now heard the blood rush to his head. Yes, when she knew the truth, he would be set free. He smiled.

She thought he couldn't touch her. Did she even think about him anymore? He didn't know. But before the game played out, she would be thinking of him, fearing him, feeling his vengeance.

Killing her wasn't the beginning, and it certainly wouldn't be the end. Many others deserved to die.

But her death would be the most satisfying.

Watching her, he noticed her hesitate as she opened the door of her black Mercedes coupe and looked around. His heart skipped a beat in excitement. Did she feel him? She couldn't see him, and even if she did, would she remember? His was an average face, the face of anybody. She knew madness, but he wasn't mad. She knew terror, but he wasn't terrifying. Not now. He skillfully concealed his excitement, his anger, his rage.

It was so much fun playing with her! A final look around; she stared right at him but couldn't see him. She must have sensed something, though, because she quickly slid into her sporty car and started the ignition. Heart pounding, fists clenched, he envisioned seizing that long, slender neck and snapping it in two.

No, I won't break her neck. Too easy, too fast.

Instead, I'll squeeze it slowly. Put pressure on her windpipe. Watch as she turns blue. Then release it, give her a breath or two. Make her think she's got a chance. That there's hope.

Then tighten up again.

He would watch her eyes fill with recognition, fear, and faint hope with each breath he allowed. And finally, the awareness: no hope. Only death. And when those pale eyes looked into his own, she would know it was all her fault.

She should have died years ago.

He stared down the road long after her car disappeared from sight. Carefully, he put the binoculars back in their case.

She wasn't going anywhere; there was plenty of time

to kill her. Walking down to his car, he glanced once again at her house before heading to the airport. There was much to do in the next twenty-four hours, but he'd be back in time to see her face when she was told what had been done.

Time to begin.

CHAPTER

1

Rowan Smith learned about Doreen Rodriguez's murder from the reporters camped out in her front yard Monday morning.

A car door slammed and she awoke with a start. Instinctively, she reached for the gun that was no longer under her pillow, searching the cool cotton sheet before remembering it was in her nightstand. Hesitating briefly, she retrieved the cold Glock. She couldn't think of a good reason for needing her gun, but it felt right in her hand.

She'd slept in sweatpants and a T-shirt, an old habit of being ready for anything, and padded down the stairs in bare feet to look out her den window and see who was visiting so early in the morning. The grating sound of a sliding van door shutting told her she had more than one visitor. She used her index finger to bend down the blinds a mere inch to peer out.

She could tell from their rumpled attire and notepads they were print reporters. Television hounds were far more concerned with appearance. Three vans and two cars crammed the driveway of her leased beachfront home. She despised reporters. She'd had more than enough of them while working for the Bureau.

The doorbell echoed, startling her. Though she could see the driveway from her den, she couldn't see the door.

Presumably one of the bolder reporters had summoned the courage to ring her doorbell.

What did they want? She'd just given an interview about the premiere of *Crime of Passion* two days ago; surely they didn't need a group session.

She started for the door, then remembered she was carrying her gun. She imagined the headline: *Paranoid Former Agent Armed for Interview.* She slid the gun into the top drawer of her desk and briskly walked to the front door, barely registering the coolness of the tile under her bare feet.

Her phone rang at the same time the doorbell repeated its obnoxious *ding-dong*. Great. Reporters coming at her from every direction. She'd dealt with them before; she'd have to again. It was only as she opened the door that she feared something bad had happened and that maybe she shouldn't talk to them.

Too late.

"Do you have a comment on the murder of Doreen Rodriguez?"

"I don't know Doreen Rodriguez," she said automatically, even as alarm bells went off in the back of her head. The name *was* familiar, but she couldn't place it. A sick feeling ate at her gut as she tried to connect the dots. As she was shutting the door, another question rang clear:

"You don't know that a twenty-year-old woman named Doreen Rodriguez was killed in Denver Saturday night in the same manner as the *character* Doreen Rodriguez was murdered in your book *Crime of Opportunity*?"

Rowan slammed the door shut. She didn't fear reporters walking in uninvited; she'd have them arrested for trespassing without a qualm. She simply wanted the resounding finality of her "no comment" to ring loud and clear.

The phone finally stopped ringing. Then, thirty seconds later, the incessant *ring-ring* started again. She ran back to her den and glanced at the caller ID: Annette. Her producer.

Picking up the receiver she said, "What in the hell is going on?" She heard yet another car screech to a halt in her driveway.

"You've heard."

"I have a bunch of reporters on my doorstep, more arriving as we speak." She peered out the blinds again. Television van. She pressed a hand to her stomach. Something was very wrong.

"I got the details from a reporter in *Denver*," Annette said rapidly, emphasizing some of her words. "A twenty-year-old waitress named Doreen Rodriguez was *killed* Saturday night. They found her body yesterday in a Dumpster outside of, and I quote, 'a small Italian café off South Broadway that could have been called quaint if not for the blood drying on the white brick façade.' "

Rowan listened to the words she'd penned years ago. Rubbing her temple, she craved a cigarette for the first time since she'd quit the FBI four years ago. "This is some kind of sick joke."

"I'm *so* sorry, Rowan."

"Dear God, I don't believe this is happening." She squeezed her eyes shut in an effort to absorb what Annette had told her. Her breath caught, and she placed a hand over her mouth. It had to be a coincidence. Some idiot reporter taking a violent crime and trying to sensationalize it by comparing it to one of her novels.

The image of Doreen Rodriguez's bloody, dismembered body flashed in her mind. She opened her eyes immediately, her vision of the murder far too real because she had created it. It couldn't have been a similar crime. Just the name was the same.

"Rowan, she was killed with a *machete* against the restaurant *wall,* her body thrown in a *Dumpster*!" Annette's voice took on a feverish pitch. "She worked in *Denver* and was born in *Albuquerque.* Some crazy person copied the crime *exactly* as you wrote it."

Rowan pressed fingers deeper into her right temple. Someone had copied her fictional crime? It couldn't be possible. How had the killer found someone so exactly like her fictional character?

More important, why?

She sunk to the floor next to her desk and buried her face in her arms, holding the phone with her shoulder. She took another deep breath and held it. She had to get hold of herself; then she'd get to the bottom of this.

There had to be a mistake.

"Are you okay?" Annette's voice was full of concern.

"What do you think?" Her voice came out a raspy whisper.

"I'm worried about your *safety,* Rowan."

"I can take care of myself."

"I'll come right over."

She almost grinned at the thought. Petite fifty-something Hollywood producer Annette O'Dell rushing over to protect her star screenwriter from a pack of vicious reporters. Rowan shook her head. "No, after my run I have to go to the studio and talk to the director about reworking a scene."

"The reporters will follow you. They're probably staked out there now."

"Damn the reporters! I have no comment. Period. Nothing, nada, zero. I don't want you saying word one about this to anyone. I am going to the studio and going to do my job. I'm not a cop; let *them* take care of this." She didn't want to play cop anymore. She didn't want any more blood on her hands.

But there it was. She wiped her hands on her sweats until Lady Macbeth came to mind, madly scrubbing her hands of blood that wasn't there.

Doreen Rodriguez. Rowan didn't kill the poor woman, but she had somehow caused her death just the same.

"Rowan, let me hire a security—"

Rowan cut Annette off with a click as she replaced the receiver in its cradle.

She took a minute to gather herself before getting up from the floor. Outside, another car drove up, more vultures ready to pounce. It made great copy, she thought wryly. Real-life murder mystery: *The Fiction Copycat. The Copycat Killer.* The press seemed to actually *like* murders. Especially high-profile, gruesome crimes. Nothing exciting in a typical domestic dispute, a hit-and-run, or a routine gang drive-by. But being sliced and diced by a machete against the side of a quaint Italian café . . .

She shook her head. Was she any better? She wrote violent murder mysteries. Even if her corpses were fictionalized, didn't she do the same thing as the reporters? Capitalizing on people's interest in gruesome crime? The human fascination with death went back thousands of years. Violent Greek and Roman myths had relieved people's fear of the unknown. Similar gruesome entertainments could be found in every generation since.

Doreen Rodriguez. Could the murder possibly have been the same as Rowan had written it? Her heart beat double-time as she imagined the pain and horror that poor young woman had suffered.

It would do her no good to dwell on the victim now. Rowan mentally summoned more than ten years of training to distance herself. When it got personal, that's when mistakes happened.

Ignoring both the door and phone, on her laptop she logged onto the local Denver newspaper website. She hoped against hope there was a mistake, some misunderstanding. But the press was on top of the story. Bad news travels fast, evidence of which was parked in her driveway.

Everything Annette had told her was there on the screen. Rowan wondered what details had, in fact, been withheld. She wondered how long it would take for the police to come and interview her. With the press already showing an interest in the coincidence, the police wouldn't be far behind. She'd get more details from them once they tracked her down.

No. No, she couldn't get involved. She had a meeting at the studio in two hours. She had made a new life for herself, a quiet life. Damn if she was going to let a murdering lunatic control her future. Again.

She started for her bedroom to dress for her run when a familiar pounding on the front door interrupted her. Cops.

That was fast.

"Ms. Smith!" a mumbled voice called. "Ms. Smith, this is the police. We need to talk."

She turned toward the door. It had started.

They sat at the dining room table, in front of the picture window that framed the blue-green Pacific Ocean. From here, twenty feet above the beach and a good hundred feet inland, one could still see the individual waves and whitecaps, tossed up by a light wind. The tide was out, the beach empty of people.

Rowan placed two mugs of hot black coffee in front of the detectives, then opened the window. The tangy, salty sea air relaxed her as she breathed in deeply. She needed to be calm and alert, but above all else, she needed to maintain control.

She sat across from the cops, holding her own coffee mug with both hands.

Ben Jackson was a short, thin man with skin the same color as the rich coffee in his mug. His poker face couldn't disguise intelligent eyes. His rigid posture and the hint of muscles under his impeccable coat told Rowan he was fit and took his job seriously. He had flown out from Denver this morning just to talk to her.

The Denver P.D. wouldn't waste scarce budget dollars. Obviously they believed the Rodriguez murder was connected to her book.

Jim Barlow was from L.A.P.D. He was older, his skin ghostly compared to Jackson's. He looked like the stereotypical, slightly overweight cop in wrinkled slacks and too-tight blazer with worn leather patches on the elbows. His pale blue eyes seemed to take in everything, while his hands fidgeted, as if he were holding a cigarette. An ex-smoker. Rowan sympathized.

She liked them both. Her instincts told her she could trust them.

Jackson began. "You've heard about the murder of Doreen Rodriguez." He motioned loosely toward the front of the house where the reporters were dissipating. The newly arrived cops' threat of arrest for trespassing had held some weight, she thought with a slight smile.

Rowan nodded. "I read the article from the Denver paper online."

"You were with the FBI."

"Six years."

"Probably made a lot of enemies. I know *I* have."

"Your point?"

"I believe your life is in danger and you should consider hiring security."

"I'm a trained FBI agent, detective. I know how to protect myself."

"You probably do. You probably still sleep with a gun under your pillow." He nodded, noting some minute reaction on her face, then continued. "This was a brutal crime and it was directed at you. You must be aware of the similarities between the murder victim and a character in your book."

"I told you I read the article."

It was all Rowan could do to maintain eye contact. She didn't want to accept the fact that this murder had anything to do with her. But her instincts shouted the contrary. This was personal.

"I wouldn't jump to conclusions," she said. "If there's another crime, maybe this maniac will pick another writer to mimic. But if it makes you feel any better, I'll be extra careful."

Damn, she sounded sarcastic without meaning to. Her defenses were up.

Jackson paused before speaking. "Did you know the real Doreen Rodriguez? Did you use her for your book?"

She shook her head. "I just made up the name. The character needed a name."

"There was one thing we managed to keep from the press," Jackson said. "Under the body, the bastard left a copy of your book."

"My book?" Her voice was barely a whisper. She sipped her coffee, using the normalcy to try to gather her thoughts.

He nodded. "*Crime of Opportunity*. In case we were too stupid to figure it out, he highlighted the passages describing the murder of the fictional Ms. Rodriguez." His deep voice was steeped in anger, the kind cops tried hard to keep in check.

Her book left at the scene. "Anything else? Any notes to me, comments, a hint that he's going to do this again?"

Jackson leaned forward. "Just the highlighted passages. What do you think?"

Rowan looked Jackson in the eye and shook her head. "I don't work for the FBI anymore, and I wasn't a profiler. You want an expert opinion? Call them."

But her mind was already working overtime. Was someone singling her out? Was one of the criminals she'd locked away carrying out some sort of twisted vendetta against her? She should get a copy of all her case files and look closely—though she remembered every violent criminal she'd helped put away.

Barlow spoke for the first time since the introductions. "I've read your books, Ms. Smith. I guess you could say I'm a faithful reader of yours. Your stories are quite horrific. Authentic." He paused. "I think he's going to strike again. Denver's looking at Rodriguez's old boyfriends, friends, colleagues," he said, almost dismissively. "But your book being put there, that sets off alarms."

Rowan breathed deeply, not saying anything. Her bells were ringing, too. A whole friggin' orchestra clamored in her head.

Jackson spoke. "My superiors are speaking with the Feds already, looking for some cooperation. But we thought you might have some insight, so I took the chance on coming out here to talk to you. Are any of those criminals you put away on the loose? Anyone threaten you?"

She couldn't help but laugh, though the hollow sound held no humor. "Threaten me? You've been a cop for longer than me. I'm sure some of your arrests didn't take too kindly to being locked up."

Shaking her head, she continued, "I'm contacted when anyone I testified against or arrested is released or up for parole. I can honestly say that everyone I arrested is either dead or in prison."

Jackson smiled slightly. "Wish I could say the same. Impressive record."

She shrugged. "Not really. I didn't catch every murdering bastard."

"What about a relative of one of these criminals? Someone wanting revenge for putting their father, brother, cousin, lover behind bars?"

Rowan shook her head. "I don't know. You'd have to go over my case reports. I can't think of anyone who stands out, but I don't have my notes and I haven't given it a lot of thought." But she knew that her days and nights would now be haunted by past cases until this murderer was found. She'd get a copy of her files herself. Make sure she didn't miss something during the seven years she'd been with the Bureau. Miss something that cost Doreen Rodriguez her life.

He might never be found. And though he had killed only one person—at least, that they knew about—Rowan's instincts told her he would strike again.

Soon.

"What about a fan? Someone who's written or called you or maybe even tried to visit you?"

"A fan? Taking it upon himself to recreate my imaginary murders?" It was possible, but she didn't think likely, and she told Jackson so. "This killer is no fan of mine."

"Why do you say that?" Barlow asked.

"He's making my fictional murders real. I didn't go far enough, in his mind, so he has to. He has to prove his own genius, that he's capable of far greater acts than a mere fiction writer."

"So he has a screw loose."

"No." She shook her head. "He's sane."

"How do you figure?"

"He planned this perfectly." She put her mug down, stood, and crossed to the open window. But she didn't see the ocean waves or hear the calling gulls. Instead, she pictured evil.

"He found a woman with the same name and occupation as one of my characters and killed her in the same manner in a similar location. Did a lot of planning and research to get all the details just right. Perfection. Next, he leaves my book with her body. Arrogance. He's smart, but he thinks everyone else is stupid and he has to give you the why or you'd never figure it out. This wasn't a crime of passion or a crime for money . . . it was a crime of opportunity." She realized, as she spoke, it was the name of her book. "This was premeditated, proving his sanity. I'd venture to state that he has an agenda, something that has nothing to do with the victims."

"Something to do with you?" Barlow asked, causing Rowan to flinch. As much as she wanted to deny it, there had to be a connection. Unless he committed another murder using another writer's book as a blueprint. She shrugged, turning a blank face to the cops, not wanting to give anything away. Not until she gave this more thought.

"I don't know."

"The FBI will probably contact you."

"Of course."

Rowan already dreaded it. Someone was playing a game with her, and she had no idea who or why. Though she had controlled her emotions throughout this interview, she felt her insides quivering. But she was the consummate professional; she would keep it together. At least until she was alone.

"Have you received any threats?"

"Nothing."

"Are you sure? What about your fan mail?"

"My agent handles correspondence. I receive reports on what comes in. I'd expect him to tell me about any threats." She'd look into that herself.

Jackson made a note. "What about the studio? The actors in the film you're working on? Anyone receive any threats, or notice anything strange?"

"The producer is Annette O'Dell. You can find her office at the studio. I don't work there, I'm just working on rewrites of my screenplay." Again, Rowan didn't think any threats had been made. Annette would have told her.

"What about a personal motive? Any former boyfriends who might turn vicious? A friend who might have felt slighted by your success?"

"To be honest, I haven't had much of a personal life since I came to California two months ago to work on this film." She sat back down and sipped her now lukewarm coffee. It landed like a lead ball in her churning stomach. "Even before that, I completed the screenplay and started working on my new book. I'm as busy now as I was working for the FBI."

"You have four published books?" Jackson asked.

She nodded. "My fifth will be released in a few weeks."

"And this is your second film?"

"Third. The second is being released in two weeks. This one won't be out until the end of next year."

"You've done pretty well since leaving the Bureau."

"Your point?" Rowan asked, irritated. She wanted to help, but these questions were irrelevant. She wanted to take her morning run, then a hot shower. Most of all, she needed time alone to think.

"We're trying to fit together all the details." But the detectives exchanged a look that meant they were through. Rowan's sigh of relief was almost audible.

She walked them to the door. Detective Jackson turned to her. "You should consider taking extra security measures. Do you have an alarm system?"

"Yes, detective, and I use it."

He nodded approval and extended his hand. Rowan shook it, feeling warmth and strength. "Call me Ben. We're on the same team here. Either Jim or I will call you later and fill you in. I'm heading back to Denver this afternoon. In the meantime, be careful."

"Thanks, I will." She closed the door behind them, turned around, and leaned against the solid oak surface. Slowly, she sank once again to the cold tile floor, her head in her hands.

One brutal murder a thousand miles away had destroyed in minutes the years of relative peace she'd painstakingly built. The realization of her complicity in the crime grew within her. She clenched her uneasy stomach. How could she live with herself if her imagination had manifested itself into evil? While someone else had stolen a life, the manner of evil was her idea, her conception. Her casual decision to name the first victim in *Crime of Opportunity* Doreen Rodriguez had resulted in the death of the real Doreen Rodriguez from Albuquerque. It was perverse and cruel.

Rowan had learned again and again that death was inequitable and brutal. It cut a path of misery in the hearts of everyone it touched. And death wasn't blind. It saw the pain, the heartache, and grew stronger.

It had started when she was ten, and it seemed it would never end.

CHAPTER
2

Michael Flynn followed the directions Annette O'Dell had given him to Rowan Smith's house, but he didn't need the house number to figure out which of the large beachfront homes was hers. Even now, a day after the story broke, a dozen cars, vans, and a single motorcycle—all sporting press credentials—lined the highway in front of number 25450.

He turned his black SUV down the steep driveway. The house looked deceptively small and nondescript from the front, but Malibu homes in this neighborhood were spacious inside and maximized their ocean view. Smith's place was at the end of a secluded row of such homes that shared a rare private beach. If he wasn't mistaken, several of these homes had been destroyed a few years back in a terrible storm. As evidence of the destruction, he noted that cement reinforcements lined the cliffs around the home to prevent the mudslides that were the primary culprit of coastal property damage.

He locked his vehicle on the chance a member of the predatory press was interested in his identity. They must have been warned about trespassing. Though they noticed him, they stayed on the street—and off Smith's property.

He breathed deeply, relishing the sharp bite of the salt air. He could get used to a place like this.

Glancing around the outside of the house, he frowned. Beachfront property was hard to protect. There were no gates or fences between houses, making the dwelling accessible on all four sides. However, the far side of the Smith residence butted up against a steep cliff. It would be virtually impossible for anyone to access the house from that direction.

That left three sides unprotected.

A bright yellow Volkswagen Beetle practically flew into the driveway, screeching to a halt behind his truck. Michael winced at Tess's erratic driving. He had been shocked when she'd passed her driver's test on the first try. She jumped out of the car, laptop computer in hand, and ran to his side, her dark curly hair bouncing. He shook his head. His sister always seemed to have energy to spare.

"Sorry I'm late," she said, her wide grin revealing two dimples.

"You're not late. You're not supposed to be here."

"What do you mean? I'm your *partner*."

"I meet clients. You run the office." The little he knew about this case troubled him. He would not endanger his sister's life. She was a computer expert, after all, not a bodyguard.

She sighed melodramatically. "Not anymore, Mickey. John's out of town, so you're stuck with me." She grinned and winked.

Michael couldn't help but smile. Tess had done everything he and John commanded for the last two years, willing to take self-defense and gun-training classes, read every book they tossed her way, and put up with the spontaneous drills they created to help prepare her for fieldwork. But neither he nor John intended to allow their baby sister to work in the field, even as she'd become increasingly valuable to their team. In the office, that is.

"This time," he said, a note of warning in his voice. "From what Annette said, I think we'll need your computer wizardry."

Tess patted her laptop and smiled brightly. "Let's go."

"Just remember who's boss."

"John is, but he's in South America."

"Tess," Michael warned, eyes narrowed.

She stood on her toes and kissed his cheek. "I won't forget, boss."

Rowan dropped the blinds in her den, cutting off the view of the two people talking on her driveway. This must be the security team Annette wanted to hire. Great. Her producer, now lurking somewhere outside Rowan's den door, expected her to consent to protection from a guy who hadn't seen a barber in months and his teeny-bopper wife or girlfriend or whoever, who drove a screaming yellow Bug, the model of discretion.

Rowan had locked herself in the den thirty minutes before because she'd finally had enough of listening to Annette treat her like a child. She looked down at the Glock now gripped with both hands.

Sometimes she wished she had died in the line of duty, because taking her life was not an option.

She'd gone round and round with her producer. Annette meant well but was so out of her element here, planting herself in the house yesterday and refusing to leave. She seemed almost excited by the whole thing, which turned Rowan completely off even though she knew it was simply Annette's way. She'd even insisted on staying in the guest room, though the petite producer was woefully ill-prepared to defend anyone. Not that Rowan thought for a minute she needed defending.

Rowan didn't know what she'd done to earn such a good friend, and she appreciated the sentiment. But Annette was driving her crazy.

Ultimately, the phone call the previous night from her ex-boss had resigned her to the fact that if she didn't accept the security offered by the studio, the FBI would assign a team to her.

"Are you okay?" Roger had asked when she picked up the extension in her den.

She heard the fear in his voice, and her heart skipped a beat. She didn't want to worry him. He'd been more than just a boss. He'd saved her life. "I'm fine, Roger."

"You're lying. How can you be fine?"

"You know the details?"

"Every last one. Had the Denver Police fax over a copy of the report. Four agents are assigned to review your old cases looking for anyone who might be capable of this, particularly male friends and relatives."

"Good. I want a copy of all my files. Maybe something will jump out at me, something I missed, an interview, a relative—hell, I don't know." She took a deep breath, then slowly blew it out. "I can't just sit around and do nothing."

"I'll contact the L.A. Bureau chief and they can download the files. You can pick them up by tomorrow afternoon."

"Thanks." She cleared her throat. "Uh, you don't think, I mean, there's no way that my father could have—"

Roger interrupted her. "I called Bellevue. MacIntosh is in the same condition."

"Thank you." Her voice cracked and she closed her eyes. *After all this time, I should have better control over my emotions.*

She hadn't expected that after twenty-three years her

father would suddenly have regained his sanity, but ever since Detectives Jackson and Barlow left the previous day, she couldn't stop thinking about him. She was relieved he was still wrapped up in his own mind. She hoped he was living through hell.

"Gracie and I are worried about you. Come back to Washington. You always have a room here with us."

"I know," she whispered. She hated that Roger worried about her; she didn't want to burden his heart. Not after everything he and Gracie had done for her. "But I can't leave."

"I'll send out a team to protect you."

"No," she said, louder than she intended.

"Dammit, I read the reports. I think this guy is after you."

She pictured Roger standing behind his big, dark, scuffed utilitarian desk, his square jaw set, his dark eyes narrowed, wrinkles of worry across his forehead.

"We don't know that," she countered. "Let the police continue their investigation. It could be completely unconnected to me." She didn't believe it, even though sometimes ex-boyfriends or violent husbands went to great lengths to cover up their crimes. Maybe that's what had happened with Doreen Rodriguez.

"You're obviously not thinking straight if you disagree. He's playing you. I won't rest until we find this bastard. I'm going to protect you whether you like it or not."

"Roger, please don't send anyone. You can hardly afford to, with the department stretched so thin after 9/11." But she knew his tone left no room for negotiation. And she knew him well enough to find an acceptable alternative for both of them.

"The studio said they'd hire a security company."

"Are you telling me the truth?"

"Annette O'Dell, my producer, wants to. I told her I didn't want anyone, but—"

"You'll take them. Right?" He wouldn't take no for an answer, she knew.

"Yes, I will," she said, resigned. "Tomorrow, Annette is sending over someone for me to interview."

"They'd better be good, Ro, not some nose-picking grocery guards."

Rowan couldn't help but smile. "Knowing Annette, they'll be good. And discreet. I don't want the press digging around any more than they already are." It was highly unlikely anyone could uncover her past. She didn't want to have to live through that nightmare in public, even if she lived with it every day of her life.

"If you think this team is inferior, let me know and I'll get a recommendation from the bureau chief in L.A. Agreed?"

"Fair enough."

"I love you," Roger said quietly. "Please be careful."

She swallowed a sob. It would be so easy to leave everything in Roger's capable hands and go back to Washington. Let Gracie baby her. Or better, hide away in her cabin. She missed the pine trees, the cool nights, the crisp mountain air of her Colorado home.

But she couldn't do that. She couldn't run when she had obligations and responsibilities. "I promise," she said.

After Roger's call that night, disturbing dreams had interrupted Rowan's sleep. She'd risen early for her morning run on the wet beach, well before the sun crested the low Malibu mountains, pushing herself until she couldn't go any farther. After showering, she holed up in the den while Annette took care of business from the dining room.

One violent murder three days ago and then nothing. *The calm before the storm.* She shuddered.

Rowan had been sitting at her desk in her locked den doing nothing but feeling guilty for a crime she hadn't committed when she heard the cars arrive. No one came to the door immediately, so she looked out the blinds and saw the two security people standing there, talking, their body language showing that they were comfortable together. A team.

She'd never had that. Even with her partners in the FBI, she'd never grown close to anyone. She couldn't. What if something happened to them?

The doorbell rang. She needed a few more minutes to compose herself. She loved Roger dearly, but talking to him last night on top of everything else had brought back black memories she needed to re-bury, at least until she was alone.

"Nice place," Tess said.

Michael looked around, frowning. He appreciated the aesthetics, but right now he was most concerned about security. "Lots of windows. Where are the blinds?"

"The owner *never* put coverings on the west-facing windows." Annette tossed her black bob with a subtle shake of the head. She was a trim and attractive woman with bright, intelligent blue eyes. "He's quite *eccentric*. So it can get hot in here in the late afternoon." The trendy producer always spoke with strong inflections. At times it was irritating.

"I thought Smith was a woman."

"She *is*. The owner's a friend of *mine*, an *actor*, who's in Australia filming. He's leasing the place to Rowan."

Michael surveyed his surroundings, absorbing the layout.

Everything was blinding white and glass. The furniture, the paint, the carpets. The only color came from bright, primary-toned abstract paintings sparsely decorating the walls. Sterile, cold. He sure wouldn't want to live here.

They stood in the large, sunken living room. Three tall windows showcased the ocean. To the right was a raised sitting area or library of sorts with a high-end entertainment center on one wall. To the left was an elevated dining room with its own picture window. All three rooms had sets of double glass doors leading to the deck.

The house was a damn fish bowl.

"What's wrong?" Annette asked.

"We need to do something about these windows." He motioned with his hand.

"Like what?"

"Anything."

"But no one can see in. The house faces the ocean."

Michael struggled to be polite. "True, but at night someone could be outside on this deck and see everything inside with the house lit up like a Christmas tree, and we wouldn't even know it." He looked around. "Where's Ms. Smith?"

"In her office," Annette said. "I'll get her."

Alone? Michael thought. Already he didn't like the feeling of this assignment. He knew nothing about Smith except that she was a former FBI agent turned writer working on a screenplay for Annette and living in a virtual glass house. And, of course, what he'd read in the newspapers about the murder in Denver.

Michael watched the producer walk down the open hall and stop at the first set of double doors. He knew Annette and trusted her for the most part, but made a mental note to have Tess do a little clandestine research on the producer and her company. While he'd never heard of committing murder for publicity, he had been privy to some illegal stunts to bring attention to a fledgling star or poorly reviewed movie.

"Rowan?" Annette said through the door. "The security people are here."

A muffled response.

Annette turned to Michael with a half-smile. "She'll be out in a few minutes."

"Look, she can't be alone. If someone is trying to kill her, she needs to be within sight at all times." He passed Annette and rapped loudly on the door. "Ms. Smith, this is Michael Flynn. Please come out."

"I said five minutes!" she called from behind the door.

"Now. You're not safe in there."

He heard her laugh, followed by the distinct sound of a round being chambered. His heart raced. *Was* she alone? He tried the door. Locked. Then one knob slowly turned. He stood back against the wall. The door opened slightly and he waited for her to emerge. When she didn't, he scooted along the wall, pushed the door in all the way.

In the middle of the den stood a tall blonde with eyes the color of the ocean. Her face was blank, emotionless, her long hair clasped in the back.

She had a gun pointed at his chest. "Bang, you're dead."

"Put the damn gun down! What in the hell do you think you're doing?"

"Protecting myself."

Michael whirled on his heel and started for the door. "Tess, let's go."

"Michael," Tess said, biting her lip.

"*Now.*" To say he was furious was an understatement. He would tolerate no one pulling a gun on him. Was she crazy?

"Please, Michael." Annette laid a manicured hand on his arm. "Rowan's upset. Just listen. She needs you."

Michael looked from Annette to the blonde emerging from the den, arms crossed, holding a Glock casually in one hand, pointed down. Her body rippled with tension, belying her casual posture. While too skinny, he noted well-toned muscles under the short sleeves of her shirt. Pale, but still a beautiful woman. Her face was as blank as when she'd pointed that damn gun at him. But her stormy eyes stopped him from walking out the door. He finally understood the phrase "eyes are windows to the soul." Rowan Smith's eyes told him she was scared but strong, troubled but defiant. A captivating combination.

"I'll give you ten minutes to explain," Michael said through clenched teeth.

It took him days to find the perfect flower shop. It would have been so much easier had she named it.

His gloved hands opened the book to the page he'd marked.

The front of the simple flower shop reminded him of the neighborhood where he'd grown up. A large picture window framed by a green-and-white awning, metal carts spilling over with an array of colorful carnations, red roses the color of fresh spilled blood, ferns newly misted, dripping dew like tears.

Perfect, down to the red roses and misted ferns.

He opened the glass door, a bell ringing overhead. The fragrant aroma of flowers, soil, and plants greeted him, along with a cheerful, "Hello, may I help you?"

He breathed in the earthy scent, looking at a display of bright spring arrangements just inside the door while he waited for two chatty women at the counter to finish their order and leave.

One arrangement in particular caught his attention: a brilliantly designed triangular piece with majestic pink and purple larkspurs framed by bright yellow daffodils, white and pink mums, and purple lilies, quivering in the air-conditioned store.

It would have been perfect for her on any other occasion, but not for a funeral. Too bad.

He turned to another worn page in the book. Though he had the passage memorized, he liked to look at the words. They gave him an almost giddy sense of pleasure, as if he were leaning over her shoulder as she typed them into her computer.

Casa Blanca lilies, carnations, roses, moluccella, snapdragons and gypsophila, all in pure white, framed the funeral wreath, soft trailing plumosus lending a green backdrop, making the white even brighter. The fragrant flowers, so alive, should never have hung next to the closed casket, a casket that held the dead, dismembered body of a life taken too soon.

"May I help you?"

He turned, smiling at the young clerk who leaned forward to wait on him. Under thirty and blonde. Thankfully, there was no other description of her in the book. Even though there were hundreds of florist shops in Los Angeles, it might have been difficult to get both the setting and the victim just right had there been more detail. It had taken him six months to track down a waitress named Doreen Rodriguez in Denver.

And he had a flight to Portland in less than two hours.

"Yes, I'd like to purchase a funeral wreath." He watched as the other customers left the store, chatting, ignorant. They had no idea they'd brushed shoulders with a god. Energized by his duplicity, he smiled at the pretty clerk.

"I'm sorry for your loss," the pretty young woman said. Her name badge read Christine.

Doreen hadn't been much of a loss. In fact, she hadn't put up much of a fight, but he wasn't about to tell his next victim that small tidbit.

Closing the book, he described the flowers he wanted in the wreath. Christine attempted to make suggestions, showing him other exquisite arrangements, flowing greenery, and explaining that wreaths had become passé. He politely demurred. "This is what she would want," he explained.

"I understand." The florist smiled warmly, with just the right hint of sympathy in her pretty blue eyes.

A shame he would have to kill her.

CHAPTER
3

"Have you been threatened?"

They sat at the dining room table, Annette providing most of the details, but Michael still had many unanswered questions. He glanced at Rowan, but couldn't get a fix on her. She'd put on small wire-rim glasses with a gray coating so he couldn't see her eyes. They weren't sunglasses, but had the same shielding effect. She sat at the far end of the table, looking out the window.

"Not directly," Rowan said in time. Summarizing what the police had told her yesterday, she was careful to leave out the detail about her book being left at the scene. "I'm perfectly capable of taking care of myself," she said, glancing at him. "What exactly would you do to protect me?" Her condescending tone irritated him.

Of course, she had been a Fed. All Feds thought they knew best, Michael thought with derision. Still, she needed protection. Some lunatic had used her book as a blueprint for murder. The killer might have his own agenda, or he might be coming for her. Increasing security around this place was a good start.

It didn't hurt that a high-profile case could really help his business take off, either.

"I was a cop for nearly fifteen years and have been in private security for two. I'm more than capable of watching your back," he told her. It was quite a nice back to watch, he thought. The whole package was attractive.

"You didn't answer my question," Rowan said, her posture rigid. "What can you do for me that I can't do for myself?"

Was she being deliberately obtuse? She had to know what a bodyguard was for. "You've worked for the FBI. You know damn well what I'd be doing. Answering your door. Escorting you when you leave the house. Locking down at night and if the guy shows, getting you to a safe place. What more do you want to know?"

Rowan arched an eyebrow and seemed about to say something when the doorbell rang. She stood, and Michael glared at her.

"I would imagine answering the door falls under my job description," he said.

She nodded, taking the Glock out of the shoulder holster she wore over her white T-shirt.

Annette looked almost excited, and Tess took out her own little snub-nosed .38.

Rowan couldn't help but smile at Tess Flynn's firearm. "Cute gun," she said before she could stop herself from being bitchy.

Michael disappeared down the hall to the foyer. He'd been a cop for fifteen years, probably joined the academy right out of high school. He had that beat-cop bravado, a slight arrogant swagger, the rigid stance. His body crackled with suppressed energy, but he had laugh lines around his green eyes and his hair was too long to be a regulation cut. He almost had a rebel appearance. She couldn't help but wonder why he'd left the force so young. He wouldn't get full retirement benefits, something very important to most people in law enforcement.

That was something she intended to look into.

But he seemed to know what he was doing regarding

personal security. It was either him or Roger would send out a pair of agents. Rowan didn't feel comfortable taking so many resources away from the Bureau. Not before they had any solid information about the killer.

She just didn't like being under someone else's thumb. The whole idea of a bodyguard irritated her. She was perfectly capable of taking care of herself, as she had told both Roger and this new guy, Michael Flynn.

She sighed, rubbed her eyes under the small glasses, resigned to the fact that it was either Michael or a former colleague. She didn't need the lenses for seeing, but she found wearing them was a good way to observe people.

A few moments later, Michael came back into the dining room carrying a huge white and green funeral wreath.

The blood drained from her face. She'd seen the wreath before. In her mind.

The sweet, cloying smell of flowers reminded Rowan of every funeral she'd ever been to. There were too many, but she remembered each and every one of them. Who thought that the overabundance of beauty somehow made violent death more palatable? Death, premature death, could never be glossed over.

"There's a card," Michael said, reaching for it.

"Don't touch it!" Rowan rushed to his side.

Michael stopped, hand in midair. "I checked out the package before I let the driver go. It's clean." He looked annoyed, his lips drawn into a tight line as if irritated that she had the audacity to challenge his ability.

"No, it's not that. I recognize it."

"The flowers?"

She nodded. "They're exactly as I envisioned in one of my books." Her voice sounded unsteady, just like she felt. This certainly wasn't a good sign, and any hope there had been a mistake in delivery quickly dissipated when she carefully pulled the card out by the corner with her fingernails.

The pre-printed message at top—IN MEMORIAM—was followed by one written sentence: *Please accept my heartfelt condolences on the death of your brainchild, Doreen.* It was signed, *A Fan.*

Rowan dropped the card on the table as if it had burned her, heart pounding. Her stomach threatened to rebel against the coffee and banana that had comprised her breakfast three hours before.

Michael leaned over to read the message. "What does it mean?"

Rowan hoped she was wrong, but feared she wasn't. "Call the police. He's going to kill again. If he hasn't already."

By the time the police left hours later, along with Annette and Tess, Rowan was exhausted. Michael didn't say anything when she retired to the den. The police would trace the flowers, but Rowan seemed resigned to the fact that someone had already died. The rancor she'd displayed earlier at Michael's presence was gone; she just closed up emotionally and told him to do what he needed to do.

Michael checked the security system and perimeter, then all windows and doors. Secure.

Long past dark, Michael's stomach growled, reminding him that he hadn't eaten since breakfast. Though the contents of Rowan's kitchen were sparse, he found some pasta—not fresh, but it would suffice. While the water boiled, he went through the pantry, pulling out basic spaghetti sauce, a jar of sliced mushrooms, a can of olives, and diced tomatoes.

He enjoyed the peace of cooking, especially in a gourmet kitchen like this. While everything simmered, he opened cabinets until he found a bottle of good red wine. He nodded at the vintage. Good stuff. He couldn't drink on the job, but maybe a glass would relax Rowan Smith.

"Glad you approve," Rowan said from the doorway.

Michael was startled she'd gotten the drop on him. He usually knew when he was being watched. "I thought you might want a glass to relax."

She nodded, slid onto one of the two bar stools. He opened the wine, poured her a glass, and handed it to her.

"Thanks," she said with a half-smile.

"It's your wine."

"For giving me time alone." The small eyeglasses she'd been wearing earlier were gone and he tried not to stare into her pretty blue-gray eyes. They were so expressive, even with her blank face and rigid posture. Right now they told him she was tired but thinking—probably running through every case she'd ever worked.

"You didn't have much by way of food, so I improvised," he said as he checked on the meal.

"Food tends to go bad. I buy what I need when I need it."

"Spoken like a true bachelorette."

"Not all of us are the marrying type."

"I suppose not." Michael went back to the stove and stirred his sauce. He'd thought about marrying on more than one occasion. Most recently, Jessica. The thought of her brought waves of anger and deep sadness. You'd think that after two years he'd be over it.

"Everything okay?" Rowan asked.

Damn, he didn't think he wore his emotions on his

sleeve. Then again, she'd been a cop and was used to reading body language.

"Fine." He kept his voice light and his back to her as he strained the rotelle, tossed everything together, and dished up two plates. By the time he slid a plate in front of Rowan, he'd forced all thoughts of Jessica from his mind.

"Normally, I would have bread and salad to go with this, but there wasn't any." He tried to make light of her bare cupboards.

"It smells wonderful."

"Thanks."

They ate in companionable silence, side by side at the counter. When they were done, Michael started cleaning, but she touched his arm. "You cooked; I'll clean."

Rowan cleaned up with quick, non-superfluous movements. He had a million questions to ask her, but decided to take it slow. There was far more to Rowan Smith than a pretty face and the ability to tell a scary story. In the few hours he'd known her, he realized she was an exceptionally private woman.

She was smart, competent, and had an intriguing past. FBI agent turned crime writer. Quiet and reserved, she seemed to have energy bottled up, simmering under her skin. An interesting contrast. He wanted to know why she'd quit what appeared to have been a promising career with the FBI. Why had she decided to write murder mysteries? What prompted her to leave Washington to move to the West Coast? Since she leased this beach house temporarily, where did she call home?

Michael would make it his mission to learn everything there was to know about Rowan Smith. For professional reasons, of course, he told himself.

After a final security check, making sure Rowan was

down for the night, and settling in one of the guest rooms, he called Tess at her apartment.

"Find anything?" He'd asked her to run a background check on Rowan Smith.

"Not much." She filled him in on the little she had learned. Rowan had resigned from the FBI four years ago. She owned a townhouse in Washington, but had lived outside Denver, Colorado, for the past three years.

Tess was right. Not much.

He lay down on the bed, one arm behind his head. "What's your take on her?"

"The jury's still out, Mickey. That power play with the gun this afternoon bothered me. I'm not used to having a gun pointed at my brother. I mean, when you were a cop I expected it, but didn't like it. Now—do we really need to take this job?"

That incident had disturbed him, too. "I think she's scared. Exceptionally private. She's used to depending on herself and no one else." He sighed, rubbed his eyes, and stifled a yawn. "The job's relatively safe. Keep her secure. Here at the house or the studio. It's not like we'll be traveling all over the city making her a target."

"I suppose you're right." She didn't sound convinced. "I think she's lonely."

He considered that. "Yeah, you're probably right."

"Mickey, don't get involved."

"I'm not. What makes you say that?"

He heard the shrug in her voice. "I know you. I know how you are with women. First Carla. Then Jessica. Rowan Smith doesn't need a knight in shining armor to rescue her."

"Don't practice your amateur psychology on me, Teresa," he warned. "I know perfectly well how to do my job. I'm not going to let a little physical attraction interfere with protecting her life." Shit, he hadn't meant to let on that he found Rowan sexy. Hell, who wouldn't? He could keep it under control.

She sighed, signaling she wasn't going to argue with him now, but the conversation wasn't over in her mind. "I'm going to dig deeper. I put out some calls this afternoon; it might take a day or two to get feedback."

"Don't break any laws."

"Who, me?" Tess laughed and hung up.

As he drifted off to sleep, he thought about Rowan Smith. She was a complex and beautiful woman, and he sensed she had a troubled past. He hoped to earn her trust so she'd share with him. At the minimum, he'd settle for what Tess could dig up.

And contrary to what his sister thought, he knew Rowan wasn't Jessica. They were nothing alike.

Tess paced half the night, wondering what she should do with the information she'd just uncovered.

Though she respected Michael's abilities, she remembered too well the times her brother had gotten emotionally involved with troubled women. Rowan's very real need of protection would attract her brother like nothing else could.

Tess had many questions about Rowan's sketchy background. Like why she quit the FBI. She wanted to know more about her cases. Rowan would be getting copies of her case files that Tess would like to go through as well. Rowan had been open about her career, but as soon as Michael's questions turned personal, she gave short, clipped answers. There was something there, but Tess couldn't figure out what. An ex-husband? She hadn't found any marriage records, but that meant squat. Ex-boyfriend? A possibility.

She hoped Michael would forgive her for calling their brother John, but she needed an unbiased opinion.

Michael was a good cop, good bodyguard, but he sometimes let personal feelings cloud his professional judgment. Rowan intrigued him, Tess could tell.

She called John's private line. "It's Tess."

Pause. "What's wrong?"

"We have a new assignment, but I think we may be over our head on this one." She told him about Rowan Smith, the murder, and the funeral wreath. "Michael asked me to do a background check."

"And?"

"Nothing."

"So?"

"Just that—nothing. It's as if she was born eighteen years old and just started college."

"Maybe you're not as good as you think," he teased lightly.

"John, I'm worried. That funeral wreath really freaked me out. I read about the murder of Doreen Rodriguez in the papers, then I read the chapter in her book. It's identical."

"What did you find on her?"

"She graduated from Georgetown twelve years ago and went directly into the FBI Academy. Graduated top of her class. She has several marksmanship awards, and I found a couple of newspaper articles where she had a hand in apprehending a criminal, but she's never quoted. She resigned four years ago, about the same time her first book was published."

"Sounds like typical burnout. It happens."

"I'm getting to that. There's a court document from more than twenty years ago. Name change."

"Oh?"

"She was a minor. And it's sealed."

"Okay, you've piqued my interest."

"I'm not done. She listed her address in Washington,

D.C., so I did a search on property ownership. The house is in the name of Roger and Grace Collins."

"That name sounds familiar."

"Roger Collins is assistant director of the FBI. There's something strange in that, don't you think? That she had a name change as a minor and was living at the home of one of the FBI directors?" She paused. "What if she knows more about this killer than she's letting on? Why would a kid need a name change? Witness protection?"

"I can think of a lot of reasons, not all of them nefarious."

Tess ignored him. "And I can already tell Michael's getting emotionally involved. I'm worried, John." She felt bad about giving this information to John before she told Michael, but she knew John's instincts were better. She'd tell Michael tomorrow.

"I'm ready to wrap up down here. Give me two days."

Tess hung up, feeling better. While she trusted Michael, John had more experience dealing with federal law enforcement agencies. Michael tended to be too trusting, while John was the exact opposite—so distrustful that it sometimes bothered Tess. She'd never met anyone so driven, so focused on his job—whatever it happened to be—than her oldest brother.

If anyone could get to the heart of the Rowan Smith case, it was John.

John snapped closed his cell phone and pushed aside Tess's worries. He had work to finish quickly if he was to get back up to California to help his brother. Though more confident in Michael's ability than Tess was, he wondered about Smith and her background. He knew how deceptive the FBI could be, especially when they protected one of their own.

He couldn't give this operation any more time. He called his DEA contact with the longitude and latitude of the warehouse where over ten thousand kilos of pure heroin was stored. He'd hoped to track down the elusive Reginald Pomera, but not this time.

He looked down and saw his clenched fists. He'd thought for sure this was the time he'd confront Pomera. He was so close. So close he could almost smell the bastard.

He forced himself to relax, taking slow, drawn-out breaths. Reminded himself that his consulting assignments for the DEA were sporadic work, at best. His new career was the security business with Michael and Tess. He was no longer an agent, no longer in the employ of the government.

Unless, of course, they needed his specialized skills in tracking down and hunting big-time drug lords like Pomera, he thought bitterly. Then he reminded himself that it had been his choice to walk away from that career.

Not as though he'd had much of a decision. Sell your soul to the devil to catch a devil. It wasn't a choice he could have made.

He paced, checking the status of the warehouse through the electronic sensors he'd planted earlier. Four guards around the perimeter, two inside. No one was on alert. Business as usual.

Even if Tess hadn't called him about returning to L.A., he would have needed to call in the raid soon, anyway. The drugs were scheduled for transport tomorrow night—and his gut told him Pomera was not going to make an appearance.

There was no way he could allow those drugs to end

up on the streets of America. It was a small blow to the huge drug cartel, but a blow nonetheless. And if one kid didn't die—it'd be worth it.

If all went well, he'd be in Los Angeles in thirty-six hours.

A quiet knock awakened Michael. Early-morning light streamed through the curtains. He jumped from bed, alert, not mindful that he wore only briefs. Rowan stood in the doorway.

She averted her eyes. "I'm going for a run."

"I'll come with you."

"You don't have to do that."

"I'm going with you. Give me three minutes."

He hadn't slept well, and it showed in his reflection. His dark whiskers made him appear even shabbier than he felt; his green eyes were bloodshot, making them seem brighter. He splashed water on his face, finger-combed his hair, and dressed in sweatpants and a T-shirt.

The smell of coffee lured him to the kitchen. Rowan stood at the sink drinking a tall glass of water, her long, straight blonde hair pulled into a high ponytail. She wore no makeup, yet Michael found her just as attractive this morning.

"Let's go," he said, pushing aside his personal interest in Rowan. He wouldn't let her distract him from the job he had to do. Not that she was doing it on purpose, he thought. If anything, she kept a wide physical and emotional distance from everyone.

"It's a three-mile run from here to the other end of the beach and back. I run it twice. Up for it?"

"No problem," he said. "Let me look around." He noticed she had a gun in a holster at her back. Not the Glock; this one was a little Heckler & Koch, the "Rolls-Royce" of 9mm semiautos. "Nice piece," he commented.

"Writing must pay well. I'm sure you couldn't afford that on a government salary."

She was beautiful when she smiled, he noted. "Yeah, it was a treat when I could walk into the gun store and pay cash for it. Maybe we should go to the range today, get in a little target practice. I'll let you try it."

"Couldn't hurt," he said.

After checking the deck and beach, he said, "In the future, you might want to consider driving somewhere else if you feel the need to run."

"Maybe." She didn't sound like she had any intention of taking him up on his suggestion, and she set off at a vigorous pace, preventing further conversation.

Rowan was surprised at how comfortable she felt with Michael Flynn. If she didn't think about him as a bodyguard, she could almost get used to the company. As long as she thought of him as merely backup, she could live with the lack of privacy. For now.

She loved running on the beach, the packed, wet sand hard enough for traction but soft enough to cushion each step. It was early and cold, the air salty and thick, the churning water caressing the land, then pulling back, a never-ending cycle of tides in, tides out. The edge of the world, where the vast Pacific met land, humbled any human who appreciated its strength.

Two laps later, she jogged up the steps to her deck. She was about to enter the house when Michael commanded, "Stop." He brushed past her, unlocked the door, and looked around. When all was clear, he told her to come in.

A reminder of who he was and why he was here.

Rowan and Michael had no opportunity to go to the shooting range that day. She was needed at the studio for a rewrite. Annette had suggested all parties involved meet in Malibu, but Rowan put her foot down, saying, "I need to get out of this house."

Tess met Michael and Rowan at her closet-sized office in the studio. Rowan looked at them skeptically. "Michael, I thought we agreed I'd be safe here."

True, they'd spoken with studio security when they'd arrived and Michael was comfortable that the head of security understood the threat. But he wanted his own person there, someone who answered to him. Since John was out of town, Tess was the only option.

"Humor me, okay?"

Rowan rolled her eyes and changed the subject. "I'm going to call the Bureau and see where my old case files are. I thought they'd have been sent over by now. We can pick them up at FBI headquarters on the way back."

"Fine. Be careful, Rowan."

"Always."

He watched Tess follow Rowan out and felt a pang of regret that he was leaving. But he wanted to check in with LAPD and see if they'd traced the flowers. It wouldn't hurt to make sure the chief knew he was on the case. Might get them better information on the status of the investigation.

Rowan would be safe as long as she stayed within the confines of the studio.

He arrived at the police station just before three that afternoon, but the chief and Detective Jim Barlow were both in a meeting with the Feds. Michael waited, chatted with his former colleagues, and grew antsy as his wait stretched into an hour.

Finally, just as he was thinking of leaving, the chief's secretary motioned to him. "You can go in now."

Chief Bunker stood behind his desk, phone tucked between his ear and shoulder.

"Flynn, good to see you. Wish it was under better circumstances." He slammed the phone down with a frown and shook Michael's hand. "Barlow just left with the Feds to a crime scene. They tracked down the flowers."

"And?"

"Shop near the San Fernando Mission. Records show that Christine Jamison sold a funeral wreath on Sunday to be delivered to Ms. Smith on Tuesday. Two uniforms went to her apartment. She's dead."

CHAPTER
4

Michael was getting into his SUV when his cell phone chirped. Caller ID told him it was Tess. "What's up?"

"Mickey!" She sounded breathless.

Adrenaline pumped. Something was wrong. "What happened?"

"Get over here quick. There was an incident on the set."

"Is Rowan hurt?" His heart pounded.

"No, she thinks it was a prank. She told me not to call you, but—"

"I'll be right there." He ended the call, then dialed the chief's direct line and asked him to send a patrol to the studio, even though he didn't have all the details.

He made record time to the studio. On the movie set, the uniformed cops were already talking to Annette, who looked like she wanted to strangle them. He spotted Rowan standing at the back of the set. Safe. Tess ran up to him, launching immediately into an explanation.

"We were watching a rehearsal here in Studio B when the actors took a break, and David Cline—he's the director—started talking with Rowan about changes and then someone screamed. I yelled for Rowan to stay put. I had my gun out, but so did she, and she led the way to the stage."

Michael's heart clenched at the image of his kid sister

running around with a gun. While he'd trained her, she was still not ready for fieldwork. He should never have assigned her to watch over Rowan today. But in all honesty, he hadn't thought anything would happen at the studio. Not with all the security measures they already had in place.

"Marcy Blair, one of the actresses, the one who screamed, was standing over a puddle of blood," Tess continued. "No one was hurt. Rowan stared at it a long time, and I thought she was going to lose it. Then she bent down and touched it. It was fake. No one saw who dumped it. Everyone was on break. Marcy Blair was the first one back."

Someone touched Michael's arm and he whirled around, tense from the news and the lack of facts.

It was Rowan. Her pale face was drawn, but determined. "Michael, trust me. There's no crime here. Send the police away."

"How do you know?" He mentally hit himself for assuming security was sound. If something had happened to Tess or Rowan . . . he didn't want to contemplate the thought. He would not leave them alone again. It was *his* job to protect Rowan, after all, studio security notwithstanding.

Rowan brought her face close to his and he swallowed. Something about this woman drew him in, but right now he was too angry and frustrated to dwell on it.

"Michael," she said softly, "I know who spilled the fake blood. He's a good kid, and I don't want him to get in trouble. I'll let you talk to him if you downplay this. Please tell the cops there was a misunderstanding."

He almost refused. He felt like scaring the living shit out of someone, and a bratty kid seemed like a good target. "You'd better be right," he said through clenched teeth.

Michael approached the uniforms, explained there was a misunderstanding, and said he would speak personally to the chief. That appeased them, and they left. Annette tried to lecture him about calling in outsiders like the police, but Michael ignored her. He'd call in whoever was necessary to get the job done.

Michael walked Rowan to her office, where she gathered her belongings. "Okay, what's going on?"

"Adam Williams is my number-one fan," she said a little ruefully. "He's nineteen and comes from a troubled home. I met him two years ago when I came to L.A. to work on my first screenplay. He started following me around and I confronted him." She locked her office and they walked outside to Michael's SUV.

"He's a good kid," Rowan continued. "A little strange, but he doesn't have anyone to talk to outside of cyberspace. When I went back to Colorado last time, we kept in touch through e-mail. I like him. I got him a job in the prop department when I came out here two months ago, saw him around Studio B today. This is something he'd do." She shrugged and gave him a half-smile. "He likes scary jokes."

"I should have him arrested." Practical joke? Perhaps. Michael would be his own judge of the kid's intentions.

"It would hurt him in ways you can't imagine," she said, a faraway look in her eyes. "You have to let me do this my way. I won't have you threatening him. Adam's not mentally retarded, but he's a little slow."

"We'll see." At her stern glare, he relented. "I'll do it your way—at least at first."

Rowan directed Michael to a small duplex only three blocks from the studio, in an older, well-maintained section of Burbank. "Adam lives in the rear unit. Please let me handle this," she repeated.

He wanted to object, but her tense jaw showed her determination. At the same time, fatigue brightened her eyes. He touched her cheek with the tips of his fingers, but it turned into a caress. He dropped his arm. "I'll be your backup."

Rowan nodded, smiling wanly. She led the way down the drive to the rear unit and knocked on the door. No answer. She knocked again. "Adam, it's me, Rowan."

Shuffling. A bolt slid out of its lock; the door opened. Looking through the screen, over Rowan's head, Michael saw a tall, skinny, pale kid with enormous brown eyes and short brown hair. He wore a black T-shirt and faded jeans. His face was clear, hairless. He looked so young Michael wondered if he even shaved.

Adam looked from Rowan to Michael and back again, shuffling his feet. "Hi."

"May we come in, Adam?"

Adam glanced at Michael, suspicious.

"This is my friend, Michael Flynn. He works for the studio." When Adam didn't budge, Rowan added, "In security."

Adam frowned at Rowan. "You knew it was me, didn't you?"

"I'd like to come in," she said.

Adam unlocked the screen door and let them in. Michael was surprised at how tidy the kid was, though the room's décor was bizarre. The worn 'fifties-style furniture was functional if unattractive; the bookshelf in the corner overflowed with books, though Rowan's four novels were stacked neatly on the top shelf. The horror posters tacked to the walls unnerved Michael, but it was the realistic dummy sitting in the corner with its head half off, blood and tendons hanging out, that made him jump. The blood looked so real it appeared wet. Upon closer examination, it was simply plastic.

"Hey, Rowan!" Adam smiled widely. "Wait here—I want to show you something." He ran to the back of the house and Michael tensed momentarily. The kid seemed harmless, but appearances could be deceiving. He stood in front of Rowan.

"I thought you said you were backup," Rowan whispered.

"I'm still your bodyguard," he said, equally quiet.

Adam bounded back into the room, holding an ordinary box. "I think I solved the problem Barry was having with the blood seepage. I made a valve here, see?" He opened the box and showed Rowan, his back to Michael, effectively cutting him off, like a jealous child. "If we create a vacuum in the bag, once you release the valve, the blood will seep out at a slower rate. I can set the valve for any rate they want."

"That's smart, Adam. I wouldn't have thought of that."

"Do you think Barry will like it?"

"Yes, I think he will."

Adam was all smiles, bouncing on the balls of his feet.

"Adam, I need to talk to you about what happened in Studio B this afternoon."

Adam frowned, a child about to be reprimanded. "I—I—I didn't mean to scare you, Rowan. I thought nothing scared you. But Marcy was really mean to Barry this morning. It wasn't his fault the vase broke before it was supposed to. He *told* her to hold it by the base, and she didn't listen. She never listens to him. Barry was really upset, and I thought it was okay to scare her because she's really mean, anyway." His bottom lip protruded and quivered.

Rowan took Adam's hand and led him to the couch. She sat down, motioning for Adam to sit as well. She nodded at Michael and motioned toward the chair in the corner, next to the beheaded dummy. He sat and frowned at the mannequin. How could anyone live with that staring at him?

"Adam, I've told you before that you can't play those kinds of jokes at the studio. Some people don't think they're funny."

"But I didn't hurt anyone! I just wanted to scare her."

"I know you wouldn't hurt anyone on purpose. But sometimes, jokes go too far." She paused. "Marcy *is* mean, and Barry didn't deserve to be yelled at. But Marcy didn't deserve to be scared. Barry told me that you are very valuable to him, that you do a good job. I don't want you to jeopardize your job, Adam."

"Th-they wouldn't fire me, would they? I didn't mean—" He was on the verge of tears.

Rowan squeezed his hand. "No, I promise you won't be fired over this. But tomorrow you're going to have to tell Barry what you did. And you have to promise him, and me, that you won't play any more practical jokes on anyone at the studio."

"I won't. I'm sorry. I didn't meant to hurt anyone." He blinked and looked like a lost puppy. "Are we still friends?"

"Of course. We'll always be friends, Adam."

He nodded. "I'm sorry."

"Adam, I can trust you, right?"

"Oh, yes. Always." He crossed his heart like a six-year-old might after making a solemn promise.

"You're going to be reading some things in the newspaper, and I want to tell you what's happening. There's a very bad man who's killing people and using my stories. He's taking murders from my books—pretend murders—and making them real."

Adam's eyes widened. "That's bad."

"The police are investigating, and the studio hired Mr. Flynn here to keep an eye out for me."

Adam gave Michael a curious, assessing scan, then frowned. "He's your bodyguard."

She nodded, though Michael noted she flinched. She still wasn't comfortable with his role. "I want you to be particularly careful," she said. "Don't talk to anyone about me. If someone seems official, ask to see identification. You know the difference between what's fake and what's real."

"I can tell the difference," he nodded vigorously.

"Good. Tell me if you see or hear anything strange, something that doesn't seem right. Call me anytime."

"I'll watch out for you. I promise."

"I know you will." She squeezed his hand and stood up. "I'm going to go now. Remember what I said."

"I will." He jumped up and walked them to the door.

From his small front porch, Adam watched Rowan and her bodyguard Mr. Flynn walk down the driveway. When he could no longer see them, he went in and ate his favorite soup—chicken and stars. He ate the whole pot of soup because it was there, then he washed and cleaned up. Rowan had told him it was important to clean up after yourself because no one would do it for you.

When he finished, he sat down with another mystery. And then he forgot almost everything Rowan had told him.

Rowan stared out the passenger window of Michael's SUV, worried, frustrated, and ticked off. They were headed back to Malibu after a long day. Between the studio, talking to Adam, and the fiasco at the FBI field office in downtown Los Angeles, Rowan couldn't wait to get to the beach house. Though she hated its sterile décor, she longed for the peace, the sound of the waves crashing against the beach, and most important, privacy.

The L.A. field director had turned over her old case files to Special Agent Quincy Peterson. He was probably waiting right that moment for her at her house. She'd told Roger not to send anyone from Washington, but he trusted Quinn. She shouldn't have been surprised Roger would want someone they both knew on the case.

She certainly didn't want to see him again. Out of all the agents Roger could have tagged to help, why Quinn?

"The FBI is taking this seriously," Michael commented.

She turned from the window and closed her eyes. She wasn't about to get into her complicated friendship with Quinn Peterson with a virtual stranger.

"They're reviewing my cases back in D.C. and checking on the status of prisoners and their families, but I asked Roger to let me go through my old cases." She shook her head. "I don't know if it'll help, but I need to do something or I'll go crazy."

"Roger Collins?"

She nodded, glancing at him. He didn't sound surprised. Then again, she wouldn't be shocked to learn he'd run a quick background check on her. "My old boss. He's an assistant director." There were several assistant directors, but it was nonetheless a high-ranking position.

"I didn't get a chance to tell you earlier, but the police found the florist." He paused. "She's dead."

Rowan had expected this, but it didn't feel any better knowing she was right. The sick dread that had started when she learned of Doreen Rodriguez spread deeper. Her meager hope that all this wasn't personal now vanished.

It *was* personal. And now the urge to go over her cases one by one to see if she'd missed *anything* was stronger than ever.

"How?" Was that weak squeak her voice? She didn't recognize it.

"Christine Jamison's throat was slit."

"With a knife from her kitchen," Rowan said, picturing the crime in her mind. Remembering her book. It was straight from her book.

"How did you—? Oh. Yeah."

"When?"

"Yesterday. About the same time the flowers were delivered to you."

The bastard had planned it all. Right down to baiting her, sending her the flowers while killing the florist. He probably got a sick thrill out of it, knowing that the police would be able to put together the timeline.

"One of your books was left behind," Michael continued. He took her hand. She glanced down, uneasy, but didn't pull her hand away. She hadn't had much comfort in the last couple of days, and this small bit of human connection gave her some strength to draw on.

"*Crime of Passion,*" she whispered. "In that book, a florist was killed so as not to be able to identify the man who was stalking his victim and sending her white roses."

"You still think this isn't about you?" he asked.

"Dammit, I know it's about me! I just don't want to accept it. It's personal, premeditated. And there will be more victims unless we figure this out. And then he'll come after me. *And I don't know why!*" She pulled her hand from Michael's and slammed her fist on the dash-board.

Rowan was grateful for Michael's silence. She stared out the window, running over every case she'd worked on. Roger would let her know immediately if one of her convicts was out. But few of them could have put to-gether these elaborately planned crimes.

William James Stanton, perhaps. A sexual sadist, he'd been sentenced by a stupid jury to life imprisonment rather than death. They'd bought his twisted sob story that he'd been so abused by his mother as a child that he wasn't actually killing pretty young moms on the East-ern seaboard, but was killing his own abusive mother over and over.

Rowan hadn't bought it. Stanton took intense plea-sure in torturing and raping his victims.

Or Lars Richard Gueteschow, the Butcher of Brent-wood. He'd hacked up teenagers—boys or girls, it didn't matter; there was nothing sexual about it—and stored their body parts in his freezer. Until one girl got away. Rowan could imagine him getting a twisted pleasure in tormenting her, the agent who'd gathered the evidence and testified against him. But he was on death row in San Quentin.

Most crimes she had investigated were jurisdictional, violent crimes the FBI became involved in because the murders occurred in more than one state. Not many of those killers could have orchestrated such a detailed op-eration as these new murders.

But where else could she look? Their relatives? Friends, neighbors, colleagues? People who had a grotesque fas-cination with their crimes? Going that route, they'd have thousands of suspects. Her head ached. She squeezed her fingers into her eyes, suddenly weary.

She just didn't know if they'd have enough time before the bastard struck again.

Rowan's hair was limp, her posture now less than rigid. She glanced over her shoulder twice, and jumped when the bodyguard touched her.

Some distance away, he smiled. She was exhausted and afraid. Good. He was giddy that he was giving her sleepless nights. He hoped that whatever sleep she managed was disturbed by nightmares of blood. Did she feel any guilt? Any complicity? After all, it was her own words that determined who lived and who died. He chuckled as he watched.

She'd come home with her bodyguard to that impatient FBI agent who'd been waiting at her door for the last hour. The agent had rung the doorbell several times, glanced at his watch even more often, and paced. The Fed didn't worry him.

The bodyguard, however, worried him slightly. Knowing Rowan as he did, he hadn't expected her to ask for help. She was so confident, so cool. Not the type to get a bodyguard. Her lover? No. She hadn't been with a man since before leaving the FBI. What was that guy's name? Oh, yeah. Hamilton. Also a Fed.

Oh, yes, he'd been watching her—one way or another—for a long time.

The bodyguard would be dealt with when the right time came. A silencer would do the trick, though he loathed guns. It made killing so impersonal.

That was for later.

First, Rowan needed to be broken. He wanted her to melt, to burn. He needed her emotion, her temper. Mostly, he wanted her fear. Then—only then—would he confront her.

Until that time, he had many things to do. He'd

marked the chosen for death. Nothing could now alter their fate. He was a god; fate would run its course. Then he and Rowan would meet again. She would know him and know fear.

And beg for her life before she died.

He waited until dark, then left. He had another flight to catch.

CHAPTER
5

He waited for Tess to close her apartment door, then clamped a hand over her mouth. Thinking fast, she swung her laptop around hard and hit him on the shoulder, but the momentum of her attack enabled him to twist her wrist. He forced her to drop the computer and cruelly bent her arm back. He felt her wince and try to pivot for control. But she'd already lost.

He let her go and flipped on the lights.

"I've told you a thousand times that an attacker can use your momentum against you."

"John! You bastard!" Tess tried to slap him, but he grabbed her arm. "How did you get in here?"

He gave her a quizzical look. "Your locks are child's play, but I actually got in through the window in the bathroom. I've told you to put a security lock on it at least a dozen times." He smirked. "Now, now, you lost fair and square. Give it up." He pulled her into a bear hug. "I've missed you, sis."

"I missed you, too, until about two minutes ago." She leaned back, surveying him like a mother would a wayward son, love and concern etched on her pretty, pixie-like face. "You've lost weight."

"South American jungles. What I can eat and drink I sweat off."

"Let me fix you dinner."

"Thought you'd never ask." He followed her to the small kitchen, checking windows as he went. "Have any juice?"

"Orange juice." She nodded at the refrigerator. She grabbed a pot out of the dishwasher and filled it with water. "You know the only thing I can cook is spaghetti."

"Some things never change. But I love spaghetti." He actually didn't care much for the eating process except to provide fuel for his body. He took out the juice container, shook it, and guzzled its contents, then tossed the empty carton into the trash and looked back in the fridge. He took out a water bottle and drank half in one gulp.

Tess watched with a half-smile. "Yes, some things never change."

"Tell me more about Mickey's case." He pulled out a chair at the small kitchen table and sat, leaning against the back until the front legs lifted off the floor.

She shrugged and poured a jar of sauce into a pot. "There's not much to tell except another woman died. A florist."

"Mimicking Smith's book?" At the airport in Mexico City he'd bought the latest bestselling Rowan Smith novel, *Crime of Corruption*. He read it cover-to-cover on the plane, hooked. He admired the protagonist, a no-nonsense FBI agent with realistic faults, and the villain was pure evil under a face as normal as, well, his.

If he hadn't known such malevolence existed, he'd have thought Smith exaggerated. But he'd known murdering bastards so twisted and deranged that he was sincerely amazed that their evil couldn't be seen on the surface.

Even Satan had once been an angel.

"John?"

He shook his head and grinned at her. "Just day-dreaming."

"More like a nightmare," Tess said. "You okay?"

"I didn't get Pomera."

Her eyes conveyed sympathy. "Was it because I called you? Pulled you out too soon?"

He shook his head. "I had to go after the warehouse or tons of drugs would be hitting our coast next week. At least we pulled a major plug. It'll take them some time to recoup their losses and rebuild inventory. One, two months maybe."

Tess's jaw dropped. "And then they'll be back in business? After just two months? What's the point? No matter what you do, how many tons of drugs you destroy, there's always more."

That was the grim reality in the war on drugs. No matter how many men they killed, how many tons of cocaine and heroin they destroyed, there were always more daring criminals, an endless supply of poor farmers, and ultimately more drugs. If he could save just one kid from making the same stupid mistake Denny had made . . .

He couldn't think about his dead friend now. Not when he'd been so close to nabbing Pomera. But the bastard was always just beyond his reach. Next time.

It wasn't his job anymore, he reminded himself, not officially. Only when the powers that be needed him, needed his connections, was he given the opportunity to legally chase Pomera. He let himself be used because each and every time he was able to destroy a shipment. Keep at least one batch of drugs off the streets of America. And maybe—just maybe—save a life.

"You're right, Tess."

"You don't have to fight a losing battle. Stay here and help Mickey."

"Speaking of Mickey—" John changed the subject. Tess wouldn't understand. Couldn't. She didn't know the evil people did to others. To people they knew, as well as to total strangers.

Focus on the case at hand. "Think he's getting too close?" It wouldn't be the first time, but Michael was a good cop. Yes, he'd let his personal feelings interfere on occasion, but he'd never screwed up on the job.

She nodded. "Just like with Jessica."

John remembered Rowan Smith's picture on the back of her book, primarily because it was so unusual for a novelist. Instead of a close-up, or half body shot, she stood in the distance, leaning against a pine tree of some sort, snow on the ground and branches above her head. It wasn't even a front shot, but her profile: aristocratic, elegant, defiant.

Most people wouldn't be able to recognize her from the picture; she was dressed all in white, with long hair so blonde it looked as white as the snow in the background. It hung smooth and silky down her back. The picture conveyed an overwhelming sense of loneliness, of separation.

"I'm worried about him," Tess said.

John took her hand and squeezed, shaking his head. "Mickey's a big boy. He's a good bodyguard. He knows what he's doing."

"I'm not talking about his professional abilities. I'm talking about his personal involvement in this case."

"It's kind of quick to make that kind of assessment, don't you think?" Even as John objected, he guessed that his sister's instincts were correct. Michael jumped feet first with women. Ever since Missy Sue Carmichael, the senior who took his brother's virginity when he was fifteen. Then Brenda the following year, Tammy,

Maria . . . hell, John couldn't keep track of all the women Michael had fallen in love with over the years.

Tess looked at him, her little nose scrunched up in disbelief. "Right, John."

Yeah, Tess knew Michael as well as he did. "Don't worry about him, Tessie. He can take care of himself."

"Maybe, but I just feel that this case is different somehow. Higher stakes."

"I'll keep an eye on him," John promised.

After thirty minutes of ultra-polite, frustrating, and tension-filled conversation with Special Agent Quinn Peterson and Rowan, Michael left the room, closing himself off in the den. He had calls to make.

The good news was the FBI had reviewed the security procedures Michael implemented and the L.A. field office was assigning two more agents though Rowan had argued against it. Tomorrow they would interview Rowan's Malibu neighbors. Four of the dozen or so houses on this stretch of beach were vacant, either vacation rentals or closed up while their owners lived in another of their homes. The FBI was alerting each property management company to watch those houses closely and notify the Bureau if anything looked amiss.

Teams would be dispatched as needed, but resources being thin they couldn't commit to full surveillance— only one around-the-clock team, aside from Peterson and his partner. But the FBI was working closely with local law enforcement to help coordinate information and offered priority use of their lab facilities at Quantico.

Peterson had brought a box packed with copies of Rowan's case files. She had kept reaching for it, obviously antsy to get started, making no secret that she thought Peterson should go.

Michael had sensed there'd been something more than a professional relationship between Rowan and this FBI agent; Rowan's invisible shield had gone back up. Michael's efforts to get inside her mind, understand her, coax her to bring down her defenses, were stymied once Quinn Peterson showed up. Michael felt a bolt of jealousy, but quickly tamped down that emotion.

He couldn't let himself get emotionally involved with another vulnerable woman. Not that Rowan was vulnerable in the traditional sense—he greatly admired her strength and focus. But she needed him, and Michael was well aware of his past with women who needed him. Two sides within him battled, and he was determined to stay his distance.

But he had to admit he was intrigued by Rowan. She was unlike any other woman he'd ever met.

In the den, Michael picked up the phone and dialed a friend with the L.A. Bureau of the FBI. "Tony, it's Michael Flynn."

"Hey, long time. What's up?"

"I need some information." He told the agent about the case and asked him to look into Rowan's FBI background, on the Q-T. Though the Feds were already working the investigation, Michael wanted to know everything they did.

Tony whistled softly. "You're asking me to get involved in the affairs of upper management. I'm just in bank fraud."

"You're the only one I know over there. Can't you see what you can find out?"

Tony paused. "I'll try, but don't count on it. Why don't you ask your brother? He has better connections, and they're probably in Washington."

"John's out of the country." Besides, Michael didn't want to bring him in. He'd ask for his brother's help if he really needed it, but not a minute before. John would take over. Like he always did.

"Hmm. Okay, Mick, I'll see what I can come up with for ya. But seriously, I doubt I'll get anything without raising a helluva lot of red flags."

"Thanks, Tony, I appreciate whatever you can dig up." He hung up. Tony was right about one thing: John had valuable contacts. It would be prudent to bring him in, but Michael preferred not to ask his brother for help.

Still, after the florist . . . he should call him, if only for advice. He picked up the phone and dialed John's home number, knowing he wasn't there but would check his messages. "John, it's Michael," he said into the answering machine. "Call me when you get back to town. I want your opinion on a new case I'm working."

Well, he should be back in L.A. in a couple of days, Michael thought. He'd talk to him then.

The phone rang as soon as Michael hung up, and he let the answering machine get it. *"Rowan, call me."* Pause. Click.

A male voice, concerned.

Michael frowned. Could be harmless, maybe an old college friend or a former colleague from the Bureau. Or not.

Was Rowan keeping something secret? Something that could get her killed?

Michael made another call.

Rowan closed the double doors of the den and breathed deeply. She'd finally convinced Quinn to leave, and she'd then asked Michael for a few minutes alone to unwind.

Seeing Quinn had brought back a flood of memories, both good and bad. They'd become friends while she trained at the FBI Academy in Quantico. For Rowan, friends were rare. She'd never deluded herself—Quinn made a point to befriend both her and Olivia because he was involved with their roommate, Miranda Moore. It wasn't exactly protocol for a field-rated agent to be romantically attached to a trainee, so making sure she and Olivia liked him enough to keep the secret was a priority.

But Rowan certainly wouldn't forgive him for taking from Miranda the one thing that mattered most to her: her dreams. After everything Miranda had been through—Rowan shook her head. It wasn't fair, and it was all Quinn's fault.

Rowan had been so caught up in her memories she missed the message the first time. She pressed rewind, play.

"Rowan, call me." Pause. Click.

Peter.

She dialed the number in Boston, her hand shaking so badly she had to hang up and redial. It was after eleven on the East Coast.

On the third ring, a quiet voice answered. "Saint John's."

"Father O'Brien, please," Rowan asked quietly. She glanced at the den door. It was closed.

A minute later, her brother's familiar voice answered. "This is Father O'Brien. How may I help you?"

Tears she hadn't realized she'd been holding back flowed freely. "Peter, it's me."

"Thank God you called. I was so worried."

"I'm sorry I didn't call you. I—I didn't think." *I didn't want you to be in danger.*

"Don't kick yourself. I saw the newspapers and couldn't reach you. I knew you were okay, but I had to make sure. I needed to hear your voice."

"I'm okay."

"You're crying."

She sucked in her breath, slowly let it out. "I miss you."

"I miss you, too. I pray for you every day."

"You don't have to do that."

Silence. "Rowan—"

"All right, I'm sorry." Rowan felt Peter's comforting presence even three thousand miles away. They didn't see each other often. Rowan's fault, she knew. Peter would have moved anywhere in the country to be near her, but she didn't want to use him as a crutch. He would fill the role all too happily, but Rowan couldn't do that to him. Or her. The only time she'd run to him was four years ago—but then it had been either Peter or the loony bin, and she wasn't ready to give up her sanity for her job. Peter had helped pick up the pieces.

"Are you taking precautions?"

"Yes. The studio hired a bodyguard and the FBI's involved." She bit her fingernail, thinking of Michael. As soon as Quinn left, he'd offered her a comforting hand. It was easy to fall into the protective trap, to hold on to someone who offered a potent dose of sanity and strength. But that wasn't fair to Michael, and it certainly wasn't what she needed right now.

"Good." The relief in Peter's voice was evident.

"I can take care of myself."

"You *think* you can."

"I can. Really. But, to be honest, I'm glad I have help. A partner, if you will. Of course, I wouldn't tell him that." What surprised Rowan most of all was that she *was* glad to have Michael around. He was smart, experienced, and gave her the space she needed. He was comfortable. Like Peter. If only she hadn't felt him watching her with more than cop's eyes.

"Independent to the last. God is with you."

"Don't preach to me, Peter," Rowan snapped, instantly regretting it. She didn't want to hurt him. He was the only person who truly mattered to her now that she didn't fight for the victims anymore.

"I'm not preaching, I'm only telling the truth." He paused. "Do you want to come out here for a while?"

"Absolutely not. I won't put you in jeopardy." Though there was nothing she wanted more than to see her brother.

"No one knows about me."

"And I don't want to change that. I shouldn't have called you from home. I need to be more careful."

"Anyway, what would anyone think if you came here? You've spent time in Boston before."

"Even if they didn't know who you really are, I still worry about my friends. Anyone I know could be a target."

"You have no friends. You're a hermit."

"That's not true. I have friends."

"Name one."

"I can name two. Miranda and Olivia."

"Your old roommates?" Peter sounded skeptical. "Do you keep in touch?"

"Of course," she said, feeling a twinge of guilt at the lie. When was the last time she'd spoken to Liv? More than a year ago, though she had sent her an e-card for her birthday just last week, before all this happened. Miranda? She'd had a hard time after being booted from Quantico. An occasional note or postcard in the mail— nothing since Christmas. But Rowan didn't blame her; Miranda was on a mission, one Rowan understood all too well.

"Rowan?"

"Sorry, woolgathering."

"You don't really have anyone to support you right now, do you?"

"I don't need anyone. Really, Peter. I'm fine."

"I doubt that."

"Don't." She wiped some tears from her face, took a deep breath, and resolved to stand strong. "I—I love you, Peter."

"I love you, too. Call me if you need anything. *Anything.*"

"I will. And Peter—be careful. Just in case."

She hung up the phone and dialed Roger at his Washington home. She had to make sure her brother was kept safe.

John whistled softly as he and Tess walked up to the Malibu house. "Nice spread."

"It's not hers. A friend or something. She has a cabin in Colorado and is just in L.A. because her book's being made into a movie."

"You sound jealous," John teased.

She shrugged and playfully hit him in the arm. "Not really. Maybe a little about the house and everything, but she doesn't seem to be the happiest woman in the world, regardless of the money her books and movies are bringing in."

Michael answered the bell, surprise in his eyes as he looked from John to Tess and back at his brother. "I thought you were in South America until the end of the week."

"Wrapped up early." He walked in, closed the door, and surveyed the surroundings. "Cush job, Mickey."

"While you were sunning it up in Bolivia, I got the call." Michael broke into a wide smile. "Glad you're back in one piece, Johnny." He embraced his brother, slapping him on the back in a bear hug.

"Me, too." John stepped back, squeezed Michael's shoulders and grinned. "It's really good to see you." He dropped his hands and looked around. Cold, sterile, artificial. He certainly wouldn't want to live in this expensive tribute to minimalism. "Can you use help?"

Michael stood back, hesitating. John understood how hard it was for Michael to ask for his help. Tess, yes. Cops, yes. His older brother, no.

"Sure, always. I left a message for you, actually. Tess didn't tell me you were coming back early." Michael narrowed his eyes at Tess, but wrapped an arm around her shoulder and kissed the top of her head.

Their brief reunion was interrupted by a female clearing her throat. John turned his eyes to Rowan Smith for the first time.

He was surprised at his reaction. He wasn't a first-sight-attraction kind of guy. But the impression he had of Rowan from her book jacket was nothing compared to the woman in person. She still had the rigid, distant look of her profiled picture. Elegant and classy. A blend of the 1930s temptress with the cool estrangement of a twenty-first-century professional. No doubt a beautiful, remarkably striking woman, but there was something more. Her intelligent, stormy blue eyes, watching and curious. John noted how she kept herself detached from them, her body turned at a slight angle, almost as if she were ready to bolt even as she looked him straight in the eye.

Captivating.

He glanced at Michael and saw the familiar look on his brother's face. He was smitten. Michael glanced at him and frowned, almost imperceptibly. He probably considered John a rival—at least as far as Ms. Rowan Smith was concerned.

They stared at each other briefly, and John tried to

judge how hard Michael had fallen. Without a doubt, his brother was in deep, but he seemed to be keeping his emotions in check. If John didn't know Michael as well as he did, he wouldn't see the competition in his eyes.

When they were in high school, they'd instituted the "First Sight Rule" to avoid fighting over girls. They were only a year apart and were frequently attracted to the same women. To keep the peace in the family, they had agreed that whoever saw the girl first had first right of refusal.

Not this time.

John dumped the rule then and there. By the look on Michael's face, he knew it too.

I'll make it up to him.

Besides, they didn't have time for fun and games while a killer was on the loose. And protecting his family—and now Rowan Smith—was John's number-one responsibility.

CHAPTER
6

She stood outside the picturesque two-story white colonial, heart pounding, a light sheen of perspiration on her back. Her skin was clammy, and she wondered if she was coming down with something.

The house was familiar, but she'd never been to this part of Nashville before. She glanced at local Agent Tom Krause, a seasoned veteran she'd worked with on another multiple homicide in Tennessee two years before.

Mature trees, evenly spaced, grew tall on the recently mowed lawn. Trimmed hedges stood sentry, marking the bottom of every closed window, every blood-red shutter. Yellow crime-scene tape slashed the serene landscape, a stark reminder of what awaited her inside.

Rowan had walked through hundreds of crime scenes. She'd seen the worst that man could do to his fellow man. Gathering her emotions, she pushed them down as far as she could, deep down, behind her soul. But today, she was having a harder time separating herself from the crime scene. Somehow, this murder was different. Familiar.

She stood in the entry hall of the immaculate home. Clean, comfortable, expensive furnishings, polished wood. There was the general disturbance associated with law enforcement presence, but the house was otherwise neat as a pin. The smell of a lemon-scented cleaner mingled with the coppery scent she knew too well, the metallic taste of blood already in her nostrils, her mouth. She closed her eyes, gathering her strength.

Why was it so hard to proceed?

"Agent Smith, you okay?"

Tom's voice cut through her hesitation. She snapped her eyes opened and nodded. "Of course, just thinking. Who were the victims?"

Tom glanced at his notepad. "Karl and Marlena Franklin and their children. Suspected murder-suicide, but the techs haven't been through the scene except to photograph it."

She nodded and continued to survey the surroundings. The bottom of the staircase landed in the foyer, curving elegantly as it approached the second floor. Displayed on the wall were pictures of a growing family, arranged step-by-step, year-by-year. The mother and father, dark-haired and blue-eyed, together. Together with an infant. Then an infant and a toddler. A toddler and a kinder-gartner. Two kids and a baby. Two kids and a toddler and a baby. Dark hair, blue eyes, attractive family.

Three boys and a baby girl.

At the top of the stairs was the last portrait this family would ever take together. Three boys, the oldest about twelve. A little girl, three, with dark pigtails and red ribbons in the hair.

Pigtails and ribbons.

Run! *Her mind screamed, but she was compelled to move forward. She heard Tom talking, but didn't hear his words.*

Run!

Her feet were rooted in the too-familiar house.

The blood in the first room was confined to the bed. Oldest boy, Packers football fan, baseball awards on his

*shelves and walls. Second room, bunk beds, more blood.
She smelled it, tasted it, breathed it into her lungs and
gagged.*

"Rowan."

*The voice was far away, and she put one foot in front
of the other, leaving Tom behind.*

"Rowan!"

*She turned into the last door, knowing before she
opened it what she would see.*

*The baby girl's room decorated in pink and white
frills, full of teddy bears and dolls. A picnic had been
laid out on the floor, complete with a Babar the Ele-
phant tea set and guests. A teddy bear, a giraffe, and
Babar preparing to partake in the meal. Left from yesterday's game.*

*An empty seat where the little girl would have sat.
Dani.*

*The little girl could have been sleeping. Would have
been sleeping until her life was stolen from her. Blood
soaked her white down comforter. Dear God, how
could so much blood come from such a tiny person!*

Pigtails.

Dani.

She screamed.

While drinking coffee in the dining room, John listened as Michael filled him in on the police investigation
and the FBI's role. Rowan had fallen asleep on the couch
in the adjoining living room less than half an hour before. She'd looked exhausted when John first saw her,
and he didn't doubt that recent nights had been interrupted by the pressure the killer placed on her.

A moan escaped Rowan, and both he and Michael
jumped up. They stared at each other for a moment,
then John sighed and sat back down. "Your case," he

said, though he wasn't sure he was making the right decision. Michael had been handling the security measures like the pro John knew he was, but whenever he looked at Rowan, a softness came over his face. A familiar expression, John thought, most recently seen when Michael was involved with that liar Jessica Weston.

Michael approached the couch cautiously as Rowan thrashed in her sleep. "Rowan," he said softly.

Suddenly, she screamed and bolted upright, her face a mask of terror as she teetered between sleep and wakefulness.

"Rowan! Rowan! Wake up!" Michael sat behind her and pulled her nearly into his lap, grabbing her waving arms. Even across the room John saw how tense Rowan was, her arms locked and quivering, almost in an empty hug.

"Dani, Dani!" she cried in the midst of her nightmare.

"What's wrong with her?" Tess asked, concerned, as she rose from the workstation she'd created in the adjoining alcove.

"Nightmare," Michael said grimly.

Who's *Danny?* John thought, frowning, his arms crossed over his chest as he rose from his seat.

Rowan quieted as Michael whispered nonsense in her ear and pulled her closer to him, patting her hair and smoothing it down her back. She shook from violent sobs, but no sound escaped.

"Rowan—"

"I'm sorry. I'm sorry." She turned into Michael's chest and her stifled sob tore at John's heart.

But John had to get to the bottom of this. "Who's Danny?" he asked, his voice harsher than intended.

Her head jerked up and she glared at him, her eyes red with unshed tears.

John ignored the signals Michael sent him to shut up. Something about this was important.

Rowan pushed herself away from Michael, reached to the small of her back, and removed her Glock from its holster. She checked the ammunition, put the gun back, and stood in the middle of the living room. John watched her control the terror of the nightmare, focusing instead on her obvious anger toward him. Why? He had only asked an obvious question. One Michael should have been asking instead of consoling her.

In the back of his heart, John wanted to wrap his arms around Rowan as well. But unlike his brother, he put sentiment on the back burner when lives were at stake.

"I need to call my boss. Ex-boss," she corrected. "I—I had a memory of a case I worked on. My last case. I'm wondering if there's some connection." She shook her head and closed her eyes. "I don't see how," she said, almost to herself, "but why else would I dream of the Franklin murders now?"

"Franklin murders?" John repeated.

She opened her eyes and looked at him. "Brutal murder-suicide. Or so we suspected at the time. There were some doubts, but I wasn't involved in the investigation. I need to see the file, though, and it's not in the box of cases Quinn brought over."

John nodded. He noted she grew composed as she became proactive. So different from the pain-filled woman who'd woken from a violent nightmare only moments ago.

"Who's Danny?" John asked again. "One of the victims?"

She looked at Michael, not John, her eyes once again shielding pain he'd seen only a moment before. She shrugged. "Another case. I've spent most of the day reviewing crime scene photos and notes. Everything's all mixed up. I don't know what I was dreaming about."

Dammit, John knew she was lying. She'd had a nightmare about Danny, whoever he was.

He sensed she wouldn't go into any more details now. Maybe it *was* all mixed up in her mind. But there was something there, something he needed to pull out. Maybe something her conscious mind didn't even realize was important.

"I'm going to call Roger," Rowan said, and she left the room without a backward glance.

Michael strode over to his brother and poked him in the chest. "What the hell were you doing? Interrogating her? Couldn't you see she'd just had a nightmare?"

John's jaw dropped. "Don't you think you're overreacting, Mickey? There's something trapped in that pretty little head of Ms. Smith's, and it's about time someone started asking the tough questions. Hell, I don't think she even knows what it is. But we need to push, we need to get to the bottom of this. The FBI is on top of it because she's one of theirs, but they aren't here in this room, are they?"

"You're doing it again," Michael said.

John blinked. "What?"

"Taking over my case."

John threw his hands up in the air, a rare outward sign of frustration, and stalked over to the dark windows that reflected Michael's angry expression and Tess's watchful eyes. This wasn't a new argument.

"I'm not taking over your case, Mickey," John said, though he itched to do just that. Michael had reasonable plans, but in John's mind they sounded like they would take too damned long to implement. Maybe Michael was trying to coddle Rowan into opening up, but John was more of a straight shooter. He expected everyone else to shoot straight as well.

"Could have fooled me," Michael said under his breath.

"There's more going on here than we know. Dammit, she knows something that could get us all killed. It's probably some damn FBI security issue, but screw it if I'm going to let you or Tess get hurt because the frickin' FBI won't share information!" John turned back to face his brother. "And if she doesn't consciously know it, it's locked in her mind and your sweet-as-pie commiserating isn't going to draw the truth out of her."

"I was a cop for fifteen years, in case you've forgotten," Michael said, taking a step toward John. "I may not have been a big, bad Delta commando, but I sure as hell know how to protect myself *and* my charge."

"Not if you can't see past her pretty face!"

Michael clenched his fists, vibrating with anger. "You just can't let me forget about fucking up with Jessica."

John mentally hit himself. He didn't want to hurt his brother. "I'm sorry, Mickey. I didn't mean to compare the two situations. But geez, can't you see there's something else here? I'm not going to let you put your life on the line for a woman—for *anyone*—who isn't forthcoming. Obviously these Franklin murders are important if she's having nightmares about them. I just think we need to find out more about Rowan Smith. She holds the key."

Finally, Michael looked at him. "You're right, John. Tomorrow morning, when we've all had some time to think about this, we'll sit down with Rowan and pick her brain."

"Good plan," John said as he approached his brother. He reached out and squeezed Michael's shoulder. "We're a team on this, Mickey. Like always."

"Are we?"

John almost didn't hear Michael, though they stood only two feet apart.

He said equally as softly, "Yeah, Mickey, we are."

But he didn't think his brother listened.

With a sigh, John whipped out his cell phone and dialed a Washington contact. "It's Flynn. I need some information."

They looked so sweet sitting on the sofa together eating popcorn and watching some stupid-ass love story on television. The popcorn came from an old-fashioned popper, not the new microwave bags that were ready in four minutes. No, the kind where you put oil in the bottom and butter on top of the lid and heated up the kernels until they filled the bowl. Like his mother used to do.

The portrait of a perfect family, the book said. Perfect? What a joke!

He thought back to his own pathetic family. His father could be strong, but most of the time had been a weak fool. Letting his mother run the roost when she was nothing but a whiny bitch. Always demanding this and asking for that. His father worked hard to put food on the table and had given them a nice house in the suburbs, and his mother just bitched bitched bitched and asked for more more more.

Money. That was all the bitch thought about.

He heard his mother's high-pitched voice like it was yesterday.

He'd been going through his mother's purse for money when he heard her coming down the hall. So he hid in the closet, keeping the sliding door slightly ajar so he could see if she came toward him. It was night and she thought he was in bed.

He was eight, but he'd been taking money for as long as he could remember. Today he needed more ammunition for his BB gun. He remembered when his dad bought it for him—it was the coolest thing his father had ever done. When the bitch protested, his father just told her if he wanted to buy his son a BB gun, he damn well would.

He smiled, knowing why he needed the ammunition. It had taken thirty-six of those little pellets to finally kill Mrs. Crenshaw's stupid, whiny cat.

For his next birthday, he was asking for a .22.

His mother went about doing all those girlie things at her table, taking off her makeup and brushing her hair, when his father walked in.

"Hi, honey," his mother said. "You're home late."

"I have children to feed and clothe," his father said, mad about something.

"I—I know, I just missed you, that's all."

She stood and walked over to him, kissed him. Yuck. They always did that kissing thing and it made him sick.

His father sighed and patted her stomach. It was starting to grow big. Another baby. Why did they have to have another one? Weren't there enough brats in this house?

His father loosened his tie and his mother said, "I looked at beds today for the girls. Since they'll have to share a room, I thought maybe getting them matching beds would be nice."

"Why didn't you ask me first? You didn't buy anything, did you?"

"No, no, I just looked. I thought—since you got that bonus—we could afford to get a few things around the house that we've been needing; you know, nothing extravagant, but—"

"Is that all you care about? Money?" His father slammed his fist so hard on the dresser that bottles of perfume and other girlie stuff crashed to the floor.

"No, honey, you know that—but with the baby coming I thought—"

Slap!

"Shut up about the damn baby!"

His mother sobbed. "You said you were happy."

Time seemed to stand still, and his little heart beat so fast from fear and a sort of excitement he didn't quite understand. What was his father going to do?

Finally, after a minute or two, his father ran a hand through his short hair. "I'm sorry, sweetheart. I didn't mean—I'm just under so much stress at work." He bent down to kiss her red cheek.

"I know. I know." She was sobbing, clinging to him. "It'll be all right. I can go back to work and—"

He pushed her away. "Work? Never. We made a deal. You have the kids and keep the house and I earn the money to support us."

"I know, and I love being a wife and mother, really, but if we're struggling, if we're going to lose the house, if—"

Slap!

"Why do you want to go to work? Does this have anything to do with George Claussen's visit last week?"

"George? I—he said I could have my old job back if I wanted it. Part-time, while the kids are in school. And when the baby comes—"

Slap!

"You and George are screwing around behind my back, aren't you?"

"No!"

Slap!

"Don't lie to me!"

"I'm not!" Sobs. More sobs. All girls did was cry. Especially his mother. She always cried and his father always gave in. Stupid!

He hated her.

"You will NOT get a job. We don't need it. I will provide. I will always provide for you. You believe me, don't you? Don't you?"

"Y-Y-Yes, I—I'm so sorry, I don't want to go to work. You are a wonderful father and husband. I love you so much." She sat sobbing on the floor, repeating garbage over and over.

"Oh, honey."

As he watched from the closet, he saw his father's rage disappear as he picked his mother up off the carpet and hugged her.

"I'm sorry, so sorry. I didn't mean to—I know you would never cheat on me. I know you love me."

"I do love you. I love you," she sobbed, clinging to him.

They'd made love on the bed as he watched from the closet. He'd heard about sex, but he'd never known exactly what it meant.

He did now.

At first he thought his father was going to kill his mother. She was grunting and crying and had this high-pitched moan. For a minute, he got a rush thinking that his mother would be dead and gone, and that stupid baby in her stomach along with her.

But she didn't die. And his father apologized over and over again. He said he loved her, loved the baby, loved everything in the world.

Wimp!

Wimp.

He shivered in the night. The wet Portland air reminded him of growing up, which reminded him how much he hated his family.

He looked back through the patio door and smiled. The picture-perfect family, sitting and laughing on the couch. He chuckled. No family was perfect. People had thought *his* family was perfect. For a while, anyway. What a joke!

Inside the house, the mother—Ms. Gina Harper, divorced—stood and stretched.

Time for bed, she mouthed.

The older girl, a teenager, yawned and slowly rose from the couch. The younger girl, five or six with dark, curly pigtails, protested. Gina Harper picked her up, tickled her, and carried her from the room. The older girl glanced in his direction, an odd look on her face, then gathered up the popcorn bowls and soda cans, turned off the lights, and followed her mother and sister.

His heart beat double-time at the thought that she'd sensed him. That somehow she knew her fate.

That she would be the next to die.

But of course she hadn't seen him, hadn't even known he stood on the brick patio outside the family room door. He'd prepared carefully.

This time there would be one minor deviation from the book, but it was one he was sure the author would appreciate.

CHAPTER
7

Rowan slept in fits and starts, her emotions raw. The nightmare stayed with her even when her eyes were open, and it didn't just concern the Franklin family murder. Evils older than four years tried to push themselves into her conscious memory; she had to fight aggressively to keep them at bay. In doing so, she developed a pounding, mind-numbing headache.

She downed two prescription-strength Motrin and went downstairs. Michael sat at the dining room table reading papers in a file.

"What's that?"

He looked up, frowned, and closed the file. "You look like hell."

"Thanks." He obviously wasn't going to tell her about the file. She imagined it had something to do with the murder of the florist, or poor Doreen Rodriguez. She didn't need to see the file, having already pictured the murders in her imagination.

"I'll make you something to eat."

She shook her head. Eating had never been important to her; during stressful times, she often forgot. "I want to run."

"That's not a good idea."

"I don't care."

The doorbell rang and she jumped. Since when had

the normalcy of everyday life scared her? She pulled her Glock from its holster and held it ready.

Michael drew his own weapon, motioning for her to wait in the kitchen.

He looked through the peephole. "Who is it?" he asked.

"Speedy Courier Service with a package for Rowan Smith."

"Who sent it?"

The man checked his log. "Harper."

Rowan peered around the corner, thought for a second, then shrugged at Michael's raised eyebrow. "I don't know," she said.

"Leave the package on the doorstep."

"I need a signature."

"Hold on a minute." Michael backed away from the door. He motioned for Rowan to stay where she was, then walked past her and out the side door.

She anxiously waited, distracted for a moment by the fact that he'd already made a pot of coffee. She poured herself a tall, black mug and sipped.

When he came back, he locked up, set the alarm again, and checked out the package while wearing gloves. Rowan watched from across the table.

"It looks okay." He glanced at her for confirmation.

She crossed into the dining room, put the mug down, and drew on the pair of latex gloves Michael handed her.

The package was light, probably not even half a pound. She put it to her ear; silence. She looked at all the seams, but none appeared to contain a hidden trigger. It would be difficult to send a bomb through a courier unless it was on a timer; packages were tossed about haphazardly, and there were no markings that this was fragile.

"It's fine," she concurred. She started to open the package and Michael stopped her.

"Let me."

Reluctantly, she put the package down and stepped back, balling her hands into fists. She hated being protected.

She watched Michael's hands cautiously work open the package, her heart beating fast, angry with herself that this delivery created an undercurrent of fear. The box inside the plain brown wrapping was white, a simple unmarked gift box the size of a videocassette. A single piece of tape sealed the edge. Michael broke it with his finger and pulled off the lid.

Two bright red ribbons, tied in bows around locks of dark, curly hair. Human hair. As if two pigtails had been cut off, preserved by a loving mother after her daughter's first big-girl haircut. Saved by a mother not wanting her little girl to grow up.

Red ribbons, dark hair.

No. No, not again.

Dani.

Tears silently streamed down Rowan's cheeks as she stared at the open box in Michael's hands. Deep sadness etched every crease of her face.

"Rowan?" He put the box on the table and stepped toward her. "Rowan?" He put his finger under her chin, lifting her gaze to his.

The raw pain in her face threw him for a loop. He had never seen such expressive eyes in his life, and they were filled with such agony.

"What does this mean?" He peered carefully at the contents to make sure he wasn't missing something. Dark hair tied in red ribbons. He put it down on the table, took her by the arms. She was shaking and he pulled her close. "Talk to me, Rowan. I can't help you if you don't talk to me."

"Dani," she croaked into his chest.

"Who's Danny?"

She didn't answer. Michael picked her up and carried her to the couch, where he held her in his lap and rocked her back and forth for several long minutes until her sobs turned to crying, her crying to whimpering, and then complete stillness. Somehow, the silence was the worst.

She'd buried her face in his chest. Michael pushed her back. "Rowan, trust me. You have to trust me."

She looked into his eyes, searching for what? Honesty? Trust? He didn't know. Her lips trembled, and he put a finger on their red fullness. "Trust me," he whispered.

She swallowed. "I—I—" She stopped, her voice hoarse.

He kissed her lightly on the forehead. She needed him. This strong, independent woman needed him, and he was filled with intense longing and desire. Every protective instinct he had was focused on her, and he half fell in love right then.

He pulled her tightly to him. "What? Tell me."

"I—I can't." Her voice came out a croak.

He turned her face to his, searching her eyes, her mouth, the worry lines on her forehead. Her lips quivered. He desperately wanted to kiss her, to show her that he could protect her, that he would always be here for her.

He couldn't kiss her. She was too vulnerable, too needy. But damn, he wanted to taste those quivering red lips, soothe the pain on her face. If only she would let him in.

She was out of his arms so fast he almost didn't feel her push off of him. "Michael, this isn't a good idea."

She had sensed their connection, too, and it gave him hope. Maybe—after all this was over—there was hope for them.

"Rowan, I can wait." Damn, that was hard to say. He didn't want to wait. He wanted to be with her completely, entirely, right now. But he wasn't going to make the same mistakes he'd made before.

He swallowed and watched her face for some of the passion he hoped simmered under her skin. He didn't see anything, but she was an expert at hiding her emotions. Surely she felt the tug at her heart as it—fate—tugged at his.

Again, the doorbell rang.

"Shit," Michael muttered as he strode to the door.

Rowan sighed in relief as she turned from Michael. She purposefully made her way to the dining room table. She liked Michael and was beginning to trust him—as a partner, not a lover. She wasn't capable of giving any man more than sex. Long ago, her ex-boyfriend had told her she was ice cold.

And she liked Michael too much to lead him into believing something about her that just wasn't true. He'd proven to be competent, giving her both the space and support she needed.

She picked up her coffee mug, averting her eyes from the box. Her hand shook. She willed for all of this to stop. She would *not* fall apart. Never again.

She heard Quinn's voice from the other room.

"There's been another murder. Where's Rowan?"

Rowan almost dropped the mug, then carefully placed it on the table before sinking into a chair. Closing her eyes, she swallowed hard. Another murder. The pigtails. She hadn't written about any of her villains taking hair from a victim, but she knew this was related to her.

He so desperately wanted to hurt her.

"I don't think—" Michael began. Rowan opened her eyes. Quinn stood at the edge of the dining room, a frown etched in his handsome face.

Quinn's partner, Agent Colleen Thorne, stood behind him. Rowan remembered Colleen from her days in the Bureau, a quiet, no-nonsense cop whom Rowan had respected, though never been close to. That wasn't a surprise; Rowan hadn't been friendly with most of her colleagues. It was easier to keep people at arm's length than to develop attachments that could hurt.

Colleen nodded her hello and Rowan returned the gesture, then turned to Quinn.

"Who'd he kill?" she asked.

"Divorced mother and two daughters," Quinn said.

"Portland. Harper. *Crime of Clarity.*" She closed her eyes, still seeing the pigtails in her mind. "Get an evidence bag."

"What's going on?" Michael asked.

"One of the victims was a five-year-old girl who appeared to have her hair cut. Brunette," Quinn added.

"Another copycat crime."

Quinn shook his head. "Yes and no. In the book, a family by the name of Harper was killed, a mother and her two teenage daughters. This is the same family name, one teenage daughter, but one five-year-old. In Rowan's novel, no hair was missing from the murdered girl."

"But you're sure this is the same person?" Rowan asked, even though there was no doubt in her mind.

"Left your book at the scene," Quinn said, his face grim. He sat down at the table across from Rowan. "The deviations from the story could be personal, perhaps his own sick fetish. Maybe he couldn't find a Harper family in Portland that matched the description, so he compromised."

Quinn put on his own gloves and slid the box, wrapping, and hair into an evidence bag. He handed it to Colleen. He mumbled something to her that Rowan couldn't hear, and Quinn's partner left the room.

Rowan's book. Rowan's fault. She closed her eyes and put her head in her hands, willing herself to keep it together. She knew the killer had intentionally deviated from the book because he knew about her past. And somehow she was sure he was going to kill her when he was done destroying her.

Who was this bastard? Who knew about Dani? She didn't believe in coincidences. He had to know about her little sister.

But no one knew Dani had been murdered.

Something clicked. What she'd been thinking about the Franklin murders the other night. That little girl was a brunette, too. It was seeing her butchered in her bed, with the dark pigtails, that had forced Rowan to turn in her shield.

Another connection to Nashville. A typical murder-suicide? Maybe not. Maybe there was something more.

"Quinn. This has to be connected to the Franklin murders. I talked to Roger about it. He said he'd get me the files."

"You didn't work that case," Quinn said, frowning. His eyes narrowed in that suspicious look he got when he interrogated someone.

She resisted the urge to clam up. She hated having to bring up her weakness again to be examined for the world to see. "It was my last case. I did the initial walk-through. Then I quit."

Both Michael and Quinn were silent, standing in front of her like questioning sentries, waiting for her to break. Maybe not. Maybe that was just her own fear. That she would break. Again.

She forced herself to stand straight, keep her hands loose in front of her on the table. Avoided fidgeting with her coffee mug. She didn't know if she had the strength to fight this unknown evil, but damn if she was going to show her weakness to the rest of the world.

"We'll get the hair down to the lab and process it to confirm that it's from the victim," Quinn said. "I've put a call in to Roger—he went to the scene—to find out what he thinks of the hair. This is the second time the killer has contacted you directly, Rowan. It's coming to a head."

He was coming after her. She knew it. If the police or FBI didn't catch him first, he would come after her. The weight of the Franklin murders rested heavily on her heart. If she hadn't quit the Bureau four years ago, would something have changed? If she had ridden the case out like the good law enforcement soldier she'd been trained to be, putting all her personal baggage aside, would there have been a different outcome? She didn't know, and not knowing added to the weight on her already heavy conscience.

So much death in her life. Maybe her own death would finally set her free.

"There will be one more," Rowan said, her voice cracking. The killer had picked one murder from each of her three books. Were they random? Or did they hold special significance for the killer? She cleared her throat. "*Crime of Corruption*. There were seven murders in that book. Can you do anything to get the word out? There are seven women in jeopardy." She picked up her coffee and sipped. It was cold, but she needed something to do with her hands.

"We're on it," Quinn said. "The D.C. police are on alert. The press is eating this up and already printed the names of the women killed in your book. I'll bet you're selling out in all the bookstores." He began to smile, then realized he'd put his foot in his mouth. "I'm sorry, Rowan, I didn't mean—"

Rowan slammed her coffee mug so hard on the table it cracked. The rage she'd focused inside, on the unknown killer, she now turned on Quinn. How could he even say it? As if she hadn't thought it herself. As if she were not physically ill over the desperately unwanted publicity. This killer had stolen the one cathartic joy she had in her life: writing, penning novels where good always triumphed over evil. She didn't know if she would ever write another word.

"How dare you! It's blood money. I will have no part in it!" She pushed her chair back and stormed past Michael, down the hall to her den.

The door slamming sounded final.

"Aw, shit." Quinn ran a hand through his hair. "I should apologize."

"Why don't you give her some time?" Michael said. Damn if he was going to let Quinn anywhere near Rowan. They obviously had a past.

Quinn looked Michael up and down. "Mr. Flynn, Rowan and I have been colleagues and friends for a long time," he said. "I'm going to talk to her."

Michael blocked Quinn's path. "Give her time," he repeated. They were the same height, but Michael had at least fifteen pounds on Quinn, all of it muscle.

They stared at each other for a full minute, Michael firm in his resolve to refuse Quinn access to Rowan; Quinn weighing the pros and cons of confronting the bodyguard.

Quinn broke the silence. "I'll give Rowan tonight, but she needs to come down to FBI headquarters tomorrow to review some of her old cases."

"She's been doing that here," Michael said.

"We've pulled out a few that merit further attention. Her insight and familiarity with these crimes is important."

"I'll bring her over."

"Thanks," Quinn said as he opened the front door. "I appreciate it."

Rowan listened to the front door shut, relieved that Quinn was gone. He was a good agent, but dammit, she thought he knew her better. Money. She didn't care about the money. She wrote because she had to, a purging of the pain she'd kept locked up for so many years. In her books, justice always won. In her fantasy world, the villains always died. Victims were avenged, good persevered over evil.

But in the real world, none of that was true. Sometimes victims received justice. Sometimes villains were punished. Sometimes good defeated evil.

But just as often, evil won.

She heard footsteps approach the door and stop. She didn't want to talk to Michael. He meant well, but he couldn't possibly understand. Fortunately, he continued on, his steps fading away on the tiled floor.

She released a breath she didn't know she'd been holding and eyed the gun in her hand. All her pain could disappear now with one well-placed bullet.

She was a coward. She couldn't take her own life. She only hoped the bastard came after her before anyone else died.

Assistant Director Roger Collins had taken the earliest flight to Portland to see the latest crime scene of the "Copycat Killer"—the name the media had attached to America's newest serial killer. Three hours later he was heading east again, but not for Dulles.

"What's the ETA to Logan?" he asked a passing flight attendant.

"We expect to land at 4:10 P.M. Eastern time."

Taking out his wallet, he extracted a card from underneath his driver's license. He stared at it for a long time before pulling out the phone from the back of the seat in front of him, typing in his credit card information, and dialing the number. He identified himself, then asked to speak to the director.

"Roger."

Dr. Milton Christopher's voice was deep and gravelly, and hadn't changed in the twenty-some years Roger had known him.

"Milt, wish I were calling to chat."

"What's wrong?"

"I'm on a flight to Boston right now and need to see MacIntosh."

There was a long pause. "There's been no change."

"I know, but I need to see him. It'll be after visiting hours."

"Does this have something to do with that serial killer on the West Coast?"

It was Roger's turn to pause. "Could be."

The doctor sighed. "I'll be here."

"Thanks."

Roger hung up and looked out the window. He had one more call to make. He dialed the number.

"Shreveport Penitentiary."

"I need to speak to the warden about an inmate."

When Roger parked his rental sedan in front of Bellevue Hospital for the Criminally Insane, he'd just gotten off the phone with the Texas Prison Authority. He glanced in the rearview mirror and wasn't surprised to see dark circles under his eyes. The gray hair Gracie always called "distinguished" today made him look older than his fifty-nine years.

Heads were going to roll for transferring that spawn of Satan without informing him. But after four and a half hours of calls, transfers, and threats, Roger had found out where he was and spoken to the warden of Beaumont, a high-security federal prison in Texas. Warden James Cullen had answers to all his questions and was overnighting a copy of all pertinent records.

Roger was getting out of the car at Bellevue when his cell rang. He almost didn't answer it; it was well after six and he didn't want Milt to wait much longer. But he glanced at the number anyway and immediately recognized it as Rowan's.

His gut clenched, knowing if the truth ever came out she'd never forgive him. The fact that everything he did was to protect her wouldn't help his case.

"Collins," he answered.

"Did Quinn talk to you today?"

"Yes." That was the reason he was in Boston, but he couldn't tell her that.

"You have protection for Peter, right? If he knows about Dani, he might know about—"

"Peter's safe, Rowan."

"I'll hire a guard if I have to. If money's a problem, I have plenty."

"It's already done."

"Thanks." She paused, and Roger felt the urge to tell her everything.

He didn't. "Anything else?"

"No, nothing."

She sounded defeated. He wished he could be there for her, be the father she needed but had never had. Even when she'd lived with him and Gracie, he'd worked twelve, fourteen-hour days. Especially in the beginning, when she'd needed him the most.

"We're going to catch this asshole."

"I know." She didn't sound like she believed it. "Good-bye."

"Wait—" But she'd already hung up.

He snapped the phone closed and hit the roof of his car with his fist. *Damn, damn, damn!*

"Anything I can do to help?"

Roger swung around. Milt Christopher had gotten the drop on him. He really was too tired to be effective. He shook his head. "Just show me MacIntosh."

They walked in silence through the grounds. The wide, lush lawns were supposed to calm the insanity that lurked within the walls.

Milt used his security pass to open a door at the far end of the courtyard. Both he and Roger had to sign in with the guard, and then they proceeded down a wide, white hallway, through two more secure doors, until they reached the entrance to Robert MacIntosh's room.

"Are you sure you don't trust me on this?"

"I trust you, Milt, but I have to see him myself."

Milt nodded, then unlocked the door with a key.

Robert MacIntosh sat in a chair facing a wide, barred window that looked out at the courtyard they had just walked through. It was nearly dark, but by the vacant look in his blue eyes, Roger didn't think MacIntosh knew or cared. He pulled a chair in front of MacIntosh and stared at him, wanting to see something, anything other than the vacuous expression he remembered.

Roger didn't believe most people were insane when they committed heinous crimes; by all public accounts Robert MacIntosh had been normal twenty-three years ago. What had caused him to break? What had severed the thin thread of sanity? Had he been insane when he killed his wife, or had her brutal murder emptied his mind to join his hollow soul?

It wasn't fair. He'd wanted to prosecute this bastard more than any other murderer he'd faced in his thirty-five years with the FBI. And MacIntosh had not spoken one word since he was found, sitting next to the shredded body of his dead wife, her blood coating him and the kitchen where she died.

"You bastard," he whispered.

Milt, the doctor, cleared his throat.

Roger searched Robert MacIntosh's unseeing eyes, finding nothing human, nothing alive in their depths. Living on the public dole at the cost of more than a hundred thousand a year, this hollow shell of a man should have been shot on sight when the first police officer arrived at the Boston death house.

He stood. "Has anyone been to see him recently?"

Milt blinked. "Actually, yes."

"I need to see the security logs."

An hour later, Roger left with copies of visitor logs from May 10 and September 23 of last year, and the promise that Milt would order up the security tapes from those days and send them to FBI headquarters immediately.

In twenty-three years, no one had visited Robert Mac-Intosh until last year, when Bob Smith came in twice.

Who the hell was Bob Smith?

CHAPTER
8

Rowan woke early with another pounding headache. She reached under her pillow and pulled out her Glock, pausing as she stared at it. She almost didn't remember switching her gun's storage spot from her nightstand to her pillow.

She didn't bother to change—she'd slept in sweats and a T-shirt. She simply pulled her arms out of the sleeves and slipped on a sports bra, then pushed her arms through again. It was a trick her few lovers admired, which should have told her they were too easily impressed.

She went into the bathroom and brushed her hair, pulling it into a hasty ponytail for her morning run. She tried to avoid the hollow-eyed woman in the mirror, but couldn't.

She'd never paid attention to her looks. Her ex-boyfriend Eric Hamilton had told her she was beautiful, like a sculpted goddess. She brushed off his compliment as a line, not interested in a man who paid more attention to her looks than her brain. Frankly, she wasn't interested in relationships. Before Eric, she'd been involved with a few men, none of them in the Bureau, none of them serious. Sex and coffee, nothing more.

How could she get close to anyone when everyone she

loved died? How could she share her past when she couldn't even think about it, except in nightmares?

Her relationship with Eric had been as close to a real one as she'd ever had, and look how pathetic that had turned out. He demanded everything from her, but still couldn't see her for what she was. Damaged. With Eric she played a part, the role of the cool, dedicated, smart FBI agent who wasn't afraid to confront bad guys in a dark alley. With Eric she was hot in bed, but cold in conversation. She knew it but couldn't change it. Didn't know if she wanted to even make the effort.

He'd asked her to move in with him. She had refused. She couldn't give up her independence, her privacy, her *home*. The life she had painstakingly built couldn't be merged with that of someone who didn't understand death and dying.

Eric was a good agent. He was smart, cocky, competent. But Rowan never felt that he tried to understand *her*. He mainly wanted her because she seemed unattainable; when she wasn't what he thought, or anyone he could mold, he sought comfort elsewhere.

And his betrayal was a relief.

In hindsight, she should have listened to Olivia. When she lived in Washington, before the Franklin murders, she and Eric had often gone out with Liv and her now ex-husband. Neither Liv nor Greg had liked Eric much. That should have told her something.

Rowan shook her head, trying to rid her mind of the past. After brushing her teeth and drinking a cup of tepid water, she went downstairs to fetch Michael from the guest room.

She was about to knock on his door when a voice from the far end of the hall said, "Good morning."

She turned to face Michael's brother, leaning against the kitchen doorjamb, steaming cup of coffee in hand.

He looked a little like Michael, but his green eyes were darker, his hair shorter, his body leaner. Rowan felt a not-too-familiar flutter in her stomach, confusing her. He was attractive, but it wasn't as if she let her hormones dictate her life. She swallowed, startled by her reaction. He was too damn sexy for his own good, and he knew it.

John Flynn was an operative. She could tell by his oh-so-casual stance. Under the seemingly at-ease posture was a man rippling with energy, exuding strength and cocky self-confidence without even trying. He wasn't as big and muscular as his brother, but Rowan knew who she'd bet on in a fight—John would win hands down.

He was dangerous. His ostensibly innocent gaze probed her inner soul. He searched for the motivation that made her tick, the mechanism that made her an agent who'd quit, who wrote, who'd attracted the attention of a serial killer.

Michael Flynn was more easily led. She could control his questions, lead him away from going too deep into her psyche. Keep the relationship professional. Straightforward.

But not John. He would not be led, stymied, or satisfied with the short answer. He was a threat. To her soul.

"What are you doing here?" she asked, walking down the hall to face him.

"Thought Mickey could use a little backup. He's been 24/7 the past few days."

She nodded toward the coffee. "Seems you've made yourself at home."

He smiled, revealing a solitary dimple that would have been endearing if he wasn't such a danger to her privacy. "You have good stuff. Real coffee beans. I like that."

She brushed past him, trying to ignore the jolt of

awareness tingling across her flesh when she touched his arm. To avoid looking at him, she poured herself a cup of coffee. She sipped, then put the mug down. Damn, his blank-faced stare made her nervous. "I'm going for a run."

He'd turned around in the doorway, but otherwise hadn't moved. "Are you?"

She narrowed her eyes and glared at him. Any other person would have feared her anger, but he only looked amused. That pissed her off. "Maybe I should wake Michael. Perhaps you can't keep up."

Annoyance flashed in his eyes, then the shield came down. So, Rowan thought, he was competitive. Well, so was she.

He approached her, stopping only inches from her face. She didn't flinch, but stared at him with an expression she deliberately kept blank.

"Who's Danny?"

She sucked in her next breath and held it, the fear of hyperventilating real. She slowly released the air and took a step toward him, shaking with anger and pain. She tilted her head up an inch from him and whispered, "Fuck you."

She started past him but he grabbed her arm. She pulled her gun and held it to his head. "Let. Go." No one, *no one,* grabbed her unless she wanted him to.

They stared at each other for a long minute before John released her. "You will tell me," he said with complete confidence. A tic in his neck told her he was angry.

She put her gun down, glad she had pissed him off. She hated him. He was a threat to everything she'd painstakingly built over the last twenty-three years. It was as if he could read her mind, see her soul. Dammit, she didn't need this! On top of everything else, she didn't need this confusion, this man who seemed to look at her and know everything about her.

He couldn't. He couldn't know her, know her past, know her thoughts. That was ridiculous, she told herself as she turned toward the side door.

"Dani has nothing to do with this. It was a case closed long ago. Roger promised me the Franklin files would be here today, and after the brunette pigtails—" her voice cracked and she mentally berated herself. "It's another connection to the Franklin case."

She didn't, couldn't look at him. She'd already said more than she intended. How did he make her do that? She couldn't remember saying Dani's name out loud for years. A virtual lifetime.

"Wait," John said, lightly laying a hand on her shoulder. "I'll go first."

She hated being the protected woman, but allowed John to leave the house, check the perimeter, and come back. "Clear. Where are you running?"

"Beach," was all she said.

He nodded. "I like the water, too."

"Navy?"

"Army."

She cocked her head. "You're no Army boy. Unless— you were with Delta." She made the statement as if she knew it was fact.

He raised an eyebrow. "I was."

She smiled as if she were in on a joke he wasn't. "Ten miles," she said and walked out the door.

She set the pace and John stayed a half-length behind her. Instantly, she knew John was far more experienced than his brother. When Michael ran with her, he watched her. John didn't. He watched the beach, the ocean, the houses. Constantly looking for a sniper, a small boat, a low-flying plane.

Much like her.

Two peas in a pod, she realized as she started the final lap. With Michael, she'd run the beach twice. With John, she ran it three times. She wasn't going to cut him any slack and suspected he wouldn't appreciate it if she did.

She tried to forget him as they ran, but it proved impossible. John's presence overpowered her, and she couldn't focus on self-preservation. He'd brought up Dani and wouldn't be as easily put off as Michael.

Michael. She felt a pang of guilt. He'd wanted to kiss her yesterday, and she couldn't return those feelings. He was kind, smart, attractive—but she didn't feel the pull. She'd learned to care for him in these few short days, but not in the way he seemed to want.

She cared for him like she cared for Peter. Like a brother.

John would not be put off for long by her refusal to talk, even though there was nothing in her childhood or Dani's murder that had anything to do with what was happening today. Everyone involved back then was dead. Except her. And Peter. Even Roger agreed it was foolish to bring it up.

But John would probably call in every favor in Washington to find out what made Rowan Smith tick. And she would have to do everything she could to stop him from getting the answers he wanted. If it all came out, she didn't know if she could rebuild her life again. Already, her past threatened her present. She had to make it stop, but didn't know how.

As she rounded the far side of the beach, her lungs burned, her skin tingled, and her hair whipped her face as the ocean breeze slapped her cheek. She never felt so alive as she did when she ran. Especially here, by the ocean. If she didn't love her cabin in the woods so much she'd consider moving to the coast.

She dismissed that thought as soon as it popped into her mind. Too many people. And she hated the house she leased—too bright, too white, too open.

But the beach: She could be at peace here. She'd been told that up the coast, north of San Francisco, there were some secluded oceanfront homes. Too cold to swim, but she didn't need to swim. She just needed the stinging salt air, the vast churning ocean, the flat wet beach. The colder the better. Being cold meant being alive.

She'd started up the wooden stairs that led from the beach to the deck of her house when John reached out and grabbed her arm, spinning her around. They stood face-to-face, she one step above him.

John breathed hard, which pleased Rowan. So did she, but she hadn't slowed during the entire run. Endurance was key.

A thin layer of perspiration affixed his T-shirt to his chest, outlining every subtle, well-toned muscle. His face was blank, but his dark green eyes flashed. Anger? Frustration?

Longing?

She blinked, and the sensation was gone. John frowned at her, and she noticed his lips—full, kissable lips. His entire face spoke of subtle masculinity, a man comfortable with himself, a man who knew his place in the world—and it wasn't at the bottom. A dimple dented his otherwise square jaw, and he hadn't shaved. His whiskers were damn sexy.

She turned her eyes to his again and wished she hadn't. Again, she sensed he saw her innermost thoughts.

She involuntarily swallowed.

"You think you're in control," he said, voice low and

gruff, as rough as the stubble on his cheeks. He leaned forward, his chest still heaving from their ten-mile run. "I will find out what you're hiding. And dammit, Rowan, if it's some stupid FBI game that's going to get my family hurt, you'll pay."

Rowan kept her face blank, but felt the steam of anger and fear rise with her words. "None of my secrets have anything to do with this." As she said it, she feared she was wrong. How else did the murderer know about the pigtails?

Coincidence. Had to be.

That was why she'd quit after the Franklin murders. Those damn pigtails haunted her sleep. She couldn't see clearly, couldn't investigate a crime that had hit too close to home. Couldn't be impartial. So she'd left.

John's eyes narrowed, and Rowan averted her head to escape his gaze. His hand shot out and held her in place. She karate-chopped his arm and he winced, loosening his hold just enough so she could jerk her arm away from him. "Don't touch me," she said through clenched teeth.

He put his hands up in a "hands-off" gesture and motioned for her to get behind him. Reluctantly, she did, but pulled out her gun, her heartbeat steadying as she held the cold metal in both hands. Her gun grounded her, made it a job. John glanced at her weapon, nodding almost imperceptibly, a hint of a smile.

She frowned when he turned his back to her and led the way up the stairs. What was with John Flynn?

When Rowan stepped in through the side door, the first thing she saw was Michael leaning against the counter, steaming coffee mug in hand. His casual stance belied his stern expression, but when he glanced at Rowan, his eyes warmed.

Guilt sank heavily in her gut. "Excuse me," she said,

brushing past John. When her arm accidentally touched his chest, she jerked as if burned.

But the heat was from within.

Brief eye contact told Rowan that John felt the same zing, and they frowned at each other. Without another word, she went down the hall and upstairs.

John absently rubbed his arm, not from pain but from a deep need to make contact with Rowan again.

"What the hell are you doing?" Michael demanded as soon as Rowan had left the kitchen.

John glanced at his brother, crossed over to the fridge, opened it, and took out a water bottle. He drained it, then tossed the empty plastic container into the trash.

"She's in good shape," John said as he folded his arms in front of him. "Gotta admire that."

Michael slammed his mug on the granite countertop and took a step toward his brother, fists clenched. "Don't think for a minute that you're taking over this case," he said, jaw set.

John put his hands up. "Hey, I'm only here to help. It's your gig."

"I saw how you looked at her."

"Whoa, brother. It's not me who has the wandering eye here. You're going to get yourself in deep shit if you don't put some distance between you and blondie." As he said it, he realized he was doing the exact same thing.

The only difference, he thought, was he wasn't afraid to hurt her to get to the truth. That thought didn't sit entirely well in his conscience.

"I don't know what you're talking about," Michael said. "I've been here for the better part of a week and you waltz in and start making demands, scaring her, and—"

"Stop right there." John pushed off from the counter and took a step toward his brother. "She's hiding something and you're enabling her. That 'Danny' she talked about, he has something to do with it. And if you don't start thinking with your head instead of your—" he glanced below Michael's belt "—you'll wind up dead."

"You know nothing about Rowan!"

"Neither do you," John said, his voice barely audible. "And you'd better start asking questions rather than letting blondie lead you around by the nose. She's using you, Mickey. She's using your obvious attraction for her to avoid answering the hard questions."

"You're the one lusting after her. Don't think I didn't see how you looked at her."

John shook his head and leaned back against the counter. "Mickey, Mickey. It's Jessica all over again."

"Don't say her name!"

"Hell if I'm going to let you make the same mistake twice! You almost got yourself killed because she lied to you. Well, Rowan Smith's closed mouth is the same damn thing as lying, and my gut tells me she knows something about this killer." John tried to pass his brother, not wanting to fight with him, but Michael grabbed his arm and spun him around.

"Let go," John said.

Michael squeezed tighter before dropping his arm. "Don't push her. She's been through hell."

You don't know the half of it, Mickey, John thought. John suspected Rowan Smith had been to hell and back many times. He saw it in her eyes, the eyes she shielded whenever possible because they exposed her to the world. But whereas Michael sought to protect her from reliving hell, John knew the only way to conquer evil was to face it head on.

To do that, Rowan was going to have to spill the beans. The only way she would, John suspected, was if he discovered the truth first.

"Stay out of this," Michael warned.

"Too late." They stared each other down. If the situation wasn't so damn serious, John would have laughed.

The phone rang, but neither man moved to answer it. When it rang a third time, Michael grabbed the wall receiver. "Smith residence," he said, gruff. "Who's this?" He paused, then glanced at his watch. "She's in the shower. We'll be there in an hour." He hung up.

John looked at him, eyebrow raised, but didn't ask who was on the phone.

"That was Agent Peterson," Michael said. "They're ready for Rowan to review the Franklin file."

"I'll leave you to it, then," John said and turned toward the hall.

"What are you going to do?"

John glanced over his shoulder. "I have some calls to make. I'll watch the house for you."

"You don't have to stay here."

John raised an eyebrow. What Michael was really saying was, *I don't want you here.*

"I know," John said, "but I want to." He started down the hall to find a bathroom to shower in, then stopped and turned back to his brother.

"Mickey," he said, "I'm sorry about the Jessica comment. That was a low blow."

"It's forgotten."

John hoped his brother meant that. Their argument was like an itch he couldn't scratch, and it bugged him. They often argued, but always came away friends. "Be careful, okay?"

"I will." Michael grinned. "And when all this shit's over, we can battle for Rowan Smith fair and square."

"There's nothing to battle." But as John said it, he realized he had some feelings for the pretty blonde that he couldn't reconcile with his desire to get her to talk.

Where Michael often let his emotions cloud his professional judgment, John vowed not to let that happen with him.

He found the shower at the end of the hall, stripped, and stood beneath the hot, stinging spray. He couldn't get Rowan Smith out of his mind. Her hard profile and soft eyes. The way she watched everything that went on around her without moving her head. She absorbed her surroundings, taking pains to blend in, but John always knew when she was in the room, even if he couldn't see her.

Yeah, he had a thing for her. But unlike Michael, he knew the difference between lust and love. He didn't believe in love at first sight or fate or any of that nonsense. He was practical, and could separate business and pleasure.

The job came first.

As he rinsed the beach run from his body, he planned exactly how he was going to get Rowan to open up. He had a feeling once she started talking, she'd have a lot to say.

CHAPTER
9

The black-and-white crime scene photos were no less graphic for their lack of color.

She stared at the picture of Karl Franklin, gun near his hand, the dark stain spread on the light carpet under his head. Half a head. The other half had been blown onto the wall when he'd shot himself.

She'd read the reports from the Franklin murders and had been surprised to learn the case wasn't closed. There wasn't enough substantial evidence that Karl Franklin indeed killed his family, then shot himself. While it was clear that Franklin committed suicide, there were some discrepancies in the physical evidence that showed he might have died *before* the other victims—and that their deaths had all been quick.

She hadn't known. She hadn't cared enough to even check.

No, that wasn't true. She cared too much. That's why she'd almost had a breakdown and ran away. She'd been too weak.

Technically, the case was ruled a probable murder-suicide but wasn't closed. After four years, it was cold. Very cold.

Unless Karl Franklin hadn't killed his family. If someone had gotten away with murder. The file was surprisingly light. No known suspects other than Franklin.

They'd interviewed neighbors and relatives and the only surviving immediate family member; Karl's son from a previous marriage was in college and had a solid alibi.

Because the timeline was so close, and establishing exact time of death difficult under the best of circumstances, the probable murder-suicide had put the case on the back burner.

Rowan slapped the file down on the conference table and the contents skidded across the smooth surface. Quinn stared at her, shaking his head as he straightened the stack. Tess frowned from her spot in the corner at her laptop, and Michael—ever diligent—stood at the door, arms crossed, watching her.

She didn't care. They didn't understand. Had her running away caused a murderer to go free? Was Karl Franklin innocent of the crime everyone thought him guilty of?

And if he was innocent, was the guilty party after her for some unknown reason?

"I was so positive something was here," she said, her voice cracking. She glanced down at the file Quinn was putting back together and saw another photo. One she had avoided. As if penance for her weakness, the picture rested on top of the stack.

"Stop." She grabbed Quinn's wrist until he pulled back.

"What?" he asked. She ignored him. Hands shaking, she reached for the image that had haunted her for four years.

And longer.

Rebecca Sue Franklin. She should have been asleep, dreaming of the tea party she'd had with her stuffed animals and dolls earlier that day. Instead, she lay under her white comforter, the dark stain a stark reminder that she was dead. Shot in her sleep. A trail of dark blood streamed from her open mouth, frozen in time.

Her dark pigtails, disheveled from sleep, contrasted with the starched white pillowcase. The dozens of stuffed animals and dolls and toys that stood sentry around her stared with blank, black eyes. Voiceless witnesses.

Rowan didn't notice the tears running down her face until one hit the photograph. It startled her, forcing her back to the present.

"Nothing. Nothing conclusive," she said, stuffing Rebecca Sue Franklin back into the folder and closing her eyes. "I think Roger should give priority to reviewing this case. I don't know why, but there's something familiar here. How else could the killer know about the pigtails? Why send them to me? I never wrote that."

"Coincidence," Quinn said as he picked up the file.

"Bullshit, and you know it. There are no coincidences."

"We could be chasing our tails, Rowan! Running after a cold case on a hunch—it's a waste of resources."

"Do you have anything better?" She was shouting, but didn't care. "Anything at all? Because none of my other cases gave us even a thread—this is the only anomaly."

"We're still running through your other cases, testimonies, everything. It takes time."

"I know it does, but this case is different. It was my last. Dani—" she caught herself. "Rebecca Sue and her pigtails. What was sent to me. There has to be a connection."

"Danny?" Quinn asked, a quizzical look on his face.

Rowan waved it away as a slip of the tongue, but didn't miss Michael's eyebrow arch up. She'd almost forgotten he was in the room.

"Don't you see?" she continued. "There's something here. I want a copy of this file. I want to read it again."

"I can't—" Quinn said, then stopped and rubbed his hands over his face. "All right. Take it."

"Thank you."

Quinn sighed. "We need to talk about protective custody."

She shook her head before he'd even completed his sentence. "I'm in this for the long haul."

"You're no longer an agent. Don't play the tough-cop routine with me. I can take you into protective custody like this—" he snapped his fingers "—if you so much as look at me wrong. And don't think I won't. Roger has given me the authority."

The audacity of him! She felt her temper reach the boiling point. "Never."

"It's for your own safety, Rowan."

"I'm not hiding. I'm not running." Not again.

Michael intervened and stepped forward, putting a hand on her shoulder and giving her a slight squeeze. "We've all been under stress this morning. It's already after noon. Why don't I take Rowan out for a bite to eat? We're done here, anyway."

"Can I stay?" Tess sat at a desk in the corner of the FBI field office conference room that had been converted into a headquarters for information about the Copycat Killer. She was typing away at the computer—doing what, Rowan had no idea. Michael had mentioned earlier that she'd been tagged as a civilian consultant by the FBI because of her computer expertise, after passing a security check. It wasn't uncommon.

"Sure," Quinn told Tess. "I have some work to do. I'll call in some sandwiches."

"I need to get out of here." Rowan pushed back her chair and stood. She picked up the file and hugged it to her chest. Tonight. Tonight she'd look at it again and talk to Roger.

She shot a glance at Quinn and walked out. She'd had enough of him today. He just didn't get it. Just like he never understood how he had betrayed Miranda. For all his brains and all his good looks, Quinn Peterson could be clueless at times.

Protective custody? Never.

Michael followed. She'd expected nothing less. Damn, but she wanted privacy. The ten minutes she'd had alone in the shower this morning was simply not enough time to think. And now with the picture of Rebecca Sue Franklin etched in her brain, she didn't want to eat, let alone have a conversation.

She pulled a Motrin out of the pocket of her jeans and dry-swallowed it.

Michael grabbed her wrist. "What's that?"

"What's what?" She jerked her arm away from him.

"That pill. It's the third time this morning that you've taken one. What are you doing?" He put both hands on her shoulders, his lips a tight line.

Rowan glanced around the office to see if anyone had heard Michael's accusation. If they had, they were wise enough to ignore the scene.

"Let go of me," she said through clenched teeth.

Michael dropped his arms and ran a hand through his hair. "What are you doing to yourself?"

She put her hand in her pocket and pulled out three more Motrin. "Satisfied?"

He had the sense to look sheepish, but she was still pissed off. "I'm sorry, I—"

"Forget it." She walked through the office and opened the main door. Michael slammed it closed.

"I go first," he reminded her.

"Shit," she muttered under her breath. "I really hate this."

"I know." His voice was laced with sympathy, but he didn't understand.

John did. John understood her. And she hated him for it.

She sensed he'd been a Fed at one time. Not FBI. Possibly CIA, but most likely DEA. He had the stealth presence and lithe movements that screamed drug enforcement, at least to her. She'd known enough DEA agents in her career that she could pick them out.

Definitely military. He'd told her Delta Force, the best the Army had to offer. He was older than Michael, but still too young for Vietnam. Delta was big in Desert Storm, and with the hostilities in the Middle East for the past two decades, the clandestine assassinations, the rescue ops—she wondered when he'd left. Why he'd left. *If* he'd left.

Perhaps he had as many secrets as she did.

"Rowan?"

She blinked, almost having forgotten where she was and whom she was with. "Woolgathering," she said, turning away from him.

"Where do you want to eat?"

She shrugged. "I don't care."

"You need to keep your strength up."

"I'm fine." She glanced up the street, motioned toward a fast-food restaurant. "That's fine."

Michael grimaced. "Junk food? I don't think so." He steered her in the opposite direction. "I saw a little Italian place around the corner."

"Sure," Rowan said, allowing Michael to lead her. It was easier than arguing. But food just didn't matter right now. Not after the murders, the pigtails, the waiting and watching and wondering when the hidden face of evil would strike next.

He'd gone through her first three books picking one murder from each. Doreen Rodriguez. The florist. The Harper family. One more book; then it was her. One more victim; then she would see his face.

Unless he wanted to toy with her more. Use her fifth book, due out next week. Wait and kill one more.

"Stop," she said, almost shouting.

Michael hovered in front of her, looking over his shoulder. "What? What do you see?"

"Nothing. Nothing. I need to make a call."

"Not here on the street."

"It's important." She pulled out her cell phone and speed-dialed Roger's private mobile line.

"Collins."

"Roger, it's me."

"Is something wrong?"

"Call my publisher and stop the shipment of books. They're due out next week."

He paused. "I'd need a court order, and—"

"No, no, they'll do it. Explain the situation and ask them to hold off. Until this guy is caught. If they don't, then we can get a court order for a delay."

"I'll take care of it."

"I need to talk to you later. About the Franklin murders."

"Did you find anything?" He sounded optimistic.

"No, not yet. But I took the file and I'm going to review it again." She glanced at Michael, who was watching the street carefully. "I'm sure I won't see anything anyone else didn't, but fresh eyes—I don't know." For the first time, she doubted herself. Maybe they were barking up the wrong tree, wasting time and resources. But what other choices did they have?

"We're leaving no stone unturned, Rowan. I promise you that." Roger's voice was forceful, even three thousand miles away. "We will catch him. It's only a matter of time."

"But who else is going to die first?"

She hung up. She'd talk to him tonight, but didn't expect anything new.

Did she know the killer? Had she seen him? Or had he affixed on her for some insane reason and learned everything about her, her past, her present? Would she recognize him if she saw the killer?

How long was he going to make her wait? The first three murders happened in a week. But she suspected this killer wanted her to suffer. To worry. Be afraid. She could almost feel him living off her fear, as if he enjoyed watching her tremble and cower. She straightened her back. If he fed off fear, it wouldn't be hers.

She wouldn't give him the satisfaction.

All week, Adam felt guilty for playing the trick on Marcy, even though she had deserved it for those mean things she said about Barry. Barry was his friend and never yelled at him and was always nice and let him hang out in the old prop room to look at all the neat stuff. But the trick upset Rowan, and Rowan was his friend too. She listened to him and cared about him like his mother never did. He sometimes wished Rowan were his mother, though that was silly because she was too young. But she would be a nice mother and wouldn't yell or say you were worthless and should never have been born.

Adam had apologized to Barry every day until today, when Barry said not to say "sorry" anymore because it didn't mean anything after awhile. Adam didn't understand that, because he really *was* sorry, but Barry was smart and knew how things worked so Adam stopped saying he was sorry.

But he hadn't seen Rowan all week. She hadn't been to the studio or to visit him or anything and he missed her. What if she was mad at him? She'd said she wasn't, but people lied all the time. Rowan had never lied to him before, but maybe she was lying this time.

He hadn't been able to eat or sleep the last two days because he worried Rowan didn't like him anymore. He had to find her and tell her how sorry he was.

Adam didn't have a driver's license, but Barry let him drive around the lot all the time. He didn't think twice about borrowing one of the studio trucks and taking it to Malibu. It was exciting to drive on the freeway. So much power! For the first time he felt almost normal, almost like he belonged.

He'd been to Rowan's house once. Last month, when he'd told her he had never seen the ocean even though he'd lived in Los Angeles his entire life, she'd driven him to her house.

The ocean was a little scary, but he didn't tell Rowan that. From her deck it was very pretty and she let him stay until the sunset, and that was the most beautiful thing he'd ever seen. Well, almost. Rowan was prettier than the sun. She had a happy smile on her face as the colors changed in the sky.

He couldn't remember how to get to her house, so he copied a map from the computer.

Rowan never treated him like he was stupid. Not like Marcy and the other actors who called him the retarded prop kid. Barry didn't like that word and talked in quiet words whenever he heard it, and Adam knew Barry tried to make him feel better, but it didn't work. Only Rowan made him feel better, because she didn't pretend. She told him what was what, and if he didn't understand, she explained it again until he did understand, and she never sighed or frowned or got that look in her eyes that said she wanted to be anywhere else but talking to him.

He turned onto Highway 1 toward Malibu and saw a flower stand by the side of the road. Would Rowan like flowers? He'd heard Barry tell one of the cameramen to get a dozen roses for his girlfriend to say he was sorry because women liked that sort of thing. Rowan was a woman and she would like flowers, too, Adam reasoned.

He pulled over onto the gravel turnout, frowning as the truck bounced so hard his head almost hit the roof of the cab. He slowed to a stop and paused, waiting for his heart to stop pounding. Maybe this driving thing wasn't as easy as he thought. He cautiously stepped out of the truck, the cool wind slapping his face. Steep cliffs only feet away dropped off to the ocean below. Adam felt woozy, and finally understood how Scottie had felt in *Vertigo*. He walked as far from the cliff as possible without actually walking onto the busy highway.

The man selling flowers had dark skin, but not black, small brown eyes, and a really nice smile that made Adam feel less nervous. After all, he'd never bought flowers for a girl before.

A dark car pulled up behind Adam's truck, but Adam barely noticed. He pointed to the roses. "Those are roses, right?" he asked.

"Yessir," the man said. "Roses. Dollar each or dozen for ten."

A dozen, a dozen. "That's twelve roses for ten dollars?"

"Yessir."

Adam had ten dollars. He had a twenty and a ten and three ones in his wallet. "O-kay," he said slowly, wanting to make sure he was making the right decision. He really liked the roses, but would Rowan like them? They were so pretty. White or red, red or white. Maybe six of each. "Can I have some white ones and some red ones?"

"Yessir."

The man from the dark car walked up to them. "Buying flowers for your lady?"

Adam glanced at the man, who looked vaguely familiar but he didn't know why. He had dark blond hair, a little long, and wore sunglasses. He was nice-looking and his clothes matched. Adam sometimes had a problem with his colors. He thought orange and brown went together, but Marcy always teased him about the way he dressed. Retro gone bad, she called it and laughed.

"N-no," Adam said, looking down and shuffling his feet. By the way he dressed, this man had money, and men with money didn't like to talk to prop boys. A lot of the men who came by the studio had money, and none of them talked to him, and if he talked to them they got mad.

"A friend?"

"Yeah." His voice was quiet and he glanced at the proprietor, who watched them.

"What were you thinking of buying?"

"The roses."

"Ah, roses. Roses are lovely."

Adam perked up. "Really? You think so?"

He nodded. Adam tilted his head, wondering how he knew this man, but he couldn't remember where he'd seen him. He frowned. He hated being dumb. That's what his mama called him. Dumb and stupid.

"Yes, I think roses are very pretty," the man said.

"I want a dozen roses," Adam said confidently to the brown-skinned man.

"But," the money man said, "I know the perfect flower for friendship."

Adam frowned. Hadn't he just said that roses were lovely? "Better than roses?"

"Oh, yes." He reached over and pulled out a stalk of a large, pretty white flower that looked almost like a cup. "Smell this."

Adam breathed in. He couldn't smell anything. But the flower was pretty. Just as pretty as Rowan.

"What's this?"

"A calla lily. And I think your lady friend will love it."

"Better than roses?"

"Oh, yes."

The man with money seemed to know what he was talking about, and Adam didn't know anything about flowers. "All right," he said slowly. "A dozen calla lilies."

"Good choice," the man said.

The brown-skinned man wrapped the flowers in paper and Adam paid him, fifteen dollars instead of the ten for the roses. But that was okay because Adam knew how to count change and took five ones from the man, carefully placing them back in his wallet before picking up the flowers.

As he started back to the truck he remembered his manners. He turned back and waved at the nice man. "Thanks, sir," he called.

The man raised his arm. "Glad to help."

Adam bounded back to the truck he'd borrowed, tickled that he'd bought the perfect flowers for friendship. Calla lilies.

Carefully, he laid them on the seat and admired them. They smelled so beautiful, and they were white, just like Rowan's hair. Yes, she was going to like them.

He started the truck and carefully pulled into traffic, unmindful that the man watched him drive away.

CHAPTER
10

John stood outside Rowan's office door, staring at the knob. Guilt nudged his conscience. He knew he shouldn't invade her space. But he'd already been in her bedroom, and there was nothing of interest there except two loaded clips for her Glock in her bedside drawer and a shotgun under her bed.

What did she fear?

She spent a lot of time in the den. Her computer was there. When she wanted to be alone, she went to the den. Why?

And why did he feel guilty? He'd done far worse in his life than rifling through the personal property of a woman he was responsible for protecting. Of course, it wasn't *his* case; it was Michael's. But she was hiding something, something important, even if she didn't know it. And Michael might be the one to pay for her omission.

Or possibly Rowan herself.

John wouldn't allow that to happen.

He opened the door before he could change his mind and closed it behind him, his heart pounding. He simply didn't want to pry into Rowan's life. Not without her invitation.

The den differed from the white starkness of the rest of the house. Dark cherry paneling, built-in bookshelves, and a large corner desk unit dominated the small room.

Two white leather love seats faced each other in the middle; a reading chair, table, and lamp were grouped in the corner. The tile from the hall extended into the den, but was mostly covered by a thick off-white shag rug.

Classic, cozy, and definitely more suited to Rowan than the bright, empty void of the immaculate Malibu beach house.

Clutter on the desk, stacks of books on the reading table, and a coffee mug with an inch of cold, congealed coffee told John this room was Rowan's home. He felt worse invading this space than her bedroom upstairs.

The books were mostly true crime, crime fiction, and literary classics. A worn copy of *One Flew Over the Cuckoo's Nest* sat on her desk. Other well-read classics littered the shelves. She may have been leasing the place, but evidently she'd brought boxes of books with her. Somehow, John didn't think the owner of this sterile abode read Steinbeck's *The Grapes of Wrath* or Capote's *In Cold Blood*.

John focused on the desk. He flicked on the computer. While waiting for it to finish booting, he searched for anything to give him more insight into Rowan and her past.

The papers on top of the stack closest to the computer were printouts from online newspapers all discussing the recent crime. Denver. Los Angeles. Portland. He'd already read them. The police had managed to keep the detail of the books being left at the crime scene to themselves, but the press had made the connection between the victims and Rowan's books.

The connection must be killing her. Spending six years fighting serial killers and mass murderers, only to end up being connected to one.

John knew how she felt. He'd lost count of the years he'd been fighting the endless War on Drugs, and sometimes he lost track of where the bad guys ended and the good guys began. But it was a battle he vowed to keep fighting until the one bastard who kept slipping through the cracks was dead and burning in hell.

The other stacks of papers appeared to be copies of bills, notes for her books, printouts of chapters. Michael had said she was working on another book, as well as the screenplay for the movie being filmed now. He'd mentioned something about how her first movie had been trashed and she wasn't about to let anyone rewrite her books into something they weren't.

John understood that as well. In fact, he found he had deep insight into Rowan that he couldn't explain. It was as if he knew how she would react, what she would think in any given situation, how these murders were eating her up inside. She was angry and rigid on the surface, but when he looked into her eyes, he saw in them so much she didn't say.

Rowan Smith kept her emotions close to the vest. Just like him.

John sat at the computer when he found nothing more of interest in the papers. Her e-mail was mostly from studio people, the majority related to the screenplay she was working on. She didn't save old e-mails. He could grab his laptop, plug it in, and run undelete on her old files, but somehow he didn't think she had anything sensitive on her computer. It appeared to be used primarily for writing.

Crime of Passion was the movie coming out at the end of the week. *Crime of Clarity* was the movie currently being filmed. Looking through her documents, he saw that *Crime of Jeopardy* was the book coming out next week, and *House of Terror* was her work in progress.

John frowned. Rowan was certain there would be one

more victim, from her fourth book, *Corruption,* and then the killer would come after her. But what about the latest book? And her current work? Her current work didn't keep the theme of her "crime of" series. He wondered why. He wanted to ask her. But if he did, she'd know he'd been on her computer.

Could the murderer have gotten a copy of the unpublished book? Was he someone Rowan knew well? Well enough to let into her house?

John shut down the computer and started going through her desk. The file drawer contained little that wasn't personal correspondence or directly related to her books.

Except for one folder.

Newspaper articles, slightly yellowed and dated four years earlier, reported a mass murder in Nashville, Tennessee.

Businessman Karl Franklin Kills Family, Self.

The story documented that Karl Franklin came home after work late one Monday night and killed his wife and four children while they slept in their beds. Everyone was shocked; he was a successful businessman, had no financial problems, and had always talked about his family glowingly.

No apparent motive, no reason. The man broke and murdered his family when nothing should have made him break. Then he killed himself, and no one was able to ask him why.

Four years ago. This was the case that Rowan had been having nightmares about. This was the case she was reviewing at FBI headquarters right now.

Something tickled the back of his mind, and he drew out his cell phone and called a contact in Washington. "Hey, Andy, it's John Flynn."

"Flynn. Second time this week. You must be working."

"You could say that. I'm helping my brother with a case. Have anything for me?"

"Nope. I told you it would take awhile. Digging into the life of the assistant director could get me fired, friend. I hope you have a job waiting for me in the wings."

John laughed. "You can partner with me next time I head down to South America."

"Hell no. I'd rather work at McDonald's. Did you want a status report? I'm empty. Call back next week."

"No, another question. Should be easy."

"Right."

John heard a vehicle slow in front of the house and he crossed to the blinds. He peered out but didn't see anything.

"When did Rowan Smith leave the FBI? It was four years ago—I'd like an exact date."

"That I can do. Hold on."

"Thanks."

While John waited, he continued to look out the blinds. He could only see the roofs of cars as they whizzed by on the highway fifty feet away, up a steep embankment that separated Rowan's house from the busy road.

Before Andy came back on the line, a beat-up truck heading south slowed in front of her house but didn't stop. If the driver was looking for a house, it could be any of the dozen on this stretch of Pacific Coast Highway. It passed and left his line of sight. But John never doubted his instincts, and he waited by the window, adjusting the blinds in such a way that he could see out but no one could see in.

"John?"

"Still here."

"She was paid through August thirty-first of four years ago, but she resigned from active duty on May second."

John didn't need to look at the newspaper article again to know that Franklin murdered his family on May first. Not only was this her last case, it was the reason for her resignation. Why? He'd read through her other cases. Some were far more brutal crimes, yet she'd investigated them without a break in stride.

"One more thing."

Andy sighed dramatically. "I *am* going to be fired."

"Can you run any similar crimes to the Franklin murder-suicide?"

"Where? When?"

"United States. Whenever."

"Shit, John, you don't ask for the hard stuff, do you?"

John couldn't help but grin. "I owe you."

"Damn straight. I'll call you back. Don't know when; that's a lot of territory to cover."

"Thanks, buddy. As soon as possible would work for me."

"I don't know if we're buddies anymore." Andy hung up.

John smiled. Andy would never change. It was nice when people were predictable.

He stood at the window and waited. Ten minutes later, he concluded that the driver was visiting someone else on this strip. Moving from the blinds, he glanced around the den one last time.

Nothing more could be learned from this space. But he felt like he knew much more about Rowan Smith.

He left the den, taking a minute to make sure it was exactly as he'd left it. Computer off, papers stacked, drawers closed. Check.

It was well after lunch and he was starving. Though

he couldn't cook half as well as his brother, he could make a mean sandwich. Tess had told him Rowan had little food in the house until Michael came by. As John looked through the well-stocked pantry and refrigerator, he couldn't help but wonder just how long Michael intended to stay. By the look of supplies, it seemed he planned on being here damned near forever.

It was Jessica all over again. And worse, Michael couldn't see it.

John fixed himself a sandwich, eating it more out of habit than because he liked the taste.

If his instincts were right, Rowan had been assigned to the Franklin case and resigned after visiting the scene. She'd probably been forced to take a leave of absence before her resignation was accepted, in the hope that she'd change her mind. John knew agents who worked hard cases often needed mental health time; otherwise they'd burn out.

Rowan Smith, classic burnout. But instead of joining some small police force as John knew others did, or working as a private consultant, or taking a desk job, Rowan had begun a second, very successful career writing crime fiction. Her books detailed the evil man could do to man, something she would have seen on a regular basis, particularly with the cases she worked.

Maybe she wasn't a classic burnout.

John heard a creak on the deck outside and paused, sandwich halfway to his mouth. His body tensed, alert. His ears practically twitched as he listened for a prowler.

Creak creak creak creak.

Someone was on the back stairs, leading from the beach.

Soundless, John put his plate down and withdrew his gun. His sneakers made no sound on the tile floor as he walked to the side door. He silently jogged down the stairs, then turned toward the beach.

Careful to keep out of sight from the intruder by hugging the support pillars of the deck, he scooted along until he reached the back stairs. He'd checked them out when he first arrived and knew that keeping to the outside of the stairs minimized the squeak the boards made.

He paused a dozen stairs from the top and peered over the railing. Intruder. The man was young, about twenty-one, tall and skinny with dark hair. He carried a huge bouquet of flowers. Had he come to the front door, John wouldn't have thought twice about him.

The boy knocked on the back door and cupped his hand to peer inside. He tried the door carefully.

Stealthily, John walked up behind him and said, "Don't move. I have a gun. Who are you? What are you doing here?"

The kid turned abruptly, eyes darting left and right. "I-I-I'm looking f-f-for R-Rowan." His eyes widened at the sight of John's gun and he clutched the flowers tighter.

"Who are you?"

"Adam. Adam. Um, Adam Williams. Four-four-five West Toluca Boulevard Unit B."

John sensed the kid was legit. There was something off about him. But the best of criminals played the game well. He kept his voice stern. "How do you know Rowan?"

"She, uh, she got me my job. I'm her number-one fan. I read all her books. She got me my job. I work for Barry at the studio. Barry is really nice but Barry got mad at me about the joke I played on Marcy, and Rowan got mad too and I said I was sorry but I thought Rowan would like flowers because she's a girl and my mama said all girls like flowers, stupid."

John holstered his gun, confident the kid was who he said. "Adam, I'm John Flynn. I'm a friend of Rowan's, too."

Adam narrowed his eyes. "How do I know you're not lying? Rowan said there was a bad man hurting people." He stepped back.

John put his hands palms up to show he wasn't an enemy. "We can call her. Do you want to call her?"

Adam nodded vigorously, then stopped and shook his head just as hard. "No, no, it could be a trap. You could be trapping her. No, she should stay away. She has a bodyguard, you know."

"I know. He's my brother, Michael. Have you met him?"

Recognition crossed Adam's face, but he was still wary. "Maybe," he said like a defiant kid.

John reached into the pocket of his jeans and pulled out his cell phone. "I'm going to call Rowan and she'll come home and talk to you, okay?" When the kid still looked undecided, John said, "You can talk to her, too. She'll tell you I'm okay, then we'll go into the house and wait."

"Okay," Adam said in a small voice.

John dialed Michael's cell, mentally hitting himself that he didn't have Rowan's direct line. "Mickey, it's John. Let me speak to Rowan."

"Why?"

"Because I have a delicate situation here that I need her help with."

"Tell me."

Damn him. He wanted to play tough guy. "Adam Williams stopped by to say hello and he isn't sure I'm not the bad guy Rowan warned him about. I'd like her to talk to him."

"Adam? The retarded kid?"

John winced and hoped Adam hadn't heard that. "Yes, Rowan's number-one fan."

"I suspected he was up to something. Keep him there. I'll call the police and—"

"No, Michael," John said, harsher than he intended. "Would you just—"

"Listen, John, I've been working this case a lot longer than you and—" he stopped, and John could hear Rowan's voice in the background, but not what she was saying. Muffled, he heard Michael's voice say, "But you don't know he's safe. Why don't we have the police talk to him?"

"Absolutely not!" Rowan exclaimed loud enough for John to hear. Another mumble, and then Rowan got on the phone.

"John?"

"It's me."

"Let me talk to Adam."

John couldn't help but smile, but a glance at Adam's scared face sobered him up. He was strangling the poor lilies in both hands. "Adam, Rowan would like to speak to you."

Hand shaking, Adam reached for the phone. "H-hello?"

John watched as Adam's expression turned from scared to worried to calm. Then worried again. "I-I didn't ask Barry. I-I watched him enough, I thought I could do it. I didn't hurt his truck, I promise!" It took several minutes, but whatever Rowan was saying seemed to appease Adam. "Can I wait for you?" The answer must have been yes, because Adam smiled broadly and handed the phone back to John. "Rowan wants to talk to you."

"Rowan?"

"John, we'll be there in fifteen minutes. I told Adam

he could wait for me. I'm going to have to get him back to Burbank. He doesn't have a driver's license."

"I'll take him."

She paused. "You'd do that?"

"Why wouldn't I?"

What did she think he was, an asshole? Obviously, Adam was a bit slow. He also worshipped Rowan. He didn't mean her any harm, and he probably didn't get a lot of breaks in the city.

"I—all right. Thank you."

She hung up, and John stared at the phone for a minute. Rowan Smith was not a trusting soul, which didn't bug him, except that she didn't seem to trust *him*.

Then again, he'd deliberately invaded her space, asking her tough questions—most of which she hadn't answered yet. And he found her captivating.

What was it about her? Sure, she was good-looking. Her white-blonde hair appeared soft and silky, something he would love to run his fingers through. She smelled fresh and natural. And her eyes—those blue-gray eyes showed him her feelings, so much better than her words and mannerisms.

She was trying so hard to figure out what she'd done to deserve the attention of this maniac. He admired her focus, her determination, her past career. He didn't understand why she'd quit, but obviously something about the Franklin murders got to her. Burnout? It was unexpected from her personality—at least the strong, independent persona she showed to the world.

But Rowan was closed and private, kept information from him that she might not think was important, but damn well could be. John didn't like deception, intended or not, and expected everyone he worked with to be on the up-and-up. To trust him. That code of honor was necessary in the jungles of South America, on the streets of Mexico, and in every drug port along the American coastline. If he couldn't trust her, what did he have?

And if she didn't trust him, how could he get closer?

He wanted to. He wanted to find out what made her tick. Like her friend Adam. Mentally slow, but Rowan had shown him some attention when it was obvious the kid had received few breaks in his life. Another facet of her complex personality.

"Adam, how about we go into the house?"

"It's locked."

"I know, but I have a key to the side door." John led the way and in just a few minutes had Adam seated at the island bar. The kid was still worrying the poor flowers in his hands. "Why don't I put those in water?"

"They're for Rowan."

"I know. But flowers need water."

"Oh. Right, they need water." He looked sheepish, and John felt bad for him. From his comments earlier, his mother hadn't been any kind of support. Rowan obviously had taken him under her wing and had the patience of a saint. John couldn't help but admire that in her.

John found a vase on the top shelf of the pantry and filled it with water, then poured in the packet of crystals that came with the lilies for preservation. He arranged the flowers in the vase and shook his head. "I'm not too good at this."

Adam moved them around a little and they looked surprisingly better. "I broke one," he said with a frown.

"That's okay, it's still standing." John picked up the vase and carried it into the dining room, centering it on the table. He called through the opening into the kitchen. "Is it okay here?"

Adam looked over the pass-through and smiled. "Yes. That's pretty."

John came back into the kitchen. "Do you want some water? A Coke?"

Adam nodded. "Milk. And Rowan said she had chocolate chocolate chip cookies and I could have one."

John hunted for the cookies and found them in the pantry, a half-eaten bag of gourmet double chocolate chip cookies. Rowan had a sweet tooth, and John couldn't help but smile. She was real after all, and not just the outer shell of a perfect woman.

Rowan walked into the kitchen, Michael right behind her. John and Adam were eating cookies and drinking milk at the island. John looked up sheepishly, a milk mustache across his top lip. He looked so silly, it made her want to smile. Big tough ex-military guy walking around with milk on his upper lip. Because she found it endearing, she quickly turned to Adam and pushed the image of John from her mind.

"Adam, why did you drive all the way out here?" she asked.

Adam glanced up at her, worrying his glass in his hands. He looked both embarrassed and excited.

"I wanted to tell you I was really, really sorry about Marcy."

"You already apologized. I told you I wasn't mad."

Adam frowned and stared into his almost empty glass of milk. "I know," he mumbled. "But Barry was mad, and he still acts mad sometimes. He says Marcy might try to get me fired."

"I won't let Marcy get you fired. I told you that."

"Or Barry?"

"Or Barry."

"Promise?"

"I'll do my best." Rowan put her hand on Adam's

chin, making him look at her. "But what you did today was wrong. I called Barry and told him about the truck. He didn't even know it was gone. What if he had called the police, thinking it was stolen?"

"I-I hadn't thought about that. I wasn't going to be gone a long time, just to bring you the flowers and go."

"I understand, but you don't have a driver's license, Adam. You could have hurt someone because you don't know all the rules of the road. I told you when you want to learn to drive, I'll teach you and help you get your license. But you can't do it whenever you want."

"I'm sorry. I'm stupid. Are you mad at me?"

Rowan tried to look stern, but couldn't pull it off. Not with Adam. She cared about him so much and wanted to strangle his mother for her cruel indifference and verbal abuse. "You're *not* stupid, Adam. I don't want to ever hear you say that again. Understand?"

"But—"

"Adam."

"Yes, Rowan. You're not mad?"

"I'm not mad. Just don't do it again."

He heaved a huge sigh of relief, and Rowan gave him a hug. She glanced at John, who had a thoughtful expression on his face. She quickly turned away. She didn't want to be drawn to John Flynn. He was dangerous. Dangerous to her.

John's cell phone rang and he answered it. Rowan couldn't hear the conversation, but John's face turned from contemplative to blank like a switch. It was about her. She wanted to confront him, but she'd do the same thing in his shoes. She didn't have to like it though.

"Thanks, Andy," he said and hung up. He caught her eye, but his expression remained closed.

He was up to something. What?

"What was that about?" Michael asked.

Rowan had almost forgotten Michael was there. He leaned against the doorway, his casual stance belying the tension she saw in his neck and shoulders. At first she'd thought John and Michael were close, but there was a growing unease whenever they were in the same room together.

"Business," John said, sliding the cell phone into his jeans pocket. "Adam brought flowers."

John had deliberately changed the subject, and Rowan was certain he was checking up on her. The thought angered her, but her impulse to push him was interrupted when Adam started talking, excited.

"John found a vase, I hope that's okay, but I didn't want them to die. I broke one, so you can throw it out, but they're still pretty."

"I'm sure they're lovely, Adam, but you didn't need to bring me anything."

Adam nodded his head vigorously. "Oh, yes. Barry always gets Sylvie flowers when she gets mad at him. And even though you said you weren't mad at me about tricking Marcy, I knew you were a little bit mad, and I wanted to tell you I was sorry, but not just say it, you know?"

Rowan smiled. "I know. That was very thoughtful." She looked around the kitchen. "Where are they?"

"John put them in the dining room." Adam jumped off the stool and grabbed Rowan's hand, pulling her into the next room. "I was going to get roses, but the man said the calla lilies were better for friends. We're friends. Aren't they pretty?"

Rowan smiled until she saw the flowers.

Lilies.

Her eyesight faded from the periphery, until all she saw were the white lilies. A dead voice, as clear as if her mother were standing right next to her, said, "Aren't they pretty? Just like you, Lily."

Lily looked up at her mother and smiled. "They're prettier, Mama."

Mama laughed and shook her head. "You'll be such a charmer with the men when you grow up, sweetheart." She ran her soft, slender fingers through Lily's hair, and Lily leaned into the caress with a smile. "You know I named you Lily because your daddy gave me lilies on our first date."

"I know, Mama." But she loved the story. She couldn't picture her father giving her mama flowers. He was so serious all the time. And sometimes he yelled at Mama. She didn't see him much. She was in bed before he came home from work most nights, and the only time she ever really talked to him was on Sundays. And sharing his attention with her two brothers and two sisters was hard. She preferred to read or play out in the backyard.

Three sisters, she reminded herself as she looked over at the bassinet. Danielle was beautiful.

"Why didn't you name the baby Rose so you can get roses all the time? Roses are prettier than lilies." Lily wrinkled her nose. She really didn't like bouquets of flowers all that much. They were nice when they were freshly cut and arranged in a vase, but they died and Mama threw them in the garbage, almost as if she didn't care. Lily didn't know why someone would want flowers around the house all the time when they died so fast.

Outside in the garden, flowers lived forever. They slept in the winter, but they came back every spring. Those flowers Lily liked.

Mama laughed and kissed Lily's head. "You are a funny girl."

Danielle started squeaking. It wasn't really a cry, just

a little squawk. "I think she's hungry, Lily. Will you get her for me?"

"Me?" Lily wanted so much to hold the new baby, but her father told her not to touch, that babies weren't dolls.

"Of course you."

Lily walked over to the bassinet and looked at her baby sister. She'd loved her the minute Daddy brought Mama and the baby home last week. But knowing that she could hold her, bring her to Mama to be fed, brought that love to a new level. She could help be the mama. She couldn't feed her because she didn't have breasts yet, but she could change her diaper and her clothes and bring her to Mama.

She smiled brightly.

"Hi, baby," she said in her best mother voice. "I'm your big sister Lily. We're going to be best friends."

Carefully, tenderly, she picked up the newborn, supporting her head just like Mama had taught her. She walked three steps to the couch.

Mama put the baby to her breast. She suckled, and Mama got a dreamy expression on her face. "Lily, there is nothing in the world better than feeding your baby. One day, you'll grow up and be a mama."

"I want lots of kids."

Mama smiled. "You can have as many as you want. You can do anything with your life, sweetheart. You can be a doctor or a lawyer or a teacher or a mother. All are important."

"But mamas are the most important because babies need them," Lily said, feeling very smart.

"Yes, babies need their mamas."

A loud thump upstairs made Lily jump, and she stepped closer to her mother.

"Stupid brat! Get out of my way."

It was Bobby. He sounded mad. Even madder than Daddy got when Mama didn't do something right.

"Honey," Mama said, worried. "Go take care of Peter. Hurry."

Lily ran from the room, her fear for Peter greater than her fear of Bobby. She stopped at the bottom of the stairs and looked up.

"No!" she screamed.

Bobby pushed Peter and his little toddler legs buckled. He grabbed at the railing as Bobby stomped down the stairs.

Lily ran up the stairs, and Bobby laughed at her. "Hope you break your neck, Lily Pad."

Lily ignored him and watched as Peter stumbled and fell three stairs, then grabbed a rail. He cried out, but she caught him. "Are you okay, baby?" she asked as she helped Peter back up the stairs. A door slammed. Bobby was gone. She hoped he never came back. He scared her so much.

She hated him.

CHAPTER
11

Rowan hit the vase with her arm. It flew off the table and onto the floor, water spraying everywhere. The vase cracked and the lilies scattered.

John frowned, uncertain of what had just happened, and watched Rowan turn to Adam, her eyes wide and terrified. "Who told you? *Who told you?*"

"I-I-I-" Adam stammered, tears streaming down his face.

John reached Rowan before Michael and grabbed her face, forcing her to look at him. "Rowan, stop. Now."

She blinked at John, her eyes wide with uncertainty. Then she glanced at Adam's petrified face.

"Adam. I'm sorry." She took a step back, shaking.

"What was that about?" John asked, his hands dropping to her shoulders. He gave her a light shake, worried. He saw the indecision on her face about whether or not to trust him. "You can trust me," he whispered.

Her eyes brimmed with tears as her hand fluttered to her mouth. She dry heaved and fled from the room.

Damn. So close! He started after her, but Michael put his arm up. "John, give her a minute."

"Shit, Michael, there's something she's not telling us that's directly related to what's going on. We can't allow her to keep us in the dark."

"Playing big bad bully isn't going to get her to open up," Michael said, his jaw twitching with anger.

John ran a hand through his hair. She'd relived some memory when she saw the flowers. She'd stared at them for over a minute before breaking the vase. What about them had set her off?

John shot a glance at Adam. He'd shrunk down against the wall, silent tears running down his face, arms tight around his legs. Rowan was going to feel awful when she realized what she'd done.

He squatted in front of him. "Adam?" No response. "Adam, it's okay."

"I'll call the studio and have someone pick him up," Michael said.

"No." John's voice was harsher than intended. "I promised Rowan I'd take him home." He reached out and touched Adam's arm. "Adam, I need you to do me a favor."

Adam sobbed. "Sh-she hates me."

"No, Adam, Rowan does *not* hate you. She cares about you very, very much. She's sorry about the flowers."

"She h-hates the fl-flowers. I shouldn'ta listened to the man."

John's instincts hummed. "The man? What man? The florist?"

Adam shook his head, still not looking at John. "No, he didn't speak English too good."

"Who? A customer?"

"I-I think s-so."

"Where did you buy the flowers?"

Adam shrugged, his shoulders heaving with quiet sobs.

"Adam, this is very important," John stressed. "I need you to show me where you bought the flowers."

"Wh-wh-why? Rowan hates me."

"No, Adam, Rowan doesn't hate you. But if you show me where you bought the flowers, Rowan will be very happy."

Adam looked up for the first time and John's heart twisted when he saw the agony on the young man's face. His dark hair was plastered to his skull, his too-white skin ghostly in contrast. "Rowan is never happy."

The reality of Adam's simple statement hit John. Rowan was keeping something bottled up inside, and there was no doubt that whatever it was, the murderer knew. He was pulling her strings. Copying her fictional murders, sending her the pigtails, the funeral wreath—

—convincing Adam to buy lilies.

The man was playing with Rowan, forcing her to re-live memories John suspected were long buried.

But nothing stayed buried forever.

"Adam, please. This is very, very important. I need you to take me to where you bought the flowers."

"Okay." His voice was quiet, like a reprimanded child.

John helped him up. Adam saw the flowers on the floor and his bottom lip quivered. John steered him out of the room and said to Michael, "I'll be back shortly. If you learn anything from her, let me know."

"Sure."

John glanced back at Michael as he left, but his brother had a faraway look on his face. What was up with that? Now was not the time or place to figure out what was going on with Michael, but he suspected it had everything to do with his feelings about Rowan. Michael was no dummy. He knew John was getting in-volved, too.

He didn't want to damage his friendship with his

brother over this case. Or this woman. But he feared it might be too late.

"Rowan? Honey?"

Michael was knocking on her bedroom door, but she didn't let him in. *Honey.* Her stomach churned. She didn't want to worry about hurting Michael. He was a good man, but he couldn't understand; he would hug her and pat her on the back like a child and tell her everything was going to be all right.

Everything was *not* going to be all right. Someone knew. Someone knew her name was Lily. And if he knew her name was Lily, he knew everything about her.

Who hated her so much that he wanted her to relive the worst night of her life?

When she was a senior in high school, she'd read *No Exit*. Three people trapped in purgatory, reliving their worst nightmare. Over and over and over—that was her life. One big nightmare. She thought it had started when she was ten, but it started so many years before. It started before she was born. It started when her father met her mother and took her on a date and gave her lilies.

"Rowan?"

She stood inside the door, put her hand up, and touched the wood. "Michael, please go away."

"You need to talk about whatever is bothering you."

"Not now."

He paused, but she didn't hear him walk away. A moment later, he said, "Rowan, please tell me the truth. Are these murders connected to whatever's been bothering you?"

Bothering her. As if the murderer were an annoying mosquito, her past that of a simple dysfunctional family. Her mere *existence* bothered her. Her life was wrapped in pain and hatred and loss that she had to keep boxed deep in her heart in order to function. But the lid had been ripped off. Her heart bled; painful memories invaded her soul. There was no fixing the box, no putting the lid back on. The secrets were tumbling out, bleeding her dry. She was going to have to face the truth. She didn't have a choice.

But she didn't know if she could move on.

"How's Adam?"

"He'll be okay," Michael said, but Rowan knew that wasn't true. She didn't know how to fix the damage, and she wouldn't forgive herself for hurting him. "John's taking him back to the studio."

Rowan suspected he would research the flowers. She'd seen how John interacted with Adam while they ate cookies and milk in the kitchen. If anyone could extract information from Adam, it would be John.

"Michael, go away," she said, wincing at her harsh tone. "Please," she added, softer.

A long pause. "I'll be downstairs."

When she was certain he'd gone, she crossed the room and picked up her cell phone. If John was in the house, she had no doubt he would listen in on any of her conversations. Michael probably wouldn't. Still, she couldn't take that chance.

"Collins."

"Roger, it's Rowan."

"What's wrong?" His voice was clipped, worried.

"Somebody knows. Somebody knows my name."

A long pause. "I don't understand."

"Yes you do. Remember I told you about my young friend Adam? Someone told him to buy me lilies."

"Can he make an ID? Get him in front of a sketch artist; I'll call around and find a good one. And don't forget—"

"Roger," Rowan interrupted, "Adam is going to take time. He's easily led, and no sketch we get will be reliable. John's going to see what he can find out."

"John?"

"John Flynn. He's my bodyguard's brother and partner. They run the security company. He's former Delta Force."

"I know him."

Roger's tone prompted Rowan to sit straighter. "Oh?"

"By reputation, not personally. Remember that drug shipment that came in through Baton Rouge six, seven years ago?"

"There were thousands of drug shipments during my years in the FBI. I didn't work them."

"No, but you'd remember this one. Billy Grayson was killed and George Petri lost his eye and leg."

Rowan remembered now. The FBI had been called to back up the sting operation, but it turned into a huge and bloody battle. Four FBI agents killed, three others permanently injured. Billy had been in her class at the academy. The DEA lost even more of their own.

"How does John Flynn fit into it? It was a royal screw-up."

"It could have been a lot worse. Flynn was undercover with Pomera's operation—he's a major player originally from Bolivia, but hell if anyone knows where he operates now. They knew about the sting and planned on taking out all the agents assigned to the case. They set up explosives in the warehouse and along the docks. Flynn almost blew his cover defusing the bombs. When they didn't go off, Pomera's men panicked and shot up the place. We got six of them. A shot set off a lump of C-4 under the dock and that's where most of our people lost their lives. Without Flynn, we'd have lost dozens more."

Roger paused, cleared his throat. "I learned more about him after that. Doesn't always play by the rules. He was in a South American jail for six months a few years back, and threatened by the CIA with jail time because he screwed with one of their operations. I don't know the details, but rumor has it that one of the CIA goons down there went bad and Flynn caught wind of it. They turned on him, left him in prison and pulled the traitor out."

Rowan could easily picture Flynn playing secret agent in the Southern Hemisphere. But prison—she couldn't imagine him locked in a cage. Too much energy, in his mind and body. She sensed that he'd rather die than be imprisoned.

"Did the CIA get him out?"

"No. He escaped. Since then, he does very little work for the government. Can't say I blame him."

Neither can I.

"Rowan, the lilies could have been a coincidence."

She closed her eyes. "No, Roger, they weren't a coincidence. Adam said something about a man recommending them. It's him."

"Who?"

"The murderer. I know it."

"I'll get Peterson on it right away."

"Okay," she said. "But tell him he can't press Adam. Adam is smart, but not in traditional ways. He's a little slow." She paused and rubbed her eyes.

"Roger, how does he know my name?" Her voice cracked.

"Let's assume this guy is after you. We don't know why. Maybe someone involved in one of your cases. He's obviously a meticulous planner. The murders are well executed, well planned, and he's psychologically torturing you. It would reason that he researched you as well. I buried your files deep, Rowan, but they still exist."

"Have you dug deeper into the Franklin murders? I read the files. It's not a closed case. There's something there. There has to be." Because if there wasn't, it meant someone who knew her as a child was killing people.

"Karl Franklin's brother has always said he was innocent. We contacted him and he was bitter, refused to talk. I'm going to Nashville early tomorrow to try to talk to him in person."

Hope. "Really? You think it's him?"

"I don't know, Rowan, but we're working every angle."

Rowan swallowed. "Roger, what if this is someone connected to my childhood? Who knows what happened—who knew Dani? The pigtails, the lilies—it's connected."

Roger sighed audibly. When he spoke, his voice cracked slightly. "Rowan, listen to me. Don't go there. You can't keep reliving the past. Everyone connected with that night is gone."

"But—"

"I promise, I'll look at the files tonight. I promise I won't leave any stone unturned. There's no one left—except your aunt in Ohio, but I don't think she's responsible."

Rowan sank to the floor. Her aunt. The woman who didn't want her or Peter. The woman who turned them away because they were devil's spawn.

"I'm not going to the premiere Friday night," she whispered.

"Of your movie?"

"Too dangerous."

"Peterson said he has it covered."

"Perhaps, but this bastard would blow the entire theater."

"Would he?" Roger asked quietly.

Rowan rubbed her head. "No," she admitted. "He has one more murder to commit. From my fourth book. But he's deviated before; he could deviate again."

"The D.C. police have issued a warning to young brunette women in the area," Roger said. "We're not sitting back and doing nothing to protect them."

"I know. But—" she stopped. How could they protect every brunette under thirty who commuted to D.C.? Not everyone listened to the news, read the papers, believed they could be in danger.

That was the crux of the matter. *It won't happen to me. I'm safe.* How many survivors had she interviewed who told her, *I didn't think it could happen to me. I never thought my daughter would be kidnapped. I was only gone a minute. My car was only in front of the building. The parking lot was lit.*

On and on. As if, if they ran fast enough, evil wouldn't see that they'd let their guard down.

She shuddered and voiced her fear. "Even though my publisher delayed the release of my next book, the killer might have been able to get an advance copy. There's been enough publicity and reviews for him to get a sense of the crimes involved. You might want to warn prostitutes in Dallas and Chicago to be extra careful."

Roger Collins hung up and sent an e-mail to his assistant to contact the Chicago and Dallas police departments ASAP. He reviewed his flight itinerary for Nashville and made notes for his conversation with Karl Franklin's brother. All the while, he couldn't get Rowan's fear out of his mind.

Lily.

Who knew about her past? He'd buried the information deep to protect her, allow her to lead a normal life. But she'd never had a normal life. Even before the violence that took her family from her, she was raised in a cruel environment by an angry father and scared mother.

He had tried to dissuade her from thinking about her childhood. He was worried for the first time in his life that the lies he'd told all those years ago were coming back to bite him. But how could he have known?

After calling Gracie to tell her he'd be late again, he went to his private safe and pulled out the thick file that contained Rowan's past. The past he had tried to bury for her. To protect her. To give her a chance.

But she'd never had a chance. And the pounding in his head made him realize he might have made a fatal mistake.

He sat down at his desk and opened the file. He had no intention of moving until he'd reviewed every damned record to see if he had missed something.

Or someone.

John glanced at Adam sitting rigid in the passenger seat of the beat-up truck. He frowned, worried about the young man's withdrawal. He didn't know Adam well, but sensed that Rowan's odd behavior disturbed him deeply.

Before Highway 101 veered east off the Pacific Coast Highway, John saw the flower stand. He'd driven past it several times in the last few days, but hadn't thought twice about it. "Is this where you bought the lilies?" he asked Adam.

Adam nodded almost imperceptibly, and John illegally cut across traffic and into the turnout. "Let's talk to the man who sold them to you."

"I don't wanna." He crossed his arms and pouted.

"Remember what I told you, Adam? This man you saw may be the man who's hurting all those people. And hurting Rowan. I know you like Rowan and don't want to see her hurt."

John didn't push Adam further, allowing him time to mull over the information. Several minutes passed; then Adam opened the door without looking at him.

Good, John thought. He slid out the driver's side.

Adam dragged his feet, but followed John to the wiry Mexican who manned the flower booth. *"Hola, señor."*

"Hola," the proprietor said with a nod. He looked at Adam and smiled. "Lady like *flores?*" He gestured to his colorful display.

Adam frowned and shook his head.

"Señor," John continued, "My *amigo—"* he patted Adam on the back both to identify him and to keep him at his side—"met a man. Do you remember?"

"Recuerde?" he repeated in Spanish. *"Sí."*

"Can you describe him? His hair?" John touched his hair. *"Pelo?"*

"Yes, hair like sand."

"The same color as sand?"

He nodded and waved toward the beach below the cliffs. Blond, John thought. A little darker than true blond.

"Did you see his eyes?"

He shook his head. "He wore *gafas de sol.* Uh, dark glasses."

Damn. "Height?" He held his hand up.

The man looked from John to Adam. "Like him," he pointed at Adam and then put his fingers together about an inch apart. "Taller."

"Do you remember what he was driving? His *coche?*"

"American sedan. Like a Ford." He shrugged. *"No seguro."*

Not sure. "Do you remember which way he went?"

He pointed toward Los Angeles. Away from Rowan. Had he been by her house? He knew where she lived, but the thought that the murderer was stalking Rowan disturbed John on several levels.

"Él compró un lirio y lo lanzó del acantilado," the small man gestured toward the cliff. *"Extraño. Pero no hago pregunta."*

He'd bought a lily and tossed it over the side. Shit.

"What did he wear?"

"Nice. *Pantalones.* Light brown. Shirt like you." He pointed at John's polo shirt. "Blue." He shrugged. *"No recuerdo cualquier cosa. Individuo que mira agradable justo cerca de cuarenta."*

About forty years of age, clean-cut guy. Nothing distinguishing. At least it was more than they had before, John thought as he thanked the man and led Adam back to the truck.

"Do you remember anything else?" Adam didn't say anything, but John pressed. "I think you do. I think there's something you're not telling me."

"No, no," Adam said shaking his head. "Don't be mad at me too."

John sighed, trying to keep his patience. "I'm not mad at you, Adam. This has been a hard day for you, I know that. But if there's anything you remember, even if you don't think it's important, I need to know."

Adam bit his lip. "He looked familiar."

"Familiar? Like you've seen him before?"

He shrugged. "Maybe."

"Think, Adam! This is important." John didn't mean to snap, but his frustration level was rising.

"I don't know. He just seemed familiar somehow.

Like I saw him before. I'm stupid. I don't remember. I'm stupid!" Adam pounded the dashboard with his fist.

John took in a deep breath as he turned the ignition. "You're not stupid, Adam. You'll remember. And when you do, I want you to call me." He wrote his cell phone number on the back of a card and handed it to him. "Call me anytime and tell me anything you remember, okay?"

Adam took the card with a frown, turning it over and over in his fingers. "Okay."

He marveled at the numbers of brunettes in D.C. who ignored the warnings issued by the police. Some traveled in groups, but most left work and headed for the Metro alone, or at least parted with their friends before boarding the commuter train.

He had to thank Rowan for this one. Four of the victims in her book were unidentified, so he didn't have to worry about finding a victim to fit the name detail. It had been harder in Portland to find a Harper family that fit, but when he saw the younger daughter he knew he could deviate from the plan and send Rowan a little memory. Adapt. He'd adapted to circumstances his entire life. Adapt, manipulate, destroy.

But to find a single brunette between the ages of twenty and thirty who commuted from Washington, D.C. to Virginia was much easier. He'd picked out a potential victim last week. Tonight he waited by her car.

Another minor deviation, but one Rowan would appreciate. After 9/11, security had changed on the Metro and he couldn't take the risk of being caught on camera. He wondered if Rowan would recognize him—it had been a long time—but he thought she would. If she didn't, certainly they could run any image through the crime lab and learn he had a record.

That simply wouldn't do. Rowan would learn his identity soon enough. On *his* terms, in *his* time.

Every one of Rowan's books fascinated him. They were so full of detail, so rich with life and death. He'd been surprised the bitch was capable of such creativity. He'd studied the protagonist and wondered if Rowan had written Dara Young to be her. Dara was nothing like Rowan; the fictional FBI agent was a brunette with brown eyes, older, and actually had friends.

No family, he thought with a wide smile.

Rowan would never suspect what he planned, but it was brilliant. Brilliant! He'd always known he was smart. Much smarter than the average schmo out there. But now . . . now he was inspired.

He would break her. Then he would kill her.

He heard the Metro pull into the station, the end of the line. He grinned at the irony of it. *The end of the line.* He looked forward to this particular story. All the victims of Rowan's fictional villain Judson Clemens were raped. He'd never thought of raping a woman. What was the point? After all, he could get laid whenever he wanted, pay for it if he had to. Not in prison, but the fags had stayed away from him after he sliced the dick of the first one who tried to fuck him. The rapist he knew in the joint had a problem with "anger management," as the shrinks called it. He laughed. He had no problem managing his anger, no problem at all.

He concealed it very well.

But he wasn't really raping the woman. He was simply following the script Rowan had so graciously laid at his feet. It was her plan, her victims.

Sorry, Melissa Jane Acker, this is the end of your line.

CHAPTER
12

Rowan dressed in a simple black gown with a single strand of pearls around her neck. She had no desire to dress fancy for this premiere; she didn't even want to go. But Roger was right about one thing. Though the bastard would deviate if he had to, bombing the theater was not his style.

Still, her stomach churned and she hadn't been able to eat anything all day. Before dressing, she drank a glass of milk to settle her stomach, but it sat like a hard lump in her gut and she prayed she could get through the evening without puking.

Normally she had an ironclad stomach. But these circumstances could hardly be called normal.

When she ran this morning with Michael, she'd missed John's presence. It wasn't that Michael wasn't a good bodyguard. Michael was more than competent, though she was uncomfortable with the amount of time he spent looking at her when he didn't think she noticed.

John was more like her. When she looked at John, listened to him, she sensed he felt the same about things as she did. Not just justice—Michael had been a cop and acted it. He believed in justice. But John understood what justice really *meant*, especially to the victims who couldn't speak for themselves.

Justice didn't always mean prison.

But it was more than that. John's worldview was unique and his own. After talking to Roger last night she'd quietly called around and learned more about John Flynn. She wasn't impressed easily, but she felt a certain pride she didn't understand knowing that John was one of the good guys, even when some operatives in government didn't think he wore the proverbial white hat. Justice came first to John. It almost made her feel guilty for quitting the agency. Justice used to be as important to her.

Now survival was all that mattered.

John had been in harrowing situations, including a South American prison, and he'd never broken. He simply changed his boss from the government to himself and went right on fighting for justice. It was damned admirable, and Rowan hated that she hadn't been able to do that four years ago.

But she had thought she was losing her mind.

She couldn't help but wonder about John's past. What did he do in Delta Force? What about after? Roger said he was DEA turned independent consultant—why had he left? To start his business with Michael? Or were there other, deeper, private reasons? Everything she'd learned about John intrigued her. She wanted to know more.

Rarely was her curiosity piqued as it was now. She didn't focus on other people, because that meant she might start to care. And if she started to care, she might care too much.

She feared she'd already crossed the first threshold with John. She already cared.

When she walked downstairs, John and Michael were standing in the foyer talking to Quinn. All three men in tuxedos, all remarkably handsome.

John caught her eye. Her breath hitched in her chest

and for a split second she saw something, sensed something, that went beyond a professional relationship.

He raised his eyebrow. He sensed it too.

Then Michael was at her side and she felt tension between the two brothers.

The last thing she wanted was to cause friction in their family. When John first came back from South America, she'd seen the quiet affection between the brothers. They would be family long after this case was settled, long after she was a dim memory.

"Rowan," Michael began, his hand on her arm.

Quinn interrupted. "There's been another victim. Melissa Jane Acker, twenty-four, brunette, picked up by the unknown subject at the Metro station in Falls Church, raped and strangled."

Rowan had tried to steel herself against the pain, but it hit hard and she almost staggered. "When?" she asked, her voice dull and clipped.

"Last night. When she didn't come to work this morning, her employer called her apartment, got no answer. Her mother went over to see if she was all right and found her." Quinn paused, his voice softer. "I'm sorry."

Rowan closed her eyes. She felt Michael's hand rub her arm, trying to support her, to share his warmth. He was a comforting presence, and right now she appreciated his coddling. The way John stared at her, he seemed to be accusing her. Or maybe it was her imagination. *You can trust me,* he'd said when she freaked out over the lilies. But could she?

How could her past have anything to do with what was happening now? Even Roger thought her fear was misplaced. He, more than anyone, should know. He'd been there—he'd fought for justice for Dani and everyone else who died.

But, dammit, that fear bubbled and brewed and threatened to burst through the surface. Just because her fear was misplaced didn't mean it wasn't real. How long could she keep it under control?

"You don't have to go," Michael said. "No one will blame you."

Rowan glanced from his concerned eyes to John's intense glare. They both waited for her answer, but John seemed to be waiting for something more.

"I'm going," Rowan said. "If he's watching, he'll know he got to me if I don't go. I can't let him see that I'm—worried." She'd almost said scared. But she wasn't going to admit it in front of these three men.

John smiled, almost imperceptibly, but Rowan felt his approval. "The place is covered. Peterson walked me through today and it's clean."

"Bomb-sniffing dogs are going through it right now," Quinn said, "and you'll go in through the back."

"The back? If he's watching, he won't see me."

Quinn glanced at Michael, his expression one of concern. "It's the reporters, Rowan. We didn't think you'd want to face some of the questions they might have."

Damn, she didn't want to, but she wasn't going to show the killer she was afraid. "I'm not going to slink around like some scared rabbit. I'll go in through the front."

"Do you think that's wise? The reporters won't be kind." Michael looked at her with a mixture of worry and something else, something more personal. Rowan quickly looked away. His emotional protection was convenient to avoid John's intensity, but she didn't want to mislead Michael into thinking she wanted more than the crutch. It was simply there and she'd been using it. Was she that shallow?

"I'm used to aggressive reporters," she said, taking a

step away from Michael. His hand fell from her back and she could breathe normally. She was making the right choice, she knew. Stand back, don't use Michael's offered strength. It wasn't fair to him. "I want to know about the case. Any evidence? Did he screw up?"

Quinn touched her shoulder. "Olivia is heading up the evidence response team," he said. "She volunteered."

Rowan felt awful. She hadn't called either Olivia or Miranda to tell them what was going on. She'd do it tomorrow. "I didn't know she was field rated."

"She's not a field agent, though she has clearance. Roger okay'd it and I wouldn't want anyone else processing the evidence. If the killer left anything of himself, Olivia will find it."

"Who's Olivia?" John asked.

"We graduated together from the Academy." Rowan shot a glance at Quinn and he turned away, jaw clenched. Still a touchy point, she thought. "Olivia now heads up the Trace Evidence lab at Quantico."

"John told us about your friend Adam Williams possibly seeing the suspect," Quinn said. "He got a description from the proprietor, but it's rough."

"I heard." John had called her after driving Adam back to the studio and told her what he'd learned. Unfortunately, the vague description rang no bells for her. It could have been anyone.

"Was Adam able to work with the sketch artist?" she asked, though she didn't have much hope.

John shook his head. "He tried. Not enough detail. Maybe if we had a photo of the suspect, but even then I'd question Adam's memory over time."

"But, if that was him," Quinn interjected, "and he was in Washington last night, it means he had to have flown out sometime after one P.M. Wednesday and arrived before five P.M. Thursday, Eastern time. That gives us a narrow window." He grew excited as he talked. "Colleen's working the airlines and we're searching the databases for lone men traveling from Los Angeles or Burbank to Dulles or National. We can then pull all the pictures from the security cams and if we're lucky and smart, get a clear shot."

Rowan's heart leapt to her throat. This might be it. He might have made a mistake. Would she recognize him? Would he be someone she knew? Someone she should have suspected, a relative, a fan? A friend? She shivered. She had few friends; that betrayal would hurt.

Not a friend. Wouldn't she be able to see it in his eyes? "You might want to broaden it to San Diego, Orange County, and Ontario," she said. "He's smart. He isn't going to do what we expect. And check return flights. Not necessarily the same airport, but he'll be around tonight. Just to watch. See if he's gotten to me. I feel it."

Damn, she was beautiful.

John's loins stirred as soon as he saw her walk down the stairs in the simple black sheath that hugged her lean, athletic body. Her long, straight blonde hair hung like liquid silk down her back, and the single strand of pearls caressed her bare neck like a lover's hand. He wondered if her skin was as soft as it looked, if her icy, hard exterior would melt when the right man touched her in just the right place.

He wanted her.

But she was a liar.

Not a liar in the traditional sense, but she was hiding something and that disturbed him down to his core. He'd seen it many, many times in his business. Deception not only by criminals like Pomera, but by his own government. Whether in the pursuit of crime or the pursuit of justice, secrets killed.

Yet he still wanted her. And he sensed she wanted him as well.

John glanced at his brother and saw Michael staring at him. He knew. He knew, and John wasn't about to tell Michael he'd keep his hands off. He didn't think he could live up to the promise, and he didn't lie to family. He felt like a damned hypocrite and that rubbed him wrong. Hadn't he just told Michael not to get too close?

Rowan had stopped leaning on Michael, John noted with interest. He wondered why. If she didn't hide behind Michael's calm understanding, John knew he could make her confess whatever secret she held locked in that beautiful head of hers. Whether or not it was relevant to the case, he needed to know.

Rowan brushed past him on her way to the kitchen. He turned to follow, but Michael crossed in front of him. Just then his cell phone rang.

He excused himself and went into Rowan's den for privacy when he saw it was a restricted Washington-area number. "John Flynn."

"It's Andy."

John straightened and crossed over to the blinds to look out onto the driveway at nothing in particular. "You have something?"

"You owe me big time."

"You know I'm good for it."

Andy snorted. "I could get fired. This goes up to Roger Collins."

"Shit. Bad?"

"Don't know. Just the facts. He and his wife Grace were the legal guardians of Rowan since she was ten." John's entire body tensed as Andy continued. "It was buried deep, but I found it on her name change papers. Her name was changed when she was ten."

"Ten years old?" John repeated.

"She was born Lily Elizabeth MacIntosh."

"Her parents?"

"You asked me to run similar crimes to the Franklin murders? Well, at first I came up with the standard murder-suicides." He paused. "You really owe me, Flynn."

"Go on," John said, teeth clenched. His head started pounding, as if sensing what Andy had discovered.

"Well, all Rowan Smith's juvenile records are sealed, but I found that name change, and then started searching MacIntosh. On a hunch."

"And?"

"Nearly twenty-five years ago Robert MacIntosh killed his wife. Two minor children were taken into protective custody. Their names were expunged, but guess who the FBI assigned to the case."

John's stomach sank. "Roger Collins."

"Bingo."

MacIntosh. It couldn't be a coincidence. Roger Collins took ten-year-old Lily MacIntosh into his home, became her guardian. Why? Witness protection program? Didn't she have other family?

What about the other surviving sibling—male or female?

"Did the father kill himself?"

"He's in a mental institution in Massachusetts."

"Are you sure?"

"Shit, John, I couldn't exactly call them and ask. Collins has markers all over these files. If I didn't trip something already it'd be a damn miracle."

John was going to have to push Rowan. Tonight. He had no other options. "Thanks, Andy. I really appreciate it."

"If I get fired, I'm coming to you for a job."

"You'll have one." John hung up and pondered the incredible information Andy had dumped in his lap. He always trusted his gut. And his gut told him Rowan's past was crucial to this case.

Lily. She'd freaked out when she'd seen the lilies, and if Adam did in fact speak to the murderer, the killer knew about Rowan's past and was using it to torment her. The surviving sibling? A brother? A brother who was possibly as dangerous as his father?

John couldn't help but wonder if the dark pigtails were connected. Or the nightmare she'd had about Danny. Her boyfriend? Husband? Son? *Brother?*

Tonight, she was going to tell him. John didn't doubt he could get her to talk as long as Michael wasn't around to hover over her like a mother hen. If Rowan didn't tell him everything, and soon, the bastard would go after her.

The thought made him ill.

CHAPTER
13

Hours after Rowan's movie premiere, Michael stepped into a North Hollywood dive spoiling for a fight.

He sauntered over to a stool near the end of the bar and nodded to the bartender. "Scotch, double. And a draft."

He was off duty, after all, put on leave by his traitorous brother. John had told Quinn Peterson, the arrogant prick, that he hadn't had time off in a week, and Peterson agreed. Dismissed him.

Leaving John alone with Rowan.

He downed half his Scotch and let the heat of the alcohol warm the icy pit in his stomach. He scowled at some hooker making eyes at him from the other end of the bar and turned away from her.

John had had the audacity to throw Jessica in his face yet again. John didn't know what had really happened between Michael and Jessica. If he had, he'd know it had been even worse than he thought.

Jessica was a beauty. Long, dark hair and big chocolate-brown eyes. She was being stalked by her ex-boyfriend. Michael had been assigned the call.

She'd been so grateful for his help, truly feared for her life, so Michael gave her his cell phone number and told her to call him anytime. She did, and he found himself going over to her house virtually every night.

They ended up in bed and Michael fell in love. She needed him, relied on him, and he relished being able to protect her.

But she hadn't been honest with him. He told himself it was because she was scared, but deep down Michael knew she'd used him. He believed she loved him in her own way, but she needed him for more than protection against a stalker. Her stalker was not her ex-boyfriend, but her husband, a low-level crime boss.

She'd ended up telling Michael that returning to her husband was the only way she could stay alive. Michael tried to convince her to run away with him, that he could protect her, that they could start over in another state, with new identities, anything. To do anything but go back to her husband.

Yet she went. Two years later, her body was found floating in a drainage ditch in the San Gabriel Mountains.

Michael tossed back his Scotch to drown the memories.

Rowan was nothing like Jessica. Yes, she needed him, and he would be there for her. But the feelings he had for Rowan went so much deeper.

John just wouldn't listen. He'd pulled Michael aside after the premiere when Rowan was talking to the producer Annette. Told Michael he looked tired and should take the night off. Michael tried to explain that he needed to be there to protect Rowan, and John threw Jessica in his face. It wasn't the same situation, but John didn't understand.

Then John pulled a fast one. The FBI relieved Michael from duty for twelve hours, but he knew it was John's doing. John escorted Rowan home.

Asshole.

He took a long gulp of beer. Sighed and ran a hand

through his hair. Michael realized that maybe he himself was the one who was being an asshole. He'd blown this conflict with his brother out of proportion, letting his ego get in the way of the truth.

It wasn't John's fault. Michael really had fallen for Jessica. Hard. He'd loved her. He might have started in the role of knight in shining armor, but somehow, over time, it had developed into much more than that. He'd overlooked so much she did, so many things she lied about, all because he had loved her.

He owed John an apology. Some of the things Michael had said tonight were way out of line. Especially about Rowan.

For the first time, he realized that Rowan and Jessica were really nothing alike. He cared about Rowan—he really liked her—but he wasn't in love with her. Maybe over time—but it wasn't the same. Not like Jessica. When he saw Rowan running with John he detected a partnership, a similar style, a streak of independence and something else. Something more.

When this case was finally put to bed, could he live with the fact that John and Rowan might have something together? That John attracted Rowan and he hadn't?

His ego might have a problem, but he was a big boy. He'd get over it. First thing tomorrow, he'd tell John . . . something. Smooth things over. Hell, he could never stay mad at his brother for long.

Someone slid onto the stool next to him, and the bartender brought over a premium Scotch.

"You look like you lost your best friend," the stranger said. "Buy you a drink?"

Michael shrugged, glanced at the guy. Suit, tie, polished shoes. Forties. Businessman. "I'm fine, thanks," he said, turning back to his beer. "Just an argument with my brother. It'll pass."

The businessman nodded to the bartender to pour two doubles. Michael shook his head.

"I'm done."

"Working tonight?"

"No, I'm off."

"Then another drink can't hurt, right?"

Michael considered. He hadn't had a night off in a week. He supposed a buzz wouldn't hurt. "Thanks, pal," he said.

"Pissed off at your brother?" the businessman asked.

Michael shook his head. "Not anymore."

When the bartender placed the drinks in front of them, Michael said, *"Salute."* He drained half the Scotch. He hadn't eaten that night and wondered what he had around his apartment to fix. Nothing. He'd been staying at Rowan's.

He finished the drink and played with a basket of beer nuts in front of him. He supposed he could walk down the street and grab fast food on the way home. The thought made his stomach queasy. But at this time of night, he didn't have many options.

Michael planned to buy the businessman a drink as he left, but when he looked up, the guy was gone. Just as well; Michael certainly didn't need another one. Two doubles and a beer on an empty stomach didn't sit well.

He stood, tossed down a tip, and left. Fast food, then home. His apartment was only two blocks from the bar; that was why he'd picked it. Then he'd sleep off the buzz and be ready to tell John that Rowan was all his—as long as he didn't hurt her. Michael cared about her, and John played hardball. In work and with women.

Michael fully intended to live up to his responsibilities as a bodyguard, and while he owed John an apology for some of the things he'd said, his brother had to understand that this was still his case and he wasn't going to be pushed aside again, no matter what John thought. Then they could arm wrestle, best two out of three, and the loser could buy the winner a six-pack.

Michael smiled. He could never stay mad at John for long.

Rowan had gone up to her room to change as soon as they'd arrived back at the beach house. John took the opportunity to secure the perimeter, get out of the monkey suit, and slip into jeans and a black T-shirt.

And stew over his fight with Michael.

It had been a low blow to pull Peterson into the mix, John admitted to himself, but Michael needed a night off. He was losing his objectivity. But when John told him as much, Michael looked ready to deck him.

John regretted his end of the conversation. He hadn't wanted to fight with his brother; he hadn't wanted to remind him about Jessica—again. He simply needed time alone with Rowan to get her to talk, knowing she wouldn't say word one about her past with Michael hovering over her.

John had to find out the truth about Lily MacIntosh and her father. How it fit in with this lunatic running around, he didn't know. But somehow, it was connected. It was the only thing that made sense.

He hoped Michael would forgive him. He was sure he would once he saw through the haze of his anger. They'd had worse arguments in the past, but when push came to shove, they stood by each other.

When Rowan hadn't come down thirty minutes later, John went up to her room and knocked on the door. "Rowan, we need to talk."

"I'm tired. Good night."

"You're not getting off the hook that easy. Open this door or I'll break it down."

"You wouldn't dare."

"Watch me. Lily." His heart raced. It was a gamble, but he needed to get her to open up to him. To trust him enough to tell him everything.

He didn't say anything and neither did Rowan. Several minutes later, he heard the bolt slide open. He braced himself as she opened the door.

Hatred was etched on her face, her jaw clenched, her neck throbbing, her hands in tight fists by her side. But her eyes—they weren't filled with hate. They showed only one emotion: pain.

"Rowan—" he began. Then she came at him with her fists, hitting his chest over and over.

"Who told you? Who told you? You bastard! How dare you invade my privacy! How dare you!" She ended in a sob and he grabbed her wrists and ushered her into the bedroom.

"Tell me everything."

"What, you don't know?" she said bitterly. "You obviously found out my name is Lily." She pulled away from him, her hair whipping his face as she turned abruptly and crossed the room to stare out the window. It was dark outside, pitch black. He saw her reflection in the glass, the agony of her defeated expression, and his heart skipped a beat.

He hated doing this to her, but it was the only option.

"Yes," he said quietly. "Your name was Lily Elizabeth MacIntosh and Roger Collins became your guardian when you were ten. You were born in Boston and your father is still there." He saw her eyes grow wide in the reflection. "And I know where he is."

She turned and faced him, her chin up. "But you don't know why?"

He gave an almost imperceptible nod. "I want you to tell me."

"Why? You know everything. How long did it take you to dig up those files? Four, five days? Nice job." Her voice cracked at the end.

"I'm afraid you don't have another day, Rowan," he said, his volume increasing. "I think he's coming after you, and I can't protect you if I don't know who I'm fighting against. I think you know. I think you know exactly who's murdering these women."

Her mouth dropped open. "If I knew, I'd tell you. I have no fucking idea who's doing this!" She closed her eyes and John watched as she gathered her strength. He wanted to go to her side, console her, coddle her.

But she'd clam up. This was the only way.

"Convince me." He sat on the edge of the bed and crossed his arms over his chest.

Rowan opened her eyes and stared at him. She hated John Flynn. All her fears, all the pain she'd buried for so long, filled her heart. She was at the breaking point. Was this what it felt like to lose your sanity? As if a million pounds of pressure pushed at you from within, threatening to explode?

Her chin quivered, and she tightened it, turning to face the window again. Everything had come down to this. No matter what Roger said, how much he'd reassured her over the last week that these murders had nothing to do with her past, she couldn't shake the feeling that someone knew about Dani. Who? She had no idea. Why? Why would he go after her now? After all this time? Who had she hurt so much that he wanted to destroy her?

Was Roger too close to the situation to see it clearly? She had relied on his wisdom and his strength for so long, she didn't question his judgment. He'd been more a father to her than her own, more a mentor than any of her many partners. She loved and trusted him. But what if he'd missed something? Something important?

She glanced over her shoulder at John. He knew about her father, but his dark green eyes weren't full of pity or disdain. They were curious, inquisitive, probing.

And understanding.

Maybe, just maybe, an impartial third party could make heads or tails of this mess.

Her voice sounded surprisingly low and calm. "I changed my name. I didn't want the name my father gave me. I didn't want his name." She saw John's reflection in the glass, unable to escape his watchful gaze. But somehow it was soothing, and she gathered the last of her strength to share her story, her past that had been buried for twenty-three years.

"I was ten years old," she began, her voice sounding unlike her, distant, flat, odd. "It was late, after eleven o'clock. I heard Johnny Carson in my parents' bedroom. Something woke me."

She leapt from her bed, heart pounding. What was that? What was that noise?

There. Again. A cry of pain.

She rushed to the toddler bed in the corner, searched for Dani amongst all the stuffed animals. There she was, between Winnie-the-Pooh and her huge giraffe.

"I started downstairs and I heard my father say, 'I can't trust you! I can't trust you!' My mother screamed."

"I can't trust you!"

"Robert, no! Please! The children—"

And she screamed, but it was cut short. The sound of silence was even worse. Then grunts and an inhuman scream coming from her father. Banging, a shout, a door slamming.

"Beth! Beth! Dear God, Beth!"

"I didn't want to follow the voices, but I couldn't help myself. They were in the kitchen."

The white walls were red, drips running down the smooth painted surface. An arc of blood stained Mama's blue checked curtains, the new ones she'd just made last month.

"My father didn't see me. He was holding a knife and it was red with blood. He was drenched, and for a minute I thought he'd been hurt."

"Then I saw Mama."

An arm draped across her face, her pink nightie stained red. It was wet and blood oozed out of her body. One blue eye stared at her. The other was missing. Her mama wasn't there. Mama was dead.

"I screamed, but Daddy didn't hear me. He dropped the knife and gathered Mama up in his arms and rocked her like a baby. But—I sensed he wasn't there. It was like he was already gone; his eyes were vacant, hollow."

"Then he came in."

"Who?" John asked, but his voice sounded so far away.

"Bobby. My brother. He was eighteen, the oldest."

Bobby stood in the door, an odd expression on his face. He was almost smiling. He looked at her and narrowed his eyes. "You. You've always been a fucking pain in my ass. It's your turn."

"Bobby picked up the knife my father dropped. He told me to run."

"Run, little bitch. I'll get you. After I take care of everyone else. One by one they'll die and then I'll come for you."

"I ran." Her voice cracked and she swallowed. She vividly remembered the terror in her chest.

Get out! Get out! She started for the front door.

"I couldn't leave the house. Not without Dani and

Peter. How could I leave them to die? I ran past the front door just as I heard the lock turning. Melanie and Rachel had been out at a movie and they were coming home. I screamed at them to run, but I don't think any sound came out."

Call the police! Please! Go away! Had she spoken? She didn't know, but the door opened and Bobby stood there, on the other side of the door, and she did scream then.

"Lily?" Rachel said, then her eyes widened as she saw Bobby come at her with the knife. She had no time to scream, but Mel did.

"He stabbed Rachel and Mel in the foyer. Over and over and I watched. It was like I couldn't move. Then he looked up the stairs at me."

"Exciting, little Lily Pad, isn't it?" Bobby was breathing hard, covered in blood, and he plunged the knife again into Rachel's body and left it there. He crossed over to the hall closet and she knew he was getting Daddy's gun. Lily turned and ran down the hall.

"He had a gun. Peter had come out of his room and was standing in the hall, shaking. I grabbed him and went into my room to get Dani. I was crying, I couldn't stop, and we all went to Mama's room."

She locked the door but feared Bobby could get in. "Lily, what's happening?" *Peter asked, his voice quivering.*

"Get in the closet!" *she told him.* "Take Dani."

Dani was crying and Peter held her close.

"I picked up the phone and dialed 911. I waited and waited and someone finally picked up. But I heard Bobby coming down the hall. He was laughing, but it wasn't a laugh."

"Nine-one-one, what is your emergency?"

"M-m-my mama's dead. Dad-daddy. B-Bobby has a

gun." She couldn't help stuttering, and hated herself for it.

"Stay on the line. Are you in danger?"

"Yes!"

A gunshot rang out, down the hall, followed by more of Bobby's laughter. She screamed and dropped the phone.

"I went into the closet with Peter and Dani and tried to keep them quiet, but I was crying and I just knew the police weren't going to get to us in time. We prayed together, Peter and I, and held Dani between us."

More gunshots, and the bedroom door burst open. "I know you're in here, Lily bitch. You think you're so smart. I see how you look at me. Well, I'm going to have the last laugh." The gun went off again and again and again . . .

Rowan turned and faced John, tears streaming down her face. She impatiently wiped at them with the back of her hand. "I heard the sirens and the shooting stopped. I didn't know where Bobby went, but Roger told me later he jumped out one of the bedroom windows to escape. They caught him at the end of the street and arrested him. Daddy—they arrested Daddy, but he was already gone. In his mind, he was dead."

She closed her eyes, saw Dani in her mind. Her beautiful, sweet little baby sister. "I didn't know Dani was dead until the paramedics came in and pulled her from my arms. A bullet had hit her and she'd died instantly. I thought the warm liquid I felt was our tears. It was her blood. All over me."

She hadn't heard John get up, but suddenly he pulled her into his arms and stroked her hair. She sank into him, gripping his back, feeding off his strength.

Then her feet left the ground and he carried her to the oversized chair in the corner, nestling her into his lap.

She leaned against him, her head on his shoulder, and felt herself marginally relax.

"What happened to Peter?" John asked quietly.

"He was adopted by a wonderful family in Boston. He's a priest now. We keep in touch, but no one knows about him. No one knows he's my brother."

"You didn't have any other family? Anyone to take you in?"

The rejection was still raw, she realized as she told him, her voice detached. "My mother had a sister. Aunt Karen. She—she came out to see Peter and me. She wouldn't take us. She—we were his children, after all. And he'd killed our mother. Her sister. She couldn't forgive us."

"You were children!"

"And then our grandparents, my father's parents. They were older, in their late sixties or so; they're dead now. They tried, but they couldn't take care of us." She took a deep breath. "I had nightmares. Peter wouldn't, couldn't talk. They didn't know how to help us."

"And Roger Collins stepped in?"

She took a deep breath, slowly let it out. "I met Roger when I agreed to testify against my brother Bobby. It wasn't an FBI case, but Roger was a crime scene investigator and had experience working with survivors. He debriefed me." Debriefed. How clinical, she thought. "He took pity on me and asked if I wanted to live with him and his wife. I agreed. But I wouldn't let them adopt me."

"Why?"

She shrugged. "I couldn't. I didn't want to love them. Everyone I love dies."

"Where's Bobby now?" John's voice was a low growl, his anger simmering beneath the surface, but Rowan felt it in his tense muscles.

"Dead." She paused, then let out a jerky breath, a sob breaking at the end. "He escaped on his way to the courthouse. Killed two guards in the process. He was shot on sight a few miles away when he tried to carjack someone. Good riddance."

"You wanted to testify," John said as he stroked her hair.

"Yes, dammit! I wanted everyone in the world to hear what he did. He got off too easy. I wanted him to suffer." Her hands fisted in his T-shirt and a low, guttural sob escaped her chest.

She stayed like that for a long time, until she could control her breathing, until the tremors in her body subsided. The hard strength of John's body beneath hers, his muscular arms holding her tight, keeping her close, gave her a peace she'd never felt before. Even if only for this moment, she truly felt safe.

She felt lighter, as if sharing her burden with John had cleansed her soul. She allowed his comfort, allowed him to share her pain. She felt almost free, and it was a heady experience.

John rocked her for quite some time, mulling over everything she'd told him. He'd suspected she'd gone through something traumatic as a child, and when he learned her father had killed her mother he couldn't imagine anything worse.

Yet it was much, much worse. It sickened him. He wanted to twist the bastard's neck himself. Both her father and her dead brother.

All that death, all that misery, heaped on a ten-year-old. It was amazing she hadn't broken down before.

"Is that why you quit the force? The Franklin murders hit too close to home?"

She stiffened in his arms, and he inwardly swore. It wasn't fair, but he had to know everything. Somehow, her past and what was happening now were connected. Maybe the Franklin murders fit in somehow.

"I almost lost my mind when I saw little Rebecca Sue Franklin dead, because she looked just like Dani. Satisfied?" She tried to sound tough and embittered, but failed. She sounded defeated.

"I'm not trying to hurt you, Rowan. But you have to face the truth. Something in your past is connected to these murders. Someone knows what happened to you. You can't tell me, after receiving the hair and the lilies, that you don't believe it."

She said nothing for a long time, and John wondered if she was going to speak at all. "I—I really thought after the hair that it was all connected to the Franklin murders. That case was why I quit the force. It was the impetus to get me to focus on writing books, because I couldn't do the job anymore. I thought for sure . . ." Her voice trailed off.

"And?"

"Roger interviewed Franklin's brother, the one who'd never believed Karl Franklin killed his family and himself. He reviewed the case files; I looked at them for the first time. He has a dozen agents going through not only that case, but all my cases. And nothing. Nothing."

She paused a long time, and John didn't interrupt her contemplation. A few moments later she said, "I asked Roger if there was someone else who knew about me, someone from the past. A relative I didn't know about, a cop who wasn't right in the head, anyone. He promised he'd look into it, but so far—" she shrugged. "They're all dead, John! Gone."

"What about your brother?"

"I told you, he's dead."

"Your other brother. Peter."

She jumped up, staggered backward. Her entire body trembled. "Peter? Are you serious? How dare you!"

"I'm trying to figure this out," he said, standing slowly, palms up. He hoped she understood he didn't mean to hurt her. She continued to back away from him.

"That is the most ridiculous thing I have ever heard! He's a priest, dammit! He's the kindest, gentlest man I know. He would never, never take anyone's life. He would never hurt me."

John spoke slowly and steadily, wanting Rowan to carefully consider all the possibilities but not sure she was ready to. "Rowan, listen to me. Someone knows about your past, intimate details about your family and your sister Dani. Hell, it took me nearly a week to get what I got and it barely scratched the surface. Someone knows what hurts you. Your brother Peter is a possibility."

She shook her head. "No. *No!* You don't know him." She put her hands to her face and violently sobbed.

John went to her. She tried to push him off, but she stumbled in her anguish and he gathered her up. "I'm sorry, Rowan. I'm sorry." He kissed her forehead as he forced her to sit with him on the edge of the bed.

"It's not Peter," she mumbled after several minutes, finally relaxing into his chest, her body still shaking. "Roger put an FBI team on him after the second murder. As protection. If he was traveling all over killing people, they'd have known."

It seemed like a logical explanation, John thought as he stroked Rowan's hair. The one person alive who knew about Rowan's past, knew what would torment her. He'd thought that as soon as he got her to talk, the answer would reveal itself. Peter was one of the few people who knew what happened that night, who knew about her sister's hair and that Rowan's name was Lily.

He'd almost forgive her for protecting her little brother, not wanting to believe it was him.

But if Peter had been under surveillance, there was no way he could have flown back and forth to Los Angeles, Portland, Washington, Boston. Yet what if Rowan was wrong? What if Peter had an accomplice? Hired someone to help him? Any number of possibilities lodged themselves in John's mind.

It definitely warranted a call to Roger Collins.

"Are you positive your father is still locked up?" he asked finally.

"Yes. He hasn't spoken since he killed Mama. Roger called the hospital right after the first murder. Just to be sure."

It had been a slim chance; now they had nothing. Not nothing—there was still Peter. He glanced at his watch. After three in D.C. He'd call Collins first thing in the morning.

He held Rowan in his arms, feeling her relax inch by inch. She felt good here with him, like she belonged. He rubbed his hands slowly up and down her back. Working the tension out of her muscles. What she'd gone through—he closed his eyes. He'd recall her pain later when he was alone and examine it more closely. Try to understand her complete and total trust in Roger Collins.

Collins was holding everything close to the vest. Why did he feel it was so important to keep Rowan's past a secret? To protect her? From her emotions—or from someone else?

Did the assistant director know more than he was letting on? John's instincts hummed. Rowan had been searching for answers and went to Collins for confirmation. He'd assured her that whatever concerns she had about her past were unfounded. She believed him because she trusted him.

John had a feeling her trust in her father-figure was about to be shattered.

He worked a hand up to her neck and she moaned a small pleasure as he kneaded her tight muscles. Feeling the dampness of her tears on his hand, he looked down at her face.

She was so beautiful. Her eyes were closed, but she leaned closer into him to allow his hand more access to her neck. Even with her pale skin splotchy from tears and emotion, her high cheekbones, elegant nose, and full red lips all beckoned to him.

He resisted the urge to kiss her and closed his eyes. He was getting dangerously close to falling for her. Just what he'd warned Michael about.

Had he fallen already?

He felt her kiss his neck, a feather of a kiss, but it reverberated below his belt. "John?" she whispered in his ear.

"What?" His voice sounded gruff and he cleared his throat, his hand pausing on her slender neck.

"Don't leave."

He tightened his grip on her and swallowed. She kissed his earlobe. He should leave. She was upset, needy, emotionally drained. He felt like he was taking advantage of her.

She trailed kisses from his ear to his shoulder. Her hand wrapped around his neck, her long, elegant fingers combing his hair, her touch sending heat down his spine.

There was no way in hell he was leaving. He put aside his feelings of hypocrisy and realized for the first time what Michael had felt for Jessica.

He should never have been so quick to judge his brother. He vowed to tell him that tomorrow.

He rubbed Rowan's back, removed her Glock pressing against his gut. She stiffened at being disarmed, but took her gun from his hand and slid it under her pillow. He took off his own firearm and put it on the nightstand, not taking his eyes from hers.

"Rowan, are you sure—?"

She put her fingers to his lips. "Shhh. Don't talk."

He wanted to talk, but didn't want to lose this connection with her. He'd felt the intense attraction from the minute he saw her, and everything that had happened since only brought them closer. There'd be time for talk later.

He held her wrist, kissed her fingers, and drew them into his mouth. The pain and tension in her face faded away. They shouldn't be doing this, but dammit, it felt right. He pulled her fingers from his mouth, tilted his head and touched his lips to hers.

There was no way one kiss could satisfy him. He pushed deeper, wanting to give her the warmth and physical contact she needed, knowing there was no going back. This wasn't going to be an easy one-night stand where he could kiss her goodbye and walk out of her life.

She was already etched in his soul.

He gently pushed her onto the bed and she wrapped her arms around his neck, pulling him closer, returning his deep assault on her lush mouth. Her mouth parted and a moan escaped. He licked her lips, her neck, behind her ear. She tasted salty from her tears. His heart twisted. No one should ever go through what Rowan had. No one. It was amazing she had come so far. She was an amazing woman.

He trailed kisses back to her lips, and plunged in with his tongue. She met him kiss for kiss, entwining her tongue with his, massaging and scratching his back.

Impatiently, she pulled his T-shirt up and he broke the kiss momentarily to whip the shirt over his head and toss it aside. She still wore her little black dress and he reached behind and unzipped it down her back. She slipped out of it and he saw her exquisite body.

She had scars. He kissed an obvious gunshot wound that had grazed her lower right rib. It looked like a knife wound had damaged her upper arm, an old one. He kissed it. Unclasping her bra, he held her breasts in his hands and caressed them. He looked down at her face. Her eyes were closed and her mouth was open. The tears had stopped.

He never wanted to see her cry again.

He kissed one breast, pulled in the nipple to suckle, and she moaned. He repeated the attention on the other breast, enjoying the way she responded to his touch. She'd been like an icicle before; now she was melting, on fire. She pulled at his jeans, and he impatiently slid out of them. He put his full weight on top of her and kissed her again.

He'd never get enough and knew he had fallen for her.

Rowan roamed her hands over John's tight, muscular body. Every hard muscle rippled beneath his uniformly tan skin. Only a line below his waist proved he didn't sunbathe in the nude.

She hadn't intended for this to happen, but as he'd held her earlier, her heart had raced and she'd felt safe. For the first time in a long, long time, she felt safe. He shared her pain and her past now seemed bearable. How that was possible after John had forced her to bare her soul, she didn't know, but getting the secrets off her chest was a relief. She hadn't spoken of any of it for twenty-three years.

A small veil had been lifted from her heart. Her burden felt lighter, as if John were carrying it with her. She was freer than she'd ever been before. Because of John.

So she had kissed his neck and asked him to stay. She wasn't sure he would. If he left, she'd find a way to live without him. She was a survivor, a loner.

But she was glad he stayed. Begging wasn't her strong suit, but right now she wasn't above it to keep John with her.

Maybe, for the first time in the two weeks since Doreen Rodriguez was murdered, the nightmares would stay away.

But more than the feeling of security, she felt a companionship and understanding with John that she'd never had before in her life. The way he looked at her, his deep eyes darkening, beckoning, promising that he was trustworthy. That he wouldn't get himself killed. That he was strong enough to take on her and the world.

He turned her on like no man had before. It was more than his dark good looks and tight, fit body. It was the way he focused on the task at hand, whether it was dragging the past out of her, pursuing justice, or right here and now making her feel whole again. Making love to her.

She had so many questions, wanted to know everything about him. And when she did, she would care about him even more. Care about him too much.

She already did.

Pushing those thoughts from her mind, she reached down and felt his firm buttocks. She dug in her fingers and he thrust forward. He was rigid against her and she wanted him. She kissed him, and he took her mouth deep in his, his hands never stopping, touching her all over, keeping her warm, making her hot. "Make love to me," she whispered in his ear, then licked the sensitive spot behind the lobe. He shuddered in her arms.

"Not yet." His voice was low and husky, and he pulled her panties off with his teeth. She grew cold without his body pressed firmly against hers, but then his tongue parted her vagina and she gasped as liquid heat pooled between her legs.

She grabbed the comforter in her fists as his tongue worked magic. She moaned, the pleasure mixed with just a little pain as her orgasm built and his mouth suckled. She arched her back, her hips rose off the bed, and he lightly bit her nub, bringing on a shuddering orgasm that left her panting and hoarse.

Then he climbed on top of her and kissed her hard. She held on to him, bringing him as close as possible. He spread her legs to enter her.

Then she flipped him.

John almost didn't know what hit him. One second he was about to sheath himself deep in Rowan's hot body, needing her, wanting her, craving her. Then he was on his back and Rowan's long blonde hair hung in his face. He spit out a strand and began to say, "What?" when she kissed him hard, then sat up.

He watched as she took him into her elegant hands and guided him into her. She gasped as his head entered, her eyes closed, her mouth parted. It was all he could do not to thrust himself completely into her at once and come. He was so close.

But he loved watching her. She was like a goddess perched above him, her back arched, her breasts firm, her nipples hard and pointed. Her skin was so white, so soft, so perfect, even with the scars.

Then she slid completely onto him and he saw stars.

He reached for her hands and held them tight. She was directing, and it was all he could do to allow it. He wanted to take control, but relished her abandon.

She ground herself into him and moaned, then pulled up until he was almost out, then slid back down.

The torture was excruciating and wonderful at the same time.

He felt her muscles clutch him as she slid down and her body quivered, sending shock waves from his balls to his brain. He couldn't wait.

Grabbing her beautiful ass in his hands, he pushed her down onto him and pumped into her. She moaned and fell onto his chest, quivering. He felt her muscles clamp down on him.

He came with more force than he had ever remembered coming, and then held her close as she rocked with her own orgasm.

He gently, tenderly, turned her over and pulled the comforter around them. He held her, kissing her hair, her face, her lips. He was already growing hard again, still sheathed in her warm body. "Rowan, I want you again."

She kissed him long and sweet. Together, they explored.

Michael staggered into his apartment, his head pounding and his stomach threatening to rebel. He should never have eaten two cheeseburgers and fries on a stomach full of Scotch and beer. Just get to the toilet, he kept telling himself. Don't make a mess on the floor.

He made it in time, and bowed to the porcelain god for a good ten minutes. When he stood, he didn't feel sick anymore, and briefly considered heading back to Rowan's to help John with protection. Naw, he'd get a good night's sleep and go back in the morning.

After drinking water directly from the bathroom faucet, he slowly walked back to his living room. His door stood wide open. "Shit," he muttered, lambasting himself for being so stupid. He crossed over and slammed the door shut.

"Hello, Mr. Flynn."

He whirled around and saw someone familiar standing in the middle of his living room. The stranger. The businessman from the bar.

Michael reached for his gun, but he already knew it was too late. Three bullets hit his chest. Excruciating heat and pain radiated throughout his body. He was on fire.

His body slammed against the wall and he fell to the floor. Everything moved in slow motion. The stranger walked over to him, light gleaming off his dark blond hair. He shook his head, a half-smile on his face, as he looked down at Michael.

"I'm sorry, Mr. Flynn. It wasn't in the book, but sometimes, we have to improvise."

The book. Rowan. Shit, he'd fucked up. *I'm sorry, John. You were right.*

A flash of light—a camera? Maybe it was a tunnel. Yes, a bright tunnel.

Then the world was gone.

CHAPTER
14

John had to force himself to do his job that morning when he and Rowan set out to jog along the beach. He wanted to watch her, but that would be dangerous. He had to watch the houses, watch the ocean, watch for anyone walking on the beach.

He craved her again. If he didn't know Michael would be at the house by the time they were done running, he might have considered making love to her on the beach. But it would be better if Michael didn't find out yet what had happened.

John wondered if he could keep his face blank.

After making love the second time, they'd slept a couple of hours. John woke with a start at four in the morning. Rowan was moaning in her sleep, crying out for Dani. He gathered her in his arms and felt a rare sense of peace as she quieted and held on to him. He didn't want to delve too deeply into his feelings. After all, he didn't doubt as soon as the murderer was caught that Rowan would go on with her life. And he would go after Pomera.

But his problems, his pain in losing Denny and others to drug-dealing killers like Pomera, seemed pitiful compared to what Rowan had endured every day since she was ten. Even before then. That Rowan had the courage to continue, albeit less than perfectly, gave him additional strength.

Rowan paused at the base of the stairs and took deep, cleansing breaths. She smiled at him, her eyes bright. She seemed almost carefree, and he was pleased he'd given her a little peace after the turmoil of the last two weeks.

"Want to join me for a shower?"

He was already semi-hard just watching her sweat, her small breasts straining against her damp T-shirt. He grabbed her and kissed her passionately, relishing the salty taste of her lips, the sweat on her back, her glow from exercise and the aftermath of good sex.

He quickly broke the embrace. This wasn't the right place. "Let's go." His voice was husky and he cleared his throat.

He didn't forget his responsibility. He checked out the deck and the house before declaring all was safe. He glanced at his watch. Seven.

"We don't have a lot of time," he said.

"Then we'd better get started." She jogged up the stairs to her bedroom and he followed, locking the door behind him. She stripped in front of him and he could only watch and admire her lean muscles. But all the right places were soft.

"Rowan, I—"

She put a finger to his lips. "Like you said," she said softly, "we don't have a lot of time."

He didn't miss the double meaning. He didn't know why it bothered him when she said it, even though he'd been thinking the same thing.

Rowan led him into the shower, relishing the connection they had forged the night before. She'd never felt so wanton, so incredibly desirous.

They began in the shower where she started to wash him, and he took over. She let him. He took the soap in his large, confident hands and rubbed her body until she quivered with more than simple lust. A longing grabbed her, a need to draw out this close intimacy. It was delicate and bright, and like anything new could easily be destroyed.

She didn't want to lose him.

He rinsed her, kissed her skin until she moaned out loud.

"Rowan," he whispered in her ear as he pushed her against the tile wall of the shower.

"I want you." Her voice was low and husky and sounded nothing like her.

He slid into her and she wrapped her legs around him, the wall holding her up. She tasted his rough, unshaven skin and moved to his lips, drawing in his tongue, loving the taste of him, wanting to stay here and forget the world outside. To give him the love she'd never been able to share before. To take his love in return.

They didn't have a lot of time. She planned to make the most of it.

Her muscles clenched and she groaned into his mouth. She pushed her pelvis hard into his, and he pulled out.

She opened her eyes and frowned. "What's wrong?"

"Nothing."

John picked her up and carried her wet body to the bed. She was more relaxed than he'd ever seen her. She reached up and touched his face, her gesture endearing, and his heart skipped a beat. Slowly, he entered her, watching her face react to his sensual invasion. Her lips parted as she closed her eyes.

"Open your eyes," he said huskily, and they popped open.

He held her hands above her head and watched her face as he made love to her. As her pleasure mounted, she wrapped her legs around his waist, meeting him thrust for thrust. When her eyes grew hazy with passion, he gathered her up in his arms as he poured himself into her. She climaxed with a moan and murmured his name.

They lay wrapped in each other's arms, breathing heavily. He pulled the sheet around them, holding her close. He knew they should get up, but he didn't want to let her go. Not now.

Her hand lay on his chest, over his heart, and he felt her own heart beating against his arm. He brushed a stray lock of wet hair from her face and kissed her forehead.

"I heard you worked for the DEA and quit," Rowan said after several moments. The change from passion to business surprised him. "I—I guess I'm just curious. What makes you tick."

She started to move away from him, but he pulled her back close to his side. If she thought she could distance herself from him now, she had another thing coming.

"After five years in Delta Force, I decided I'd had enough and sought one of those cush government jobs." He tried to laugh, but it fell flat.

"Hmm. And I joined the FBI because I wanted to be Dana Scully."

A joke? From Rowan? But John didn't smile. He saw Denny's empty-eyed death stare as if he'd found his body yesterday.

"I had an idyllic childhood," he said after a moment. "A regular *Leave It to Beaver* house. My dad was a cop, straight as an arrow, honorable. My mom stayed home. Baked cookies, drove us to every activity under the sun, always there to listen. It was a good life. Hell, it was perfect."

He missed his parents. They'd died less than a year apart. His dad from an unexpected heart attack, his mother—John suspected—from a broken heart. That was three years ago, but it still hurt.

"They're not around anymore?" Rowan asked softly.

"No." He cleared his throat, swallowing the sudden sorrow that had crept up. "My best friend was Denny Schwartz. He lived down the street and we did everything together. Michael usually came with us, but Denny and I were the same age, in the same classes; we both liked the same games. Mickey always wanted to be a cop, like our dad. So when we played cops and robbers, he was always the cop."

"You were the robber?"

"Sometimes. Usually, I found some other role to fill, sometimes siding with Mickey, sometimes with Denny. We had other guys in our little gang as well, but Denny was—the best."

Denny had always come up with the most original and complex role-playing games. Had always smiled. Always made him laugh. John was surprised at the intense emotion that swept through him when he almost heard Denny chuckle in his ear. *Can't believe you're mourning me when you have that hot mama in your arms.*

"Denny was a joker. Practical jokes. My mother didn't particularly cotton to him, but she accepted him into her house because he came from a broken home. His father left when he was five and he had two younger sisters. His mom worked two jobs to make ends meet. It wasn't easy, but Denny never complained."

I have a plan, Johnny. I'll take care of Mama and the girls, you'll see.

"I wanted him to join the Army with me. I enlisted when I was eighteen. Didn't really care much about going to college, though I did end up there after my five years, courtesy of the GI Bill."

"Good program."

He shrugged. "Yeah. Well, Denny didn't want to go. He had plans. Always a new scheme." He paused, stifled an urge to scream. Had he known what Denny's big plan was, he would have quit the Army and hauled him as far from L.A. as he could.

"This big plan of his involved drugs. Big-time."

"You didn't know."

"I didn't even suspect." He was still disgusted that he'd been so clueless about his friend's illegal activities. "We were young, didn't write back and forth much, e-mail wasn't around yet. Tess wrote, told me Denny had gotten into a rough crowd, but she wasn't that close to him, didn't know how rough, how bad. And Mickey was still in high school, then the police academy and night school—Denny didn't have anyone else."

"You blame yourself for leaving."

Of course John blamed himself. Had he stayed in Los Angeles, Denny wouldn't have died. He'd never have gotten involved in drugs, sold them to kids, gotten himself killed for stealing from the hand that fed him.

Rowan's hand roamed his chest. Not in lust, but in understanding. He took it with his free hand and brought it to his lips. She smelled of soap and sex and he couldn't imagine being anywhere else but here, with her. Sharing a story he hadn't shared with anyone, not in any detail.

"I came back to L.A. and started classes at UCLA. Looked up Denny. He wasn't living at home, and his ma hadn't seen much of him. Which was strange. He'd always been close to his mother and sisters."

Mrs. Schwartz looked tired, worn out, from years of two jobs and raising three kids on her own. "Johnny, I don't know where he's living now," she said with a shrug. "He comes by every now and then, hands me a roll of money, and leaves. I don't know where he gets it." She paused, looked at him with watery eyes. "I can't spend it. I think—I think he's doing something wrong."

"I tracked him down through old friends. Right away I knew he was up to something. One of his get-rich-quick schemes. One of his big plans. Of course he didn't tell me about it. Didn't clue me in to the fact that he was hawking drugs to high school kids. And younger." His voice cracked. "No, I had to learn that on my own. When I followed him."

"I'm so sorry. That must have hurt."

"No, it didn't hurt. I was too pissed off for it to hurt. I brought my father down to talk to him, straighten him out, when I couldn't do it on my own. Dad could do anything. He was that kind of guy. Knew how to talk sense into young punks who thought they knew everything. Punks like Denny. Because that's exactly what he'd turned into. A drug-dealing punk."

"Denny boy," Pat Flynn said as he looked around the opulent house in Malibu that Denny had somehow bought at the age of twenty-four with no known job or means of support, "I think you've gotten yourself in too deep."

John watched from his father's side, positive he could talk sense into Denny. His arms were crossed, defiant.

"Uh, Mr. Flynn, you shouldn't be here." Beneath his cockiness, Denny looked scared.

He should be afraid, John thought. He was getting kids killed over a temporary high. Using the stuff himself, judging by his runny nose and red-rimmed eyes. Dammit, they'd made it through four years of high school, never giving in to drugs except for one time when they were sixteen and pretty Mandy Sayers shared a joint.

"Denny, I can help you. I can get you out of this mess."

"I don't know what you're talking about, Mr. Flynn. I'm not in any trouble."

Denny ran a hand through his hair and grinned while his other hand played behind his ear. He'd always been a damn awful liar.

"My father tried. Damn, he tried. I'd never seen him so frustrated. He ended up yelling at Denny. My dad never yelled. Not in anger like that. But Denny was in total denial that he was doing anything wrong. Lying to my dad. Lying *to me.*"

"It was like he'd betrayed you."

John squeezed her hand. "Yeah," he said softly.

"What happened to him?" Rowan asked after a time.

"He was executed."

He'd spent a week trying to convince Denny to turn over his dealers and be the good guy for a change. When that failed, he just wanted him to get out before it killed him. Denny never even admitted he was dealing, never admitted he was in too deep.

"It was my fault."

"How? Denny made all his own choices. No one forced him to start dealing."

"Neither my dad nor I gave up. One night, the night before Denny was murdered, he told me he was a marked man. That his boss had seen the cops at his house. I knew he meant my dad, but he didn't say it."

"I'll lay it straight for them. It's not what you think, Johnny. But—but I think you'd better stop coming around, okay? Just steer clear for a while, okay?"

"He wanted me out of his life, told me as much. I left. I was hurt and angry and didn't know what to do. I went back to my dad. That's when he told me he'd told Narcotics about Denny. They were tailing him, hoping to catch Reginald Pomera."

"Pomera," Rowan muttered, familiar with the name.

"Yeah. He wasn't top dog back then, but he was lethal. The major courier from South America into southern California. My dad didn't tell me the details. Not then, not ever. I learned later that Pomera was in the country and they hoped to catch him. Denny was their best lead. He'd been approached with witness protection but denied he needed anything, that he was doing anything wrong.

"The next night, I couldn't stand it. I didn't want to betray my father, but I knew something was wrong with Denny. He had to get out, and fast. I didn't have much money, but enough to take us to some hole-in-the-wall city where I could talk or beat sense into the jerk." His voice cracked again, the hot sting of unshed tears caking his throat.

A memory of him and Denny. They were twelve. Riding bikes in the flood control channel. Laughing, taking jumps they had no business taking. They were lucky they hadn't broken an arm or leg or worse. Denny always kept his hair too long, and it would hang over his eyes like a sheepdog's.

"I went back, one last time, and that's when I found him."

The house blazed with light, as if on fire. But it wasn't fire. It was cold death.

The smell of death wasn't foreign to him. He'd lost a friend or two in the line of duty. The coppery scent of blood, mixed with the foul stench of bodily fluids at the moment of death when the body relaxed . . . death surrounded Denny's house.

Denny's death.

"He'd been shot execution style. I touched him, flipped over the body, to see if I could save him."

The glassy eyes stared at him, dark and empty. He stared back, as if seeing his best friend for the first time.

"He was already gone. But his body was still warm. I'd missed his killer by minutes."

"You would have been killed, too," Rowan said, her voice tinged with emotion.

"I know." He took a deep breath, finished up. "Against my father's wishes, I did my own undercover work. Found out Pomera was in town. Learned from Denny's lowlife friends that Pomera had ordered the hit because Denny was stealing from the deals.

"But," he continued, his voice laced with intense hatred, "I think Pomera pulled the trigger himself. From everything I've learned about the bastard, he'd have gotten a sick thrill out of killing a pathetic, doped-up, mid-level drug dealer like Denny."

"And that's why you joined Drug Enforcement."

"Yeah."

"And why did you leave?"

Shit, she asked the hard questions. He hadn't thought about this in so long, but he owed it to her, especially after dragging out her past. After what they'd shared.

And didn't they say confession was good for the soul?

"It's sort of complicated."

"You don't have to tell me."

"I want to."

The doorbell chimed, breaking the moment. Rowan stiffened next to him, then extracted her limbs from his and jumped up. She hurried to the walk-in closet and closed the door firmly behind her.

Bad timing. Bad planning, too, he thought as he picked up his dirty sweatpants, still damp from their run. He quickly slid into them, pulled on his T-shirt, grabbed his gun, and jogged downstairs. Sex, then purging demons— he pulled himself together and hoped Michael couldn't read every minute of the last twelve hours on his face.

He peered through the peephole and frowned. Quinn Peterson, the Fed. His disheveled appearance and day's growth of beard suggested he hadn't slept much the night before.

Not another murder. That meant Rowan was next. He stiffened at the thought. No, not Rowan. He wouldn't let the killer even get close.

He braced himself for the bad news and opened the door. "Peterson."

"Flynn." Peterson stepped in and John closed and bolted the door behind him, reset the alarm. "Where's Rowan?"

"Shower," he said.

"I'm here," Rowan called as she came down the stairs.

John sneaked a look at her. She was composed, dressed in jeans and a white T-shirt, her hair brushed and pulled into a wet ponytail. A flush that hadn't been there yesterday coated her skin. He couldn't help but be pleased he was the cause of her improved mood.

But her glow disappeared when she looked at Peterson's face. John glanced back at the Fed. "What's wrong?"

"Let's sit down." He crossed the foyer and walked over to the windows facing the ocean. He didn't look at them.

"Quinn, what happened? Did he kill someone else?" Rowan's voice cracked.

Peterson turned to face them, eyes red. "It's Michael. The bastard shot him."

John barely heard Rowan's shocked gasp. His heart pounded; his ears rang. His brother. No.

"What hospital? Where—"

"He's dead."

"No." John shook his head. "Goddammit, *No!*" He

kicked the glass coffee table with his bare foot, and it toppled over and shattered against the end table.

Michael. Not Michael. John stared at Peterson and knew there was no mistake.

Michael was dead.

An intense, physical hollowness spread through his chest, ten times worse than anything he'd ever felt before. His father's death had been a shock that jolted the family. His army buddies who'd died had hurt his soul. Denny's senseless murder had rocked everything John believed in, had finished forming his path.

But Michael. His best friend. His brother.

All the death, all the pointless drug murders. He'd seen more blood and guts than most people see in their lifetime. Nothing had prepared him for this.

He pictured Michael, blood seeping from his lifeless body. His eyes open, glassy . . . He shook away the vision, his eyes blurry with unshed tears.

"What. Happened." His breath came in ragged gasps as he tried to control his rage.

"He went to a bar last night, a few blocks from his apartment. The Pistol; apparently it's a dive bar that doubles as a cop hangout."

John knew the place. Michael went there when he was troubled. And he'd been plenty pissed last night.

"He was there for an hour or so, drank on the heavy side of moderate. The bartender didn't think he was drunk, just tipsy. He went to a fast-food restaurant, ate there, walked home. He was talking to someone at the bar for a short time, and the police are working with the bartender on a description. The guy—dark blond hair, forties—left before Michael, but . . ."

Quinn paused, cleared his throat, then continued. "Michael entered his apartment and the police believe an intruder was waiting for him. He was shot three times in the chest. Died at the scene."

John's fists clenched at his side. He wanted to punch someone. He wanted to kill someone. "No. I don't believe it." But his tone said the opposite.

"He didn't bother hiding it. Three neighbors called in gunfire to 911. I would have been here sooner, but it took time for the local police to realize there was a connection. It was the chief who ultimately called me less than an hour ago. I came straight here."

Quinn stared at him, his own face twisted with hurt and regret. "It's the same bastard. He—left a note. I'm sorry, John. I'm really sorry."

John's mind was a jumble of memories and plans and vengeance. The killer went after Michael. Why? It wasn't in the books. He did it because he could. To show Rowan he could get to her.

He whirled around and stared at Rowan. Complex and conflicting emotions assaulted him. Anger. Grief. Pain. Guilt. It was his fault. He'd sent Michael away to get Rowan to talk.

To get her into bed.

He'd wanted her from the beginning, knew there was an invisible bond joining them from the moment they met. Michael had cared for her, but John didn't give him any credit for knowing his feelings. He threw Jessica back at him. He pushed Michael aside, manipulated him out of the picture. They fought and John pulled his ace, got the FBI to insist Michael take time off.

John had sent his own brother to his death.

He could never tell Michael he was sorry.

A deep, low, guttural moan escaped John's throat and he couldn't look at Rowan or the tears that streamed down her face. He needed air. He had to get out of here.

"Tess," he said, his voice hoarse with barely constrained grief.

"She doesn't know. She's meeting me at the headquarters at nine, but—"

"I'll tell her." He passed Rowan without looking at her. He left the house without another word.

Rowan watched John leave, agonizing for him. For herself.

It was all her fault.

The bastard wanted to hurt her, but he was hurting innocent people in the process.

Who was it? Who knew about her past? She had to call Roger. She had to find out what he knew, what he'd found out. He was the damn FBI! They couldn't be in the dark for this long. They had to suspect someone.

And if the killer knew about her family, he might know about Peter. If anything happened to him—

But she couldn't stop thinking about Michael.

John. Tess.

Dear God, why? Why did he go after Michael?

Because he could.

"Rowan." Quinn walked to her side, crunching glass into the carpet. He frowned at the mess, but said nothing. "We need to put you into a safe house."

"No." She closed her eyes and rubbed her forehead. Her headache that had disappeared sometime last night was now back with a vengeance.

"Be reasonable! Roger would not allow you to—"

"Just, no. The killer will come for me. I'll kill him."

"He's elusive. Smart. I can't let you put yourself in danger." He put a hand on her shoulder; she shrugged it off.

"It's not your choice. I'm not going to run so he can kill more people. If he can kill Michael"—her voice hitched and she swallowed back a sob—"he can get to anyone. You. Tess. Roger. But it's me he wants. He's deviating to show me he's smarter. Stronger."

She took a deep breath and squared her shoulders. "He doesn't know who the hell he's up against."

Rowan sat on hold for a good five minutes. Finally, Roger came on the line.

Without preamble, she asked, "What have you found out?"

"Rowan, I spent all night going over your files. I have a team tracking down every cop who was assigned to the investigation. And—well, the thought came to me last night. What about the families of the two guards Bobby killed? I can't see how or why they would go after you, but it was the only thing that came to mind."

Her heart beat faster. Revenge. They were tormenting her because her brother had brutally killed their father, their brother, their son. It was plausible, especially since Bobby was dead and in hell and they couldn't go after him. But why now? Why like this?

There had been many, many nights over the years when Rowan had woken in the dead of night, wishing Bobby were alive so she could kill him herself. He'd stolen everything from her, everything but her life, and her very existence felt hollow since Bobby had killed her sisters.

If it connected to Bobby somehow—that would make more sense to her.

"You're checking?" She was desperate. Desperate and grasping at straws. "But why wait twenty-some-odd years? Why wait at all?"

"I have Vigo working on a profile, but he hasn't come up with anything useful yet." Hans Vigo was the top profiler in the agency. But Rowan knew a profile was only as good as the information given to the profiler.

They were missing a lot of information. More than they should. For the first time in four years, she regretted quitting the Bureau.

"What about the Franklin murders? You said you were going to talk to Karl Franklin's brother. Did—?"

Roger interrupted. "Nothing. I visited him, talked to him. The man is in a wheelchair. I went to his doctor and it's legitimate. He can't walk. He couldn't be involved, even if he had the motive. Everything else in Nashville— a dead end."

Dead end. And she'd been so sure this had something to do with the Franklin case. The pigtails.

Dani.

It was about Dani; it was about her family.

"It's about the past. Roger, you have to find out what's going on. And tell me right away. I'm serious, Roger, don't try to protect me. I have to know the truth."

Next she tried Peter at the rectory in Boston, but he was in church. She left a brief message, their personal code, then sank into the oversized chair in the den. Burying her face in her hands, she allowed herself a moment of self-pity, to mourn her life. Her dead family. And now, Michael.

And the loss of something she had almost had with John, a connection she felt with him that she'd felt with no other man. Something that for a short time she thought might become bigger, better than she deserved.

But it was gone. Like a life ended before its time, whatever fleeting connection that existed between her and John had been abruptly severed.

What did she expect? She didn't deserve John. She'd often thought of herself as half a person, incomplete. Less than whole. What she missed she couldn't lay a finger on, but she knew she lacked something. Why else could she not bond with others like a normal person? Why did she find it so hard to stay in contact with her few friends, like Olivia and Miranda? Why couldn't she form relationships with men?

Already she had developed a stronger bond with John than any of her previous lovers, but look where they were now.

John wouldn't forgive her. She couldn't forgive herself.

The ringing phone startled her, but she grabbed the receiver on the second ring.

"Rowan, it's Peter. What's wrong?"

He knew she'd never leave a message unless it was an emergency.

"The bastard killed Michael. My bodyguard."

"Dear Lord." She could picture Peter making the sign of the cross. "Were you—hurt?"

"No. He was killed during his night off." *While I was making love to his brother.* Her entire body shook with restrained guilt.

"I can be out there in a matter of hours—"

"No! Stay there. You're safe." She hadn't meant to shout, but if anything happened to Peter—she couldn't think about that. "Isn't there some nice, safe monastery you can hang out in for a week or two?" She tried to make her voice light, but failed miserably.

"If he hasn't come for me, he doesn't know about me."

"If anything happened to you, I don't know what I would do."

"I'll be on alert. And there's a couple of your FBI friends parked in a very obvious unmarked sedan across from the rectory. I'm sure I'm perfectly safe here."

That's what Michael had thought. She shuddered. "Peter—"

"I'm staying. Unless you need me there."

"Stay far away from me."

"I'm worried about you."

"I can take care of myself." She sounded like a petulant child. "I think this guy knows everything about what happened to Mama and the girls. Everything. For some reason, he's after me. Can you think of anyone— no matter how far-fetched—who could be doing this? Do you remember anything from that night, that time, anything at all, to give to Roger for follow-up?"

"Roger already called me the other day."

"The other day?" She frowned.

"Yeah, Wednesday I think."

Wednesday? But that was before Rowan had talked to him about her new suspicions. Maybe he came up with them himself and hadn't wanted to worry her. But he didn't mention that when she'd talked to him earlier.

"What did he want?"

"Exactly what you asked. Memories. And I told him I didn't have anything. Bobby's dead, and he's the only one who I can think of who could kill so mercilessly."

Heart pounding, John paced Tess's small apartment like an irate tiger trapped in a cage. His skin burned. Every breath shot hot, piercing pains into his gut.

Michael was dead.

When he told Tess, she became hysterical. Gut-wrenching sobs, agonizing cries. For an hour, she clung to John. She blamed Rowan.

"It's my fault," John told her. "I insisted he take time off." *So I could screw Rowan.* Black guilt squeezed his heart.

"No, no, it's *her!* Y-y-you s-said she was k-keeping se-crets! She killed him. *She killed my brother!*"

It took John a long time to calm Tess enough to convince her to lie down. She quietly sobbed, and when she stopped John checked on her. Asleep, her splotchy face bore her grief.

His rage, his anger, and his guilt ate at his gut until all he saw was red, his fury consuming every pore. He paced. Back and forth.

I will kill the bastard.

It's my fault.

Michael would have been at Rowan's if John hadn't interfered. If he hadn't been so damned confident he could get Rowan to talk and that Michael would only have been a hindrance, his brother would be alive today. If they hadn't fought, Michael wouldn't have been drinking. He could have fought back if he wasn't impaired. In the back of his mind he remembered Peterson saying he was shot instantly, by an intruder in his apartment.

No time to react. But Michael was trained. If he hadn't been mildly intoxicated, he might have had a chance.

Maybe.

An agonized groan escaped John's throat and he swallowed back stinging tears. There'd be time to grieve later. He had a killer to find.

Calling in a favor, he obtained Roger Collins's cell phone number and dialed.

"Collins," the assistant director answered after three rings.

"Mr. Collins, this is John Flynn."

Long pause. "I heard about your brother. I'm sorry."

"And I heard about you."

"What's that supposed to mean?"

"I know all about Lily MacIntosh and that you were her guardian."

"Rowan told you?"

"Eventually. I had to drag it out of her, but she told

me everything." John stared out Tess's apartment window, not focusing on anything but getting information. "You know the details of this case. The bastard knows about Rowan's past. He knows about her family. He knows her name was Lily!" He didn't mean to shout, but his nerves were frayed. *It won't help Michael to lose it now.*

Calmer, John said, "I know Peter MacIntosh is alive and goes by the name Peter O'Brien. He's supposed to be a priest in Boston. He would know enough about Rowan's past."

"Peter? You're way off base, Flynn."

"I don't think so. Unless you have another idea."

Another long pause. "I've had a team watching Peter since the second murder. He hasn't left Boston."

"I think you need to double-check."

"Don't tell me how to do my job, Mr. Flynn."

John ignored the threat in the assistant director's voice. He couldn't care less about pissing off high-ranking officials.

"You know this guy is out for Rowan. And he's going to get her unless you figure out who knows about her past. You appear to be the only one who's in a position to do anything about it." He paused. "My brother is lying in a morgue because you and Rowan hid her past. All the resources spent going through her cases wasted time. We should have been going back even further. Full disclosure. Instead, you kept your mouths shut. My brother's death is on your conscience."

"Don't you dare lay this at Rowan's feet, Flynn. She's been through hell and back, and—"

"I don't give a damn." John squeezed his eyes shut and pinched the bridge of his nose. All he saw was Rowan's wretched face when she'd told him about her mother's murder. Shit.

But Michael was dead.

"Why didn't you dig deeper, Collins? Even if Rowan didn't know or understand the full implication of what happened to her as a child, you certainly did."

"I've been looking at the old files, interviewing people—"

"Obviously, that wasn't good enough."

"I have six agents tracking down the family of the two guards Bobby MacIntosh killed when he attempted to escape."

"It should have been done at the beginning." John's jaw was so tight he could barely speak.

"Flynn, we're doing everything we can. Can't you see this is a complex situation?" Roger sounded frustrated, speaking too loudly and too quickly.

Complex? "What are you hiding?" John asked. Something wasn't quite right.

"I don't know what you're talking about," Roger snapped back. "I've been working this 24/7 since Doreen Rodriguez was killed. Don't think I've been slacking off. I care about Rowan more than you can possibly imagine. As if she were my own daughter."

Daughter. That reminded him about the priest. "I expect that Peter O'Brien will be checked out in full, and that you'll look into the murder of Rowan's family a little more closely. Someone who has intimate knowledge of her family killed my brother.

"And," John continued, his voice low, "he will kill Rowan if we don't find him."

"I know." Collins's voice shook with anger.

Good, John thought. He needs to be pissed off.

"Flynn, I know this is a difficult time right now, but are you staying on the job? Do I need to replace you?"

John closed his eyes. The revenge he sought felt thick

on his tongue, clouded his judgment. Could he do it? Could he protect Rowan?

Or would he, too, end up dead, his reflexes hindered by rage instead of alcohol? But what else could he do? Without being a part of this, he'd be out of the loop. He couldn't stay on the outside looking in, wondering if Michael's death would be avenged, or if the bastard would get off with life in prison.

Or if Rowan would end up dead, too.

His emotions were too raw where she was concerned, so he banished her from his thoughts and said to Collins, "Tomorrow I'll be back. Today I need to take care of my family."

"I understand."

"Keep me informed," John said as he hung up.

He couldn't think about Rowan. Not now. This was a job, and more than just a job. He'd keep her in the back of his mind, at least for today.

He went to Tess's room. He'd thought he heard her stirring when he was on the phone and wanted to make sure she was all right. "Tess?" He knocked lightly.

No answer.

He opened the door and stared at the rumpled bed. She wasn't there. A quick look through the apartment showed that she'd left.

He knew exactly where she'd gone.

Rowan heard the familiar buzz of a Volkswagen in the driveway and suspected Tess was here to say her piece. She closed her eyes and leaned back into her favorite chair, the overstuffed reading chair she'd loved since walking into the sterile beach house with Annette months ago.

She'd planned to be here through July, then go back to her cabin outside of Denver. She missed the only place she'd ever considered home since that fateful night twenty-three years ago.

But would Rowan be able to leave in two months? Would this killer be caught? Or would she be his next victim? Would she be the last?

It might be worth sacrificing her life if she were the last. If she could take him out at the same time.

The thought actually soothed her. Revenge, justice, peace. After Michael's murder, nothing short of death would give her peace. Though she hadn't pulled the trigger, how could she live knowing she was responsible for his death? Michael's murder sat raw in her soul, a wound she doubted would ever heal. Michael had joined Dani. And Rachel and Mel and her mother.

While she'd been content in John's arms, Michael had been gunned down.

She didn't know if she even could face John again. The pain and agony he must be experiencing—the grief on his face. She knew exactly how he felt. Her stomach churned painfully.

The den door swung open so hard the knob hit the wall and dented the paneling. Tess stomped in, her face wet with tears but set with determination. Pain. Hatred. Her short dark hair was a mess, her clothing wrinkled.

Quinn was behind her looking concerned, but Rowan gave him minimal attention. She focused on Michael's sister.

"It's all your fault!" Tess screamed.

"I'm sorry," Rowan said. "Believe me, I am sorry." She stood, turned to face Tess, ready to take any punishment.

"You *lied!* You kept secrets and Michael is dead. John told me everything. I-I-I'll never forgive you. I hope he gets you. I hope you both burn in hell!"

What could Rowan say? She hoped he came for her,

too. Then she would have a chance to stop him. And if she died in the process, what loss to the world would that be?

"I know," she said simply.

"Tess, you don't mean that," Quinn said, putting his hands on her shoulders. She shrugged him off and stepped forward.

"Yes. I. Do."

Rowan hadn't noticed before, but Tess had the same green eyes as her brothers, only lighter. They all looked alike. Tess. Michael. John. She couldn't think about John or what they'd done last night. What a foolish, selfish mistake! A mistake that cost Michael his life. Michael should have been here, safe.

But if John had gone home, would the bastard have gone after *him?*

Michael wouldn't have been preoccupied, angry at his brother for forcing him to take a break. Angry at John because of *her.*

The realization hit her and she stumbled backward. Michael had known, at least sensed, the tension and attraction between her and John. He was jealous. He'd fought with his brother because of *her,* not just because John insisted he take time off.

It was her fault.

She tilted her chin up and nodded at Tess. "I don't blame you, Tess. Michael was a great guy, and I'm—"

"Don't!" she screamed and approached Rowan, hands bunched at her side. "Don't talk about him! He was *my* brother! You bitch!" She started pounding Rowan with her fists and Rowan let her. She was numb, dead inside. Did she have any grief left to give? The pain from the punches couldn't compare to the agony of death, the added nightmares, the guilt seizing her soul with its piercing grip.

"Tess, please." Quinn rushed over and tried to gently pry her off.

The front door slammed, and Quinn pulled his gun and ran from the room. A moment later, John burst in, Quinn behind him.

"Tess!" John grabbed her and spun her around. Tears streamed down her face and she pounded her brother in the chest. He took hold of her wrists and gently wrestled her under control. "Tess, honey. Stop. Please, sweetheart, stop." His voice was calm, soothing, very much in control.

Tess's bottom lip quivered; tears streamed down her face. She collapsed into his arms, sobbing.

John caught Rowan's gaze before he led Tess from the room. The mixture of pain and rage she saw in his hard, chiseled expression stabbed her heart.

Quinn crossed to her, put an arm around her shoulders, and eased her into the reading chair.

"Rowan, it's not your fault." He rubbed her back and brushed a loose strand of hair away from her face. "Don't blame yourself."

She didn't say anything. What could she say? The last two weeks were one big living, breathing nightmare. Would it ever end? Would he finally come after her so she could have peace?

Justice.

She couldn't let him get away. When he found her, would he glowingly tell her of his crimes, seeking her praise? Her horror? Her anger? Whatever he wanted from her, she wasn't going to give him anything but a bullet.

But first, she had to make sure Roger had done what she'd asked.

"Rowan, Tess didn't mean any of that. She's distraught."

Rowan looked up at Quinn. His handsome face was long with sadness and worry. "Protect her, Quinn. When people get upset, they do stupid things. And call the Dallas and Chicago police and Bureau field offices. Make sure they understand the seriousness of warning prostitutes. Particularly high-paid call girls."

"We already took care of that—"

"Do it again!" Rowan yelled, then pinched the bridge of her nose. It didn't do any good to yell at Quinn. It wasn't his fault.

"All right," he said quietly. "Rowan, it may surprise you, but I know what I'm doing. I've been an agent for fifteen years. And Roger hasn't rested since the beginning."

"I know. I'm sorry." She rested her hand on Quinn's arm. "It's just—" She absently waved an arm toward the shelf that housed copies of her books. She walked over to them and stared.

"It felt so cathartic to write these books, to always have good triumph over evil when we both know the bad guys often win." She stared at the shelf. *Crime of Opportunity. Crime of Passion. Crime of Clarity. Crime of Corruption.* And her latest book, the one they were holding until this bastard was caught, *Crime of Jeopardy.*

Twenty advance copies had been sent to her, but she had only brought five to Malibu, in case she wanted to send them to someone. She'd given one to Adam . . .

There were three on her shelf.

She stared at them, her heart beating fast. Three left. There should have been four.

"Rowan—" Quinn began.

"He's been here." Her voice was barely audible.

"Who?"

"The killer. He's been here. Right here." She pointed

to the shelf of books. "He has the last book. He could kill anytime."

Three more days.

He stood at the window and looked out into the blackness. It was three in the morning and very, very dark here on the coast. He hated it. Hated the ocean, hated the cold, foggy mornings, hated the salt air. How she ran on the wet beach every damn morning in the soggy air was beyond his understanding, but she'd always been odd. His opposite.

Except for one thing. She came up with exquisite ways to murder.

In *Crime of Jeopardy,* Rowan's counterpart, Dara Young, investigates the murder of a prostitute in Dallas that is linked to an unsolved series of murders in Chicago. The victims are mutilated and vital organs removed with precision.

He'd been studying basic surgical procedures in anticipation, but he read the good parts—the details about each murder—three times to get it just right. Exactly as Rowan envisioned.

Turning from the window, he crossed the spacious, sparsely furnished living room and finally went upstairs to bed. He pulled a book off his nightstand and caressed the cover. *Crime of Jeopardy.* It wouldn't be in bookstores for another three days, but he had taken this copy out from under Rowan's cocky little nose weeks ago. Weeks. Before Doreen Rodriguez took her last breath. Before he'd finished planning each payback, before he planned what he would do to Rowan.

But he knew now, and it would be good. Very, very good.

But first, *Jeopardy.* Dallas or Chicago. Chicago or

Dallas. Hmmm. He was a little nervous about going back to Texas, but the challenge thrilled him as well.

Chicago, Dallas. Dallas, Chicago. It made no difference to him. Some stupid whore was going to die and lose her innards, one way or the other.

He lay back on the bed dressed in nothing and pulled the warm comforter over him. He had some serious planning to do.

He was running out of money. He couldn't very well take out the whore when he didn't have the plane fare to get to Dallas. Robbery really wasn't his thing, but every few months he hit a couple stores and pulled in enough money to get around. The trick was to pick businesses with women behind the counter. They'd fork over the money quick and easy and he'd be out in less than five minutes. He'd only had to kill once.

Tomorrow he'd take care of his finances, then finalize his plans for the whore.

How much did they know? Obviously enough to keep Rowan under lock and key.

There were several Feds watching Rowan. A pair outside her house in a so-called nondescript sedan, and they rotated every twelve hours. That agent she was friendly with. And the bodyguard's brother. He was a little worrisome. Elusive, harder than the bodyguard he killed. More like a seasoned Fed, an undercover cop.

He wouldn't underestimate the brother. No, that might be a mistake. But he had time. One whore in the Midwest, and then Rowan was his.

He smiled as he drifted off to sleep.

CHAPTER
15

It was after hours when John went to the morgue.

He'd asked his aunt to stay with Tess, then spoke to the chief of police, Michael's old boss, to arrange the viewing.

John barely registered the cold temperature of the basement as the assistant coroner led him down the hall and into one of the many body storage rooms. He unlocked drawer B-4, second row from the bottom, but didn't open it.

"I'll give you a few minutes," the assistant said, then crossed the room to give John privacy.

John stared at the drawer.

Michael. Michael was in drawer B-4.

John reached down, clasped the handle tightly, and closed his eyes. *How can you be dead? How can you be gone?*

They hadn't always had an easy relationship, even in childhood. They weren't much more than a year apart in age, rivals in both sports and women. But they'd always been friends, even when they sparred. John went Army, Delta Force, and Mickey became a cop. Both had their father's strong sense of justice; both had their mother's compassion for victims. When their dad died of a heart attack at the age of fifty, they'd bonded to take care of their mother and sister. And when their mom died the following year, they remained close. Started their business. Watched out for Tess.

Sure, they'd had disagreements. Jessica was a major one. John had never trusted her, but Michael was convinced she'd change. A few other big fights, here and there. But when they fought, they always made up. Like partners in a good marriage, they didn't go to bed angry.

Until last night.

A hollow sob escaped his throat and John squatted next to the box. The last time he'd spoken to Michael was in anger. He'd outmaneuvered him, and Michael knew it. John always won because he played the game better. He knew which buttons to push and he pressed them just right to get the reaction he wanted.

And when Agent Peterson saw Michael lose his temper, he'd agreed that Michael needed a night off. Perfect timing. Timing John had set up. Now Michael was dead. And he couldn't tell his brother he'd been wrong.

John slid open the drawer, cold air rushing out to slap him in the face. The familiar chemical smell mixed with death assaulted his senses. He'd seen plenty of dead bodies before. In the morgue, in the battlefield, in the jungles.

But none had been his brother's.

The three dark holes in Michael's chest stood out against the blue-white pallor of his bloodless skin. His body seemed smaller as it lay there on the steel tray. Michael's dark hair was damp from the icy cold. It was too long, but he'd never liked the short military cuts John preferred. Michael, who'd been so full of life and laughter, always liking a good joke, now lifeless.

John didn't realize he was crying until a tear fell onto Michael's neck. He put his hand over his eyes, squeezing them shut, holding back the hot sting of emotion. His breath came deep, in hitches. His heart beat painfully in his chest.

"Michael, I'm sorry," he whispered, his voice cracking. "I will find your killer. I will have your vengeance. I promise. I won't let you down again."

John watched her sleep.

She was curled into the reading chair in her den. By all appearances, Rowan hadn't left the room since yesterday. She looked vulnerable. Her long hair hung over her face and she rested her head on her arms, which were folded on the armrest. Her feet were tucked under her. Not at all comfortable. Even in the dim light coming from the hall, she seemed too pale. He wondered if she'd eaten, then asked himself if he cared.

He couldn't care. Not now.

John glanced at his watch. Five-thirty. He hadn't slept more than an hour, and at four had given up on sleep completely. He couldn't get the vision of Michael lying cold and dead out of his mind. Yet somehow, he felt calmer. He had a purpose, a goal: revenge.

He'd relieved Peterson minutes ago and brewed a pot of coffee. Collins had called and told him Peter O'Brien, Rowan's brother in Boston, couldn't have committed any of the murders. He had a pretty good alibi—daily Mass. John had sensed that O'Brien wasn't involved, especially after hearing he was being watched by the Feds, but he had still insisted that the assistant director look into him and anyone he could think of who might have a motive for going after Rowan in such a sick and sadistic manner.

Collins was checking into the records of the MacIntosh murders and would be faxing over all newspaper articles, photos, everything that might be of use, to the FBI headquarters.

John wished there were another way, but hours of tossing and turning, pacing and sitting, left him with the only possible conclusion: Someone Rowan knew well had killed Michael, and that someone had been in Rowan's life twenty-three years ago.

Rowan needed to look at the reports and hope something popped so they could get this bastard. Peterson had agreed to bring in Adam Williams to look at photos as well. John was too distraught to feel guilty, though a pang of remorse hit him. The poor kid wasn't going to be comfortable at headquarters looking at crime scene photos, but John could think of no other way. Adam was the only one who'd for sure seen the killer. He was their best hope of identifying him.

John cleared his throat quietly, not wanting to startle Rowan, but she jumped up, gun in hand. He hadn't noticed she was sleeping with it.

"John." Her voice was thick and groggy. She slowly sank back down into the chair to steady herself.

"I made coffee."

She nodded. "Thanks." She coughed to clear her throat. "Where's Quinn?"

"I relieved him."

Her eyebrow went up as she stared at him. "I-I thought—"

"I'm on the case until we catch my brother's killer." His voice sounded harsh, but his emotions were raw and close to the surface.

"I—uh, I guess a run is out."

"You want to run, we run." He stared at her, careful to keep his face blank.

"I need a minute," she finally said.

"I'll be in the kitchen." As soon as he closed the den door, he breathed regular again. He hadn't realized he'd been so tense talking to Rowan. He hated seeing her so scared, defeated, hollow-eyed. But he couldn't think about her, couldn't care about her, and sure as hell couldn't worry about her.

He would protect her life. Nothing more. Nothing less.

Because if it weren't for her and his damn hormones and his stupid fight with Michael, his brother would still be alive. He'd accused Michael of letting his emotions cloud his judgment, but he had done exactly the same thing. Not only did he think *he* was the only one who could get Rowan to spill the truth, he had wanted not only her honesty, but her body.

Rowan watched John leave and stifled a cry. She brought her hands to her mouth in a vain attempt to trap the sound. She didn't know how she was going to get through the day, but she needed to get a grip on herself.

How could she forgive herself? How could John forgive her?

She went up to her bedroom and splashed water on her face. She stared at the ghostlike reflection in the mirror. Was that her? Her pale blue eyes were grayer than usual, dull and lifeless. Her skin had a sallow appearance, her hair was stringy, her breath awful. She brushed her teeth twice, washed her face with soap, and brushed her hair before pulling it back.

She really didn't want to run, but somehow it seemed important to hold up in front of John. If she broke down, he would have one more thing to worry about. She didn't want him to be concerned about her. She was a big girl; she'd been living with pain and guilt most of her life. One more murder wasn't going to break her. She'd simply add it to the chamber in her heart that held the memories of everyone she'd inadvertently had a hand in killing.

Michael was in good company.

She pinched the bridge of her nose and took a couple deep breaths. It was foolish to run, she knew; she hadn't eaten since Friday night. But maybe it would help numb the pain.

John looked forward to the run. He needed it. Anything to compete with the pain in his heart. Three laps would be a start. Four might fight the pain. Five might drown it out.

But it would be foolish to get that exhausted. If they were being watched, it would be a good time for the killer to attack.

John peered out the kitchen window, but all he saw was the wall of the house next to Rowan's and about eighty feet of the sandy, concrete-reinforced cliff between them.

He was on his third cup of coffee and he'd forced down a piece of toast. It tasted like paper and left a lump in his stomach but was doing its job of soaking up the caffeine. He was beginning to feel half-human.

Rowan came into the kitchen and poured herself a glass of water. She looked better than twenty minutes ago, but her face was still pale. Her little dark glasses covered her eyes. But she seemed ready. Rigid. Cold. Expressionless.

A worrisome thought flitted across his mind. Rowan was not as cold as he'd believed when he first met her. It was an act to cover up her feelings, just like the glasses she wore covered her eyes. Maybe all this was getting to her.

Dammit, he couldn't care. He had a job to do: catch Michael's killer and keep Rowan out of the crossfire. He didn't have the energy to worry about her feelings.

"Let's go," he said.

On the wet sand, he pushed her pace. He maintained his protective spot two strides behind, but he breathed down her neck, urging her to move faster, harder. How could he purge the pain at this slow pace? He needed the cold air to replace the hot grief, the sting of salt in his lungs.

So he pressed her. When she wanted to stop after two laps, he wouldn't let her. He wasn't even winded. He knew she could handle three or more laps. They'd run many times, and Rowan was in fabulous shape. Did she think he couldn't handle it? Did she think he was going to break down? Not him, not now.

They were almost back to the stairs of her house. Rowan was slowing. "Come on, run!" he shouted in her ear like a drill sergeant.

She stumbled and fell to her knees. He swerved and leaped over her, but made contact with her body and tumbled himself.

He quickly stood in a crouch and surveyed the scene, gun out. Trap, was his first thought. The murderer planted something on the beach to trip them up. Was he waiting to pounce?

He saw nothing but quiet homes set far from the beach. He heard nothing but the roar of the ocean, the breeze, the squawk of gulls searching for fish. No glint of a sniper rifle, no trace of a trap.

Then why did the hair stand up on the back of his neck?

"It's clear, but we should get back," John said.

Rowan was on all fours, panting heavily. He put his hand out for her, but she didn't take it.

"What the fuck?" he said. "We need to get going. You're a sitting duck out here."

"Let. Him." She sank down into the sand, her head buried in her arms.

"What are you talking about?" He reached down and used his strength to haul her to her feet. She'd lost her glasses in the fall, and her eyes swam with tears. She staggered, unable to get her footing, and fell against him, pushing him back at the same time.

"Let me go," she whispered, trying to free her arm.

She had little strength. He easily held on to her. But he let her go. She fell back into the sand, her legs like noodles. "Just leave me. He'll come. You can watch from my deck and when he comes, kill him. There's a sniper rifle in my closet."

What in the world was she talking about? Using herself as bait? If Rowan died, he'd lose someone else. He couldn't, wouldn't let her die.

He stared at her face, red from exertion and half covered with sand from her fall. She wasn't looking at him, but at the ocean, tears spilling from her eyes. Her breath was still coming out ragged, her cheeks hollow.

He didn't want to think about her pain. He didn't want to be reminded of what he'd been doing when Michael died. How he'd manipulated his brother, sending him to his death.

How he had loved being wrapped in Rowan's arms, holding her, being in her.

This was neither the time nor the place for a relationship, or even just sex. But Rowan had no one. He wouldn't let her offer herself up to the murderer like a sacrificial lamb.

He scooped her into his arms and carried her to the house. When she didn't so much as protest to being cradled like a baby, he knew she was not herself.

He hadn't given any thought as to how she felt about Michael's murder. It slowly dawned on him that she was as agonized as he. But Michael wasn't her brother, her best friend. He'd only been her bodyguard.

Still, in her mind, she was responsible for whomever the bastard killed. John should have made that connection sooner, but he'd been so wrapped up in getting her to tell him the truth, and then in grieving over Michael.

Rowan was in pain, too.

He put her on the couch, but she wouldn't look at him, just lay on her back staring at the ceiling. He watched her work to control her emotions, to bring down the shield she'd erected so well.

She was exhausted from his pushing her on the run, on top of little sleep. Had she eaten? He doubted it. He hadn't been able to eat yesterday. He'd only had a couple of sips of soup, and only because he'd forced Tess to eat something.

He left her and went to the kitchen to pour himself more coffee. What was he going to do? He could barely keep himself together; how was he going to keep Rowan together?

Focus. Dammit, he could focus. All those months— years—tracking Pomera and his operatives. After Denny died, infiltrating the drug gang and slowly, painstakingly, taking the dealers down one by one. Focus. Perseverance. Patience.

He would do it. For Michael.

Which meant he needed Rowan and whatever information was trapped in her brain, information she didn't know was important. And he wouldn't be able to get anything out of her if she made herself sick from guilt.

Food was nothing more than fuel—a good thing, because John couldn't cook. He toasted some wheat bread and made a peanut butter and jelly sandwich. He assumed Rowan liked peanut butter and jelly because it was in the house. He poured her coffee and brought it out to the living room.

She wasn't there.

"Shit." He went to the den and sure enough she stood in the corner, looking out the front windows through partially opened venetian blinds.

"He's been watching me."

She spoke without turning around, her voice soft, gravelly.

"How do you know?"

"At first, a feeling. I didn't realize it before, but every so often I'd feel prickly. A tingling in my spine, but I didn't notice anyone paying undue attention to me." She shook her head, looked down at her feet. "He's been here, John. In my house."

"What?" His body tensed, instantly on alert.

She finally glanced at him over her shoulder before turning to her bookshelf. In that moment, her face exposed all the tumultuous emotions she usually kept in check. "He took one of my books. I know it was him. I told Quinn; he had the house dusted, but so far, nothing.

"I don't know if I can get through this, John."

He strained to hear her. He put the sandwich and coffee on the desk and stood behind her.

"You will." He shuddered at the thought that Michael's killer had been in Rowan's house. Had he broken in while she slept upstairs? When? How long had he been stalking her before devising this vicious, cruel way to torment her?

"I'm not as strong as you think. I quit the FBI because I was weak."

"You quit because you had to take a break. Everyone needs a break, especially doing what we do. Surrounded by evil. Fighting evil and not always winning."

She turned and looked at him, her eyes surprisingly blank. What was she really thinking? Had she given up?

"You never gave up," she said. "You never gave up fighting for Denny."

"That's different."

She nodded slowly. "Don Quixote and windmills. I'm another windmill, John. Go back to your sister. She needs you. The FBI isn't going to leave me unprotected."

She wanted him to leave? "No," he said. "I'm here until the end."

She stared at him, her face firm, a slight frown pulling down the corners of her lips. "I can't live with another death on my conscience."

"Nothing is going to happen to me." He took her by the shoulders. He didn't mean to shake her so hard, just give her a little jolt so she'd know he was serious. But her head jerked forward and he saw some of the fire back in her eyes.

Good. She needed to know he meant business.

"Rowan, I am here until the end. He killed my brother. He's killed six other innocent people. He's tormenting you. I will not rest until he's dead." He'd meant captured, but didn't correct himself.

"Or you are," she whispered as she pulled away from him. She paused by the desk where the sandwich and coffee sat. She looked at the food for a long time, but didn't touch it. She crossed to the door. "I just talked to Roger. I asked him to send over all the files of my mother's murder and Dani's. He told me he'd already done it." She looked at him, not accusing, but knowing. "When do we leave?"

He should have told her. "I was going to tell you."

She nodded, didn't say anything.

"Two hours. Peterson's putting the files together as they get them from Washington."

"I'll be in my room." She walked out.

Damn. What had just happened? What was she thinking? She had to know he would protect her to the end.

* * *

She dreamed.

Powerless to stop the dream, it played in her mind, almost soothing, a lullaby. She stood outside her Colorado cabin, the A-frame she considered home. Peace and joy. Home. Alone at last. Death and violence and blood a distant memory.

It was light when she stood outside the cabin, but when she finally went inside it was dark. None of the lights worked, but she heard someone upstairs. Downstairs. Intruders? Her heart pounded.

Rowan, it's me.

Michael? She said his name out loud. *Michael, you're dead.*

He laughed and she couldn't help but smile. Dead men didn't laugh. They didn't talk and make her feel like everything was going to be all right.

It was all just a nightmare. Everything. None of it happened. No one is out to get you. You're going to be okay.

Thank God. Maybe Peter's prayers worked, and the God she'd thought was cruel and vicious had a streak of kindness.

Lily! Play with me!

Dani ran up to her and entwined herself between her legs. She was three, her dark, curling pigtails bouncing up and down.

Dani? But—

It was all a nightmare, Michael said, stepping out of the shadows. He wore a tuxedo. The red stain spreading across the front drew her attention.

Michael, you've been shot. Was that her voice? It's a dream, she reminded herself. None of this is real.

It's real, Lily. Dani looked up at her with wide blue eyes. Rowan squatted down and reached out to her sister.

Dani, I love you.

She playfully pulled on a pigtail like she used to, but it fell off in her hand. She stared at the hair she clutched, then dropped it as if it burned her skin. She looked at her sister, saw the dark stain on her blue jammies, the glassy gaze in her pretty eyes. Dani fell into her arms, her blood seeping through Rowan's fingers, and she screamed.

Don't scream! He'll hear you.

Michael again. Michael was dead and he was talking to her.

He'll hear you.

It was Doreen Rodriguez from the couch. Or, rather, her head. The rest of her body was strewn across the room. A severed hand reached for Rowan and she ran to the other side of the room, Dani in her arms.

Lily, sweet Lily.

Mama?

Mama was in the kitchen. She came out, covered in blood. *Lily, Lily, I'm sorry.* Mama cried tears of blood.

Oh, Mama. I miss you so much!

She pulled Dani close to her, but when she looked down again, it wasn't Dani.

It was Tess.

No, no! She'd killed Tess. No, not her. She didn't. *He* did. But John would never forgive her. First Michael, then Tess. Who else? Who else had to die in her name?

Why, why, why? She squeezed her eyes shut.

She was falling and she opened her eyes. She was in her bed, her own bed in the cabin's loft. She wasn't alone. John lay next to her, touching her breast, her stomach. His hands were warm and she sighed, content. This was where she belonged. She snuggled up against him, feeling a peace and longing she'd never known, a deep desire to be close to someone.

John.

He made love to her. Slow, warm, affectionate. It was beautiful, like nothing she'd ever before experienced. He was a part of her. They were inseparable. They needed each other. She needed him. She needed him like she'd never needed anyone.

She rolled over to face him, her movements slow, awkward, like she was underwater, water as thick as blood.

John?

She reached out to touch him. Her hand came back warm and sticky. Wet. She brought her fingers to her face. Blood. John's blood.

She sat up and stared at her bed. John lay there, butchered. His head hung from his spine, an arm was missing, his torso a bloody mess of guts and muscle. He stared at her with dark, glassy green eyes, accusing her.

It's all your fault. It's all your fault.

Suddenly, his exposed heart pounded in his chest, spraying blood all over her. He sat up, his intestines spilling out and crawling toward her. His arm pointed at her. *It's you. You did this. You, Lily Pad, you.*

His intestines crawled up her legs and she screamed and screamed and screamed.

CHAPTER
16

He was staring out the living room window thinking about Michael when he heard her scream. It wasn't just any scream: It was full of stark terror and pain. He drew his gun and took the stairs three at a time, throwing his weight against her locked door.

She was thrashing on the bed, sobbing. He quickly determined no one else was in the room. When he reached her side, he slapped her to shock her out of her nightmare. But when her eyes opened, he saw she was still wrapped in whatever terror she'd imagined. She stared at him, eyes wide, her entire body trembling so violently her teeth rattled.

"You're dead! You're dead!" She pounded her fists against his chest, and he held her close as she broke down.

Her anguished sobs broke his heart. He'd never heard so much agony in a voice. But she didn't allow him to hold her for long. She pulled herself together quicker than he thought she should have and pushed him away. "I need a shower."

"What happened?"

"Nightmare." Sliding out of his arms, she disappeared in the bathroom. He heard the lock click into place.

Fifteen minutes later, she came downstairs—freshly showered but still pale and exhausted.

"You need to eat." He maneuvered her into the kitchen, where he managed to get her to eat half a sandwich and a glass of milk.

They'd just sat down with a fresh cup of coffee when Peterson called to tell John the files were ready for Rowan. John was having second thoughts about this idea. He feared Rowan was on the edge and this might push her over.

But he had to find his brother's killer.

When there was a battle, justice had to prevail. Any way he could get it.

"You don't have to do this," he told her thirty minutes later as they sat in the almost empty underground parking garage of the FBI's field office in Los Angeles. Sundays weren't big overtime days.

She stared at her hands, clasped tightly in her lap. "Yes, I do. You know it, and I know it." Her voice was quiet but firm. She looked at him, her eyes blank. "Don't worry about me."

A knife twisted in his heart. *Don't worry about me.* She said it as if she suspected he wasn't worried. And the irony was, when he set this up, he hadn't been. He hadn't cared what it would do to her.

Now he did.

He reached out and took her hand. "Rowan, you're going to be okay. Say the word and I'll take you home."

"I have to look. If only I'd figured it out earlier. But I never—never—thought it had to do with my past. My cases, the Franklin murder, a deranged fan—but n-n-not my family." She took a deep breath and swallowed a sob. "If I had, maybe we could have stopped him before—"

She looked down at their hands but didn't finish her sentence.

He took his free hand and pushed her chin up, forcing her to look at him. "It's not your fault. You approached this logically, methodically." Leaning forward, he gently touched his lips to hers. "You're not in this alone."

When he pulled back, he saw her eyes register surprise; then she brought the shield back up, calm coldness radiating from her tight, lanky body. She slowly extracted her hand from his. "Let's get this over with." She opened her door.

When they arrived in the conference room, John was surprised to see Tess sitting at the desk in the corner, her fingers flying over the keyboard. Her short hair was limp but clean, her face devoid of makeup and set in determination.

Tess looked up, met his eyes, and gave him a weak smile. Then she saw Rowan and quickly turned back to her work.

She needed time. But time didn't heal all wounds. He hoped Tess wasn't one of the unlucky ones.

Quinn Peterson sat at the large table, looking through a thick file folder. He stood when John closed the door. "Roger faxed everything we couldn't download from the archives," he said. "I sent my partner to pick Mr. Williams up."

Rowan stiffened. "Adam?" She looked from Quinn to John, unconcealed anger on her face. "You're dragging Adam down here?"

"He might be our only hope of identifying this guy before it's too late," John said quietly.

She squeezed her eyes shut. "He's never going to recover." She released a long breath. "But you're right," she said, her anger either dissipated or buried; John didn't know which. "John, could I ask a favor?"

"Anything."

"Would you go down and meet Agent Thorne and Adam when they get here and explain what's going to happen? He's going to be freaked out, being picked up at home and brought here." She glanced at Peterson. "I wish you'd have told me; I would have talked to him."

"I don't think he would have talked to you," John said, and her attention snapped back to him. Her eyes widened, not in anger but surprise and something more. Disappointment? Hurt? "After the incident with the lilies, I think Adam is a little intimidated."

Hurt. Definitely hurt in her stormy eyes. She nodded and turned away, but not before he saw the glistening of tears.

"I'll talk to him," John assured her and left the room.

Rowan stared at the thick file folder, her heart pounding so loudly she thought for sure Quinn and Tess would be able to hear it. She was so scared, but she wouldn't admit it. Not now.

"I never knew," Quinn said, resting a hand on her shoulder. She shrugged, worried if she spoke her voice would quiver. "Miranda knew, didn't she?"

Rowan nodded and let out a long breath. "Most of it. The first week we were at the academy, Miranda, Olivia, and I talked about why we wanted to become agents. We were drinking margaritas. I rarely drink." She almost smiled, remembering how good it felt to find two women who understood her. "I'd never talked about it before, not even to Roger. Roger didn't want to talk about it, I don't think. It was over and I needed to move on. I—well, I had some issues back then."

"That's not surprising."

She waved off his comment and sat down at the table, not looking at the file across from her. She'd have to go through it, but needed a minute. She glanced at Tess, who still appeared to be working on something, but Rowan sensed she had an ear cocked toward their conversation. What did it matter? The truth was going to come out anyway. It was just as well. It wasn't like Tess could hate her any more than she already did.

"Miranda had been upfront with us from day one. That's one of the things I love about her."

Rowan looked up at Quinn who stood with crossed arms and a tight jaw, his dark eyes unreadable. Did he feel guilt or anger over what happened with Miranda at Quantico? Rowan wished she could ask, but Quinn would accuse her of evading.

"Anyway," she continued, "we were drinking and Miranda asked us why we were there. It just came out." Rowan paused. Even after telling John everything, it was still hard to talk about what happened that night.

"Why did you want to be an agent? Because of Roger?"

"Partly. He saved my life. Not physically, but psychologically. He gave me focus. He cares so much about justice."

"So do you."

"Yes, I care. But he wants to punish criminals. I want to avenge the victims." She paused. The difference was so subtle, she didn't know how to explain it.

"I never understood how my father could kill my mother," she said. "Even with the repeated physical abuse, I never thought—I mean, I really thought he loved her in his own warped way. But I was a kid, I didn't know any better. I know now after years of psychology and criminology classes that domestic violence isn't love. But I had to try to find out why my father lost his mind. How Bobby could be so cruel. If I knew why,

I could be a better agent. I could better fight for the victims if I understood their attackers."

"Did you find the answers you sought?"

"No. Every criminal I interviewed I asked why. I never got an answer I understood."

"Maybe because you're not a killer."

No, I'm not a killer. My father is. My brother was. Not me. Not yet.

She stared at the file, dreading what was inside, knowing the pictures and reports would hurt and bring back memories she'd tried to keep buried. She couldn't run anymore. She had to do it. To stop the insanity.

She opened the file.

The documents, either printed from the computer archives or faxed from Roger, were in little semblance of order. The first page was the original police report. *Multiple homicide.* The victims were listed by name, age, location, and apparent cause of death.

Elizabeth Regina MacIntosh, 46, white female, found in kitchen. Multiple stab wounds, deceased.

Melanie Regina MacIntosh, 17, white female, found in entry. Stabbed multiple times, deceased.

Rachel Suzanne MacIntosh, 15, white female, found in entry. Stabbed multiple times, deceased.

Danielle Anne MacIntosh, 4, white female, found in master bedroom. Shot once in chest with 9mm handgun, deceased.

Rowan took a deep breath. She felt like a child again. Saw her mother's dead and bloody body. Watched her sisters die. Ran with Peter and Dani to the closet.

But Bobby came after them.

Turning the page, she saw her father's commitment papers. She'd read them so many times before she had them memorized, so quickly turned the page.

Bobby's arrest.

Suspect in multiple homicide escaped through second story window and was pursued to the corner of Crestline Drive and Bridgeview Court where he was apprehended without further incident. Read Miranda warning and suspect asked for an attorney.

His description was listed in clinical terms. Robert William MacIntosh, Junior, 18. Blond hair, blue eyes, six feet one inch, 170 lbs. No distinguishing marks. No tattoos. No piercings.

Bobby looked like a nice guy, but Rowan knew the truth about him. She'd known forever that Bobby was evil. Thank God he was dead.

Yet from the grave he'd pursued her. In her nightmares. In her choice of career, both to join the FBI and ultimately to quit the FBI. He'd been controlling her life since the beginning, more now that he was dead than he ever could when he was alive. How could she not see it? How could she have lived for so long under his evil shadow and not seen how much he still controlled her?

Now she knew. She wouldn't let him do it any longer.

She turned the page.

"You okay, Ro?" Quinn asked quietly as he slid a glass of water in front of her.

She nodded and gratefully accepted the drink. She sipped, the cool liquid soothing her raw throat. Quinn stood behind her like a soldier. She felt his gaze boring into her back. She heard the click-click-click of Tess on the computer. Pause. Click-click-click. It'd be annoying if it weren't so rhythmic.

She turned another page.

Photos.

She carefully put the glass down, afraid her shaking hand would spill water on the file. The kitchen. Mama wasn't in it, but she saw the starkness of the black-and-white imagery, the blood-spattered walls, the overturned chair. Some artists chose black and white because its impact was far more powerful than color. There was nothing to compare with blood in stark gray. You expected it to be red in color; you didn't realize it had such depth until the color was leeched from the image.

She rapidly flipped through the photos. She couldn't look. This was what she was here to do, but she couldn't do it. Quinn took them from the stack and placed them face down, away from her. She wiped her face, surprised to feel damp cheeks.

Focus on the reports. Pretend she hadn't been there. This was simply another investigation, the family strangers.

She didn't know if she could finish, but she had to.

She picked the pictures up again and took a deep breath.

She noticed the room had become silent. Quinn watched her closely. Tess had stopped working and was staring at her, a frown on her round face. Damn. If the answers were here, in this damned file, she had to find them.

Quinn's cell phone rang and he answered. "Peterson. . . . All right, thanks for the heads up." He slammed the phone shut.

"What's wrong?" Rowan asked, fearing the worst. *Not another dead body.*

"Colleen has Adam in the garage with John. They'll be up in a few minutes."

She nodded and turned back to the files. The words were a blur. Was she losing it? No. *Tears.* She absently rubbed her eyes and took a deep breath.

She had to focus, read the reports like the agent she was trained to be. Look for clues. Like this crowd shot. She looked at each face closely. Were any familiar? Had she known these people as a child? Were they somehow in her life now?

She had to pretend this wasn't her family slaughtered so mercilessly. Pretend they were strangers.

Right. Strangers who haunted her in her sleep.

She looked up and noticed Tess was still watching her, an odd expression on her face. The door opened and Tess turned back to her computer. John led Adam into the room, a hand on his shoulder. The kid looked terrified and glanced at John for reassurance. When Adam's eyes rested on Rowan, he visibly recoiled, drawing closer to John. Rowan felt small and miserable. She'd hurt someone she cared about and didn't know how to fix it. Or if it could be fixed.

John murmured something in his ear and Adam marginally relaxed, but he avoided looking at Rowan. John sat him down at another desk facing the wall.

"The pictures?" he asked Quinn.

Rowan sighed in relief as Quinn picked up the folder in front of her and handed it to John.

He opened it, glanced through it, and pulled out the crowd shots.

"Adam, remember what I told you," John said, leaning over the desk and looking the scared kid in the eye. "I'll be right here. All I want is for you to look at these pictures and tell me if you've seen any of these people before. Remember, they might not look exactly the same, but older."

"Yes, John," Adam said, his voice quivering.

Rowan tried to focus on her task and tore her eyes away from John and Adam.

Her heart felt heavy in her chest. John looked at the pictures with Adam, glanced at her. Was that pity she saw in his eyes? His jaw clenched, and she saw his pulse throbbing in his neck.

No, not pity. Rage. It wasn't directed at her, but it made her uncomfortable. She didn't want anyone, particularly John, fighting her ghosts. But dammit, if she couldn't get herself under control she'd be no good in battling her demons, the real demon killer and those in her nightmares.

She focused again on the file.

The room was silent for a long ten minutes. Adam was the first to speak, his head hung low. "I'm sorry. I'm sorry. He's not here. I swear, John, he's not here. I would remember. I would, I would!" His voice rose in frustration.

John rested his hand on Adam's shoulder. "It's okay, Adam." He glanced at Quinn. "Peterson, did you get that photo I asked about?"

"O'Brien? Yeah." He reached across Rowan and handed John a thin folder.

Rowan's head shot up and her eyes narrowed. "I told you Peter had nothing to do with this!"

"Collins cleared him, but I'm just double-checking."

She turned her back to him, squeezed her eyes with her fingers until they hurt.

Peter had nothing to do with any of this. But if she didn't know him as well as she did, wouldn't she, too, think he was the logical suspect? "You're right, John," she whispered, her admission shredding her heart. *Peter, please forgive me.* "We have to rule him out."

John took the folder to Adam and said, "Adam, do you recognize this man?"

He showed Adam a photo. Rowan couldn't resist standing and looking at the picture herself.

Peter looked nothing like her, except maybe for the eyes. Peter had dark hair like Dani. The picture showed him out of his clerical collar, in a button-down shirt. Where had Quinn gotten it? It appeared recent.

She missed him. Seeing his photo reminded her that she'd intentionally separated her brother from her life. He had the Church, his adoptive family, his own life. She was a reminder of the past for him just as much as he was for her. But she still loved him.

"Adam?" John prompted.

Adam shook his head. "I'm sorry. I'm really, really, really sorry. That's not him."

Rowan relaxed. She knew it wasn't Peter, but couldn't help being relieved at Adam's affirmation.

"What if he had sandy hair?" John asked. "Like he colored it. Remember, you saw him wearing sunglasses."

Adam still shook his head. "It's not him, I know. The man I saw at the flowers had a crooked nose."

John glanced up at Quinn. "A crooked nose? Like maybe it had been broken? Like Agent Peterson here?"

Adam turned to inspect Quinn. He cocked his head to the side, seeming to see something no one else in the room did. Rowan tensed.

"Yeah, like his nose," he said, almost in awe that he had recognized something. "It wasn't straight like this," he gestured to the picture. "And the man I saw had a pointier chin."

"I'm proud of you, Adam. You remembered a lot."

"But I didn't see *him*." He pointed to the picture of Peter.

"That's okay. What else about this picture and the man you saw is different?"

Adam frowned as if not understanding. "I dunno."

Damn, they'd come so far. If they had a picture of the suspect, Rowan didn't doubt Adam would recognize him.

"John?" Tess said excitedly. "John, Quinn, I think I found something."

The men rushed to her desk. "What?" John asked.

"I did the search on Robert MacIntosh in the medical database Quinn gave me access to. Look."

They were silent. "Holy shit," John said. "Rowan, come here." It was a command, and Rowan obeyed. But her feet felt heavy, her whole body sluggish.

She peered over Tess's shoulder at the screen. At first she didn't see what John saw. Each line appeared to be a medical entry on Robert William MacIntosh. Her father. Each procedure was carried out in Boston at the Bellevue facility. Except one for surgery two weeks after the murders. Multiple gunshot wounds. Release date was four weeks later, federal custody.

"My father wasn't shot."

"But your brother—also named Robert MacIntosh—was when he tried to escape."

She shook her head. "Bobby was killed trying to escape."

"Not according to these records."

Rowan started shaking uncontrollably. Bobby couldn't be alive. He couldn't be. How? Where had he been all this time? Wouldn't Roger have told her? Had he been lying to her all these years?

John reached for her, but she pulled away.

Roger had to have known. All along, he had to have known that Bobby was alive. And if Bobby was alive, he was perfectly capable of killing all those people. Doreen Rodriguez. The little Harper girl with the pigtails. Michael.

She grabbed the stack of photos from the table and flipped through them, discarding most, not caring when they drifted to the floor.

Bobby.

She took the one clear photo of Bobby from the stack. He was handcuffed and held by one cop while another opened the rear door of a black-and-white. Bobby had blood on his clothes, Mel and Rachel's blood. No one could stab another human being and walk away unsoiled.

He had blond hair, a couple of shades darker than hers. His eyes stared at her. Cocky. Unremorseful.

She swallowed bile at the thought he was still alive. It just couldn't be. That meant Roger had been lying to her since he met her.

She slapped the picture in front of Adam. "Is this the man you saw?" She couldn't keep the fear and anger out of her voice.

"Rowan." John was at her side, his hand on her arm. She tried to brush him off, but he squeezed her wrist. "We need a recent photo. It's been twenty-three years."

Twenty-three years. Yes, Bobby would have changed, she thought. What did he look like now? Had she seen him and not known? Not known that her evil brother was alive and walking the streets?

Adam was mumbling something and she turned to him. "Adam, I'm sorry. I-I, just, oh hell," she concluded lamely.

"Maybe," Adam whispered.

Rowan pulled out her cell phone and dialed Roger's direct line.

"Collins."

"Why didn't you tell me Bobby was alive?" Her voice was cold, detached, as if someone else was using her mouth.

He said nothing for a long, long time. "Rowan, he threatened you. I sat across from that devil's spawn and listened to him tell me how he was going to kill you. When he escaped, he killed two guards. We tried him on those deaths so you didn't have to testify. Plenty of witnesses, and with two peace officers killed, he easily got life without parole. He wasn't getting out, Ro. And you were having such awful nightmares, Gracie and I were worried. If you thought he was dead, what was the harm? I didn't think—"

"He's been in prison all this time and I didn't know? How dare you! How dare you keep something so important from me. I'm not some weak-kneed child anymore. I could have handled it."

"But—"

"Where is he? Right now, where is he?"

"Texas."

"I want to see him."

"I spoke with the warden after the first murder and—"

"You suspected him?" Her world spun around her. She felt John's hands on her arms, grounding her, easing her into a chair. But she didn't see anything; rage the color of dried blood blinded her. She pictured Roger, the man she had often wished were her real father, sitting at his desk, telling her he'd lied to her for twenty-three years.

"No, no, not really. I was just checking. Making sure there wasn't a mistake. He's in maximum security, no escapes."

"I want to see him. Now."

"Rowan—"

"With or without you." She couldn't talk to Roger. She thrust her phone in John's direction and dropped it. He grabbed it.

"Collins?" he said into the receiver. "What prison?" He paused. "We're leaving on the next available flight." He hung up. "Rowan, if—"

"John." Tess interrupted. "Look."

Both John and Rowan turned to the computer screen.

Tess had brought up Bobby's mug shot. "This was taken five years ago."

Bobby had aged remarkably well in prison, Rowan thought. His blond hair had grown darker and was cut military style. His face was hard, his eyes cold, his skin pale. But, really, he looked like anyone. An average person. Normal.

"I wanna go home," Adam wailed from his desk.

John turned to him and helped him up. "One more picture, Adam. One more."

"Promise?" he said, sulking.

"I promise."

Adam allowed himself to be led to Tess's computer. He stared at the screen. "Adam, is this the man you saw at the flower stand?"

Adam nodded, tears filling his eyes. "Can I go home now?"

Quinn motioned for Colleen, who'd been quietly standing in the corner since bringing John and Adam up earlier. "Adam, Colleen will take you home."

Rowan stared at the picture on the screen. Was he responsible for all this? How? If he was rotting in a prison cell, how could Adam have seen him in Malibu?

"Thank you, Adam," she said, trying to convey her appreciation. Adam left without looking at her.

"I'm putting out an APB on Robert MacIntosh," Quinn said. "Good work, Tess. If you ever want a government job, let me know."

"We need to go," Rowan said. "I need to see him behind bars. What if he's not there? What if he escaped?" But that was impossible. Roger would have known. The entire country would have been on the lookout for an escaped convict.

Nothing made sense.

John agreed. "Quinn, how fast can we get out there?"

"First available flight. Get over to Burbank and I'll bump passengers for us if I have to."

"Thanks." He turned to Rowan. "Ready?"

She nodded. Ready or not, she had to confront Bobby.

CHAPTER
17

Rowan didn't speak during the drive to the airport. John was grateful Peterson had moved heaven and earth to put them on a flight that left in less than an hour and worked security to rush them all through.

Peterson himself sat in the air marshal's seat near the front since he was a federal officer and there was no air marshal assigned to this flight, while John and Rowan had seats in the back.

John gave Rowan the space she obviously needed. He ached for her. Why had he dragged her down there? He could have handled Adam himself. He'd had some vague idea that going through the reports would trigger some repressed memory, prompting her to remember something.

Then he reminded himself Rowan had wanted to do it. Needed to do it.

He'd never imagined Bobby MacIntosh was alive. But now there was no doubt in his mind that whoever sat in that Texas prison cell under the name "Robert MacIntosh, Junior" was not Rowan's brother.

He glanced at Rowan. She suspected the same thing.

Almost immediately after they'd boarded, the plane taxied and left. Rowan still hadn't spoken and John was getting antsy. With a sidelong glance at the businessman who sat on the aisle seat next to him, John leaned toward Rowan and spoke quietly in her ear.

"Are you okay?"

She didn't respond, just stared out the window.

"Rowan, talk to me." He didn't mean to sound so gruff, but dammit, he couldn't stand the silence or the blank stare in her eyes.

"It's Bobby. I know it."

"We'll know soon enough."

"Roger lied to me. From the beginning." Her voice vibrated in anguish. John knew exactly how she felt. Lies, deception, betrayal. He pushed those thoughts aside—this was neither the time nor place. He longed to take her into his arms and hold her, just hold her so she'd know she wasn't alone. But he was walking on eggshells. After the emotional trauma of reviewing the photos of her family's murder and discovering the father-figure she trusted had lied to her about something so important, he didn't know how much more she could take.

"When Roger interviewed me," she continued, "after they told me Bobby had been caught and was in jail and couldn't hurt me, he was honest. He told me the case was solid, but I was the only eyewitness. My testimony would ensure Bobby would stay in prison for the rest of his life."

He took her hand and squeezed. She finally turned from the window and looked down at their clasped hands, but didn't make any move to break the connection.

John didn't know why he felt relieved.

"How did you feel about that?" He tried to remember that Rowan had been only ten back then. He'd seen the pictures. What a senseless tragedy! A little girl who'd lost nearly her entire family in one awful night. Was rejected by her aunt and grandparents. He could almost picture the courageous child Rowan had been.

"Angry. Confused. I wanted to hurt him for what he did, but I didn't understand the process then." She paused. "Roger was also the one who told me about my father, that he hadn't spoken a word since the police found him in the kitchen. I insisted on seeing him. So Roger took me to Bellevue. He didn't want to, but he did."

She caught his eye. The misery in her face made him want to pull her into his arms and tell her he would protect her.

But she didn't want his protection. She wanted his understanding.

"Roger was right," she said, her voice barely audible. "I completely broke down when I saw my father's hollow eyes. He wasn't there anymore. He wasn't possessed by the devil, he didn't have an evil look in his eye, he didn't rant and rave. He just *wasn't*." She looked out the window again.

"I suppose that's why Roger lied to me," she said. "He didn't think I'd be able to handle testifying, no matter what I said."

Rowan would never forget seeing her father that last time. He didn't look like the strong, sometimes angry, sometimes wonderful man she'd grown to admire and fear.

"Mama, why does Daddy hit you?"

She'd been seven when she'd asked that question. She was rocking Dani to sleep in her mother's chair in their bedroom, cooing sweet nothings into the baby's ear.

Her mother dropped her hairbrush on the vanity table. "Why would you ask such a thing?"

"I—I'm sorry."

She rocked Dani, hoping her mother wasn't angry

*with her. She'd never spanked her. Her father had, twice.
Once when she broke the crystal cake plate that had
been her mama's favorite. Then last year when she'd run
away. She'd moved all her things into the shed.*

Because of Bobby. He scared her.

"Honey," *her mother said, coming over to them. She
kneeled in front of the chair, stopped the rocking.
Forced Lily to look into her mother's eyes.*

*Such pretty eyes, Lily thought. Daddy said they were
like sisters. She only hoped she grew up as beautiful as
her mama.*

"Honey, you're too young to understand. Daddy
doesn't mean to hurt me. And—and it doesn't really
hurt."

*Mama glanced down at Dani and Lily knew, but
didn't understand, why her mama was lying.*

"Okay," *she said, her voice small and shaking.*

Mama squeezed her hand. "Sometimes I say or do the
wrong thing. Daddy gets upset. He works very, very
hard, you know. Very hard. Six kids cost a lot of money,
you know." *She was speaking fast.*

"Okay, Mama."

"But Daddy loves me. Very, very much. And I love
him. And it isn't all the time, just sometimes. Rarely."

*Mama wasn't making sense. Then she leaned over and
kissed Lily on the head and the world got a little better.*

"Rowan?"

John's voice was soft but urgent.

"Rowan, are you okay?"

"Just thinking." She took a deep breath. He knew
everything already. Only one more secret to share. "My
father abused my mother. Hit her. She always justified it.
Said it was her fault. When I asked her about it once, she
just said she did things wrong. Stood up for him."

Her knuckles were white from clenching her hands

into fists. She consciously worked out the tension in her muscles.

"I didn't think killing her came out of nowhere," John said. "You know, it's a pattern. Abusive relationships often end in death."

"They'd been married nineteen years. Six kids. And—and she stayed with him the whole time, no matter what he did." She remembered the flowers he always brought. The kisses he bestowed on her when he came in at night. "It was like Jekyll and Hyde. He hit her. They argued so much. But I couldn't believe he killed her. Didn't want to believe. He used to call her his queen."

She took a deep breath. She didn't realize she'd been crying until John wiped the tears from her cheeks.

"I loved my father and hated him. He could be so wonderful—playing games, taking us to the park, out for ice cream—but he hit my mother." Her voice hitched. "I was so confused. Then seeing him so—so—so empty." She took a deep breath. "That, I didn't know how to accept. Not then."

"You were a child, Rowan. A child forced to grow up very fast."

"Bobby was different."

Rowan never forgot Bobby's cruelty. The silent terror he'd inflicted on all of them. Even Mama.

"Some people are just born evil," John said.

She didn't disagree. "I think Bobby took the worst of Daddy and twisted it. I mean, he was the oldest. He knew what was going on. He used to push Mel and Rachel around just like Daddy did to Mama. He'd hit them."

"And no one did anything." John's voice was full of shock. Not a surprise. After all, he had had a perfect childhood.

"Once Mel went to Daddy. Told him that Bobby had

hit Rachel so hard she fell down the stairs. Daddy and
Bobby had a huge fight in the garage. Bobby left for
days. And I was glad. So glad.

"But he came back."

With a vengeance, Rowan thought. That was a year
before the murders. When he turned eighteen, she had
hoped he'd move out for good. But he didn't.

"Bobby called my father weak and pussy-whipped. I
didn't know what that meant at the time. But he never
challenged him to his face, except that one time. It was
when Daddy wasn't home that Bobby terrorized us. He
broke Peter's arm when he was a toddler. I saw him do
it. But he told me if I told the truth, he would kill me. I
believed him and told Mama it was an accident."

"No one would blame you, Rowan," John said.

"Would anything have been different if I'd told the
truth then?" she continued, almost as if she hadn't heard
him. "Would Bobby have been sent away? Punished?
Anything?"

She shook her head and released a deep, weary sigh.
"I'll never know." She laughed, but felt no humor. Only
a deep, pervading emptiness. She wondered if she'd ever
feel whole again.

John squeezed her hand, held on with both of his. She
felt cold to the touch. His throat was raw and scratchy.
Tears of anger and rage threatened and he swallowed
them down. No child should ever have to go through
what Rowan did. The senselessness, the horror of everything she'd endured stabbed at his heart.

But what really angered him was not simply young
Bobby's evil. It was her parents. What had they been
doing living with an abusive son, a young man who tor-
mented them and their other children? How could they
do nothing? How could her mother sit in the house, let

her children witness her abuse, and not get them out of there?

There were two older girls. Couldn't one of them have gone to the authorities? Surely they witnessed Bobby's anger; they'd obviously been subject to it themselves. Yet Rowan placed everything on her own shoulders, as if she were the only one who could have done something yet had failed to act.

If only he could explain to her, reassure her, that her actions and inactions had nothing to do with what happened.

"Rowan, none of it was your fault," John said quietly.

She shrugged. Had she even registered what he'd said? "I guess what I'm saying is that I expected Bobby to do something bad. Real bad."

"Why do you think your father broke?"

"I just don't know. It's why I studied criminal psychology in college. It's why I joined the FBI. For answers. And I found answers. But not about my daddy. Just the standard: Abusive spouses often kill or are killed."

John pulled her to him. He couldn't stand to hear the self-torture in her voice. Evil knew no bounds. Rich or poor, male or female, old or young. He didn't know what made Robert MacIntosh kill his wife, but it had broken him forever. Twenty-three years without speaking, without even acknowledging the presence of another human being.

But Bobby MacIntosh was another story. If he was right and Rowan's brother was the cause of the three-week, premeditated, expertly plotted killing spree, then his evil heart was more twisted, and far saner, than his father's.

*　　*　　*

Roger Collins paced the waiting room of Beaumont, the maximum-security prison where Bobby MacIntosh had been incarcerated for the past year. The warden was transferring him into a private conference room, but Roger waited for Rowan.

He wanted to strangle John Flynn, but at the same time feared his theory was right. That Bobby MacIntosh was not in Beaumont, but instead was free and terrorizing Rowan.

Good intentions aside, he'd made a big mistake. A mistake that cost seven people their lives. And maybe more.

Bobby MacIntosh at eighteen—hardly a man—was more dangerous than most hardened criminals with decades of assaults under their belts. No remorse, and he certainly took a special glee in his killing night.

"Well, well, well, if it isn't Special Agent Roger Collins," Bobby MacIntosh had said twenty-three years ago when Roger interviewed him in a Boston jail cell.

Roger stood outside the cell and stared at the kid who'd killed three of his sisters.

"Lily is going to testify against you," he'd told Bobby, wanting to see him squirm. "She's alive and well and wants to send you to the electric chair."

Bobby's eyes narrowed as he glared at Roger.

"Massachusetts doesn't have a death penalty. It's unconstitutional," he mocked.

"Too bad. I would have happily flipped the switch. Lily would have, too. You tried to break her, but she's strong. Stronger than you think. Stronger than you've ever given her credit for. When she gets on the stand, not one juror is going to vote to acquit. You are going to spend the rest of your life in prison."

He'd approached the bars, stood inches from them.

He'd never felt such loathing toward a suspect in his life. After listening to Lily's story, Roger hated this kid.

"And if you think you'll be living for long behind bars," he said, his voice low and even, "think again."

Bobby just stared at him, his eyes mocking, casually reclining on the cot. "You don't know me," Bobby said, shaking his head. "I'm a survivor. And if *you* think I'm spending the rest of my life behind bars, you're the one who's deranged."

Bobby sat up, put his hands on his knees, and narrowed his eyes. The hard anger in his face made Roger involuntarily swallow. This was the man Lily feared, the brother she had lived with for ten years, who killed without remorse. He did it for sheer pleasure.

"I will kill Lily. Not now, not tomorrow. Someday. I'll take her scrawny neck and break it in two."

"Don't count on it," Roger had said through clenched teeth. He turned and stormed out of the jail. But he heard Bobby MacIntosh's final words.

"Don't underestimate me, asshole."

The next day he took Lily to see her father. And the strong little girl completely fell apart and needed to be sedated. It was only then that he feared she wouldn't be able to take the stand, that testifying might permanently harm her. And after everything she'd gone through, he didn't want her to face even more.

Bobby attempted to escape on the way to a preliminary hearing. He'd shot and killed two guards and had been gunned down. While he was in surgery, Roger prayed to a God he barely believed in that He would send Bobby to hell, where he belonged.

But the young killer lived.

Fortunately, the circumstances were different this time. Bobby had killed two cops. Roger convinced the D.A. that Lily wasn't strong enough to withstand a trial.

They tried MacIntosh for the murders of the cops instead of the murders of his family. Life in prison, no possibility of parole.

Damn Massachusetts; he should have gotten the death penalty.

Roger went to Lily and told her Bobby had been killed trying to escape.

Thinking back, it had been a good plan. MacIntosh was in prison, Lily spared the agony of the trial and the fear that her brother was alive and would hurt her. She grew up believing he was dead and couldn't harm her. And she'd grown up lovely. Beautiful, smart, devoted. He'd pushed her into the FBI because she had the empathy and brains to make an outstanding agent.

It was only when she resigned after the Franklin homicides that Roger wondered if he hadn't made mistakes with Rowan. Like bringing her into protective custody without telling her, under the guise of guardianship. Encouraging her to limit contact with Peter. Convincing her to change her name.

Everything he'd done, Roger had done because he loved her. Rowan was the child, the daughter, he and Gracie could never have. When her grandparents called him and said they didn't know how to handle her and Peter, that the children had night terrors and the psychiatrist wanted to try drug therapy, Roger made a decision. He contacted a cop who'd told him he and his wife would adopt both Lily and Peter.

But after a trial period, they wanted only Peter.

Rowan didn't make it easy on anyone back then. Who could blame her? She was torturing herself that Dani had died. That she couldn't save her family.

So Roger took Rowan in. And had lied to her ever since.

A guard opened the door of the waiting room and escorted Rowan, Quinn Peterson, and a dark-haired man he presumed was John Flynn into the room.

One look at Rowan and Roger no longer wondered if he'd made a mistake. He knew it.

Still embarrassed about her emotional breakdown on the plane, Rowan vowed to keep herself under control. John had been surprisingly understanding, considering that her brother might have killed his brother. John listened, asked simple questions, and didn't tell her everything was going to be okay.

Nothing was ever going to be "okay."

She stared at Roger and frowned. "You lied to me."

Roger nodded. "I thought it was for the best. I'm sorry. I was wrong."

What an understatement! She shook her head, unable to trust herself to speak. If she said anything to Roger, it would be replete with cursing and venom. He'd lied to her forever, didn't trust her with the truth. Probably thought she'd end up in a loony bin like her father. Maybe she would have. Maybe she still would.

But his betrayal would stay with her until she died. She didn't know if she'd ever be able to forgive him.

She turned from Roger and ended up staring into John's deep green eyes. He squeezed her arm and she leaned into him just enough to show him she appreciated his support. For the first time in this long, long day, Rowan felt she might survive.

The warden came into the room, a surprisingly small, balding man who walked tall and wore a nervous smile. "Assistant Director Collins, I'm Warden James Cullen. The prisoner is ready for your visit."

He glanced at Rowan and John. "Ms. Smith, correct?"

She nodded. "This is my partner, John Flynn." Partner? It just slipped out. She'd meant to say bodyguard.

She wasn't even a damned agent anymore. She didn't *have* a partner.

No one said anything, but she felt a subtle shift in John's stance. She didn't look at him, but wondered what he was thinking.

Rowan followed the warden out, John right behind her in his subtle protective mode. Roger and Quinn trailed them. They traveled down a long, wide corridor, making several turns, and the warden typed security commands at three separate gates. They were accompanied by two armed guards.

The clear window looking into the brightly lit interrogation room showed a forty-something man shackled at his wrists and ankles. He had short-cropped sandy blond hair, a pointed chin, and blue eyes. He was average height and build, with the sunken look of defeat seen in many lifers.

He looked like Bobby MacIntosh. At first glance, Rowan was certain it *was* her brother in chains behind the table.

But it wasn't.

Roger spoke, his trembling voice deep and filled with anger. And fear.

"That's not MacIntosh."

CHAPTER
18

"Uh, sir, we double-checked his records and it *is* him," Warden Cullen said with a stiff nod, running his hand over his smooth skull. "He's been here for fourteen months. Our new security protocols have us take a DNA sample on arrival. When you called three weeks ago, we took another DNA sample. It's definitely Robert MacIntosh."

"He must have made the switch during transport," Roger said, almost to himself.

"Excuse me?" John said.

Warden Cullen explained. "Security is very tight. For the past two years, new prisoners must provide their DNA for the file. In addition to a recent photograph and fingerprints, of course. In the past, fingerprints and identifying marks were the main distinguishing characteristics.

"Everything is in the computer," he continued, confidence growing. "So when we received Robert MacIntosh into the facility fourteen months ago, we compared his photograph, distinguishing marks, and fingerprints with the computer records. Perfect match."

"What about his DNA?" Roger asked.

The warden frowned. "We took his DNA sample upon admittance."

"So you had nothing to compare it with."

"DNA sampling is expensive, Director Collins. New prisoners are done routinely. MacIntosh has been in the system for over twenty years. Existing prisoners are added as funds become available.

"MacIntosh had been in Louisiana since his conviction until fourteen months ago, when he was transported here. They didn't have a DNA sample on record," the warden explained.

"I didn't know he'd been transferred until three weeks ago," Roger said, not looking Rowan in the eye. He stared instead at the imposter.

"Transferred," John repeated, failing to contain his frustration.

Roger nodded, looked sheepish. "I had a copy of the file sent to me. He'd been beaten by a prison gang, and it wasn't the first time. Louisiana has been having some problems, and MacIntosh's attorney petitioned for a transfer. It was granted. I was supposed to be notified, but I wasn't."

"There was no reason to believe he's anyone other than Robert MacIntosh, Junior," the warden said, his voice tight with indignation. "All the files matched."

"Computer records," John mumbled, running a hand through his short hair. "They could have been switched."

"I beg your pardon, Mr. Flynn," the warden said, "but computer security is tight. This is a federal penitentiary. We protect ourselves against hackers."

"No system is secure," John said, jaw clenched.

Rowan nodded to the man on the other side of the window. The man posing as her brother. "He knows the answer."

Two minutes later, Rowan sat across from the man who'd passed as Bobby for fourteen months. John stood against the wall next to one of the two guards, Roger sat to Rowan's right, and Warden Cullen stood nervously at her left.

"Who are you?" Rowan asked.

"Bobby MacIntosh, but ya know that," the imposter said, staring at her and trying to look fearsome, but failing.

Rowan shook her head. "No, you're not Bobby. Bobby is my brother. I know him. You are not Bobby."

"Hey, babe, I've changed."

"Tell me how you made the switch," Roger said.

"I don't know what you're talkin' about." He shuffled his feet, the chains clinking together, echoing in the silence of the sparsely furnished room.

Rowan glared at him. This man had helped her brother commit murder. "Did you plan it with him? Accomplice to murder. Hmmm. Texas has the death penalty, doesn't it, Warden?"

"Well, uh, yes we do."

"I don't suppose an accomplice is eligible," Rowan said, her voice flat and hard.

"Well, there are extenuating circumstances where an accomplice may be eligible," the warden said.

Rowan controlled her reaction. It was bullshit, but the imposter wouldn't know that. Play up whatever angle they had. Besides, everyone knew Texas had one of the strongest death penalty laws in the country.

The imposter fidgeted, crossed his arms over his chest. "I don't know what you're talkin' about."

"Well, let me spell it out. We have your DNA. My DNA is on file with the FBI. Assistant Director Collins," she motioned toward Roger, "already called for my profile to be faxed here. If you really are my brother, the DNA profiles will prove that." She glanced at Warden Cullen, who quickly picked up the thread.

"Guard, please call up to my office and see if the fax has arrived from Washington."

One of the guards left the room and the imposter became visibly agitated. Certainly he had heard of more than one criminal who'd been caught because of DNA. DNA was king at enough trials to make any prisoner wary.

"I, uh—" he began, then stopped.

"Tell me where Bobby MacIntosh is," Roger said.

"I don't know," the prisoner whispered. His eyes darted from Rowan to Roger to the warden. "I think I need a lawyer."

Roger slammed his fist on the table. "No!"

Warden Cullen frowned at him. Rowan leaned forward. "Sir," she asked, "what is your name?"

"Lloyd," he answered, his shackles rustling.

"Lloyd, my name is Rowan Smith."

He shrugged. "I know."

"I'm the reason Bobby wanted out of prison, right?" she prodded.

Lloyd hesitated, then nodded.

Her head spun. It *was* Bobby. All along it was him, and he wanted to destroy her. Take from her what he hadn't twenty-three years ago.

She kept her voice firm and modulated. "Bobby told you about me."

He hesitated. "I really think I need—"

Warden Cullen interrupted. "Look, Lloyd, I'll tell you what. Anything you tell us here won't be used against you, okay? Just answer their questions."

Lloyd didn't look convinced. "He'll kill me if I talk."

Rowan stared at him. "I'll kill you if you don't."

"Ms. Smith—" Warden Cullen warned.

The guard returned with two pieces of official-looking paper. He handed them to the warden, who read them and nodded. Lloyd paled, his pasty complexion becoming even whiter.

Cullen spoke. "This proves you're not Robert MacIntosh. Do you want to cooperate or be charged with accessory to murder?"

"Murder? But she's not dead!"

"Bobby started with others," Rowan said. "He plans to end with me. But I have no intention of letting him kill me." She kept her face rigid, her eyes shielded. She knew she looked fearsome; it was an expression the press had loved to comment on when she'd been with the Bureau. It also worked well on criminals.

She couldn't afford to break down now. Not when they were so close.

Lloyd swallowed, glanced at the warden, then back at her. Rowan didn't move a muscle, but her heart beat so loudly in her ears she thought for sure everyone could hear. She couldn't blow this. Wouldn't blow it.

"I want in writing that I'm not gonna be charged for any of this." He leaned back in his chair and closed his mouth.

Roger looked at the warden, who sighed and pulled out a legal pad. He hand-wrote a promise on two sheets of paper, signed both, and handed the pen to Lloyd. Lloyd signed them awkwardly with his hands bound and the warden took them. Rowan glanced down. He'd signed them "Robert MacIntosh."

They weren't legitimate without his legal name, but no one said anything. Stupid idiot, Rowan thought. No wonder Bobby had so easily manipulated him.

"I met Bobby in the joint in Louisiana. Right when he came in. Young punk kid. We hit it off right away. We looked kinda alike. He told me about you," he said with a nod toward Rowan. "He hates you."

"The feeling is mutual," Rowan said through clenched

teeth, her mouth dry. She refused to let this guy get to her.

"Well, I got out after ten. He told me to find you. Sure, why not? I had nothing better to do. But you were fuckin' hard to find. Then Bobby turned me on to Roger Collins here and told me you might've changed your name. But he had your social, and that's what led me to your college transcripts." He smiled, obviously pleased with himself.

"Well, I sorta followed you. Not all the time, didn't have to. I knew your name, could check up on you from time to time. Kept Bobby informed."

"You. Stalked. Me." It was all she could do not to reach over and squeeze the bastard's neck.

"Hell no, I didn't care about you. And it wasn't like I was always around. I had to keep a low profile, ya know. Work, pay taxes. I landed back in the can on some stupid trumped-up charge, in upstate New York. Was in there for nearly two years. Time off for good behavior." He chuckled. "Realized something important, though."

"What?" Roger asked, impatient.

He shrugged and gave a half-smile. "I really like being in the can. Don't have to work if I don't wanna. Three squares. Place to live, live for free. I never killed no one, so don't have death row over my head. I mean, freedom is overrated. I tried to explain it all to Bobby, but he don't listen.

"I lost track of you for a time and Bobby was antsy; when he heard you were some hotshot writer making big bucks, he sorta flipped. He came up with this all, but it took time. Two years to plan it and have it all come together."

"How did you trade places?" Roger asked.

"That was easier than I thought. I didn't think Bobby'd be able to pull it off, but he was so sure it'd work and I thought, what the fuck? If I was caught, I'd get what I wanted, another stint in the joint. If it worked, I'd get to come here to Beaumont. Nice place. Helluva lot better than Louisiana."

"How?" Roger repeated, his anger evident.

"Bobby staged an accident, gang fight I think. He was taken to the hospital, all cut up. There was a guard outside his room, but not inside. We switched places. I just dressed up like a fuckin' janitor and walked right in. 'Course Bobby had to cut me and I didn't like that too much, but it worked and I came here and he walked outta the hospital. It was damn perfect."

"What about your fingerprints?" Warden Cullen asked.

"Before Bobby left Louisiana, he hacked into the computer system and swapped our IDs. You know, fingerprints and whatnot. It's all there, in the computer. And Bobby is really smart. He played the inside good. Got access to the library and offices. He had some guy in the pen for computer fraud help him."

"Who?" the warden asked.

Lloyd shrugged. "Didn't ask."

Rowan couldn't believe what Lloyd was telling them. Bobby had been walking free for fourteen months. He'd probably kept a low profile for a while to make sure the prison system hadn't caught on, and when he didn't see anything in the news, he started following her. Read her books. Planned how to torment her. How to kill her characters and make her suffer.

"You bastard." She spread her hands on the table in front of her, her knuckles white.

"Hey! I didn't kill anybody. I don't kill people. I'm a thief." He said it with pride, and Rowan just shook her head and pressed her fingers to the bridge of her nose. Bobby was alive. He was walking the streets and killing people.

"Do you know where MacIntosh is now?" Roger asked, his voice low.

Lloyd shrugged. "He didn't keep in touch, if you know what I mean. Why would he? He had what he wanted, I had what I wanted."

"Take him back to his cell," Warden Cullen said with obvious disgust.

The guards hoisted Lloyd up and walked him out. Over his shoulder, he glanced at Rowan. "Bobby told me you were a weak bitch. I dunno. I think he underestimated you." He paused. "But I know you shouldn't underestimate Bobby."

Warden Cullen allowed them to use his office while he went to another room to talk to his people about the situation.

Roger reinforced the APB Quinn Peterson had put out earlier, sent a team over to watch his house and protect Gracie, and when he didn't have any more calls to make, sat down and finally looked at Rowan.

"I'm sorry, Rowan."

"You bastard. I trusted you."

He closed his eyes. When he opened them, Rowan was surprised to see tears. He swallowed. "I only wanted to protect you. Rowan, you're the daughter I never had. But damn, I was an awful father. I was never there for you. I pushed you to go into the FBI, pushed you into the business, and tried to push you into staying. I thought—hell, I don't know what I thought. Retribution, justice, what did I know?"

Rowan was surprised when the hot sting of tears crept into the back of her eyes. She wanted to hate Roger for keeping something so important from her, for lying to her, but she couldn't hate him.

She was sorely, irrevocably disappointed in him. The

system had known Bobby was alive, and Roger should have come clean when this entire charade started to unfold.

They might have learned the truth sooner. And saved someone's life. Like Michael's.

"Roger, you were the father I needed. I never believed you'd lie to me. That you'd keep something so important a secret. And what about the people who died because you remained silent? What about Michael?"

"Believe me when I tell you I checked and double-checked Bobby's status. I had no reason to believe he wasn't in prison."

"But when all the leads dried up? When the tiny hope that someone related to the Franklin murders was involved didn't pan out? What about then?"

She swiped at her face, impatiently slapping the tears aside. A quick glance at Quinn and John standing to the side reminded her she wasn't alone with Roger. They'd been so quiet, she'd forgotten they were in the room.

"I don't know," Roger said quietly. "I don't know that we could have stopped what happened."

"You're right. We don't know. We don't know because we never had the chance to try." She stared at him and saw a man she no longer recognized. He looked like Roger Collins—dark, graying hair, clear blue eyes, hint of wrinkles edging his eyes and mouth. But he wasn't the Roger she spent half her childhood with. The man who taught her truth and justice were worth fighting for. The man who stood before her was a liar, and his betrayal stung.

"Peter." Her eyes widened as she realized that if Bobby knew about her, he had to know about Peter. "Peter—he's going after him!"

Roger shook his head. "No. He thinks Peter is dead."

She looked at him quizzically. "Why?"

"He believes Peter was killed that night, that you were the only survivor. He alluded to that when I interrogated him, and I never corrected his assumption."

"Certainly he went through the newspaper archives and found out it wasn't true!"

"Peter was listed in critical condition, and there was never any press account of his death or survival."

"Critical?" Rowan remembered that Peter had been so emotionally distraught he'd been sedated after the murders, but he hadn't been physically injured.

She took a deep breath. "We need to check on this jerk's story, try to retrace Bobby's steps for the past fourteen months." She slammed her fist on the desk as she sunk into a chair. "Bobby has been free for fourteen months and no one fucking knew!"

John put his hand on her shoulder as her breath came in rasps. Amazingly, she felt better. His calm presence throughout the plane ride, the interrogation, and now— it was just what she needed. She glanced up at him and he gave her a nod.

"There's something else I need to tell you," Roger said as he sat in the warden's chair.

She turned to him, bracing herself for the worst, but was surprised when Roger said, "I think Bobby visited your father twice last year."

Her eyes widened. "And no one noticed?"

"He used a false name and identification. Bob Smith. I tried to get the tapes, but protocol is that they overwrite them every three months. They are digitally preserved in an out-of-state archive and are being sent to me. I should have something tonight or tomorrow."

"We don't need the tapes. It was Bobby."

"I agree, but we may get a recent photograph."

Rowan took a deep breath. "I want to go to Boston."

John spoke for the first time. "That's not a good idea."

She turned to look at him. His jaw was set, his mouth a thin, angry line. Angry? Maybe worried. It didn't matter. She had to do it. "I need to see my father. Maybe he has an idea what Bobby's plans are. That sounds like something Bobby would do. Brag." She paused. "He thought our father was weak. Bobby'd want to rub his nose in the fact that he's stronger. That he killed without breaking and enjoyed it. That he planned on killing the rest of us."

"I want you in a safe house tomorrow," Roger said. "We'll have dozens of agents all over the country hunting for MacIntosh. But he's coming for you. I need you out of harm's way."

"No," Rowan said. "I'm going to Boston. I'm going to see my father, then I'm going to call Peter and tell him the truth. I have to. I can't let him believe the lie anymore. And even though Bobby doesn't know about him, he knows enough about me that he might be able to track him down. Peter needs to be on alert."

"I can't change your mind," said Roger. It was a statement.

She shook her head. "Tomorrow morning I'm flying to Boston. With or without you."

John leaned over and whispered in her ear. "You're not going anyplace without me, Rowan. You still need a bodyguard."

She turned and searched his eyes. He'd been quiet all day. He blamed her for Michael's death, and he blamed himself. She'd seen that for herself yesterday. But now? He grieved; he wanted revenge. But he'd also sent out this invisible protective shell to surround her. She felt stronger in his presence, like she could get through this. Alive and well.

"Thank you," she mouthed, then turned back to Roger. "Six A.M. Lobby. And don't let Dr. Christopher tell him I'm coming. The element of surprise might work in this case."

Monday morning, Bobby MacIntosh went to a major bookstore in Dallas for a copy of *Crime of Jeopardy.*

Not that he needed it. But he wanted another copy. To follow the pattern, leave it with the victim. Though he was confident Rowan, no matter how stupid she was, had figured it out by now.

Rowan. Where had she come up with a stupid name like that? Probably thought she'd fool him. That he'd never find her if she changed her name. He smiled. *You can run but you can't hide, Lily.*

The end was near. One more book, one more murder. He'd already picked the perfect victim, arranged the perfect crime, and was almost giddy with anticipation. This was it. One more victim and then he could confront his sister.

He couldn't have been happier if he'd been able to choose all the variables. Of course, Doreen Rodriguez had taken the most effort and planning. But that murder had to be perfect to show Lily he was smarter than she was.

By now the bitch must be terrified. She'd hired a bodyguard, but he'd taken care of him. Weak. Worthless.

So smart. He'd learned the little pixie who'd been hanging around was the bodyguard's sister. He'd followed her around a bit. She'd be easy to get to. If he needed her.

Security. What a joke! Security was nothing for a genius.

He'd debated taking out the other guy. *John Flynn.*

While he'd been waiting for the idiot bodyguard to come back from the bar he'd done a little search of his own, learned a little about the brother. Just in from South America. Bobby wondered why.

John Flynn was more elusive. But he'd be going to a funeral soon, right? Hmm. That might interfere with his current plans. He'd have to rush. And hurrying caused mistakes. He couldn't afford a mistake, not now when he was so close to getting exactly what he wanted.

Retribution.

Besides, killing Flynn in front of Lily had its advantages. It would force her into compliance if she got it in her head to fight him. Not that she'd win, of course. No matter how well trained she'd been in the fucking FBI, he'd been trained in prison. He'd win, hands down.

But first things first.

He hadn't found Lily's book in the new-release section. Frowning, he searched the store, his frustration growing.

"May I help you find something?" The clerk was young, blonde, and petite.

"Where's *Crime of Jeopardy*?"

"Pardon me?"

He let out his breath. Stupid bitch. "The book. Rowan Smith. It was supposed to be released today."

"Uh, I'll ask my manager. I haven't seen it." She scurried off.

Couldn't deviate from the plan. The bodyguard was special, to show Lily how close he was, that he could get to anyone. But now he had to play by the book.

He chuckled at his pun. As soon as his sister was taken care of, he'd be free. What a heady thought! Everyone in his stupid family would be dead where they belonged and he could finally start living without their mightier-than-thou faces haunting him in his dreams.

He could hardly wait to watch Lily Pad die. The last of the line. And because he'd been so successful, he might just take care of dear old Dad as well.

But where's the fun in killing someone who doesn't know who the fuck you are?

It had been mind-blowing to him that his father was a catatonic zombie sitting in the loony bin. When he'd first seen him from the back—sitting in an outdoor chair watching the garden—he'd thought, what a scam. His dad had beat the system and just had to pretend he was a basketcase. He'd planned on helping him escape.

Then he saw his eyes. His father wasn't even there in that skinny body.

His father had always been weak. It figured he couldn't handle payback. Still, Bobby had hoped that they would work together, that he could share with his father how incredible it felt to take Lily's mind and bend it. To take her characters and make them real. To see her suffer.

They'd worked together before, hadn't they? His father had started it, and Bobby had finished it.

But his father would never have finished it, Bobby realized, a hot pit of anger rising to his throat. His father was a fool. Always apologizing. Always getting down on his knees and asking forgiveness.

Fucking asshole.

When he was fourteen, Bobby remembered seeing his father do just that—get on his knees in front of his mother. They'd been in the backyard and the bitch did something stupid. Forgot something. His father belted her across the face good; blood trickled out the side of her mouth.

Her look of fear made Bobby's heart race. To have that much power, to be looked at with such intense fear, must be awesome. He longed for the day his mother would cower at his feet and realize who really ran the house.

Then his father did the unforgivable. He took her hands, got down on his knees, and said he was sorry.

Sorry!

He'd kissed her hands, begged her forgiveness, tears streaming down his face. He was crying. The rage Bobby felt then was nothing like anything he'd ever experienced. Seeing his father cowering in front of a stupid female, on his knees no less, turned something in his gut from anger to raw rage.

He'd gone into the house, unable to watch the spectacle, as his mother got on her knees and kissed him. *I know, honey, I know. I'm sorry, too.*

They both deserved to die.

Something rubbed against his feet and he looked down to see the puppy his father had brought home for the family two weeks before. It looked at him with such pathetic brown eyes Bobby wanted to kick it across the room.

Instead, he picked the mutt up and left the house.

No one ever saw that stupid dog again.

Bobby shook his head, looked around. He wasn't fourteen and at home. He was in the middle of a stupid bookstore, waiting. Where was the blonde?

He glanced at his watch. Ten minutes! He fidgeted.

He crossed over to one of the counters and cut in front of the line. "I was waiting to find out about *Crime of Jeopardy*. It was supposed to be here today. Do I have to find another store to buy it?"

The skinny boy behind the counter looked at him oddly, and the little blonde girl hurried up to him. Why did everyone have to be so young?

"I'm sorry, sir, but the shipment hasn't come in. My manager says that it was postponed and won't be here for at least a week, maybe longer. Can I help you find anything else?"

Postponed? Why? Was it accidental—or on purpose? Did the cops think that if he didn't have the book he wouldn't complete his mission?

Fools. He'd show them he was smarter than all of them.

He stormed out of the store without another word. Maybe this was meant to be. Yeah. Leave her own copy of the stupid book on the whore's body. He'd already targeted the prostitute.

Sadie.

If they thought they could beat him, they were sorely mistaken. As soon as the whore was dead, he'd confront Rowan. *Lily.*

Almost sad that the game was ending, he went back to his hotel room to finish the preparations.

CHAPTER
19

Boston was unseasonably cold. Instead of a light breeze, blooming trees, and clear skies, everything had a gray pallor; a frosty wetness quickly penetrated layers of clothing, sinking deep into the bones.

Neither John nor Rowan was dressed for Boston. They'd left sunny Los Angeles with the clothes on their back and bought only essentials in the hotel gift shop when they arrived in Dallas. But they both forked over money for overpriced clothes at Logan Airport, including sweaters and windbreakers.

Rowan hadn't spoken much on the flight or the car ride to Bellevue. John gave her the space she needed. But not too much. He kept an eye on her, staying close so she knew she wasn't alone. He was her bodyguard, after all. And more.

But he didn't dwell on that right now.

He didn't know if he was helping, though every once in a while he caught her looking at him, an odd expression on her face.

He'd never had problems reading people before, but Rowan wasn't just any person. She'd spent years shielding her emotions to protect herself. He saw that now. There was something in her eyes that called to him. Her eyes showed him her pain, her anger, her fear, her uncertainty. He also saw intelligence, hope, and strength—a vitality that kept her from giving in to despair, turning a ten-year-old trauma victim into an unrelenting FBI agent and an agent into an author. Even though Rowan believed she was weak, hammered with nightmares that caused her to quit the Bureau, he saw a woman who was smart enough to know when she needed a break. Before the job broke her.

She was stronger than him. John was still tilting at windmills, knowing that the biggest windmill—the so-called War on Drugs—was a losing battle. Every time they stopped a shipment, another twice as big came to shore.

But it was what he did. He couldn't give up, at least while Reginald Pomera still drew breath.

Bellevue Hospital for the Criminally Insane looked serene against the misty gray sky. Roger drove, and Rowan sat next to him. Agent Peterson had taken a flight back to Los Angeles to coordinate the search for Bobby MacIntosh.

Even though John couldn't see her face, he watched Rowan's jaw clench and felt tension radiating from her entire body. He wanted to comfort her, to tell her she didn't have to do this, that he would take her away from the pain.

But she wouldn't appreciate it. Not now. Maybe later, when it was done, she'd want someone to lean on. He planned on being there for her.

"Rowan," Roger said as he turned off the ignition, "are you sure?"

She didn't respond, but shot him a cold look. As she moved to open the passenger door, John quickly jumped out the back and opened it for her. She seemed surprised, then sighed and allowed him to escort her to the main door.

Roger scrambled to follow them. He'd called ahead, and Dr. Christopher met them in the lobby.

"Collins," the doctor said with a curt nod. Then, "You must be Rowan Smith."

"I am."

"I can only allow two visitors with Mr. MacIntosh. I need to be in the room to observe."

"I'm her bodyguard," John said as he stared pointedly at Collins.

"I'll wait here," Roger said, defeated. He'd screwed up big time, losing Rowan's trust and respect. John almost felt sorry for him. Until he remembered Michael was dead.

John followed Dr. Christopher and Rowan down the wide corridor. Silence filled the halls, an eerie emptiness that surprised John. Shouldn't there be orderlies milling around, nurses with medication, patients making demands? It was as if they were the only people alive in the complex, and it made John nervous.

"Where is everyone?" he finally asked when they went through a secure door and still no one had greeted them since their arrival in the lobby.

"We have minimal staff on this end," Dr. Christopher said. "Our patients are on a strict schedule. They are not your typical mentally disturbed individuals. Everyone here is required to be by court order. Most will die here. The violent patients are in the north wing. That area has far more personnel and is much noisier than this wing. But every room, every hall, is monitored by security." He gestured to cameras in every corner. "A trained and armed medical team can be anywhere in this facility in sixty seconds or less."

Dr. Christopher stopped outside a wide door. Through the window, John saw the back of a skinny man sitting hunched in a chair facing a large plate-glass window that looked out onto lush greenery. He glanced at Rowan. She stared at her father, fear making her shake.

John cupped Rowan's jaw, forcing her to look at him. He caught her eyes and held them. "You can do this, Rowan. I will be with you the whole time. He can only hurt you if you let him."

"I'm ready." Her voice was shaky but clear.

"Very well." Dr. Christopher palmed his badge on the security panel and the door clicked open.

Mind numb, Rowan didn't move to enter. All she saw was her father, but not here, not in this sterile, sparsely furnished room. She saw him drop a bloody knife and pick up his dead wife. *Beth. Beth. What have I done?*

"Rowan?"

John's voice came from far away, at the end of a tunnel, basked in light. She faced him, wanting—needing—his strength. His dark green eyes held hers, sending her his vitality.

"Rowan, I'm right here," he was saying.

She felt John squeeze her hand. She didn't know if she'd reached for him, or he for her.

It didn't matter. She wasn't alone.

Rowan placed the only other chair in the room in front of her father. With a deep breath, she sat down and forced herself to look into his eyes.

He didn't see her.

His blue-gray eyes, so much like her own, stared vacantly beyond her. They didn't see her, didn't see anything. Her father was still gone, his body an empty shell, just as it was twenty-three years ago after he killed her mother.

"Daddy," she whispered, her voice a croak. "It's Lily."

No recognition. No movement. Nothing but the blank stare.

She tried again. "Daddy, I know that Bobby came to visit you."

Nothing.

Nothing! How could he sit there and not *be* in there somewhere? "Daddy, I need you!" Her voice rose. "Wake up, dammit!"

"Ms. Smith, he can hear just fine," Dr. Christopher interjected. "His brain has stopped making connections between speech and thought."

"What, he's brain dead? In a coma?" she asked, incredulous.

"No, nothing like that. Though it's more like a coma than anything else," Dr. Christopher explained. "Your father's condition is purely psychological, and technically a coma is caused by an internal or external injury to the brain. A car accident or a tumor, for example. Your father has a neuropsychological disorder, quite rare but there are several documented cases. Your father hears everything, but can't understand it. He sees, but can't process the images. He's locked himself in his mind because of the trauma of the crime he committed. If he hadn't, he likely would have committed suicide when he realized what he'd done. In all likelihood, if your brother hadn't picked up the knife, your father would have used it on himself."

Rowan listened to what the doctor said, but all she could think about was *why?* Why did her father kill his wife? Though her years of training reminded her that abusive husbands often killed, she still found it difficult to reconcile the abuse with murder, the violence with her parents.

She wanted to end that part of her life and start over. But as much as she'd become her own person, separate from her upbringing, she was so intricately tied to her father. Her mother. Her dead sisters.

Bobby.

"Why, Daddy?" she said, surprised that her voice sounded so young. "Why did you kill Mama?"

He blinked. She sensed rather than saw the doctor come to attention. No one said anything.

"I saw you, Daddy. I saw you stab Mama."

"Beth."

Rowan sucked in her breath. Her father had spoken her mother's name.

Rowan looked like her mother. Only she and Bobby were fair-haired like her. She nodded. "Yes, Robert, I'm here."

He blinked again. This time, a single tear ran down his cheek. Rowan watched as it hung off his jaw for a second, then fell onto his hands.

"Robert, I need your help." He didn't say anything, but Rowan continued. "Bobby came to visit you. He talked to you. What did he say?"

"Beth."

This was impossible. She resisted the urge to reach out and slap her father. Instead, she said, "Robert, Lily needs your help. Bobby wants to hurt her. What did he tell you?"

Nothing.

She heard Dr. Christopher writing frantically and he passed her a note. *Ask him why he killed you.*

She closed her eyes. She could do this. She could. Tears stung the back of her eyes, her throat.

"Robert. Why did you kill me?"

He blinked and turned his eyes toward her. His expression wasn't normal, but it wasn't the empty stare he'd had when she first walked in.

Her heart beat so fast her chest stung. She kept her expression blank, firm. She would *not* break down. Not here. Not now.

"Bobby saw you with him again. I told you to stay away from him, but you didn't."

Bobby. She stifled a cry and felt a hand on her shoulder. John. Sharing his strength. She took a deep breath.

"Bobby wants to hurt Lily. Please help me stop him."

Her father shook his head very slowly back and forth. "Bobby killed our children, Beth. Lily's dead."

"No, no I'm not, Da—Robert. Lily is alive. Bobby is trying to kill her."

His head rocked back and forth, very slowly. His voice was as petulant as a child's. "She's as good as dead. Bobby said so."

Rowan wanted to scream, hit him, shake him until he started making sense.

She tried everything she could, but her father didn't say another word. He sat there, staring at her with odd eyes, eyes that saw and didn't see at the same time. His head moved back and forth, back and forth, until Rowan couldn't take it anymore. She jumped up and ran to the door. It was locked; she couldn't get out. She pounded her fist against the door. John was at her side, his arm around her shoulders. Dr. Christopher let them out.

The doctor was excited. "I never thought you'd visit, but you helped him make an incredible breakthrough. Incredible." Dr. Christopher bounced on his heels. "Will you come again? We can work together to bring him out. For the first time, I think we might be able to reach him."

Rowan stared at the doctor, her mouth dropping open, eyes wide. "Are you serious? I hope he rots in hell."

The doctor frowned and blinked. "He's mentally ill, Ms. Smith. He didn't know what he was doing when he killed your mother."

"I don't believe that. I hope he's suffering in the world he's created for himself. He used to hit my mother. Hit her until she bruised and bled. She stayed because she said she loved him." She laughed without humor. "And she's dead. He killed her. I hope he burns hot when he finally dies." She paused and stared at the doctor defiantly.

"I never thought there was a worse punishment than death. But maybe there is."

"Are you okay?" John asked as they waited for a table in the hotel restaurant.

After leaving Bellevue, they went directly to the local FBI office where Collins had set up a temporary operations room to coordinate with Los Angeles and Washington. The number-one priority was to distribute Bobby MacIntosh's photo to all airline security personnel in the country. After 9/11 there was a mechanism in place to do just that, but the success still relied on the competence of local officials.

After Rowan told Collins about what her father had said, she clammed up. John didn't blame her. He'd want time alone after something like that. Now they were alone. Collins had retired to his room, though John didn't think he'd be sleeping. Guilt was a powerful insomniac.

"I'm okay," Rowan said.

"You know you can talk to me, right?"

She looked at him quizzically and John frowned. Didn't she trust him? After everything they'd been through?

Yet he'd treated her like crap after Michael was killed on Friday.

Friday. It had been three nights—seventy-two hours since Michael was gunned down. And John was here eating dinner in a nice Boston restaurant with the woman Michael had half fallen in love with.

"John?" Rowan asked, concern in her voice.

He didn't want to talk about Michael, but she had a right to know what he was thinking. "I don't blame you for Michael's death. Please believe me. I wasn't myself, and I said some things I didn't mean. I was out of line."

She absorbed what he said and he watched her shake her head slightly. "You may not blame me, but that doesn't make it any less my fault."

"Rowan, you had no idea the killer was your brother. You had every reason to believe he was dead."

Tears welled in her eyes, but they didn't fall. "I can't believe Roger kept this secret for so long."

The hostess approached. "Your table is ready," she said. "For three?"

John nodded. "Yes, thank you."

"Who are we waiting for? Not Roger. I—I can't deal with him right now."

"Not Roger. Peter."

Her eyes widened in concern. "Peter? But he has to keep a low profile, what if—"

He put his finger to her lips. "Rowan, I got his number from Roger and called him. He wants to see you. I think it would be good for you, especially after today."

The indecision on her face was clear. She loved her brother, but feared for him.

"He has an FBI escort, if that makes you feel any better."

"A little," she admitted.

They sat at the table and Rowan kept turning her head to look for her brother.

She drew in a deep breath, a hitch in her voice. "John, I cared for Michael. I liked him. I'm so sorry he's gone."

"Stop." His voice was harsher than he'd intended. "I

don't blame you, Rowan. You have to stop blaming yourself."

He took a deep breath. His hands had become tight fists and he slowly flexed them, trying to ease the tension that had been building since Michael was killed. It was more his fault than anyone's.

He didn't want to yell at her, but he had to make her understand. "I'm just as responsible for Michael being there as you. I should never have taken him off that night. It was me being selfish and judgmental." Damn, it hurt to say it out loud, but there it was.

"Who's Jessica?"

John blinked, surprised at the change of subject. "A woman Michael was involved with."

"I overheard you and Tess talking about me being another Jessica. What did you mean?"

John mulled that over. He couldn't tell her everything without betraying Michael on some level, but he didn't want to lie to her. Couldn't lie to her. He opted for a sanitized version of the truth. "Michael was a cop and caught the case. Jessica's ex-boyfriend was stalking her. Some badass junior Mafia goon. Michael helped her, continued to see her. Fell in love. It didn't work out. Jessica went back to the guy, ended up dead." He paused. "He has a thing for damsels in distress."

"I'm hardly a damsel in distress." She glanced down, and John couldn't read her expression. It was hard enough with all her self-imposed barriers, but if he couldn't see her eyes he didn't know what she was thinking.

"No, but you're a beautiful woman who needed someone to watch over her," he said softly. He reached over and took her hand. "Rowan, I'm not going to get over Michael's death anytime soon. It's my fault he was alone. I didn't think—no one thought—that Bobby would go after him." He put his free hand up when she looked like she was going to interrupt him. "But," he continued, "I'll deal with it in my own time and my own way."

She nodded, understanding in her pretty eyes.

"Rowan," a voice said behind her.

Rowan felt John tense, but she smiled, let go of his hand, and stood. "Peter," she whispered, turning to face her baby brother.

Peter wore a simple, dark sweater over his cleric's collar, his gray eyes shining bright with concern. He held out his arms and she stepped into his warm embrace, breathing in his safe and familiar scent, her cheek on his chest. He was quite tall, taller than John, and on the thin side.

She stepped back and inspected him. Definite worry in the faint lines of his handsome face. His dark hair had started graying on the sides, a few white strands intermingled here and there. He was only thirty; where had the gray come from?

She touched his face. "It's so good to see you." And it was. More than good; seeing him was almost like healing.

He kissed her on the forehead, then stepped back and extended his hand to John, who had stood and assumed his bodyguard stance behind her and to the side. "John Flynn?"

"Yes, Father."

Peter smiled wide, a touch of humor glimmering in his eyes. "Peter will suffice. Thank you for calling me."

John nodded, motioning for him to sit. Once they were all settled, the waitress took their orders and left.

"What did John tell you?" Rowan asked, breaking an awkward silence. Both Peter and John seemed to be sizing each other up. It made her feel strange.

"I suppose I should ask what he *didn't* tell me." Peter frowned. "Why did you come to Boston?"

Rowan closed her eyes. "To see our father."

"What?" The quiet shock in Peter's deep voice surprised Rowan. "But—I never thought you—" He stopped himself. "Why?"

"Bobby is alive," she said quietly. "Alive and killing people. He's the killer, Peter."

Rowan told Peter everything, from beginning to end. About the murders, the pigtails, the lilies, Roger's lies. Their food came and they picked at it, no one in the mood to eat.

When she was done, Peter turned to John. "I am so sorry about your brother."

"Thank you." Rowan thought John sounded a little gruff, but what did she expect? She'd just recounted how Michael had been killed.

"Dad talked?" Peter sipped water. "I'm surprised."

Rowan nodded. "Me, too. You know, I keep playing over and over in my mind what he said. Bobby told him my mother was with someone. Did Bobby set this whole thing up? Did he want to cause problems between Mom and Dad? I just don't understand."

"Bobby always got a perverse pleasure out of hurting people. Physically and emotionally," Peter said. "I was too young to understand how deep his anger and hatred went, but I knew enough to stay as far away from him as possible."

"I think Bobby had to have been manipulating Dad for a long time. Maybe he never thought he'd kill Mama, just wanted to cause problems for the pleasure of causing problems, but something happened to Daddy and he broke."

She pushed her plate away. "Or maybe I'm just making excuses for him."

"Because he hit Mama."

Her eyes widened. "You knew? You never said anything."

Eyes swimming with grief, Peter nodded. "I knew, but didn't understand. I was seven when she died. I heard fights more than saw. Except the bruises." He took a deep breath. "Mama chose to stay. That makes everything harder to deal with."

A tear slipped down Rowan's face and she wiped it away. "You should have talked to me. Maybe we could have helped each other."

"Maybe we could have, if we were older. And together. But when the O'Briens adopted me and Roger took you in, we didn't see each other and then—time. Time is cruel, Rowan. I've dealt with everything the best way I could, and I'm at peace with it. What else can I do? Except try to help you. But you never let anyone in." Peter looked at John. "At least, you didn't for a long time."

Rowan stole a glance at John. His jaw was tight, posture stiff, but his eyes looked at her with compassion and something more. Something binding. Her heart paused as she realized in that moment that John had grown to be such an important part of her life so quickly, she hadn't seen it happen.

That wasn't an entirely comfortable thought.

"Why didn't the O'Briens adopt Rowan?" John asked, turning from her to Peter.

Peter paused a long time. "It was a difficult time for both of us, I think. They're good people, but two damaged kids would be trying on anyone. Aunt Karen, our mother's sister, refused to take us in. Rowan and I overheard her call us the 'Devil's spawn.' "

Rowan would never forget that. It reminded her always of where she came from. The loins of a devil.

"Our grandparents were old," she said quietly. "We were with them for a week, but—I didn't make it easy."

"Who could blame you?" Peter snapped, rare anger in his voice. "When are you going to stop blaming yourself? What could you have done as a child to stop our father from stabbing our mother to death? What could you have done to protect Dani? You did everything you could. You saved my life."

She stifled a sob, and Peter's hand shot out and squeezed hers. "You have to let the past go."

"I know," she whispered. "But not until Bobby is caught. He's on the loose, killing people to get to me. Please be careful, Peter. If he finds out you're still alive, he'll go after you."

"I'm ready, Rowan. I'm at peace. The question is, are you?"

After Peter left, John escorted Rowan to her room. He had the adjoining suite, and made sure the door was open in case she was in trouble. He doubted Bobby knew where they were, but if he had help or access to airline records—illegally—he might be able to track them down.

John couldn't sleep. He lay on his back and stared at the acoustic hotel ceiling, the dim light from the street casting shadows across his room. He thought about everything Peter had said. Rowan's guilt and frustration. He understood that. He had plenty of guilt and frustration of his own.

He missed Michael. Wednesday was his funeral, and he didn't want to go. He hated funerals. He'd been to too many in his nearly forty years. His mom. His dad. Colleagues. Criminals.

Denny.

He'd already said goodbye to Michael in the morgue—

face-to-face. He closed his eyes and saw his brother's cold, lifeless body in the steel drawer.

But he would go. He had to. For Tess. For Michael.

A faint movement from Rowan's room caught his eye and he silently slid from his bed, gun in hand.

"It's me," Rowan said as she stepped through the doorway. Her long white hair fell down her back and shimmered in the shadows. She wore a long T-shirt that barely touched the top of her thighs, and her long, shapely legs were bare.

He relaxed, put his gun by his side. "Is everything okay?"

She nodded. "I just—Can I sleep with you tonight?"

The words were like a child's, but her voice was husky, sexy. His body instantly responded. "Are you sure?"

She walked over to him, laid a hand on his chest. Her lips were inches from his. "Yes, John. I'm sure."

Rowan hadn't been sure of a lot in her life, especially since she quit the FBI, but right here, right now, she was confident that she needed John. More than a need. A desire deeper than anything she'd felt for a man before.

How could something that felt so powerful, so right, happen so fast?

"Rowan." His voice was dark and shaded with desire. He stood still, trembling slightly beneath her hands spread across his wide, muscular chest.

She couldn't imagine being anywhere but here. *With John.*

She kissed his chest, his heat radiating through her lips, down her throat, to the center of her soul. Her breath hitched as she realized her feelings for John went deeper than she'd thought. She wanted to scream with the injustice of it all—that she very well could die. Or that John could.

Dear God, no. Not John. She'd never be able to live with herself if he died protecting her.

"What's wrong?" he asked as she feathered kisses on his chest, up his shoulder.

He was too perceptive for his own good. She didn't say a word, just continued to kiss him. She didn't want to talk. She just wanted to *feel*.

He stepped back, tilted her chin up with his finger. "Talk to me."

But she couldn't talk about it. Not her fears, not what her heart was clamoring for her to say.

She couldn't say it. Everyone she loved died.

"Make love to me," she said and touched her lips to his.

"Row—"

"Shh," she murmured into his lips, gently pushing him back onto the bed.

He hesitated only a moment before deepening the embrace. Like a switch, he went from soft caresses to hard passion. Her hands roamed the long, firm length of his body. Rowan couldn't touch him enough. As if it were the last time, she needed to touch all of him, from his cropped hair to his broad shoulders to the jagged scar that ran from mid-thigh to his knee.

Her mouth trailed down his chest to his stomach. He quivered, his hands wound tightly in her hair. She kissed his navel, licked him from his hard stomach down to his pelvis, her hands reaching for his long hardness, and taking it into her mouth. He moaned and she drew him in deeper.

Sweat and raw masculine need wafted through her senses. Never had she felt so passionate, so desirable.

"Row-an." He pulled her up and off him, rolled over on top of her. "You're driving me crazy."

He sank into her. His lips onto hers, his tongue dueling. Chest against chest, pelvis against pelvis. He slid comfortably into her, drawing out a long groan from deep in her body.

They quickly found their rhythm. Fast, hard, intense. She couldn't get close enough to him; he pulled her closer, plunging deeper, until they pushed each other into orgasms, clinging and almost frantic. As if it were the last time.

No. It couldn't be the last time. She couldn't lose him now that she'd found someone who fit so well into her tainted and troubled life.

Unless—

She didn't want to think about John's feelings, but she had to. He was comforting her, caring for her, loving her—for tonight. Tonight they had. Tomorrow—maybe. But forever?

She couldn't even imagine forever. There had never been a forever in her life, and it was foolish to think of one with this complex and tough man with the tender soul.

She breathed deeply and tried to roll away from him.

"Not so fast." John cleared his throat. If Rowan thought she was going back to her bed she had another thing coming.

He scrambled to the center of the bed, bringing Rowan with him, covering their naked, sweat-coated bodies with the sheet. He didn't remember ditching his sweats or pulling her nightshirt off. Maybe she had.

He relished the closeness they'd shared, but felt her pull away shortly after, as if closing herself off from the warm afterglow. As if it were just about sex.

It wasn't just about sex. And it hadn't been since the first night they made love. Was it only three days ago?

He kissed her forehead, felt her tense up. "What's wrong?"

"Nothing," she said, much too quickly. She kissed his throat. Already he knew her M.O. She was trying to distract him to avoid talking. Avoid his questions.

Not this time. "Tell me."

She didn't say anything for a long minute. Then, with a voice as soft and quiet as a spring breeze, she whispered, "Everyone I care about dies."

His heart clenched. He wanted desperately to reassure her, but she wouldn't buy it. Not after what she'd been through in her life.

He would have to prove it to her. "Bobby will be caught."

She shrugged into his body, but her skin grew cold to the touch. He'd said the wrong thing. "I'm sorry, Rowan, I—"

"No, you're right. He *will* be caught. It's just a matter of time. And death."

"I won't let anything happen to you. You know that."

She didn't say anything and he forced her to look at him. The tears swimming in her eyes threw him.

He'd never let anything happen to her. He'd die first.

That was the crux of the problem. She knew it.

"You have to let me do my job, Rowan."

She nodded, then turned away. When he pulled her close, spooning her body into his, she didn't resist. Her compliance wasn't a reassurance. If anything, it worried him even more.

CHAPTER
20

The morning of Michael's funeral was overcast, perfect for the mood but unusual for southern California.
One of those odd coincidences that made Rowan think
there might be a God and that sometimes He did care.

Then she remembered that God had been absent
when Michael was murdered.

She stayed in the back of the church during the funeral. Quinn and Colleen flanked her, and several security teams were positioned both within and outside the
church and in Tess's apartment, where the mourners
would gather after.

John sat with his sister in the front pew, his arm
around her small shoulders, his head bent close to hers.

Rowan didn't think Bobby would try anything here.
Not only were there Feds all over, Michael had been a
cop and dozens of uniformed officers were in attendance
to pay their respects.

It was all Rowan could do to keep her emotions under
control. She felt such an outsider.

John gave the eulogy.

"Michael is my brother," he began. "And I love him."

Tears silently streamed down Rowan's face.

"Michael was born a cop. He was a damn good one.
When he left the force to open shop with me, the
L.A.P.D. lost a good man. Honorable and steadfast.

Michael believed in justice and the firm line between right and wrong.

"But the Michael you might not have known was a man I called Mickey, my brother and best friend. He loved to fish and could sit still for hours waiting for a bite. When I'd fidget and break a line in my haste, Mickey would shake his head and say, 'Patience.' He'd laugh because he always caught the biggest fish."

Rowan stayed for John, but didn't hear any more of his stories about Michael. She hated funerals, hated saying goodbye to good people. John's bravery shone through. Standing and speaking about his dead brother must have split his heart.

She had Quinn and Colleen take her back to Malibu as soon as the funeral ended. She caught John's eye as she was leaving and he frowned. She turned away, tears in her eyes. That couldn't be a good sign.

She didn't do relationships well. What was going on between her and John? She had no idea, but deep down sensed it wouldn't last. How could it? John's brother was dead because of her. His sister was in danger because of her. While John made his own decisions regarding the situations he placed himself in, his life was in jeopardy because of her.

Bobby was going to come for her. She had to make sure he hurt no one else.

Bobby MacIntosh looked downright debonair Wednesday night, if he said so himself.

The mirror reflected a tall, sandy-haired cowboy complete with faded jeans, crisp new button-down shirt, and a bolo tie with a turquoise clasp set in silver. Yes, mighty handsome. Reckon on having some fun tonight, he thought with a smile.

He was meeting Sadie in thirty minutes and escorting

her to a lovely dinner, then a little roll in the hay in businessman Rex Barker's hotel room. Sadie wasn't *just* a prostitute. She was a *high-class call girl.* The kind of girl wealthy businessmen took out for dinner and drinks, to business conventions and the theater and art exhibits.

And, when you're smart, you get a referral from a regular customer. Of course, sometimes you have to make it up as you go along. Being an ex-con helped in this case, though Bobby didn't use his real name. He'd called other ex-cons and eventually learned of an escort service that fit his needs. As an added bonus, he used the name of a prominent federal judge as a referral.

Smart, very smart.

He finished preparing his briefcase—a scalpel, medical scissors, garbage bags, scarves, and nipple clasps. My my my, when he'd read how Rowan's villain killed his victims he was shocked that she could come up with something so twisted.

He was giddy with anticipation.

He closed his briefcase and left the hotel room.

Tonight, he'd be on a flight back to Los Angeles. By Friday, Rowan—*Lily*—would be all his.

He couldn't wait to strangle the bitch.

Susannah Darlene Pierce, Sadie to her clients, learned early on to use her looks to get what she wanted. When her stepfather stole her virginity at age fourteen, she could have buried her head in the sand and bemoaned the fates.

Instead, she took matters into her own hands. Starting with her beloved stepfather.

No one knew who set Stuart Price up on embezzlement charges. No one except Sadie, of course. She figured five years in prison and a quarter million in restitution to his clients would buy her the time to get out of the Bible Belt and make it in Hollywood.

She never did make it to Hollywood.

In Dallas, she met Bridget Carter, a beautiful brunette with designer clothes Sadie coveted, a million-dollar house in a ritzy part of town, and the poise of a starlet. Bridget explained Life to Sadie, and Sadie got it.

Control. Power. Security.

Being an escort afforded her control over men she'd always desired but never knew how to get. What did a seventeen-year-old high school dropout from Arkansas know about the power of womanhood? Because that was what being an escort—or call girl, or hooker, or prostitute—meant. Power.

Bridget taught her everything from dressing properly to manners to safety to culture—an escort should know about current events, but always agree with her man. An escort should know all about popular music, art, and theater in order to blend into society. And Sadie ate it up. That's why she was double-majoring in art history and business. Art history for fun, business for—well, business.

At $250 an hour, four hours minimum, Sadie worked only two nights a week and made more money each month than her waitress-mom saw all year. And had her mama stood up for her when she told her about the rape, maybe Sadie would have sent her enough so she wouldn't have to work twelve-hour days, six days a week.

But her mama called her a whore and didn't believe her. So Sadie had no qualms about keeping all her whore-tainted money to herself.

Now, five years later, going to college, escorting old men part-time, and living in a beautiful condo, Sadie had it made. She figured three more years and she'd retire with enough money that she wouldn't have to work if she didn't want to. Bridget, who was over forty, was training her to take over the business, and Sadie thought that might be a fine way to retire. Fifteen percent of her girls' business, taking clients only when she wanted to, living in a mansion and being married to a successful businessman. Yep, what a life!

She normally didn't work Wednesdays, but Bridget had called and said Judge Vernon Watson had recommended her to a friend who was visiting on business and would only be in town tonight. Sadie liked Vern, who paid her $1,500 once a month for nothing more than dinner and a show, then a blow job in his chambers. Because Vern had recommended Mr. Barker, she agreed to work.

Rule Number One: Never let your client know where you live. So Sadie met him in the bar of his hotel, the Adam's Mark, an exclusive hotel near downtown.

She couldn't help but be surprised—Vern was well into his sixties, but his friend was only about forty. And he dressed like a northerner thought a cowboy would dress. But he was pleasant looking—not drop-dead gorgeous, but nice looking—and younger than most of her clients.

She smiled and extended her hand. "Mr. Barker, I'm Sadie Pierce."

He smiled in return, took her hand, and kissed it. "The pleasure's all mine," he said with a slight drawl, though it wasn't a Texas accent.

She didn't think twice as he took her arm and led her to the front of the hotel, where he hailed a taxi.

Conversation at dinner was typical, a little on the quiet side. Barker seemed to be people-watching, noticing everyone who came in. While that would annoy

most dates, it didn't bother Sadie. She, after all, was
paid to cater to his needs.

In the taxi, he said, "I know I promised you a show,
Miss Sadie, but you are just so dang beautiful I was
wondering if you'd mind if we just went back to my
room."

He was actually kind of cute when he asked. As if she
would mind. That was her job, one she performed quite
well.

"Not at all, Mr. Barker."

It was odd how he never told her to call him Rex. All
her dates had her address them by their first name. It
made the men believe she was there because she enjoyed
their company, not because they were paying her. But he
wasn't a regular, and he probably hadn't hired an escort
often.

In his room, she asked to freshen up. "Right through
the bedroom," he told her. "What can I fix you to
drink?"

Rule Number Two: Never drink alcohol while working.

"Perrier or mineral water, whatever you have."

"Wine? Something stronger?"

"Sweetheart, you're man enough to turn me on without an artificial stimulant." Always make them seem
like they are in charge.

He seemed unsure, so she smiled, leaned up, and
kissed him lightly on the lips. "Three minutes and I'll be
ready for whatever you have planned."

He smiled. A trickle of fear slid down her spine. She
blinked, and whatever it was she'd seen or sensed was
gone.

She ignored Rule Number Three: Trust your instincts.

Winking at him, she turned and waltzed into the bathroom.

After taking care of business, she pulled her makeup from her small purse and noticed that the message light was flashing on her phone. Normally she'd ignore her messages while working, but the caller ID showed Bridget's number—three messages, all from her. Sadie hoped nothing was wrong as she punched in her password and listened.

"Please please please, Sadie, get out as soon as you can. I don't trust this guy. I just talked to the judge and he didn't recommend anyone. I'm sorry I didn't check it out first, but I just assumed—it's all my fault. I'm so worried—remember that warning from the cops I told you about?" She paused, breathless. "Just tell him your mother died and you have to go and he'll get a full refund. Okay? Please call me as soon as you can. *Please*."

Sadie's heart beat frantically. She'd never heard Bridget so scared. Bridget, the classiest, calmest, most proper woman she knew.

She glanced at her surroundings. Bathroom. No way out. She was on the edge of panic as she shakingly put her phone back. Would the lie work? She didn't see any other way. She couldn't very well just walk out.

But he'd *lied* about Vern. They'd even talked about the judge over dinner, and Barker made it sound like they were close friends. That really burned Sadie. Some men—like her stepfather and this bastard Barker—thought they could manipulate women into doing what they wanted because women were stupid.

Sadie was anything but stupid.

Temper up, ready to tell *Mr. Barker*—if that was in fact his name—that the gig was up and she was leaving, she swung open the bathroom door and strode across the bedroom into the living room of the suite. "Mr. Barker? I'm sorry, but—"

A big hand clamped down around her mouth and she

struggled. "You were taking a little too long in there," a voice low and rough said in her ear, sounding nothing like the semi-drawl Barker had used earlier.

She struggled, realizing she very well might be in a fight for her life. The warning about some serial killer who might be coming after prostitutes flashed in the back of her mind.

She'd never thought it would happen to her.

Some of her escorts got a little rough, and she had no qualms about using her self-defense skills on them. But this was different. Barker used raw strength to subdue her.

Cold metal brushed against her wrist and she heard a "click" as handcuffs locked into place on one wrist. Her instincts screamed, "No!" She couldn't let him gain control.

She fought back. Drawing on all her self-defense training, she used his strength against him. She kicked back and up, right into his balls, and he screamed. He pushed her down on the floor. As she stumbled, trying to get up, he pounced on her.

"Bitch!" He slapped her.

She struggled and he grabbed her arm with the handcuffs dangling from the wrist. From the corner of her eye she saw the floor lamp. She reached for it—her fingers brushed the base, but she wasn't close enough to grab it.

Remember your training!

Training. Right. She took her free hand and went for his eyes, clawing at the one closest to her hand, grabbing onto the outer lid, and pulled.

He screamed, and released her other arm to hit her. Her head jerked to the side and she instantly knew her nose was broken.

She was scared, but she was also pissed off. He was just like her stepfather. Any woman who didn't fall to her knees and comply with whatever sick game he had in mind was ripe to use as a punching bag.

She wasn't going to die at the hands of some sick bastard who wanted to dominate women. She took her right hand, the one with the cuffs dangling from it, and with all her strength whacked him on the side of the head with the metal. Again. Again.

His cry of rage and pain scared her more than the threat itself. This man was not right in the head. She felt his hands on her throat, his thumbs pressed into her windpipe.

He was going to kill her.

No! She refused to die. She brought her hands up through the V his arms made and reached for his eyes again. She was gasping, her vision began to fade, but she grabbed the small bones on the outside of his eyes and squeezed. She didn't know if the maneuver would work when Mr. Wolfe taught it to her all those years ago, but she felt the bones crack in her fingers and she held on. Barker screamed in pain and let go of her throat, reaching for her hands.

She whipped the handcuff again and it cut his face. His body shifted enough and she kicked and scrambled out from underneath. She didn't worry about her purse. She ran straight for the door, jerked it open, and bolted down the hall. Screams failed to sound from her raw and bruised throat.

She ran to the staircase, unwilling to wait for the elevator. She didn't know if he was chasing her, but she sprinted for her life down ten flights of stairs, not stopping until she burst into the lobby and into the arms of a very surprised hotel assistant manager who just happened to be walking by.

"Good God, ma'am, what happened?"

Her voice raw, blood from her broken nose clogging

her throat, she sputtered, "My. Date. My date tried to kill me." She gave the room number and the assistant manager carried her to the couch in his office while calling security to the room.

And fifteen minutes later, he was the one to tell her the man was gone.

CHAPTER
21

Rowan didn't see John after the funeral. She didn't understand why she felt oddly empty. After all, John had family and friends in from all over the country to pay respects to his brother. And Tess needed comfort and strength, something that John had in abundance.

But at three in the morning when Rowan woke from another nightmare, she wished he were there to hold her.

Foolish, she thought as reached under her pillow for her Glock and sat up in bed. She'd lived with her nightmares on and off for twenty-three years without relying on a man to comfort her. Why now? Why John?

She held the cold gun in her hands and stared into the darkness outside the large picture window. It was a moonless night, but the stars were so bright they seemed touchable.

Bobby, come for me. Please. I need this to be over.

Her inner strength began to melt. The carefully constructed wall that had protected her for so long crumbled at her feet. She was a trapped animal, pacing, pacing, pacing. Waiting for someone to come and shoot her. A mouse being toyed with by a cat. As soon as the mouse lost hope and cowered, the cat killed its prey.

Was that what Bobby was doing? Toying with her until she broke? Playing with her until she screamed with rage or retreated into her mind with insanity?

Did he want to turn her into their father? A hollow shell of a man, a victim of his weak mind and guilty conscience?

What if she didn't give him what he wanted? What if she didn't plead for mercy or beg for death? What if she simply stood there and took whatever he intended to give her?

It wasn't John she thought of just then. It was Michael.

And Doreen and the Harpers and the florist and pretty Melissa Jane Acker.

She wouldn't let Bobby win. Not for herself. For *them*. The victims of his glee, the down payment for his plans. They deserved justice. They deserved peace in the grave.

Peace would only come when Bobby was dead and buried and rotting in hell.

Sleep wasn't going to come, she realized, as she threw back the covers and swung her legs over the side. She slipped into the running shoes that always had a place by the side of her bed and laced them in the dark.

Four in the morning. She couldn't wake Quinn now for a run, but she'd love one as dawn crested over the Malibu mountains and lit the ocean. Five-thirty. Until then, maybe she could get some writing done. It had been weeks since she'd been able to write a word.

She quietly walked down the stairs and let herself into the den. She closed the door and booted her computer.

She wasn't working on a fictional *House of Terror*. At least, she wasn't writing the book she'd started three months ago. She'd realized after Doreen Rodriguez was killed she couldn't write fiction anymore, at least not now. Maybe not ever. Not pretend murders and unreal evil.

But her new work was still called *House of Terror*. And her new work had the same crime.

Only the victims were real, the murderer real, the survivors real.

For the first time, she was writing true crime.

A huge weight lifted from her heart.

It was seven when John knocked on Rowan's door. Quinn Peterson answered immediately, expecting him.

"Collins talk to you?" Peterson asked as he locked the door and reset the alarm, his voice rough from lack of sleep.

"Yep." John glanced around the room, not realizing he was looking for Rowan until he didn't see her. "Where's Rowan?"

Peterson nodded toward the closed den door. "She's been in there since four this morning."

John frowned. He didn't like Rowan's habit of locking herself in her den. "Have you checked on her?"

The agent nodded as he led John into the kitchen. "I was sleeping on the couch and the sound of the computer woke me. She said she was writing and wanted to go running at six. But when I went in then, she hadn't moved and told me to give her ten minutes. But then Roger called, and—" he ended with a shrug.

"You told her?"

"Oh, yeah. She'd strangle me if I kept any news from her. I told her everything we know about Bobby and the woman in Dallas." He handed John a cup of hot, black coffee and refilled his own mug.

"And her reaction?"

"At first angry, then pleased that the woman got away. Almost emboldened. Then she went back to writing."

"I'm going to talk to her." *I need to see her.*

"Did Collins ask you about going to the safe house?"

John nodded. "I agreed."

"Good."

"I don't think Rowan is going to feel the same."

John walked down the hall and stood outside the den. Faintly, he heard fingers tapping on the keyboard in spurts of speed.

He hadn't wanted to agree with Roger Collins's request that he escort Rowan to a safe house while the manhunt for Bobby MacIntosh raged. He wanted—needed—to be there when they caught Bobby. The bastard who'd killed Michael. The bastard who had been tormenting Rowan until she almost broke.

He almost wanted Bobby to break into the house so he had an excuse to kill him.

But he didn't want to endanger Rowan. Keeping her safe had become more important than anything else. Keeping her alive until Bobby was caught or killed, then keeping her by his side. How, he wasn't sure. These feelings were new to him, confusing. Disconcerting.

He couldn't just walk away with a kiss and goodbye.

She had become important to him in a short period of time. If anything happened to her, he'd never forgive himself. He trusted no one else to protect her, no one else to ensure her safety. So he agreed to escort her to the safe house and stay with her until MacIntosh was caught. It was one of the hardest decisions in his life, but he felt it was right. Keep her safe.

After the fiasco in Dallas, MacIntosh would be enraged. More likely to make mistakes. So it was only a matter of time.

The prostitute was under twenty-four-hour protection as well, Collins told John, in case MacIntosh went after her to finish the job. Apparently, she'd taken extensive self-defense training and had been warned by a friend that the man she knew as Rex Barker might be dangerous.

That knowledge probably saved her life.

John stared at the door, dreading talking to Rowan about the safe house, but the clock was ticking. It had to be done. He knocked once on the door and opened it.

Rowan sat at her computer, hands poised above the keyboard as she glanced over her shoulder. She caught his eye, and John saw a side of Rowan he'd never seen. A spark in her eyes, a light in her face—something was different. Maybe it was the slight smile on her lips—was she happy to see him?

He'd missed her. The realization hit him with an almost physical force and he would have taken a step back if he hadn't stopped himself.

Yesterday, he'd seen her in the back of the church and wanted her at his side. For comfort. Had she been with him, the entire day would have been a little easier. But she'd left at the end of the service, and he had too many obligations to follow her.

It left a hole in his heart. Something he desperately wanted to fix now. Seeing her this morning almost made up for being apart the night before.

She'd said something, but he'd missed it.

"I'm sorry, what?" he asked, feeling like a lovestruck teenager.

"Is the girl okay? Sadie Pierce?" Rowan swiveled the chair to look at him. She wore gray sweats and a faded blue T-shirt, her hair pulled back, and she had on no makeup, but Rowan couldn't have looked more appealing to him.

What was wrong with him? He didn't form romantic attachments, especially with women he worked with. Or protected. That wasn't his M.O., and he didn't want to start now.

"She's under protection," he said. "Spent the night in the hospital and was released, minor injuries. She's resilient."

Rowan closed her eyes and smiled. "Good. I can't tell you how happy I am that she got away." She paused, looked pointedly at him. "Roger told you about the medical bag. The book. The book Bobby stole from my shelf."

John nodded. "There's no word on Bobby."

"I'd hoped. Roger pulled out all the stops." Her voice held a tremor.

He shook his head. "The cops are out full-force in Dallas; L.A. transportation hubs are looking for him. It'll be hard for him to get back here undetected."

"But not impossible," she murmured.

"No, not impossible. He's proven to be pretty smart, so unless he does something stupid, he'll be here. For you, Rowan. We have to protect you."

"You are. There are two unmarked sedans on the highway, and Quinn is holed up in my living room. We're ready for him."

"We need to do more."

"What?"

"I spoke with Collins this morning."

Her body stiffened. She was still raw over Roger lying to her. John didn't blame her. He'd had a hard time being civil to Collins over the phone.

"And?"

"He wants you in a safe house."

"No." She crossed her arms as if her answer were final.

"You don't have a choice."

"Like hell I don't!" She tossed her arms into the air and crossed over to the phone, picking it up and pointing it at him. "I will not run away and cower. Bobby's going to come for me now. Good. We're prepared. We'll catch him, and that will be the end of that."

She started punching numbers into the handset. John reached over and tried to pull the phone away, but she karate-chopped his arm.

"Dammit, Rowan," he said, rubbing his wrist. "You know it's for the best. They're going to put a lookalike in the house, set a trap."

"I want to be here. I need to be here!"

"You can't. You're too close to this."

"I'm a trained agent, dammit." She said into the receiver, "Roger, I'm not going to a safe house." She listened, her face registering her anger. "You can't do that!" A moment later, she yelled, "Damn you!" and slammed down the receiver.

She whirled on John, hit him in the chest. "You're in on this!"

"I think it's a good idea."

"Like hell it is! I want to be here when they take him down. I can't believe you'd rather run away."

John steeled his jaw, his anger building. He grabbed her wrists and held them tight, pulling her close. His lips were inches from hers.

"I'm not running away, Rowan," he said, keeping his voice low and calm. "I'm protecting you. Collins put you in protective custody for your own good."

"Don't tell me what's for my own good," she said, her voice vibrating, her eyes dark with pain and anger.

"Look at your behavior right now, Rowan. You've just proven you're too close to the case. Don't do this."

"After everything that's happened, I deserve to *be here*!" Her body shook, her eyes pleading with him.

John didn't disagree with her. How could he? He understood vengeance. Justice. Doing something yourself because he was *your* enemy.

But Bobby MacIntosh had proven to be shrewd. He'd planned four of his murders perfectly. The escape of the last victim was partly his bad luck and partly his choice of Sadie Pierce.

John didn't doubt that MacIntosh had a plan to get Rowan alone and kill her. After hurting her.

He couldn't let that happen. John was confident in his abilities, but more important, he trusted his instincts. MacIntosh would blow up the damned house if he could. Anything to get Rowan. And John wasn't going to lose her.

"Well, you don't have a choice," he told her quietly. "You have one hour to pack your things and then I'm taking you away."

She stared at him with a savage look of betrayal. Why couldn't she understand this was for the best? It wasn't perfect, but it would keep her alive until they caught her brother.

Without another word, she brushed past him and left the room, slamming the door.

What had he expected? That she'd willingly go with him up the coast? Consider it a vacation? That they could take long walks on the beach and make love in front of the fire? They weren't going to some damned lover's nest, it was a safe house. And he wasn't her lover, just an available partner in bed when they both needed someone.

It was best not to think of his time with Rowan as anything else.

He turned to leave, but the glow of the computer screen caught his eye. He crossed over and read what she'd last written.

My idyllic childhood was anything but. I thought, in my young girl's mind, that the love of my mother could keep the monsters at bay. Monsters weren't real, after all.

But we lived with monsters. Not only my brother, whom I had always feared, but a monster masked with the face of a loving father. He never raised his hand to us, his children. But my mother didn't escape his wrath. And now I can't help but ask why. Why did she allow herself to be repeatedly hurt? Did it take her death to end her pain?

And why did no one else see my father's abuse?

It had been a lovely spring day, the white cherry blossoms exploding with life . . .

She was writing an autobiography, John thought, incredulous. He was sure she hadn't considered this before. Because she didn't discuss the past. Now, it seemed, she'd been set free.

He started to have doubts about the safe house. Maybe Collins was wrong and she *could* handle a confrontation with her brother. Then again, her reaction five minutes ago told him she was too close, too emotionally involved to think straight.

Torn, he looked at the closed door. No, he couldn't risk it. He couldn't risk her life.

If he lost Rowan, he didn't think he would recover. He just hoped he wasn't making a huge mistake.

Rowan remained silent on the lengthy drive up the coast, which took longer than it normally would have because John took several precautions to ensure they weren't followed. The safe house was near Cambria, a small town north of Santa Barbara.

Rowan thought it ironic that only a few weeks ago she'd thought about spending some time on California's north coast because it combined the ocean, the woods, and the privacy she craved. The central coast was much the same, and Cambria was an idyllic, quiet vacation community where they would be safe.

Yet she disliked everything about it.

She expected this overprotectiveness from Roger. After all, he'd lied to her from the beginning—in order to protect her. While she despised the lies and the betrayal, at least she understood his motivation. She'd been a different person at ten, barely more than a baby, really. What knight in shining armor wouldn't want to protect a young damsel in distress? And back then, she'd thought of Roger as her rescuer, her white knight.

But she hadn't expected this from John. Of all people, she thought John would understand. He wanted justice for Michael as much as—or even more than—she did. And for all Bobby's other victims.

The sacrifice John had made hit her hard. He'd left to protect *her*. He'd given up his chance to avenge his brother's murder because he wanted to keep *her* safe. She glanced over at him with renewed appreciation. And something deeper. A feeling that had been invading her mind and body since the first night they made love.

John was irrevocably a part of her soul. She couldn't lose him. She'd finally begun to accept and deal with what had happened so many years ago. Losing John was unthinkable.

When it came right down to it, Rowan hated running. It reminded her of the Franklin murders and the lowest point in her life since Dani had been killed.

She didn't have the urge to run anymore. Her demon had a face: Bobby. She wanted to fight him herself. She wanted to see the look on his face when he realized she wasn't the young, weak, frightened little girl he'd confronted twenty-three years ago. Despite her youth she had beaten him then, and surely she could beat him now.

But the opportunity to catch Bobby had been taken away by the erroneous whim of a man who had lied to her and the complicity of a man she had trusted.

It felt wrong, even though she knew it was really their only option. She hadn't done or said anything to make John or Roger believe she was strong enough to handle a confrontation with Bobby. Was she? If Bobby found her, would she be able to fight him and win? Or would she cower in a closet like her younger self, waiting for him, letting him kill those she loved?

She hoped—no, she *believed*—that if Bobby found her, she would rise to the challenge. She wouldn't let him get to her. Couldn't let him defeat her.

But running kept John safe as well. While she had no doubt he was capable of leading an operation while driven by emotion, here in the safe house, he, too, would be protected. The thought gave her a modicum of peace.

"I'm sorry," she said to John when he stopped in front of a locked gate down a private drive.

He turned in the seat to look at her, the engine idling. "You don't have anything to be sorry about."

She shook her head. "Yes, I do. I acted like an immature kid back in Malibu and I sulked all the way here."

"You do have sulking down to an art. I don't think I've ever been around a woman who could be quiet for three hours." He was actually joking. It made her heart a little lighter.

She wrinkled her nose. "Well, I appreciate you coming here with me. Roger would have assigned an agent. You didn't have to do this. You could have stayed back in L.A. Avenged Michael."

John didn't say anything for a long moment, then took her hand and squeezed so tight it almost hurt.

"You mean a lot to me, Rowan. I'm not going to trust your safety to anyone else. Michael is dead." He swallowed, raw pain clouding his eyes. "You are alive. I need you to stay that way."

His voice was full of quiet emotion. He put a hand behind her neck and pulled her face to his, kissing her hard on the lips. Then he stepped from the car to unlock the gate.

She closed her eyes and hoped Bobby was caught fast. Not only because he was a vicious murderer who deserved to be locked up in prison—or worse—for the rest of his life, but because her life was in limbo—professionally and personally—until he was apprehended.

Five minutes later the road dead-ended in front of a cabin. The safe house. It didn't have a view of the ocean, but through the trees, Rowan could hear the distant roar of water breaking against rocks. It didn't sound far away at all. This was exactly the location she had dreamed about.

The cabin itself was open and spacious, with two private bedrooms downstairs and a loft upstairs. Everything else—the living room, dining room, and kitchen—was in the open, one large room with tall windows looking west into the woods and toward the unseen ocean.

It was similar to her cabin in Colorado, just bigger. She felt like she'd come home.

John finished his security check, then brought in their bags. She had packed light: one overnight bag and her laptop. John had two bags as well—one for clothes, one for weapons. She had her Glock and knife on her.

John unloaded his firearms. "I'm going to put this little .45 in the kitchen here on the other side of the bread-box," he said as he crossed into the small kitchen area. "And," he continued as he crossed over to the larger of the two couches, "the nine-millimeter under this cushion." The butt barely jutted out, and you couldn't see it unless you knew it was there.

Rowan nodded. John had his favorite ten-millimeter holstered in the small of his back, and he took the collapsible rifle and another gun into his bedroom, along with extra ammunition.

She watched him walk down the short hall and turn into the bedroom on the right. They were in a fortress, but someone else was taking her place. Someone else was making her kill.

That didn't make her feel any better.

Adam dreamed the same dream again that night.

He'd been having the dream ever since seeing the picture of the man who told him to buy lilies for Rowan. At the flower stand by the ocean he'd thought something was familiar about the stranger, but he didn't know what or why.

It always started with the flowers. Adam wanted to buy roses. The man wanted him to buy lilies.

In the dream Adam said no, Rowan didn't like lilies. She broke lilies and got mad. He didn't want to buy them for her.

"She likes lilies, she just doesn't know it," the man said, his voice sounding odd, through a fog.

Adam shook his head back and forth. Then, as happens in dreams, he was no longer at the flower stand but sitting on Rowan's deck watching the sunset. Rowan was happy and smiling. She was holding a thick green stalk with a white calla lily on the top.

He frowned at her. "You hate lilies."

"No, I just didn't know how pretty they were."

He listened to the waves break and run up the shore. It was soothing.

And then he would wake up and have to go to the bathroom.

He had the dream every night, and sometimes more than once. But he always woke up and felt like he was forgetting something, something very, very important.

"Stupid," he said to himself. "You're just a stupid kid."

CHAPTER
22

Rowan lamented the fact that she wasn't good with relationships. She was angry with John about the safe house, but understood its necessity. She'd tried to explain this in the car, but she hadn't seemed to do a good job.

He'd made no attempt to come to her room last night.

Of course, he was in full protection mode, leaving the cabin every hour to prowl like a cat through the wilderness for ten minutes before coming back.

She'd asked to go with him and he simply said, "No."

But she was going stir-crazy, and it was obvious John was, too. Rowan typed. John paced. Rowan stared out the window. John checked the perimeter. Rowan cleaned the guns. John paced.

Quinn had checked in that morning and said there was no news. Bobby hadn't surfaced, but the decoy was in place.

Finally, Rowan had had enough. "Let's run."

"We can't leave."

"We've been cooped up in this damn cabin for the whole day. We have at least a good hour of daylight left, and running will do us both good. Besides, you're wearing the finish off the poor hardwood floor."

John frowned, obviously debating her suggestion. "All right," he snapped. "We'll go. But I'm in charge."

"Of course you are," Rowan mumbled, irritated.

They changed into sweats and running shoes. It was cooler up the coast in the evening. John had checked out the perimeter—again—and brought a map. The beach was a quarter-mile walk through the woods. He led the way, his whole body tense. Rowan resisted an urge to massage his shoulders; certain they would feel too tight and rock hard.

Not being in the action was hurting him as much as it was her. The sacrifice he'd made to protect her both disturbed and warmed her heart. She didn't want to think he cared. After all, with Michael's death on their conscience and the reality that when this was all over they wouldn't be together, she could hardly afford to think that there was something more than physical desire between them.

Last night, before she'd drifted off to sleep—alone—she couldn't help but think about what might have been. If Michael hadn't been killed. If Bobby weren't after her. If she were certain of her sanity.

John Flynn was a man she could love.

But love wasn't for people like her. John had helped her start putting together the pieces of a life that had been shattered years ago, but now she could do it herself. And in doing it, she acknowledged that she wasn't whole and it would take a lot more than accepting the past and focusing on the future to make her a complete, viable, lovable woman.

She would never forget what John had done for her.

They walked to the shore and stopped at the edge of a cliff. The beach looked clean and unused. Serene. The ocean here was more volatile than at Malibu, the waves crashing hard against the wet, rocky sand, violently claiming the land. They walked along the rim of the cliff until they found a slope easy to scramble down, then without talking they ran.

She breathed in the cold, wet air. The spray from the breaking waves caressed her skin, and the sensation invigorated her. She was alive. Free. Her heart felt lighter somehow, and she owed it to John. He couldn't possibly know or understand the transformation she'd gone through over the past few days. Reliving the murders, feeling Dani in her arms again—even if only in her mind. Her willingness to confront Bobby. All of that, together, freed her soul.

She'd written more in the last two days than she had in months. Seventy pages, and she had more in her.

She felt guilty for her elation. Michael was dead. She wanted vengeance, justice, and for the first time truly believed it would happen. Bobby wouldn't get away with his crimes. He would be punished—both Colorado and California had the death penalty—and he could rot for ten years in a ten-by-ten cell until he finally fried in the electric chair.

For the first time in a long time, she had hope. Not only that justice would be served, but that she would be complete. Healed.

She didn't know the distance they ran, but suspected it was nearly three miles by the time they got back to the ledge they had descended. She started up first, John right behind her. The setting sun caught her eye and she turned.

"John," she said quietly, nodding toward the sky.

He turned and looked. "It's beautiful," he whispered, then looked back at her. "Just like you."

Her breath caught in her throat. "John, I—"

He put his finger to her lips, took her arm, and motioned for her to sit. She did. Together, they watched the sunset. Such a normal thing, really. Why did it feel so odd? So different?

Because she didn't do normal things. She didn't have a normal life. She didn't watch sunsets with handsome men she loved—cared about, she corrected herself.

She wanted to freeze this moment in time, as John wrapped an arm around her, squeezing her close to his side. Sighing, she let her head rest on his shoulder. This quiet affection was something she'd never had, but she could live with it. Forever.

"They're going to catch Bobby," John said quietly as the sun began its descent, seeming to sink into the ocean.

"I know."

"You being here, safe, is the right thing. I know you're torn up about not being in on the op, and I'm sorry I wasn't more—uh, sensitive—about the way I told you."

He was worrying about her feelings when she'd acted so irresponsibly. "No apologies, John. I'm okay."

"Are you?"

"Yes. I am. For the first time in a long time I'm okay."

Acknowledging that she *hadn't* been okay for a long time was the hardest part. But once she'd said it out loud, she felt at peace.

John fidgeted next to her. She glanced over at him. He was frowning slightly, his brows furrowed in some sort of deep thought, and she wondered what was going on in his mind.

She was also curious about what Roger had told her about John's past, the sting operation that had gone bad.

"Roger told me what happened in Baton Rouge."

John tensed next to her. "Did he?"

"Roger was impressed."

"Not many people were."

She sighed, looked at his hand on the ground, and

took it into her own. Rowan surprised herself; she'd never considered herself a comforting sort of person.

"It seems to me," she said after a moment, "that you risked your own life to save your fellow agents. At least, that's how Roger portrayed it."

She paused, glancing at him. "Did that have anything to do with you quitting DEA and going freelance?"

He didn't speak for a long time, only staring out at the setting sun and the vast array of bright colors that shaded the sky. "Someone had to do it."

Rowan had a dozen questions, but remained silent. Momentarily, John spoke, his voice reflective.

"I was in Pomera's inner circle. It took me three years. Three years to gain the trust of his people, to become part of the team. I had to break a lot of rules to get there, doing some things I'm not especially proud of."

"I can imagine."

"Can you?" John said, his voice full of venom. "Look the other way while your *comrades* kill innocent people?"

She knew he wasn't angry at her, but at himself. "We do what we have to do, John. Sometimes the lesser of two evils is the only choice we have."

Silence descended, and as the sun disappeared on the horizon the air grew cooler. Still, they stayed on the edge of the cliff, and John didn't doubt that Rowan understood.

"I could have taken down Pomera then. But that day, in Baton Rouge, the lesser of two evils was letting him go. And we still lost eight men and women." He'd never forget the brief moment of indecision, and the guilt that the two minutes he'd wasted in pursuit of Pomera had been two minutes taken from saving his colleagues.

The guilt had never left him. John would never know if he could have saved more of them.

"Many more lives would have been lost had you not diffused those bombs," Rowan said.

"Maybe fewer would have died had I not debated my duty."

"I don't understand."

"I started to go after Pomera. I could have gotten him, and I went after him. But—"

"But you thought twice and ended up doing the right thing." She squeezed his hand and forced him to look at her.

She hadn't worn her little shaded glasses, and the compassion—and love?—he saw in her stormy blue eyes told him she *did* understand. Some choices were almost impossible to make. Some choices were between wrong and wrong, and there was not a damned thing you could do about it.

Yes, he'd saved lives. But how many lives had been lost because Pomera got away that day? He'd never gotten that close to him before.

Too often, he doubted he'd ever be that close again.

"Yeah, I did the right thing," he said softly. "But I had to quit. There was a mole in the operation, someone my boss trusted, and he protected the bastard. Too many people died, and 'I'm sorry' didn't hold any water with me. I got fed up with the bureaucratic nonsense, the waste, the damn walking on eggshells trying to play by the rules."

They sat in silence, John thinking about the choices he'd had to make. Were they the right ones? He didn't know. But at the time, it was the best he could do.

Much like Rowan's choices.

Rowan wondered about the recent decision John had made.

"John? Are *you* okay? I mean, about not being there to apprehend Bobby?"

He looked at her and his eyes flashed anger and something else, something personal, that warmed her. "You don't even have to ask, Rowan. I wouldn't be anyplace else except here with you. Can't you see that I care about you?"

He didn't give her a chance to respond. He kissed her hard on the lips, a groan escaping his chest. She wrapped her arms around him and in his urgency to get close, they toppled to the ground. His hard weight pinned her down, but she relished the closeness, the desire radiating from him.

Suddenly, he jumped up, pulling her with him.

"We can't do this here," he said, his voice rusty and his eyes dark as he set a vigorous pace back to the cabin.

John was certain about two things. One, that Rowan believed he would walk away when this was over. And two, that he wouldn't allow her to leave him. Somehow, some way, she had to remain in his life.

He didn't quite know how it would work. The next time there was a shot at Pomera, he'd take it. He'd be in South America for as long as it took to get that murderous bastard. It could be months, or years. It wouldn't be fair to ask Rowan to wait for him.

But he wanted her. Now and forever. He couldn't imagine making love to another woman. She'd become a part of him. Through the pain of losing Michael, the betrayal of her guardian, the confrontation with her father, he saw her foundation and it was solid. She was rebuilding her life. He saw it in everything she did. She thought she'd been weak when she quit the FBI, but if anything, it was self-preservation.

Even he had burned out once.

But he'd come back from that defeat to fight again. So would Rowan. Because that was what she did. He wouldn't be surprised if she went back to the FBI when this was all over. Her sense of justice was too important to lock herself away in seclusion, writing. But even if she didn't return, even if she continued her writing career, it wouldn't be from fear. It would be because she wanted to.

And that made all the difference in the world.

So he'd kissed her. But one taste wasn't enough. One taste reminded him of making love to her, of touching her, of holding her lithe body in his arms after sex, both of them satiated.

Not for long. He always wanted more of her.

He couldn't get back to the cabin fast enough, but he had protocol to follow, though that had certainly slipped his mind for the moment he almost made love to her there on the cliff.

"Wait here," he told her as he did a security check around the perimeter.

Surprisingly, when he finished his check he found her waiting right where he'd left her. He almost smiled, but as soon as her eyes narrowed with desire and she took a step toward him, he couldn't wait any longer. He dived in.

Her lips responded to his with passion, spurring him on. Parting for him so he could go deeper. He pulled in her tongue, playing with it, trying to possess her. To bring her closer. To make her truly his. She kept the pace, her arms wrapped around his neck pulling him closer. Her nails squeezed his neck and he shuddered.

He could take her right there, right then. But he didn't. He wanted to do it right. Show her feelings he wasn't ready to express out loud. Show her the depth of his desire, that this wasn't the last time, but the first of many.

That the end was nowhere near.

She reached down and pulled up his shirt, still damp from their run in the cold. He moaned when her fingers kneaded his back and roamed up to his shoulders, never stopping, pulling him in to her.

He whipped off his shirt and tossed it aside. Her hands splayed across his chest, her thumbs making circles over his nipples, sending jolts of energy to his loins. He was already hard and wanted to speed things up, but he stopped himself. He wasn't going to rush this. He took a deep breath and pushed himself off her.

Her skin was flushed and her nipples poked through her damp T-shirt, hard and pointed. He swallowed, bent down, and picked her up. She really didn't weigh much, but she was solid muscle from running. Muscles tense with anticipation as he carried her into his room and laid her on the bed.

She looked at him with eyes so clear and serene, his voice caught in his throat. She trusted him. It was written all over her face, in her expressive eyes, that she'd put her life, her body, in his hands.

That meant more to him than anything she could say because he knew how difficult it was for Rowan to have faith in anyone but herself.

He slid out of his pants and stood naked before her. She watched him, a half-smile on her face. Her perusal was almost as much a turn-on as her touch, and his penis jerked toward her. He reached over, pulling off her T-shirt at the same time she unhooked her bra.

She wasn't large, but her breasts were perfect handfuls, her nipples hard. He took one into his mouth and tasted.

Rowan was in heaven. She'd never imagined that making love could mean so much more than physical release. She had an emotional attachment that heightened every touch, every sensation, every murmur of affection.

She moaned as John sucked her breast, his tongue flicking her nipple already aching with need. She rubbed his shoulders, his head, his arms. She couldn't get enough of him. Last night she had almost gone to his room, but she wasn't sure how he would respond. He was trapped up here as much as she was, though it was by choice.

She'd wanted this, his touch, his kiss, a physical connection that told her she was alive and healthy and whole. But his assault on her senses was more than physical. She felt something else, something possessive and loving.

She didn't dwell on it, because she knew it couldn't last. But for now she could bask in his affection, his touch, his desire.

He switched to her other breast while kneading the first. Hot liquid pooled between her legs. A mere touch would set her off. Something about John's caress, his kiss, his firm and seductive confidence.

She couldn't define the feeling, but deep down she sensed she could give her body to no other man but John. He had claimed her soul when he saved it; it belonged to no other. She didn't realize she was crying until tears pooled in her ears.

John must have sensed something, because he looked at her face. "Rowan? Honey, what's wrong?"

She shook her head. Nothing she could put into words. "Kiss me," she murmured, her voice husky.

But he didn't. He looked down at her with dark green eyes full of desire, of concern, of love.

No. Not love. Everyone she loved died.

"Rowan, I—"

She cut him off by pulling his lips to hers and kissing him hard. She reached down between them and took him in her hand. He felt his pulse throbbing between her fingers. She took her thumb and rubbed his head. He moaned and ground into her as he returned her kiss.

It wasn't just a kiss. Their lips joined in a passionate mating game, mimicking the act of making love they both urgently craved, a ravenous need that would never be completely satiated.

His hands roamed down her bare chest, under the waistband of her sweats, and touched her wetness. She arched her back, wanting him. He broke the kiss and pulled off her sweats. When he kissed her toes she sighed, stifling a moan. When had her feet become so sensual? His hot breath between her toes sent chills down her spine and heightened her desire.

When she didn't think she could stand it anymore, his mouth left her toes and kissed her calves, then under her knees, trailing wet kisses all the way to her clit.

She came as soon as his tongue plunged into her. Her body rocked against him, her hands holding his head, his tongue circling her nub, prolonging her intense pleasure. She'd just begun to come down off the fabulous orgasm when he pulled up and put his hands on either side of her head.

"Oh, John," she said, her voice breathy and not at all sounding like her.

His eyes were dark and heavy-lidded. His face was twisted with restraint. Then, in one swift motion, he plunged deep into her and she cried out. Not from pain, but the exquisite pleasure of taking John completely within her. He stopped, his face clearly showing he was trying to stay in control.

Here, with John, she could be out of control. Out of control in a good way, a way to purge and please, hope and yearn. She reached down and squeezed his firm ass, pushing him even deeper. His face strained and she felt his penis jump inside her, bringing her pleasure again. She felt another spiral begin within her, and he wasn't even moving.

Then he withdrew and plunged again.

Holding back was driving him crazy, but John wanted to prolong the connection he'd made with Rowan. No rushing; he wanted to slowly make love to her, show her his feelings, feelings he struggled to voice, though every time he tried she stopped him.

She couldn't stop this.

He pulled out and plunged again, relishing her tight core that accommodated him perfectly. He felt thicker than he had in a long time, harder than he'd ever remembered being. He squeezed his eyes shut, trying to hold back and keep this union.

But her hands squeezed and touched, pushing him closer, caressing the sensitive skin behind his penis, touching him. He moaned and pushed deeper, felt her writhe beneath him.

He couldn't hold back, didn't want to hold back. He wanted to claim her, bring her to orgasm, share her heat with his own. He pumped into her hard and fast and she panted beneath him, letting herself go, losing control.

With each thrust he ground into her clit and she gasped and pushed into him. She arched up and clutched him with her muscles and came around him. With a final thrust he poured himself into her. He loved the way her body met his, loved the way she kept up with him.

Loved her.

He moaned and collapsed onto her, sweating and completely satiated. He kissed her neck, her shoulders, her ears. Her lips. She held on to him tightly, as if trying to get closer, and he relished their connection. Even though she wouldn't say it, wouldn't let him talk about it, they had bonded so deeply even death couldn't separate them.

Where had that thought come from? He shivered.

Rowan felt John tense after the most incredible sex

she'd ever had. Incredible because she felt something other than the physical act between them, which was glorious. There was something more, something deeper, as if they'd committed to something without speaking.

Then he'd tensed.

"Is something wrong?" Her voice was low, barely a whisper.

He rolled over, pulling her on top of him, and kissed her lightly on the lips. "No," he said and kissed her again. "We fit well together."

She smiled slightly. "Yes, I suppose we do."

"I've never found anyone I, um, fit so well with." John looked at Rowan with questioning eyes and she sucked in her breath. She couldn't miss the double meaning.

"Nor have I," she said quietly, turning her eyes from his.

He forced her to look at him. "Rowan, after—after everything is over, I want to—"

"John, please, let's not—"

He cut her off with a kiss. "Rowan, this isn't going to end. *We* are not going to end. I don't know exactly what's happened, but you are a part of me in a way I can't explain, and I'm not going to let you walk away."

The pain she felt in her heart told her she loved him. She knew because the thought of him dying was the foremost thing on her mind.

Everyone she loved died.

"John, let's talk about this later. After—everything is over."

He stared at her for a long time and she couldn't read his expression. Was he angry? Upset? She didn't want to hurt him, but it would hurt more if she lost him. Yes, she was being selfish. But the great strides she'd made at putting the past behind her would be shattered if she cared too much and the worst happened. No plans for the future, nothing to wrap her heart around, not now. Maybe not ever.

In the back of her mind, a whispered thought murmured *It's too late. You care. You love him.* But she didn't—couldn't—acknowledge it.

"I understand," he said, then kissed her.

She believed he did.

The whore should be dead, but she'd beaten him.

The fucking slut fought like a cat, and Bobby sported two black eyes to prove it. They hurt like hell, and his vision was blurred in his left eye. If he had time—if he hadn't been identified—he would go back and finish the job. He'd beat her to a pulp before slicing her throat and watching her bleed like a stuck pig.

But he couldn't go back to Dallas. He was holed up in some fucking motel in the Arizona desert waiting for dark so he could steal some bitch's car and get back to Los Angeles.

Lily was there. She was waiting for him.

And this time, the little cunt wouldn't survive.

CHAPTER
23

Bobby trained his binoculars on the beach to watch Rowan run with Agent Peterson.

It didn't take long for him to realize they thought he was stupid. The blonde was a fake.

Fools, all of them. They thought they could trick him. Find a Lily lookalike, make him think she was just living her life the same as always. But she'd run, hidden from him, just like when she was a punk kid who irritated him with her narrow-eyed glances and perpetual frown. As if *she* could scare *him*.

Right.

The woman who *looked* like Lily didn't *run* like the bitch. When Lily ran, her arms were bent at perfect ninety-degree angles. Her strides were long, straight, and steady. No hesitation. And she watched directly in front of her.

Even though the fake blonde ran differently, it wasn't until he saw her pause at the end of the beach before turning back toward the house that he realized the woman wasn't his sister.

Lily never stopped. When she reached the end, she turned immediately and ran back, barely slowing her stride.

So he watched closely as she came back up the beach, stared at her face as she walked up the stairs.

She looked like Lily. Same hair. Same height. Same basic facial structure. But she wasn't his stupid sister.

It was in the eyes.

He grabbed his rifle and snapped on the scope. He almost took her out right there, but it would blow his hiding place. While he'd kill the decoy, he'd lose the chance to find Lily.

Lily was too important. She would be begging him to kill her by the time he was through.

He put down the rifle and winced as his fingers brushed against his bruised eye. It had been three days since the stupid whore hurt him, but his left eye still hurt something awful. As soon as he'd served retribution on Lily he'd go back and take care of the whore in Dallas. Wake her up in the middle of the night so she knew he was going to kill her, then slash her throat and watch her bleed to death.

Then he'd take care of his father.

He should have eradicated him all those years ago, cut him up like his mother. And he'd missed the opportunity six months ago when he saw the weak bastard comatose and hollow. Security had been tight, and he didn't want to draw attention to himself.

But he would go back. He'd get rid of the last remnant of his past. Then he would finally be free.

First things first. Lily Pad would die.

So he watched the house all day. And waited. And learned one very important fact.

The bodyguard's brother was nowhere to be seen. Where the bodyguard was, so would be Lily Pad.

He knew exactly how to ferret them out of hiding.

"Are you settled in for the night, Ms. Flynn?"

Tess sighed and tried to smile at the bodyguard John had hired to sit in her living room, but she was too tired.

Ever since Michael had been killed, disturbing dreams interrupted her sleep. She could be in bed for twelve hours, yet wake up as if she hadn't slept a minute.

"Yes, Philip. And I told you to call me Tess."

He shuffled his feet and shrugged. "Right. Tess. I'm going to check the doors and windows and make sure everything's closed up for the night."

"Thanks." She walked down the hall to her bedroom and closed the door. She wasn't used to having another person in the apartment with her, but she did feel better knowing someone was looking out for her.

John had been gone for nearly four days, staying at some safe house outside of Los Angeles. That was all he could tell her. It wasn't enough. She was worried sick over him.

She realized she wasn't cut out for security work. Not the hands-on work she'd thought she wanted when she first began helping Michael and John with their new company. Fieldwork, Michael had called it. Give her a computer and some research and she'd be happy. In fact, Agent Quinn Peterson was working on getting her into a training program for the FBI in their high-tech crimes unit. The opportunity was the only bright spot after two weeks of darkness.

Michael's death had blown a hole in her heart that would never heal. She would live with his absence for the rest of her life. The thought made her weary and sad, adding to her inability to sleep well.

After taking a long, hot bath with lavender oil in a futile effort to relax her muscles, she slid into her pajamas and lay on the bed.

"God, watch out for John, please. I can't lose two brothers." Tears slid down her cheeks and she rolled over on her side.

John had come over before leaving for the safe house

and introduced her to Philip, who'd be watching her along with his relief guy, some ex-Marine named Jim Jones. *If* that was his name. John had some strange friends.

She hadn't wanted him to go. "Can't the FBI take over? I mean, this is their case, isn't it?"

John simply shook his head. "I have a responsibility to protect Rowan."

"Michael's dead because of her!" She knew she'd sounded childish, but she didn't care. She grieved for her brother. If it wasn't for this stupid job he'd still be alive.

"Tess, please don't say that."

She wiped away her tears and glared. "You're sleeping with her, aren't you?"

"I don't want to do this now. We'll talk about it later."

"Which means yes."

"Please, Tess. Drop it for now. I need you to be strong and alert. Don't worry about me."

"I can't help but worry. Some maniac is after Rowan and you'd die for her."

"I have no intention of dying."

"Neither did Michael."

Tess knew she'd hurt John, and she felt bad about it, but there wasn't anything she could do now. She certainly didn't like the idea of John and Rowan Smith being involved. John didn't throw his emotions around lightly.

Tess wasn't sure she could live with that. At the same time, she felt bad that she couldn't just wish her brother happiness and accept Rowan. But how could she? She couldn't imagine sitting across from her at Thanksgiving dinner. What would she say?

Rowan was withdrawn and unsociable, and she had more baggage than anyone Tess knew. While on the one hand she felt sorry for the woman who'd lost her family so brutally and at such a young age, she couldn't imagine having her as a permanent part of her life as John's wife. John needed a nice, well-balanced, understanding woman. Someone more like their mother.

Wife! What was Tess thinking? It couldn't be that serious. Just a physical-attraction kind of thing brought on by danger. She could hope, couldn't she?

She must have dozed off, because suddenly she jumped up and sat on the edge of her bed, her heart pounding.

She'd heard something. But what? And why did it wake her?

Her digital clock blinked on and off. 12:07. That meant the power had gone out and come back on seven minutes ago. Had that woken her? She glanced at her wrist out of habit, but she'd taken off her watch in the bathroom. She had no idea what time it was, but it felt very late. Everything was dark, except for the shadows cast by the light she'd left on in her bathroom.

Scrape.

What was that? Philip?

With shaking hands, she reached for the little gun in her nightstand drawer. She'd never shot anyone before. What if it was Philip? Dear God, she didn't want to accidentally shoot him.

Adrenaline coursed through her body, ringing in her ears, and the gun wavered in her hands.

Her door opened.

"Who's there?" she demanded, her voice quivering. Why couldn't she sound strong?

Whoosh! A sharp pain pierced her shoulder.

I've been shot. Her hands felt numb and she dropped the gun on the carpet. She reached for her shoulder and felt something protruding, but had no idea what she'd been shot with.

"Good evening, Ms. Flynn." The deep, masculine voice chuckled, but her blood ran ice cold. "Or perhaps I should say 'good night.' You'll be taking a little nap for our drive."

"Wha—?" Her voice wasn't cooperating. Now her legs felt numb and she slid off the bed onto the floor, frozen. She was completely paralyzed and at the mercy of this unknown intruder.

"Shh, don't talk." She couldn't see more than his shadow, and her vision began to blur. He moved toward her. "If you cooperate, I promise that if I have to kill you, it'll be painless. But if you give me one ounce of trouble, you'll suffer."

"Y-You."

"How—articulate. Yes, it's me, Bobby MacIntosh. Nice to meet you, Tess Flynn. You're just what I need to get my bitch sister out of hiding."

No! She tried to scream. No sound came out. Her eyelids felt heavy, refused to stay open. Sandbags held down her limbs. Why wouldn't they cooperate? *Move!*

She reached out, her hand feeling disconnected from her body. "Agh." She couldn't talk, her vocal chords thick and not working properly. What was wrong with her?

I don't want to die.

She collapsed in a heap on the floor, and Bobby smiled. That was easy, he thought, as he picked up the unconscious woman and turned to the door.

"Too bad I'll have to kill your other brother, too."

CHAPTER
24

John slammed his cell phone shut. He saw nothing but hot, red anger.

The bastard had Tess.

He stared at the directions he'd written down, but they were already etched in his mind. MacIntosh had contacted Roger Collins to arrange an exchange—Rowan for Tess—and the FBI was planning a sting operation. John feared Tess would be caught in the crossfire.

"John, what happened?" Rowan sounded worried.

"He has Tess."

The color drained from her face as she sank onto the couch. "How?"

"He shot her bodyguard, a guy I was in Delta Force with, and kidnapped her from her damn apartment!" John tried to temper his anger. It wouldn't do Tess any good if he lost control.

"Phil's going to be okay. The bullet missed major arteries, clean exit. The evidence suggests Tess was shot with a tranquilizer and carried from the apartment, between three and three-ten this morning. He cut the power to the entire apartment building to disrupt the security system. He shot Phil through a window with a silenced gun, broke in, and took my sister."

Rowan's mouth dropped open during John's recitation, which he kept even and professional. He had to; otherwise he'd lose his focus.

John took a deep breath but kept his voice steady. "He called Collins and wants to swap you for Tess." He sounded so matter-of-fact, when inside he screamed with rage.

First Michael. Now Tess. He squeezed his eyes shut, held the bridge of his nose. No, no, no. Not Tess. She was alive right now. Dead hostages were no good. He had to make sure she stayed alive.

Rowan jumped up, pulled out her gun, and checked it. "Okay, what's the plan? Who's backing me up, and are you—?"

"Stop. You're not going anywhere."

She stared at him and blinked. "What?"

"You're staying right here. Collins called in a guard, he'll arrive in less than an hour, and then I'm going to—"

"You're leaving me here?"

"I'm not risking your life, too! It's you he wants. You can't be anywhere near the trap."

"You're right about one thing. It's *me* he wants. He's not going to be fooled. He wasn't fooled by the first decoy; what makes you think he'll be fooled with the second?"

"We don't know what he thought of the decoy. He could have planned this all along to lure you out into the open. He wants to get to you through me—through my sister. I won't let him. I can save Tess."

Even as he said it, ice cold fear ran down his spine. Bobby MacIntosh shot Michael in cold blood and John didn't doubt for a minute that he'd kill Tess as soon as her usefulness expired.

"Our number-one goal is to rescue Tess." *If she's still alive.* John pushed all thought from his mind that she could already be dead. "Orders are to shoot at the first clear shot."

Rowan shook her head. "I have to be there," she said firmly.

"Like hell you do!" He crossed to her and grabbed her arms. "I'm not going to lose you too! He'll kill you as soon as he sees you. Then he'll take out everyone else. With you gone, Tess is of no use to him. Right now she's alive because she's a bargaining chip."

"Let me trade myself for her," Rowan said through clenched teeth, determined. "I'm a trained agent. I can protect myself."

John laughed without humor. "I'm not sacrificing you for Tess. Or Tess for you. I'm going to get my sister out alive, and then I'll kill the bastard for touching her."

"He'll know. Trading me is the only chance that everyone will make it out alive."

"Everyone except you!"

"I'm prepared—"

"What? You're prepared to die? Stop it, Rowan! You don't need to sacrifice yourself for anyone. There'll be more than a dozen agents—trained as well as or better than you—who will be around to make sure no one gets hurt. Sometimes, you just have to realize there are people as good as you out there who can do the damn job!"

He hadn't meant to yell at her, but he was so stressed and worried about Tess he couldn't think straight.

Her eyes narrowed and she pulled away from him. "You're wrong. About this, you're wrong."

"You don't have a choice." He worked to control his fear. Scared people made mistakes. He couldn't afford to make any mistakes. Not when the women he loved were in jeopardy.

Tess. And Rowan.

"Rowan," he said, his voice softer, "please don't

make me worry about you. I couldn't bear it if anything happened to you."

She stared at him for a long minute before saying, "And how do you think I'll feel if Bobby kills you? Or Tess?"

There was a knock on the door and they both drew their weapons. John glared at her, and she stepped into the kitchen while he returned the knock.

Knock knock. Pause. Knock. Pause. Knock knock knock.

John opened the door. "Flynn?" the large, beefy man asked, his voice deep and low.

"Yes."

"I'm Reggie Jackman. Collins sent me."

John opened the door all the way and let Jackman in as he holstered his gun. Jackman was a large, broad man who looked like he could break someone's neck without much effort. He extended his hand and John shook it.

"Thanks for coming on short notice."

"No problem."

John glanced at Rowan. He hated to do this, but it had to be done. "Ms. Smith isn't too happy about being kept out of the op. I'd keep a close eye on her."

Rowan's eyes widened in surprise, then narrowed. John had expected her to be pissed off. He didn't expect her to look so betrayed.

But what choice did he have? She was safe here in Cambria. She'd be a sitting duck in L.A. He had to rescue his sister, but he couldn't keep an eye on Rowan at the same time.

Without a word, Rowan left the room, quietly closing the door behind her. It sounded final.

Forgive me, Rowan. It's for the best.

Reggie nodded. "You can count on me. No one gets the drop on me, Mr. Flynn."

John packed his weapons and ten minutes later was ready to go. He started for the door, then stopped.

He dropped his bag and strode to Rowan's room. He didn't knock, just let himself in. She sat in the lone chair in the corner, her laptop on the nightstand she had pulled over and converted into a makeshift desk. But the screen was blank.

When she looked at him, he saw her struggle to control her emotions. Her eyes brimmed with tears, but none fell.

He pulled her out of the chair and kissed her hard, holding her face in his hands. He didn't want to let her go, but he had to. He hoped she understood. And would forgive him.

He looked her in the eyes. "I love you, Rowan. I will return. I promise."

Before she could say anything, he turned and left.

Rowan sank back into the chair, her hand touching her lips. She still felt his kiss and heard his voice.

I love you, Rowan.

She breathed deeply, a hitch in her chest forcing a sob from her lungs. *I love you, too.*

Everyone she loved ended up dead.

She closed her eyes and allowed the tears to fall. Trapped, alone. Stuck in the middle of nowhere with a bodyguard she didn't know, who didn't understand her. John off fighting her battles, his sister held hostage by her sick, twisted brother.

She wouldn't let them die.

It didn't matter what John thought; during the last few weeks Rowan had learned an awful lot about her brother. And she had her memories. Bobby wouldn't be fooled by a decoy. He'd want proof. Certainly Quinn and Roger knew that!

They probably thought they could talk him down. Or find a clean shot. And most of the time, either of those scenarios would work. But Bobby had been planning this for years. He'd been in prison. He probably had skills and ideas they couldn't plan for. Tess was a hostage; he would not give her up.

Roger would understand that. Shoot to kill.

Rowan didn't feel good about this. Something was wrong. Bobby wouldn't walk into that situation without complete confidence he'd be able to walk out—with Rowan.

He wouldn't kill her on sight. No, he wanted to play with her. Torture her. Show her who was boss, who had won, who was going to kill her. Had she been in her house last night, he wouldn't have kidnapped Tess. He would have tried for *her*. The ordeal would be over right now—or just beginning.

She slammed the laptop closed. Damn, she should have been there!

She didn't fear him anymore. Not personally. But she feared what he would do when she didn't show up at the exchange. She wanted no more dead bodies on her conscience.

John had written the directions on a notepad next to the phone. He'd taken only the top sheet. She had one ace up her sleeve, and she was going to use it. *And he told Reggie Jackman to watch me.*

She rose and crossed to her bag. Pulling out her toiletries, she found the bottle of prescription sleeping pills a doctor had given her years ago. She rarely used them, because she feared sleeping too deeply would prevent her from pulling herself from the nightmares that hounded her. But it had become a habit to take them with her, a reminder of her weakness.

Silently, she locked the door. Then, she took out her

knife and cut the pills as best she could, pounding them to dust with the dull end.

She didn't want to hurt poor Reggie Jackman. He was a big guy. Four pills should knock him out.

Roger paced in the Dulles terminal and waited for his flight to be called. His assistant stood several feet away, knowing better than to disturb him when he was in this pensive mood.

Once he landed in Burbank, he'd have six hours to orchestrate the trap. Bobby would be expecting something, so he had to make it *look* like there was nothing to expect. Roger alone would escort the decoy to the meeting place in the middle of a damned field in Ventura. There would be a full SWAT team completely out of sight, arriving on foot in case Bobby was casing the area.

Roger's gut churned knowing that Bobby had Tess Flynn captive. He had no doubt she was alive at this point, but for how long? And in what condition? He should have killed Bobby MacIntosh when he had the opportunity twenty-three years ago. It would have cost him his job, his career, and his family, but the bastard would be dead and all these people wouldn't have suffered. His quiet complicity in their deaths would haunt him to his grave. While he'd never lied to his boss or the government, he'd made several missteps over the last few weeks that could still cost him a reprimand or worse.

He should have checked on Bobby after the first murder, but Roger never thought he could orchestrate such an elaborate, undetected escape.

Rowan might never forgive him for his original lie. She might never forgive him for locking her in a safe house and keeping her out of the action. Had he failed her again? Gracie insisted Rowan would understand over time, but Roger didn't think so. Gracie hadn't seen Rowan, listened to her, talked to her. She didn't know Rowan like he did.

He'd been lying to Rowan since he met her, and now they were both paying the price.

The speaker system buzzed, then a generic female voice announced, "Attention passengers. Flight 337 for Dallas, Burbank, now open for boarding."

"Sir?" His aide, a skinny young guy right out of the academy, approached.

"Five minutes," he said and pulled out his cell phone.

Roger had an idea. He didn't know if it would work, but time was running out. He punched in a number from memory.

"Saint John's, may I help you?"

"I need to talk to Father O'Brien. It's an emergency."

CHAPTER
25

Adam woke up in the middle of the night with a memory within reach, but as soon as he saw his digital clock telling him it was 3:35 A.M., he lost it.

But it was important. He knew it was important, something he had to remember.

For Rowan.

He got up and poured himself a glass of milk. The dream was the same. He was at Rowan's house at sunset watching the pretty colors and listening to the ocean. Something had caught his eye.

Something. But what?

He was determined to remember. He began going over that day in his mind. Over and over, from beginning to end. He'd woken up. Drank milk. Cereal. What kind of cereal? Rice Krispies. He smiled. Snap, crackle, pop!

Don't get off track. You have to remember, Adam!

Cereal. Then cleaning up his dishes. Rowan told him it was important to clean up after yourself. He had watched part of *Attack of the 50-Foot Woman* on DVD before leaving for the studio. He loved that movie.

He'd gone to work. What had he done? Think. Think. He put together the blood packet for the gunfight. It wasn't Rowan's movie, but an action movie, and Barry

was letting him help. Barry said he followed directions
well.

Then why couldn't he remember this thing that he
knew was important? Think, stupid!

He sat and he thought. And when he got to the end of
that day in his mind and it didn't come to him, he
started again.

4:50. And counting.

They grouped at FBI headquarters at three that afternoon. John was beside himself about Tess. Though Collins had spoken to MacIntosh earlier and was able to
talk briefly to Tess, Bobby was too volatile, too violent,
too unpredictable. He could have shot her as soon as
he'd hung up.

But John felt she was still alive. She had to be. It had
been his responsibility to protect his sister, and he had
failed her.

The ground game was set. The SWAT team had already moved into place. Roger would escort the decoy
to the exchange point and Bobby had agreed to bring
Tess with him.

John wanted to drive Roger's car, but Roger tagged
Quinn for the assignment, ordering John to stay at the
command center they'd set up down the road. If anything went wrong . . . Roger didn't need to say more.

Get back to Rowan and hide her.

Nothing would go wrong, John told himself. Not
with Tess in the middle of a hostage situation. Not with
Tess being held by a murderer.

Not with Rowan waiting for him.

Please forgive me for leaving you. It's for your safety.
He hoped Rowan had accepted it by now. Realized it
was for the best.

Even John had his doubts. Were they doing the right

thing in keeping Rowan in the safe house? Was she right about the trap? She was safe now, but for how long? If this went bad, who would protect her?

I love you.

He had a lot of reasons to get out of this alive, not the least of which was saving Tess. But also important was to build on this precarious relationship with Rowan. He didn't want to lose her.

So he sat in the command center a half-mile away with Colleen Thorne, Quinn Peterson's partner, and waited. Two other agents and a pair of SWAT team members hunkered down over communications equipment, but everything was quiet, tension simmering hot and silent beneath the surface.

The exchange point was in the middle of a fallow field outside of Ventura, accessible from all sides. The soil was dry, hard, and lumpy, the landscape impossible to position support troops in. Bobby had insisted that Collins and Rowan drive to the field from the north and when he saw them, he would drive in for the exchange.

The SWAT and FBI teams had changed into dark fatigues, but they couldn't get too close—barely close enough to take a clean shot.

So many things could go wrong. John stood rigid at the edge of the makeshift command center, where he could observe and hear what was said. He was used to being responsible—for himself and his small team of loyalists. He hated not being in control.

Nearly six o'clock. Time for action.

"Has the suspect been identified?" Agent Thorne asked the field.

"Negative," the SWAT commander stated. "Hold on." He listened to someone talking in his earpiece.

John's skin tingled. This was it.

"We have a possible approaching from the northwest. Dark green sedan."

John frowned and glanced at the map. That part of the field was impassable with a car. You'd need a four-wheel drive to get through the rough terrain and irrigation ditches.

"It's not him. The car stopped. A lone driver emerged. Female."

"Tess?" John asked, but doubted Bobby would have let her go.

"Negative." The commander called in for a description. "The female is approximately five foot eight, wearing jeans and beige jacket. Blonde."

Rowan. John slammed his fist on the table. "God-*dammit!*"

Roger Collins called in from the far north of the field. "Eighteen hundred hours," he said. "We're proceeding to the exchange point."

Agent Thorne said, "Sir, we've just identified a lone female on foot approximately half a mile from your location who may be Rowan Smith."

The SWAT commander spoke. "Possible suspect vehicle coming from the southwest. SUV, tinted windows, Arizona plates. Heading straight for the exchange point."

Silence. "Flynn?" Collins's voice commanded.

John didn't need to hear the question. "I'm on my way."

It had taken a lot longer than Rowan anticipated for the drug to affect Reggie Jackman. Reggie drank coffee like water, downing two pots over the course of the night and not sleeping a wink. Finally, she added more powdered sleeping pills directly into the pot. By one that afternoon he was out. By one-fifteen she was on the road in his car, headed down to Ventura County.

She got stuck in afternoon commuter traffic in Santa Barbara and ended up a half-mile or so from the field just before six. She was cutting it close, but she didn't dare park any closer. This was the nearest approach from her direction, but there was no way she'd make it over another irrigation ditch. She'd almost bottomed out on the last one.

She checked her guns and pulled on a lightweight beige windbreaker to better blend into the surroundings. She dreaded the weight of the jacket, however minimal. It was a hot day, and the heat radiating off the dry soil made it seem even hotter, with no breeze carrying in the nearby coolness of the Pacific Ocean. The cloying air sat in her lungs and she breathed through her mouth, tasting dirt.

On foot, she headed to the field, keeping low.

She spotted one of the SWAT teams about a hundred yards west of the field, but couldn't see any other men. That was good. An SUV was already there—Roger. She saw him in the passenger seat. Waiting. Waiting for Bobby.

There was no way Bobby could escape. At least in theory. The whole exchange plan smelled rotten. Bobby wouldn't come here if he thought he couldn't get out. He had a hostage, which increased his chances, but there were likely dozens of men in the area waiting for a clear shot. Bobby had to suspect it.

He had something planned, and she feared for Tess's life.

And John's. She hadn't seen him, but she sensed he was close. Tess was his sister. His responsibility. Just like Dani had been hers.

She'd failed Dani, but she wouldn't fail Tess. John might blame himself, but Rowan knew exactly who was responsible. And she wouldn't be able to live with herself if Tess died.

Keeping low, she scurried closer. To her right, she saw dust being kicked up by another large vehicle.

Bobby had arrived. Her stomach churned uncomfortably at the realization she would soon be face-to-face with her murderous brother, but she pushed on.

Someone had to stop him.

John spotted Rowan lying low on his left at the same time Bobby MacIntosh's SUV came surprisingly close on his right. John hugged the ground, gun in hand, hoping for a clean shot but knowing he couldn't take it without knowing exactly where Tess was.

He caught a glimpse of the driver, and it wasn't Bobby. It was Tess. In the brief moment he saw his sister's drawn face, he realized she was terrified.

Bobby had to be in the passenger seat. He called in the information to headquarters.

"Did you get a visual on the suspect?"

"Negative. Must be in the passenger seat."

"Hold your position."

"Like hell I will," John muttered.

Rowan had already moved much too close to the exchange point for his comfort. He followed parallel to her path. It was difficult to stay near to the ground, but tumbleweeds and low-lying brush obscured him, as well as Rowan.

A hundred yards in front of him, Tess stopped the SUV. John sucked in his breath but felt surprisingly calm. This was an op, after all. Something he was trained for. As long as he could separate his emotions from action, he would be fine.

The passenger door of Roger's SUV opened and the assistant director stepped out, staying behind the door.

He put his cell phone to his ear. Through his ear communicator, John heard the conversation.

And broke out in a cold sweat, even in the dry heat.

"Prompt."

It was Bobby MacIntosh on the phone.

"We're ready."

"So am I. I want to see Lily."

"I want to see Tess Flynn."

"Can't you see her? She drove in."

"I want to make sure she's okay."

Bobby sighed. "What, you don't trust me?" His voice was mocking, overconfident.

"Let me see her."

"Very well." He hung up.

"MacIntosh?" Roger said into the dead receiver. "Shit, where is he?"

A minute later, the driver's door of MacIntosh's silver SUV opened. Tess slowly got out of the car and shut the door behind her.

"No!" John exclaimed, breaking into a run toward her.

"Goddammit," Roger said over the mike. He punched numbers into his cell phone. "Bobby, pick up the damn phone!"

Tess stood next to the car wearing a vest wired with explosives. Even from his distance, John saw her visibly shaking. She made no move toward Roger. He had no doubt Bobby controlled her every move.

He had to get to her. He could disarm any bomb if he had the time. Just a few minutes. That was all he needed.

He scrambled as close as he dared but lost sight of Rowan. His eyes searched for her. Dammit, where was she?

Over the mike, Bobby finally picked up Roger's frantic call. "What fucking game are you playing, Bobby?"

"My, my, losing your cool, Mr. Big Shot." He laughed.

The SWAT commander broke in through the secure channel, where Bobby wouldn't be able to hear. "Another car, a van, has come within the half-mile radius. Lone male driver."

"I'm coming to get my sister," Bobby said. "And if you try to pull a fast one on me, know that there's enough explosive on cute little Ms. Flynn to take out her and everyone else you have hiding within a quarter-mile radius. Of course, that might have something to do with the explosives I packed into the SUV."

"You changed the rules," Roger said, voice low. "This wasn't what we agreed to."

"You're hardly in the position to complain, Roger. Give my sister the keys to your car. Little Tess has the instructions, though I'm sure your wonderfully trained FBI agents have already figured out where I am. Tell them to hold off, or I detonate Ms. Flynn right now."

"Bastard."

"*Tsk, tsk.* You're not in a good mood, are you, Roger? As soon as I have my sister, I'll set the bomb. You'll have ten minutes to disarm it. I'm sure that'll be enough time for a brilliant FBI agent such as yourself."

"But," Bobby continued, his voice low, "if you try to screw me, I'll detonate it immediately. Understand?"

"Yes." Roger's voice was strained.

"Send Lily to me now. If I don't see her in three minutes KA-BOOM."

John realized that Bobby was too far away to see what was going on at the exchange site. He had a chance to get to Tess and start dismantling the bomb. Three minutes? Next to impossible. But he had to try. He didn't believe for a moment that MacIntosh would give them the full ten minutes. He listened as Roger told the commander to clear the area of all personnel, back at least two hundred yards.

Rowan watched John sprint toward Tess, who looked like she wore several pounds of plastic explosive wired into a vest. At the same time, the decoy emerged from the rear passenger door. From a hundred feet away, she could pass for Rowan.

Bobby wouldn't buy it when they were up close and personal. He'd blow up everyone here.

Quinn got out of the driver's side of Roger's car and the decoy started walking toward John and Tess.

Rowan would give anything to know what was going on.

Tess was sobbing silently when John rushed to her side.

"Go away! Go away!" she cried, her face a mask of terror. "He's going to kill us all."

"Shh, Tess, I know what I'm doing." John had dismantled more complicated bombs, but this one could be detonated by remote or misstep. He had to proceed with caution.

"No, no, you can't. Please, go away. Save yourself and everyone else. It's my fault." She was shaking and tears streamed down her face.

"Tess!" He didn't want to yell at her, but if she panicked they would all end up dead. "Look at me." He held her face in his hands.

She did, her green eyes wide with shock and fear.

"I can fix this. But you can't move. You have to remain as still as possible, understand?"

She nodded, almost imperceptibly, but still shook in his hands.

"Th-there's more in the truck," she said, her teeth chattering.

"I know. One thing at a time." He let go of her and pulled his fully loaded Swiss army knife out of his pocket. Not ideal, but it would do. It had to.

"Ms. Flynn?"

John glanced over his shoulder and did a double take. For a brief moment he thought she was Rowan. She wasn't.

"Tess, where does Bobby want her to go?" John asked.

"It won't work. He'll know she's not Rowan and you'll die, John. We'll all die. He'll kill us!" Tess was shouting hysterically.

John slapped her, wincing at the sound his hand made against Tess's cheek. Her head jerked back and her hand came up to her face. "Hey!" she said, frowning.

"Tess, I'm sorry. You have to stay with me here." He started separating the wires so he could see how the bomb was put together.

"I'm Special Agent Francie Blake, Ms. Flynn. I need to know where to go. Now."

Tess pulled a piece of paper out of her pocket and handed it to her. "Be careful. When he realizes you're not Rowan, I don't know what he'll do, but he won't be happy. He knew there was a decoy at her house."

"What?" John asked, pausing briefly in his assessment of the bomb. He resumed.

"He watched the house somehow. Saw her running and he told me he knew she wasn't Rowan. That Rowan had run away. Francie, you can't go. He'll kill you."

"I'm trained, Ms. Flynn." She was reading the note.

John had a bad feeling. He turned on the mike so he could speak to Collins and the rest of the team. "Collins? Tess said MacIntosh knows about the decoy in Malibu. Saw her running."

"That can't be. We had three teams covering the outside of the house, one inside."

"Boat? The cliffs? I don't know." He clipped one wire, bracing himself. Good. The right one.

"How fast can you diffuse the bomb?"

"I think I can get Tess done, but not in three minutes. Correction, ninety seconds. We need that extra ten minutes."

He snipped another wire and swore. There was a fail-safe. He had to start from square one.

"He's not going to give you ten minutes, John. He's not," Tess said. "Go. Please. I—I'll be okay."

John ignored his sister's pleas. "Get out of here, Blake. Stall as best you can. I need at least five minutes for Tess's vest, then we'll run like hell."

"I'm outta here. I'll give you as much time as I can." She sprinted back to Roger's car.

John moved Tess fifty feet from the SUV, but he couldn't work and talk at the same time, so he focused on the bomb. But a familiar voice came through on his mike.

"Roger, I have to go," said Rowan.

"No," Collins said.

John glanced over his shoulder. There she was.

"Dammit, Roger!" Rowan snapped. "When he sees it's not me, he's going to detonate the bomb."

"Blake, go."

A moment later, Roger's SUV passed John, heading southwest across the dry field.

"Roger, he's going to kill her! Call her back."

"Francie Blake is suited up. She's going to buy us time to dismantle the bomb, and then—"

"Get out of here, Rowan," said Roger. "Peterson, get her out of here."

"Let me go, Quinn!"

"Rowan," Collins said, "there's a bomb in that SUV over there. As soon as Ms. Flynn is in the clear, we're all running."

John wanted to wring Rowan's neck for leaving the safe house, but right now he had too much to worry about. Sweat poured off his face as he unscrewed the faceplate of the timer with the tiny screwdriver in his knife. He dropped it to the ground and concentrated on the remote timer.

"John?" Tess asked, her voice high-pitched and soft.

"Two more minutes." He hoped.

"Two minutes?" Collins repeated over the mike.

"I think so. Maybe three."

The next minute passed too quickly, but he made some progress. Collins, Peterson, and Rowan approached and stood a few feet away. He spared a glance at Rowan. She was covered in dust, her face cold and unreadable. Except her eyes.

She was frantic.

"You should have stayed at the safe house," John told her, his voice low and angry. He turned his attention back to the bomb.

"You shouldn't have left me there."

He couldn't rush the procedure, but he worked as fast as possible. Faster than he would have liked.

A shotgun blast resonated through the still air and Tess screamed. It took John a second to realize she hadn't been hit. The blast was too far away.

Agent Blake.

He heard the chirp of a cell phone. It wasn't his.

Roger answered. "MacIntosh?"

"She wasn't Lily. I want to talk to my sister. Now. Ten seconds or I blow the SUV. Nine. Eight. Seven. Six."

Rowan wrestled the phone from Roger's hand.

"Bobby, it's me. Stop the bomb. You don't want to kill me like this, do you?"

"I knew you were there. Sending another woman to die in your place."

"That wasn't my choice."

"Right. We all have choices."

"I'll come."

"No!" John shouted.

"Stop the bomb."

"When I see that it's you."

Rowan mouthed to John. *How much time?*

He held up two fingers, then moved his hand back and forth. *Give or take.*

"Where are you?"

"Follow the car tracks that your fake left. Quarter-mile."

"It'll take me five minutes."

"I'm giving you three. Better run fast, Lily Pad."

He disconnected.

Rowan looked at John and saw the conflict on his face. "You have three minutes, John. That's the best I can do."

"Don't you dare go with him."

"I'll do what I can. But he *will* blow up the car. Run fast."

"Rowan, wait!"

"I can't." She caught his eye. *I love you,* she mouthed. Then Rowan turned and ran.

Bobby kicked the fake Rowan's body. He wasn't positive she was dead, but her face was bleeding and she was definitely unconscious. He raised the shotgun to take another shot when he glanced up.

A lone woman ran toward him. He checked his watch. Two minutes, fifty seconds.

He lowered the shotgun to watch her run, making sure this time that it was his bitch sister. Yes, it was Lily. No doubt about it.

She stopped fifty feet away and stared at him.

"What are you waiting for?" Bobby yelled. He pulled the remote from his pocket. "This?"

He smiled and pressed the button.

An explosion rocked the earth. Wow, he was better than he thought. What an impact! No one within two hundred yards would escape that blast, he thought gleefully.

Lily's screams echoed in his ears, making him smile. She reached into her jacket—did she plan to shoot him? Ha.

Not so fast. He pulled the tranquilizer gun from his pocket and fired. Lily got off a shot, but it missed. He laughed as she crumpled to the ground, the yellow feathers of the tranquilizer dart protruding from her chest.

The game isn't over until you're dead.

CHAPTER
26

John didn't know how long he'd been out, but a group of SWAT members were reviving him with water.

He sat up quickly, his ears ringing. Tess. He looked around and saw her lying more than twenty feet from him. He tried to stand and swore as his stomach threatened to rebel.

"Whoa, Mr. Flynn," a member of the team said. "You were out for a good five minutes."

"Tess."

"She's fine. Possible concussion, and it looks like she broke her arm in the fall, but she'll be fine. An ambulance is on the way."

Rowan. Slowly John stood, gathered his wits, and spotted Roger, who lay several feet away, awake. He approached him. "Rowan."

"We lost them." Roger's face twisted in pain, both physical and emotional.

"*What?*" No, dammit, they couldn't have lost her! He had ached to go after her, but couldn't. He hadn't had a choice.

Tess would be dead right now.

But Rowan could be dead. From what he'd seen and heard about Bobby MacIntosh, her death would be slow and painful. Some twisted sort of retribution.

John's fists clenched.

"In the chaos after the explosion, only one team followed. They got a license plate, ran it, tailed them. Lost them momentarily when he got off the freeway, then found the car ditched."

"Idiots!" John ran a hand through his hair, dirt raining down on him. He didn't care about his filth; he needed to find Rowan.

One of the SWAT team members approached. "Director Collins, you need to lie still."

Collins winced as the cop inspected him.

"What's wrong?" John asked.

"Possible broken vertebrae," the cop said.

"And Quinn Peterson?" John asked.

"Nasty-looking head wound, but he should be fine. Our medics are with him now."

John would never forget the last three minutes before the explosion.

Not being able to follow Rowan killed him inside. His stomach felt ill, hollow. He was lost—the thought of Rowan in the hands of Bobby MacIntosh made him want to hit someone.

Or kill someone. Namely, the bastard who'd taken her.

He remembered it now. Out of the corner of his eye, John had watched Rowan jog away with a glance at her watch. She'd give them the full three minutes. If it didn't take that long to dismantle this device on Tess, then he could follow her.

Quinn Peterson had gone over to look at the explosives on the truck.

"Peterson! Leave them alone, unless you know how to dismantle them," John had called, his voice strained as he unscrewed the final panel.

"No," he'd said, voice as tense as John felt. "Just wanted to verify the explosives."

Good idea. John continued to work on Tess's bomb, relieved that the failsafe was standard. Ninety seconds. Then they'd run.

Only he planned to run after Rowan.

A few seconds later, Peterson swore loudly. "He has an arsenal of explosives in here! It's set on a remote detonator only."

"No time delay?" John asked.

"None."

"He never was going to give us the ten minutes," Tess said, trying to control her sobs. "I told you. Please, John."

"Shush. I'm almost done. Then run as fast as you can."

Two minutes left. John asked Collins to count down every ten seconds. Each interval seemed to go by so slowly he wondered if time had somehow stood still, locking him in this hell of risking Tess's life and fearing Rowan would be shot on sight.

"Ten."

Snip. Five more wires to go. What order? Right, right. Standard. Snip. Four more wires. Separate. Unscrew the switch. Snip. Three more wires.

"Twenty."

Rowan, please be careful. Stay far back. As soon as the three minutes are up, get away. He's going to blow it. No matter what, he's going to blow it and you need to run fast. I know you can do it, John willed.

"Thirty."

Snip. Snip. One more to go, but this was tricky. If he cut the wrong one—no, he knew. It had to be the white one. It was connected—shit, double-check. White, beige, black. Black? No, definitely white. Connected there. Don't snip too close to the switch.

"Forty." Collins called to Peterson. "Quinn! Get back here."

John braced himself. Snip.

Nothing.

"Got it," he said, under his breath. He quickly helped Tess out of the rigged vest and gently dropped it to the ground.

"Fifty," Collins said.

"Peterson!" John yelled. "We're clear. Run." He grabbed Tess. They had one minute, ten seconds, and John sensed Bobby MacIntosh wouldn't give them a second more.

Two hundred yards? No, they wouldn't make two football fields. He hoped a hundred would get them in the clear.

The explosion shook the earth and threw Tess away from him. John felt his feet leave the ground and he was flying. Then everything went black.

He now cleared his mind of the nightmare they'd just lived through and checked his watch, which was surprisingly undamaged. It wasn't even seven.

"I'm going to find Rowan," he said.

"Flynn, be careful. Every available team is looking for her." Roger Collins then talked into his transmitter. "Agent Thorne, are you available?"

"Yes, sir."

"How's Francie? Is she—" Roger swallowed, glanced at John.

"The vest saved her life. She's being looked at by medics and will need minor surgery, but she'll pull through."

"Thank God." Roger drew in a breath. "Thorne, bring a car out here and pick Flynn up. Help him any way you can."

"ETA two minutes. Out."

"Thanks," John said, and meant it.

"Find her. Before Bobby—before he kills her."

"I will."

But he had no idea where to start.

Father Peter O'Brien landed at Burbank Airport after eight that night, having traveled more than ten hours. He hadn't had much opportunity to sleep. On the leg from Boston to Chicago, he sat next to a ninety-year-old widow who asked him to pray the Rosary with her—all twenty decades. Each ten prayers, he asked for Rowan's safety and Bobby's soul.

In Chicago they were delayed three hours because of a security problem. He ate in a café in the airport and was subjected to the ridicule of a young couple who found his Church lacking in many ways. On the connecting flight he sat next to a woman diagnosed with stage-three breast cancer and was humbled by her strength of character and quiet confidence that God would use her doctors to make her well. She wasn't Catholic, but her faith was strong and gave Peter hope.

It was a long trip, and he dozed maybe forty minutes before landing in Burbank. He attempted to contact Roger Collins in Chicago to tell him of the delay, but without success. Once he'd landed, he tried Roger again. Still no answer.

Roger had made it clear that if Peter couldn't reach him, something had gone wrong.

He took out the note he'd jotted down after his conversation with the assistant FBI director last night.

John Flynn, 818-555-0708.

Flynn was protecting Rowan. But since Roger couldn't be reached, Peter feared Rowan was in danger.

He dialed the number. After the third ring he became more worried; then someone picked up the phone.

"Flynn."

"John, it's Peter O'Brien."

"What's wrong?"

"I'm at the Burbank Airport. Roger was supposed to pick me up, but I can't reach him."

There was a pause. "Roger's in the hospital with a broken back. Why are you here?"

Peter crossed himself. "Roger felt I might be helpful in negotiating with Bobby if it came down to that. Bobby doesn't know I'm alive."

"He has Rowan."

"Dear God," Peter said, grabbing the side of the phone booth. "Where?"

"Hell if I know. I'm heading down to FBI headquarters now, but I'll swing by and pick you up. I think Roger may be right. Throw MacIntosh off balance. If we can find him. Meet me outside of the terminal."

Black. Cold. Very, very cold.

Rowan tried to open her eyes but they felt weighted down with wet sand. Even the smallest effort resulted in a massive headache. She tried to take a deep breath, but her chest was constricted. Her numb fingers and toes began to tingle as she tried to move, and the tingle turned to pain.

It was then that she realized she was trussed up like a pig, her arms and legs pulled behind her and tied together. No wonder she ached.

It smelled like vomit. Very likely, she thought, as she remembered the sting of being shot with the tranquilizer dart. Heavy-duty narcotics could make anyone sick. At first she thought the cold was an aftereffect of the tranquilizer, but the floor was cold. The faint hum of an air conditioner ran behind the walls. Someone had turned it on full blast. She involuntarily shivered.

Her mouth was dry and foul tasting, her body racked with pain as she slowly wriggled, trying to loosen the binds. As sensation returned to her fingers, she felt nylon rope. The more she tugged, the tighter the rope became, so she stopped moving.

At least she was alive. Alive and thinking.

Bobby.

When she'd first seen him holding the shotgun, she'd frozen. This was her brother, whom she hadn't seen in over twenty years. He looked completely different. She doubted she'd have recognized him on the street. He was forty-one now, a man. His hair was short, cropped. His face fuller, his body broader. He even seemed taller, which wasn't unusual. Many boys grew well into their late teens and early twenties.

But it was him.

Then he'd pressed a button and her entire life blew up.

John had to be dead. There was no way he could have gotten away so fast. She'd felt the explosion nearly a quarter-mile away.

The guilt hit her first, then a deep, physical sadness that started in her chest and spread out, making her feel more tired, her limbs heavier, her heart weaker.

She hadn't told John she loved him. But she did.

And he went to his grave not knowing how important he'd become to her in such a short time. How she didn't want to say goodbye, that he was now an irrevocable part of her life. Her soul.

Bobby had stolen John from her. Her future, however tentative, was shattered without a thought by the one person who knew how to destroy mercilessly.

She choked out an uncontrolled sob, grief causing her to shake, her heart pounding painfully in her chest. What did she have to live for? The memories of everyone Bobby had killed? Her mother? Her sisters? Michael and Tess?

John.

I love you, Rowan.

Another sob escaped her throat, but turned into a moan. Her cheek rested on a hardwood floor. She listened, waiting for Bobby to come and kill her. She had nothing left to live for. But all she heard was the dull, static noise of the waves crashing against the beach below.

Waves. Ocean. The familiar rhythm was soothing. They were on the coast. She breathed deeply, ignoring the stabbing pain in her chest. The house smelled musty, stale. Closed up. The artificial Lysol smell of unused house.

As the tranquilizer wore off, her eyelids became lighter and she managed to open them. Pitch black. She could see nothing. But it felt like she was in a large room with high ceilings. As her eyes adjusted to the darkness, she saw a faint change in the shades of black. Curtains, drawn over windows. That was the direction of the ocean.

Unused house. The house next door? Could he have been in the vacant house next door to her rental all this time? The property management company aired it out once a week, but other than that, no one would have been around.

If he had been living next door, he'd know the shift changes of the FBI agents. Michael. John. Recognize everyone who visited her. Know how to get to Tess.

He'd been watching her.

He'd seen how his actions affected her. He'd been playing his game, using her. He relished it. The control, the power. How long? Had he been to her cabin in Colorado? Followed her to Malibu? Been to the studio to watch her work?

Had he broken into her house and gone through her clothes? Her computer? Her papers? How close had he been without her knowing it? He'd been in her house to steal the advance copy of her book. When? While she slept? While she was working? While she ran?

The emptiness in her soul slowly filled with red rage, so hot it began to physically warm her. Bobby had been in control all this time. She'd been a pawn, reacting to every one of his moves on the chessboard he'd created. Bobby had won each and every move, except the attack on that brave prostitute in Dallas. Now, he was taking his final turn.

She would stop him.

She had to find a way to take him down with her. He wasn't going to kill her outright. If he were, he'd have done so already. He would have killed her with a bullet in the back instead of drugging her. Because of that, because of his propensity to play with her mind, she had a chance.

Her survival meant nothing to her anymore. But her death would mean something if she dragged Bobby down to hell with her.

Footsteps on hardwood. Stairs. He was coming upstairs toward her. *Tap. Tap. Tap. Tap.* Closer, heavier. Pause. Rattle. He was behind her. A lock turned and she strained to face him, but couldn't. The door creaked.

Her heart beat so loudly it drowned out her thoughts. She broke out in a sweat despite the too-cold air conditioning.

Lights blazed and she squeezed her eyes shut, but not before pain shot through her head at the sudden brightness.

"Hello, Lily. I know you're awake."

She heard her brother cross the floor toward her.

Bobby grabbed her hair in his hand and yanked. She tried to open her eyes, but the light blinded her.

He laughed, dropping her head. He untied her, pulling hard on the ropes in the process, but she refused to cry out. She wouldn't give him the satisfaction of breaking her. When her limbs were free, the blood rushed to her hands and feet in a painful flood. She tried to get up but failed, collapsed, breathing heavily.

"I'll let you pull yourself together, Lily Pad. It really wouldn't be that much fun to kill you now when you don't even have a chance." His voice was older, but still held the singsong taunting of his youth.

"I. Will. Kill you." Rowan's uneven breath sputtered a curse.

He laughed again. "Hope. Enjoy it while you still have some. I have . . . things to get ready for you down-stairs. So just relax while you can."

She heard him cross the floor and close the door be-hind him. The lock turned. He'd left the light on and she slowly opened her eyes. She was in the middle of a large bedroom. Though her vision was blurred, she made out the bottom of a bed, a pale blue dust ruffle ten feet away.

Gradually, she pulled herself on all fours, ignoring the ache in her chest, the throbbing of her shoulder from where the dart had hit her, the hot, painful tingling in her hands and feet. She remained in that position for quite some time, until the nausea passed and she could sit up.

Her vision cleared, and it looked as if someone were lying in the bed. Who? The owners of the house only stayed in the late summer and fall. Someone would have noticed if anyone from the property management com-pany were missing.

She pushed herself up, ignoring the woozy sensation, a leftover from the narcotics. "Hello?" Her voice came out a croak and she cleared her throat.

She looked. Lying on top of the covers was a fifty-something woman. Her vacant eyes stared directly at Rowan, locked in terror. Small flies buzzed around her face. There was a single bullet hole in her forehead.

The pillow was stained dark red. Dried blood. But this woman had been awake when she died. She'd known her fate, her eyes reflecting her fear. Even as Rowan turned away, she knew who the woman was. She and John had seen her picture in the news while at the safe house in Cambria. She'd been driving from the hospital after visiting her first-born granddaughter somewhere in Arizona when she disappeared. Rowan hadn't thought anything of it at the time, but like any good FBI agent, she made a mental note of her photograph.

Arizona, on the way from Texas to California.

She screamed.

On the other side of the door, Bobby laughed.

Adam dreamed.

He was driving Barry's truck. He stopped at the flower stand and the man with money was there. But he saw him now like the picture. The picture John had shown him. Blond hair, blue eyes. But they weren't nice eyes. They were cold. Blue and cold.

"She likes lilies."

Adam shook his head. "No. No, she hates lilies. She broke the vase last time."

"Trust me."

"No, I want to buy roses. White roses."

And he did. But when he turned into Rowan's driveway, he wasn't driving Barry's truck and he didn't have white roses.

He was in Rowan's car and he had lilies. He hid them behind his back so she couldn't see them.

"I can't believe you've never seen the sunset over the ocean," Rowan told him as she unlocked her door. Adam followed her to the deck, and at first he was a little scared. The ocean looked awfully big. He couldn't swim.

"Do you want some cookies?"

He nodded and smiled, and Rowan went back inside.

He stared at the ocean, scared and in awe at the same time. He had never seen anything like it before. He'd seen it in the movies, of course, but nothing like this. He stood on the edge of the world, and that felt powerful.

Something burned his eyes, like a reflection. He turned in the direction it came from. The house next to Rowan's. He looked up at the second-floor windows, and the drapes fluttered.

He saw him. The money man.

Rowan cowered in the corner for several minutes before gathering her courage. The shock of seeing the dead grandmother had worn off and the viciousness of Bobby's crimes hit her.

Someone had to fight for the victims.

How many innocent people had Bobby killed, all because he wanted to torment her? All because she was the one who got away?

"I will kill you, Bobby MacIntosh," she said out loud to no one, except the dead.

She searched for anything that could be used as a weapon. Anything. But there was nothing. Bobby had stripped the room. There wasn't even bathroom cleaner remaining in the cabinets, a razor blade stuck between drawers, or a wire coat hanger hanging in the closet. There was nothing.

She would have to rely on her own strength and training. She positioned herself inside the door and listened. Waited.

John slammed his fist on the table in the FBI conference room. It was after midnight and they had nothing.

A madman had Rowan somewhere, and John had no idea where to start looking. It was as if they'd disappeared off the face of the earth.

Peter O'Brien sat at a desk, quiet and solemn. John almost forgot he was in the room until he said, "Rowan is strong. She's not going to give up."

"He's been tormenting her. Sending her proof of his crimes. Mementoes," he said bitterly.

"But she didn't break." Peter paused. "Four years ago, when she left the FBI, she thought she was losing her mind like our father and that solitude was the only way to keep her sanity. I tried to explain that she was stronger than she thought, that knowing she needed time away proved she was saner than most people." He shook his head. "Rowan didn't understand."

John caught Peter's eye. "I think she understands now. But MacIntosh is a violent killer. Smart. Shrewd." He sank into a chair and leaned forward, helpless. He banged his head against the polished surface of the conference table, trying to figure out where he'd gone wrong.

"I should have brought her with me," John said. "I should have known she wouldn't stay put."

Peter nodded. "Rowan doesn't like people to fight her battles. But she sure takes them on for others."

John leaned back in his chair and looked at him. "What did you know back then? Did you know your brother was so twisted?"

Peter frowned and closed his eyes. "Bobby took pleasure in tormenting the women in the house. And me, but mostly the girls. He called our mother a whore. Accused her of sleeping with the neighbors, Dad's boss, anyone. She would turn away and cry, but never correct him. Never punish him. She probably couldn't.

"She loved us, but worshipped our father." Peter paused. "Dad hit her. I didn't see it happen more than twice, but I saw the aftermath many times. He was always so sorry afterward, and she never said anything about it.

"But once I heard Bobby yell at Dad to stop apologizing. Saying she deserved it. Dad hit him, and Bobby left for days. Though my mother was worried about him, it was like a dark cloud had been lifted from the house. We all breathed a little easier.

"Then he came back. And it got worse."

Peter opened his eyes and looked at John. "I've counseled women in abusive situations. I've explained to them that just because their husband is head of the house doesn't mean he can hurt them. I've helped several women leave their husbands and find help. I hate splitting up the family, but I know if they didn't leave, they could end up just like my mother. Dead. Their innocent children orphans. Or worse. When they leave, they leave for their kids. Not for themselves. Somehow, deep down, they think they deserve the abuse. Or that their husband will change. Or they believe he's truly sorry.

"In all the years and the families I've counseled, dozens of them in abusive situations, only one husband has ever repented and gotten beyond his violence." Peter sighed, sounding weary. "The statistics aren't promising."

"How do you do it? How do you face those women and not relive what happened to your family?"

"Remembering what happened to my family propels me forward. It's what drives Rowan, though she buries her feelings. I'm hurt and angry, but I can help other families escape the violence. Rowan's hurt and angry, so decided to fight for families who never escaped. The victims. The difference is she never understood why she did what she did. When she saw the family in Tennessee, the hard reality of her life overwhelmed her and she quit. To survive."

John mulled over everything Peter had said. He had an uncanny way of pegging things just right. He understood Rowan, her motivation and her conflicts. Yet

Rowan admittedly kept her brother at arm's length. Why? Because Peter reminded her of the past? Or because he knew her so well?

He was about to ask how often they spoke when his phone rang. He grabbed it immediately. "Flynn."

Silence on the other end.

"Rowan?" he asked, jumping out of his chair, hopeful.

"N-no," a small voice said. "It-it's Adam."

"Adam?" John sank into his chair, his brow furrowed. "What's wrong?"

"You gave me your number. Is-is it okay to call?"

"Of course. Of course you can call me anytime. Are you okay? Did something happen?"

"I remembered something."

John stiffened, fully alert. "What? What did you remember?"

"I told you the man at the flowers looked familiar, right?"

"Yes."

"I've been having this dream. Over and over. But I didn't know why. Until tonight. See, I thought all day about the first time Rowan took me to her house. We watched the sunset together. I'd never seen one before, and she—"

"Adam," John interrupted, trying to keep the frustration from his voice, "where did you see the man?"

Adam paused, and John feared he'd scared him.

"Please, Adam," he said, forcing himself to remain calm. "This is very important. Where did you see the man?"

"The window. In the window of the house next to Rowan's."

CHAPTER
28

"Haven't you ever wanted to kill someone? Just for the sheer pleasure of it?"

Bobby stared at Rowan with a sparkle in his cold blue eyes.

She was tied to a chair in the dining room and Bobby sat at the head of the table, drinking Scotch and holding a gun on her.

She'd lost the battle.

He'd anticipated that she would attack him and was prepared. She couldn't even land a single blow. He'd come in low and spun around, grabbing her.

She'd been too emotional, too unfocused.

She wouldn't make the same mistake next time. If there was a next time.

"Well?" he prodded, swirling his Scotch, the ice rattling around in the glass, much in the same manner as it had in their father's years ago.

"I saw him," she said.

"Who?"

"Daddy."

Bobby scowled, his face full of contempt. "Weak fool! He couldn't stomach that the bitch was finally dead. He was pussy-whipped. Nothing like the man I thought he was."

Rowan worked to control her expression. She could not allow Bobby to bait her if she hoped to defeat him.

Sitting here in the formal dining room, at a highly polished and rarely used table, with her lunatic brother felt surreal. She reminded herself Bobby *wasn't* a lunatic. He was a coldblooded killer who'd planned vicious, brutal crimes and followed through with precision.

And he was her brother. They'd been born to the same parents, had been raised in the same house. They'd both witnessed their father's abuse of their mother, but Bobby enjoyed it. Relished it. She abhorred it.

Had Bobby been born evil? Or had he watched their father's extreme mood swings and been affected? Did he have a twisted gene that turned evil when he witnessed it? Or did the circumstances of their upbringing turn him into a killer and her into a cop?

She reminded herself that she wasn't a cop anymore. And if she had any control over it, Bobby's killing spree would end here, tonight.

"Daddy spoke to me," Rowan said.

"Dad? Bullshit." Bobby laughed, shaking his head.

"He called me Beth."

"He's lost his fucking mind. I saw him, too. Stupid fuck. His mind's gone, he lost it twenty-three years ago. He could have pled temporary insanity. Bet some bleeding-heart jury would have bought it. But he's fucking insane."

"You're not," Rowan said.

"Damn straight I'm not." He slammed his glass down on the table. "I think you're playing me. The fucker didn't say a word."

Rowan would never forget what her father had said when he thought she was her mother. *Bobby saw you with him again. I told you to stay away from him, but you didn't.*

"You told him that you saw Mom with another man. Not for the first time."

His brows furrowed and he looked pissed. "I don't know how you know that, but it didn't come from *him*. He was as crazy as a loon when I saw him."

"When you saw him, you told him I was as good as dead."

"And you will be soon." Now Bobby looked more than a little pissed off. His blue eyes took on a violent darkness. Rowan wondered if he'd tried to bait their father into talking and failed. The fact that their father spoke to *her* must irritate him.

"Yes," she said a moment later.

Bobby narrowed his eyes. "Yes? What the fuck does that mean?"

"You asked if I ever wanted to kill someone for the sheer pleasure of it. Yes." Rowan glared at him, trying to keep her emotions under control. She wanted to scream and rage and tear at these binds, but knew that was what he wanted.

"I would get intense pleasure killing *you*, you bastard."

He reached over and slapped her, knocking her over. She struggled, tied to the chair. The coppery flavor of her own blood poured into her mouth and she swallowed, gagging.

Bobby laughed. "Such spunk. You were always a brat. But you were scared of me. I knew it. You're scared of me now. I see it. And you will die." He stood and stared down at her, his cold blue eyes vindictive. "But you will beg for mercy before I'm done." He kicked her and walked away.

She closed her eyes and took deep breaths. It hurt, but there was no real damage. She needed to loosen the ropes, break free when he least expected it. But she had no intention of escaping.

Not until she killed him.

She wished she knew his plan. She thought he'd just use her as a punching bag. Literally beat her to death. She wouldn't break. She'd been trained to withstand torture. To retreat into her mind, force herself to think of something other than the situation.

But Bobby wanted to break her. He'd started by sending her the funeral wreath, the hair, the lilies. He fully intended to kill her, but first he wanted her fear. Her tears. She mentally prepared herself for the worst.

She had no idea.

He came back, untied her from the chair, hoisted her up, and half-carried, half-dragged her to the living room. He tossed her onto the couch and righted her so she sat up as straight as possible. She felt the ropes on her wrists loosen. Just enough to give her hope that she could manipulate the binds and free herself.

"This is your life, Lily bitch." He sat down in a recliner and turned the television on with the remote control.

It was one of those large-screen televisions, fifty or so inches across. When the screen lit, Rowan was staring at a wedding picture.

Her parents.

"Robert MacIntosh married Elizabeth Pierson on June first," Bobby said, his voice singsong, mocking. "Typical spring wedding for a boring couple. He had a future, could have gone places and done things with his life, but the bitch kept him tied to home with a bunch of brats."

Bobby glanced at her. "You all should have been killed. Six fucking kids. What were they thinking? The house was a fucking zoo all the time. If I didn't keep you all in line, there'd never be any peace and quiet." He paused, a gleam in his eye as he glared at Rowan. "But I know why. She did it to keep Daddy with her. Got herself pregnant every time he had a thought of leaving the whore."

Rowan was careful to show no reaction. She wouldn't allow Bobby's words to affect her. She looked at her parents on the screen. Her father's dark hair and brilliant blue eyes. Her mother's fair skin and white-blonde hair.

It was like looking at herself.

They looked happy. At least when they first got married. You saw it in their eyes, in the way her father beamed at her mother, in her mother's half-smile, half-laugh, caught forever in time.

What had happened? Had her father started hitting her mother after they were married? After they had children? When did the abuse start, and why did her mother stay with him for so long?

"Did you know the bitch was pregnant when they got married?" Bobby said, his voice spitting out venom that made Rowan unconsciously shiver. "She got herself pregnant, trapped him into marriage. I was born in November. June, November. Hmmm. All their hypocrisy. Church on Sundays, no swearing, no fun. Yet they were out screwing around. Good enough for them, wasn't it?"

Rowan didn't think the hypocrisy had anything to do with church or swearing. It had to do with her parent's relationship. With her father hitting her mother and her allowing it. With her accepting all his apologies. With their all going to church as a family and pretending they were normal.

They were anything but normal.

Rowan hadn't realized the image on the video was paused until Bobby pressed "play" and the image switched to a baby. He paused it again.

"Me," he said, with both disdain and pride in his voice. "The only MacIntosh worthy of being born. The bitch should have had her fucking tubes tied, but no, she couldn't keep Daddy trapped if she couldn't get herself knocked up."

The baby was beautiful. Bald, with startling blue eyes. Round and chubby. Bobby sat in a little baby chair in front of a Christmas tree, about a month old. He could have been the Gerber baby.

Bobby. How could a beautiful, innocent little baby turn into a monster? Rowan closed her eyes.

"Open your eyes!"

She felt the sharp sting of something on her face. Tears sprung to her eyes at the sudden, unexpected pain, but she swallowed them. She glared at Bobby. He had a whip in his hand.

"Don't close them again. You don't want to know what I'll do."

"You can torture me, but I won't break," she said through clenched teeth, anger seething beneath the surface.

"We'll see." He grinned.

The videotape started rolling again. The baby picture stayed on for another minute, before switching to a picture of Bobby, Melanie, and Rachel. A portrait, taken at the shopping mall. Bobby was three or four, Melanie a year younger, and Rachel a baby.

They were three beautiful children, Bobby fair, Mel and Rachel dark-haired like their father. Young, happy children.

Bobby didn't look cruel. But was any four-year-old capable of knowing he was going to grow up and kill his family? Kill innocent human beings in his warped sense of vengeance and revenge?

Bobby didn't pause the pictures. Several snapshots of

the three oldest MacIntosh children rolled across the screen. At birthday parties. At Christmas and Easter and wearing their Sunday best. Playing in the yard, in the park, having a tea party in the backyard.

Rowan searched Bobby's eyes for the turning point, when he had changed from a happy little boy to a murderous thug who terrorized his younger siblings.

Then she saw it. Not in Bobby, but in Melanie and Rachel.

They were young girls, four and six or so, and Rowan saw *their* eyes change. Bobby's didn't. Bobby looked the same. But one snapshot of Rachel showed fear as she glanced at him, the photograph preserving her emotion for all time. Another showed Mel hugging Rachel. It could have been the sweet scene of two sisters embracing; instead, Rowan saw anger in Mel's eyes and tears in Rachel's.

Had their mother known? Had she known what Bobby did to her other children? She would have had to, Rowan thought. Rowan remembered many times when her mother had told her to take Peter outside, away from Bobby. All the times Mel had taken them for ice cream. The sullen look in Rachel's eyes whenever Bobby had been in the same room.

Her mother had known. Yet she kept them all in that house. Knowing Bobby terrorized them. Taking the abuse of her husband yet welcoming him in her bed. Rowan would never understand her mother. She couldn't hate her, though she wanted to. After all, she was dead. Murdered by her abusive husband.

They were all dead.

Except Bobby and her. And Peter, Rowan thought gratefully. Peter was safe in Boston.

If Rowan died at Bobby's hands, she would die knowing Bobby hadn't won. Peter was alive. And because Bobby thought he was dead, he was safe.

The images started flashing by rapidly, pictures of Mel and Rachel and Mama. Where had they come from? As she watched, she realized that the same ten or so pictures repeated. Over and over. They looked familiar to her, but why?

Her photo album. He'd found her cabin in Colorado and stole the one thing she had left of her family.

Suddenly it stopped on Mama's bloody body.

Rowan screamed, then closed her eyes.

Bobby whipped her across the neck and she winced. "Open them!"

"Go ahead, whip me to death! I don't care!" She tried to control her pain and anger but couldn't.

"Open them, or your lover will be next."

Her eyes shot open and she glared at him. "I don't know what you're talking about."

Though Bobby didn't know it, John was dead. He'd never have left Tess.

She quickly blinked back her tears. She couldn't think about John now. She wouldn't be able to focus on what she needed to do.

Bobby leaned back, smirking, tucking the whip into his lap. "Yes you do. Watch."

Stone-faced, preparing herself for more bloody images of the family she loved, she stared at the television.

Music started. Loud, surrounding her through speakers in all corners of the room. Some unidentifiable rap tune with verses that highlighted the word "kill" and a beat she felt in her gut. She wanted to vomit.

Mama's picture was in black and white. The shades of gray did nothing to mask the terror of the scene. The blood almost black against the pale gray of the linoleum, arcs and splatters across the too-white cabinets, the stark lighting giving everything an unreal feel, like a bad B-movie.

Mama was followed by a picture of her father taken recently. His dark hair gray, his eyes vacant, empty, hollow. *Bobby must have taken it when he visited Daddy.* He looked just like Rowan remembered seeing him last week.

Then Mel and Rachel, together, smiling. Then lying dead and bloody in the foyer.

Kill, kill, kill the bitch!

Rowan shivered at the lyrics, wondering how Bobby had obtained the crime-scene photos. She almost laughed out loud. She could hardly believe he'd escaped from prison and had found a fool to replace him. Stealing crime photos would be child's play.

Peter at five, his kindergarten photo. Then Peter dead.

No, not dead, Rowan reminded herself. He wasn't dead.

There was a photo of a cop carrying Peter out of the house. Peter wore his dinosaur pajamas and they were covered in blood. It was Dani's blood, not his. *Dani's blood.* But Peter's eyes were closed and his mouth was open and he appeared lifeless.

The image changed to Dani. *Dani.* A whimper escaped her throat but she forced herself to look. Beautiful Dani as a baby. As a toddler. At three, playing tea with her stuffed animals.

Then the small body bag. Somehow, the black bag was worse than seeing her dead again. So generic, so sterile.

Rowan didn't know she was crying until her cheeks felt hot and damp.

Her tormentor grunted. "I never understood why you liked that little crybaby so much. Oh, well, she's dead and buried, isn't she? You couldn't protect her. What'd you do? Put her body in front of yours? So she'd die in your place?" Bobby barked out a laugh, and Rowan wanted to strangle him with her bare hands. She had never hated anyone so much in her life. Black fury burned as she steadily worked on the ropes that bound her, careful not to let him see what she was doing.

The music changed to the Beatles' "Paperback Writer," the upbeat tune paradoxical to the gruesome photos that followed.

A bloody body massacred, cut into bits, lying in a Dumpster. It took Rowan a moment to realize this was Doreen Rodriguez. Bobby had taken pictures of his crimes. Bile rose in her throat and she swallowed it back.

The florist, stabbed to death, pretty blonde hair matted with blood.

The Harpers. The little girl while she still had her pigtails. The mom staring dead into the camera.

Pretty Melissa Jane Acker, raped, strangled, her body left spread-eagled in the signature style of Rowan's fictional killer in *Crime of Corruption*.

"You're sick," she muttered.

Bobby laughed, and her fingers continued working on the ropes. Were they looser? She thought so. Her fingernails were raw and wet with her blood as they broke in her quiet fury.

Then she stopped.

Michael.

He was half lying, half sitting against the wall in what she presumed was his apartment, his chest a bloody mess, his eyes unfocused. Dying.

A sob escaped her throat and Bobby said, "I thought you were screwing him. But you're the ice princess." His tone was mocking. "Ice cold, no feeling. The press didn't like you. I don't think you've made any friends now, have you?"

Michael. He didn't deserve this. None of them did. "You fucking bastard," she whispered. "I'll kill you!"

The whip stung the back of her neck again and she felt warm blood ooze down her back.

"You're hardly in a position to threaten me, Lily Pad."

The videotape rolled. Images of Tess. John. Roger. Herself. Many taken from the vacant house next to hers. Roger in Washington. Tess going into her apartment.

He paused it.

"Well, she's in a bazillion pieces, or burned to a crisp. Either way, your lover's sister is dead. Along with Roger Collins. Asshole. He deserved it. His fucking mocking attitude, thinking he was so much better than me. Well, I showed him, didn't I? Didn't I?" Bobby lashed out with the whip again, this one cutting across her arm.

"Yes, you sure did." *Oh, Roger! I'm so sorry.*

"I was going to get his stupid wife, but didn't have the chance. Now it won't be any fun to knock her off. So, I guess she's going to live." He sounded almost sad.

"You *are* sick," she said quietly. That they shared the same parents, the same blood, made her nauseous.

"No, Lily Pad, I'm not sick." He paused the videotape and turned to her. "Look at me."

She did, her hatred for Bobby filling her soul.

"Our father is sick," he said, his voice bitter with hate. "Weak, pathetic, sick. Stupid fuck let that woman pussy-whip him into getting her way every fucking time. When he finally stood up to her and slapped the bitch down, he cried and apologized. Of course she forgave him. What's one bruise when she had whatever she fucking wanted? If he'd only showed her who's boss, she'd never have gotten away with screwing around."

"She didn't. That's your own twisted logic."

"Oh, Lily, you are naïve. Dad finally confronted her

that night. They were in a huge fight when I walked into the kitchen. Dad pounding on her and I thought finally, he was going to kill her."

"What?" Rowan wasn't sure she was hearing Bobby correctly. He saw their father kill their mother? But—hadn't he come in later?

"You heard me. I told him to kill the bitch. And you know what the fucker did? He hit *me*."

Bobby sounded surprised. Rowan was stunned.

"So I did what he never had the balls to do. Took Mama's biggest knife and sliced her open. And he just watched. Stupid fool."

"You? You killed Mama?" Rowan's stomach dry-heaved. She'd *seen* her father with the knife. Saw him kneeling over Mama's body. Saw him drop the knife. Watched as Bobby walked in and said *The bitch is finally dead.*

"Of course I did. He'd never do it. All he ever did was beat up on her and then cry and apologize and whine. Over and over. I was sick and tired of it. I'd have killed him, too, but he wasn't putting up a fight. Just knelt there and picked up the knife and held it. Lost it completely, by the look of him."

"You're sick."

"You think I'm sick? What about *you*? I've read all of your books, Lily. All of them. You came up with crimes so horrific I was shocked." Eyes wide, he splayed his hand across his chest in mock surprise.

"Really, Lily," he continued, "your mind is twisted. I only did what you are too weak to do. Made your fantasies real."

She turned from him, hot with rage she couldn't act on. She started working the ropes again. Almost free. *Patience, Rowan. Patience.*

He'd killed their mother. Her father was no murderer. It was Bobby. She hadn't seen her father stabbing Mama, but assumed it because she'd walked in right afterward and he had been holding the bloody knife.

But it had been Bobby all along.

He started the video again and demanded she watch.

Running on the beach. Taken from this house. "I never understood why you run on the beach when there's a perfectly good gym two miles up the road. It's cold, and that awful smell of kelp and salt. Fucking gross." Then a picture of her and Michael on the beach. Then her and John.

Then her and John on the stairs leading up to her deck. John's hand was on her cheek. She remembered that moment. When she first realized there was a connection between them.

I love you, Rowan.

She willed herself not to show any emotion. It was so hard not to break.

Then the image changed and she was kissing John again, in the dining room. The picture was fuzzy, taken through the window, but it was obvious they were in a passionate embrace.

Her stomach rolled at the thought that Bobby had watched an intimate moment between her and John. That he'd photographed it.

She still felt John's phantom kiss on her lips. She'd take that last taste of him to her grave.

Bobby stared at his little sister. "Well? Do you have anything to say?"

"No."

"Oh, come now, Lily. You must be all torn up inside. Knowing that you're responsible for the deaths of all those people. Doreen. Gina and Natalie and Kimberly Harper. Michael Flynn, your stupid-ass of a drunk bodyguard. He was practically crying in his Scotch that night. Pussy-whipped, just like Dad. Pretty much accepted the fact that you and his brother were doing the dirty deed and he should step out of the way."

What? Michael had actually talked to Bobby? But he wouldn't have known Bobby from a stranger; they'd just been two guys drinking at a bar.

Rowan squirmed with frustration. "You asshole! You know nothing about Michael or anyone else. You're going to rot in hell, you pig."

Bobby laughed, feeding on her rage. "Oh, yeah, bring it on, babe. Bring it on. I knew that ice-cold exterior would melt. I'll bet you're just itching to get to me. After I break your scrawny neck, I'm going to shoot your lover in the back. Seems fitting, doesn't it? Sort of a re-done 'Romeo and Juliet.' Too bad you won't have time to write about it."

She leapt from her seat, hands free. She launched herself at Bobby, oblivious to the sting of the whip across her chest. She didn't realize a scream came from her lungs until she heard it, loud and ringing in her ears.

She had the element of surprise. She put her arms together and swung them at the side of his head. He fell out of the chair with the force of her blow, swearing.

She lunged at him and grasped his neck, pushing her thumbs hard into his windpipe. He thrashed and kicked, throwing her off him. She tried to scramble away, but he grabbed her legs and pulled her back.

Screaming in anger and pain, she fought to escape.

"Bitch, you'll pay!" He slammed her head into the floor. Her vision blurred. He flipped her over so she faced him, then slapped her. "You're going to die. Then I'll get your boyfriend."

He swung, missing as she kicked him hard in the

groin. He grunted and she scurried away, running toward the door.

She had it open, but he slammed it closed behind her and knocked her down.

Then she saw it. The fireplace.

She crawled toward the fireplace and he kicked her.

"Oh, this is too much fun!" Bobby yelled. "Run again."

He kicked her in the side. She hissed, sucked in her breath. A sharp, knifelike pain dug into her side. She lost her breath and willed herself to breathe again, focus. Control.

He pulled her up, his breath heavy and ragged. She stared into familiar blue eyes, eyes filled with a wild, sick pleasure. A slight smile turned his lips up.

Bobby took a gun out of his waistband and pointed it at her face.

"Run," he said, laughing. *"Run!"*

John jumped from the car before Agent Thorne stopped and ran down the sloping driveway. There was a crash from inside, and then the door swung open and he saw her.

Rowan. The dim streetlights cast odd shadows on her face; then he realized it was blood. A man loomed behind her and slammed the door shut.

He's killing her.

Peter was right behind him by the time John reached the door. He turned the knob with his left hand, his gun in his right. The door was unlocked and he swung it open.

"Run!" he heard MacIntosh scream at Rowan.

"MacIntosh!" John yelled.

Bobby swung around, blood streaming from the side of his head. He had a gun.

Rowan slipped from his grasp and stumbled into the brick fireplace, her head hitting the hard surface with a sickening thud.

John's heart jumped as he watched, out of the corner of his eye, Rowan fall. He didn't take his gaze off of Bobby.

"I was going to get you next," Bobby told him. "Now Lily can watch you die."

John started to pull the trigger when Peter stepped from behind him.

"No, Bobby."

"Peter! Get back!" John snapped, trying to block the priest with his body.

A hint of recognition flickered across Bobby's face. "No. It's not possible. You're dead. I saw you."

"You saw what you wanted to see," Peter said. "This must end now. No one else needs to die, Bobby. Put down the gun."

Bobby's features twisted in rage. John kept trying to maneuver in front of Peter, but the damned priest wouldn't stop moving.

Rowan moaned from the fireplace as she tried to sit up, and Bobby's attention momentarily wavered. John rushed him.

Bobby caught sight of the movement and turned, firing his gun at the same time. The force of the bullet struck John's right arm and his gun flew from his grasp.

Bobby laughed and took two steps over to him. "Now you die. And it's even better than I thought—Lily Pad can watch her lover die. Oh, Romeo." Bobby aimed.

"And then *him*." He sneered, jerking the gun toward Peter. "You were supposed to be dead!"

Peter stood in the foyer.

"Bobby, stop this insanity. Now."

Peter's voice was firm, strong. Rowan opened her eyes. *Peter?* What was he doing here? Her vision was blurry, clouded. She fumbled around for something, anything to defend herself with. To defend Peter.

John was unarmed, blood dripping from his arm. Shot. But he was alive. A huge weight lifted from her heart and soul. John hadn't been killed in the explosion.

Everyone I love dies . . .

Not anymore. Bobby's killing spree would end here. Tonight. Now.

"What, preacher man, you going to send me to hell?" Bobby spat out, waving the gun between Peter and John. "Whatever happened to forgiveness?" He barked that cruel, wild laugh he had. It grated on Rowan's mind, her head pounding, echoing. She shook it, trying to regain her full senses.

Weapon. Weapon. She spotted John's gun, but she had double vision. She tried to focus, but it was too far away.

"Bobby, you must want forgiveness. You have to be repentant."

Again, that wild laugh. "You want me to be *sorry?* Okay, I'm sorry." He giggled. "Sorry you were all born."

Rowan finally felt something solid. Metal. Glancing to her right, she saw she was holding a fireplace poker. She tightened her grasp. She had only one chance.

The two men she loved—John and Peter—would die if she didn't succeed.

She couldn't let Bobby win.

Through her failing vision she noticed John moving carefully away from Peter, away from her. She could attack without Bobby's full attention. And keep his gun away from Peter.

She inched forward.

"Bobby, the FBI has surrounded the house," John said. "You won't get away."

"I have hostages," he said mockingly. "Worked with your sister, eh? Sorry she had to be blown up, she was kind of cute. Too bad I didn't have time to screw her."

Anger spread across John's face. "She didn't die," he said. "She made it. I disarmed your amateur attempt at making a bomb. You failed."

"You lie!" Bobby pointed the gun straight at John's head.

Rowan screamed and lunged at Bobby, the poker in her hand.

A gun went off. Bobby's? Then another shot. A third explosion. Rowan didn't know where the sounds were coming from; they seemed to be coming from everywhere.

Bobby turned, eyes wide in rage and pain, and fired as she ran straight at him with the poker. A hot flash of pain hit her left shoulder but she kept moving forward. If she failed, John and Peter would die.

The sick sound of the poker cutting into Bobby's flesh was followed by an inhuman scream. She stumbled and fell on top of him. Each breath hurt her chest.

Large hands pulled her off. She looked up through the haze. "Peter," she whispered. "Run. I couldn't . . ." she coughed and sputtered.

"Shh," he told her and laid her down gently. His lips moved in silent prayer, but Rowan didn't know if he was really quiet or if she just couldn't hear him. He turned to Bobby and made the sign of the cross.

John interrupted Peter. "Don't you dare pray for him," he said as he knelt at Rowan's side.

"He's dying," Peter said simply.

"I hope he burns in hell," John said.

Bobby tried to speak as he clutched the poker sticking out of his stomach. Nothing came out but a gurgle and blood. He sputtered, convulsed, then lay still, his eyes open and fixed.

"John," Rowan murmured, eyes closed.

"I'm here. Open your eyes."

"You're—you're alive." Her eyes fluttered open, then closed again.

"Yes. So are you. Peter, call an ambulance."

"Why—Peter?"

"Roger called him to come out. We didn't know where you were. Tess is safe. You bought us enough time." He leaned over and kissed her, his tears falling on her face. He took off his shirt, wincing as the material pulled out of his wound, and pressed it against the gushing hole in her left shoulder.

"I—I thought you were dead. The bomb." She coughed, her voice weak.

"Stay with me, Rowan. Don't let him win."

"I-I—" She coughed again.

"Shh. Don't talk."

"The ambulance is on the way," Peter said as he squatted and handed John towels. John quickly tossed his shirt aside and held the towels to Rowan's bleeding wound.

Agent Thorne and two other Feds John didn't recognize were searching the place. One knelt beside Bobby and confirmed he was dead.

"How is she?" Thorne asked, worried.

"She'll make it," John said through clenched teeth. *She has to. I don't want to live without her. I don't know if I can.*

"John." Rowan's voice was weak, her breathing shallow.

"Shh. Save your strength."

"I-I love you."

Tears rolled down his cheeks. "Rowan, you know I love you. Stay with me."

"Yes."

"Don't talk." Her blood spread under his fingers, but he kept firm pressure on her shoulder. "Don't you dare die on me."

She closed her eyes and gave an almost imperceptible shake of her head. She coughed.

"It's over, Rowan," John said. "It's over."

CHAPTER

29

Rowan woke up numb and burning at the same time. Her mind was foggy. She tried to open her eyes, but failed. Everything seemed fuzzy and gray. She had to be dead.

Sounds. *Beep-beep-beep.* A low-level hum. Even breathing. Smells. Clean, antiseptic, sterile.

She tried to speak, but it came out a hollow squeak.

"Rowan?"

His voice sounded far away, down a long tunnel. She tried to answer, but her throat was raw and dry. She'd give anything for water. Was this hell? An eternal thirst . . .

"Rowan, it's John."

Suddenly she was back in the beach house, the smell of death surrounding her. Everything came back. The videotape of all the people Bobby killed. The whip. Peter. The gunshots. Stabbing Bobby with the poker. Pain. Intense pain in her shoulder. She'd been shot before, but nothing felt as awful as this. It was as if her arm had been severed and reattached to befit Frankenstein's monster.

John. John had been shot. "J-John." Had she spoken? She couldn't tell; her ears throbbed.

"Shh, honey. It's me. It's me. You're okay. You're going to be okay now." He sounded greatly relieved. Worried and tired, but relieved.

She felt him grasp her hand. She was alive. And John was alive.

Bobby was dead. She'd killed him.

Maybe there was a God after all.

"I'm sorry."

"Stop. There's nothing for you to be sorry about. Bobby's gone. And you're okay."

She started coughing. "Wa-ter."

Something touched her lips. A straw. She sucked as hard as she could and managed to bring up a sip of water. It coated her throat and she was grateful for its coolness.

"Tess is okay?" She vaguely remembered John telling her Tess was alive, but she had to hear it again.

"Yes, she's fine. Broken arm. Both Roger and Quinn are going to make it, too."

"But—how—?" Then she remembered John saying that she'd bought them enough time. Enough time to get away from the bomb.

She felt tension leaving her body, as if the uncertainty had kept her worried even while she'd been unconscious.

"How long—?" How long had she been here? A day? Two? Longer?

"Shh. Don't talk, sweetheart." She felt a feather of a kiss on her hand.

"Rowan, I want you to listen to me. Don't talk, just listen. You had nothing to do with Bobby's crimes. Nothing. I know you, I know the guilt is eating at you. But you must not blame yourself."

He squeezed her hand. "Rowan, I saw the video Bobby forced you to watch. Please, please don't let it torment you."

The images on that videotape would forever be etched

in her mind. She would have done anything to spare John the pain of seeing his brother like that.

She forced herself to open her eyes. Slowly. As they adjusted to the bright lights, she focused on John.

He hadn't shaved in two, three days. His hair even looked longer, not the perfect military cut he'd maintained for the three weeks she'd known him.

Three weeks. Had everything happened in that short a time? It didn't seem possible. It was as if her entire previous life had been a short prologue leading up to a long, torturous book she'd been forced to read.

So much death. So much blood. But it was over. Truly over.

"Peter?" She was certain she'd seen him there, at the house with Bobby. Heard his familiar, kind, loving voice.

"He's fine. He's here, waiting for you to recover." He brought her hand up to his lips and kissed it, then brought the straw to her mouth. She sipped, feeling a tad stronger than the first time she drank.

"You've just been through hell and back. You're alive. I'm alive. We've made it. We're going to get through this because we're together."

"John—"

"Rowan, you love me. You told me so, and you can't take it back."

"I do. I love you," she whispered. But how could she explain that she still wasn't a complete person? That she needed time to think about everything that had happened, to really and truly put it behind her? She'd never forget, but she felt hope that she could move on. Move forward.

"But—" she began.

"No buts, I said." He leaned over and lightly kissed her. "Together, Rowan. We've been loners for so long, both of us. But together we're stronger."

Together we're stronger. She smiled weakly. "Yes, we are."

John tensed when someone knocked on the door. Still in protection mode. Surprisingly, the thought didn't bother her like it did before. It was comforting to have someone care about her. Especially someone she loved.

John turned without letting go of her hand, relaxing when Quinn Peterson walked in. A large swatch of gauze was taped above his left eye, partially covered by his sandy hair, and his wrist was wrapped in an ace bandage.

"You're awake," Quinn said, relieved.

"You thought I was a goner?" she asked. Her voice wasn't strong, but at least she was coherent.

"No, you're a survivor." He sighed and ran a hand through his hair. "The Butcher is back."

Rowan closed her eyes. "Dammit. She doesn't deserve this!"

"Am I missing something?" John asked.

"My roommate at Quantico, Miranda Moore, lives in Bozeman, Montana," Rowan said. "She'd been attacked by a serial killer and lived. Years ago," she explained quickly when she saw the shock on John's face. "That's how we know each other. After her attack, she decided to join the FBI."

"Oh, she's one of yours."

"No, she never graduated Quantico." Rowan glared at Quinn. He stared back at her. She shook her head. No, he didn't understand. Maybe he never would. It sure didn't help that he and Miranda were both so stubborn.

"What happened?" she asked Quinn after an awkward silence.

"Another college student is missing, but the sheriff is

certain it's the Butcher. He called me this morning and asked me to go up there and help. I've already cleared it with my office." He paused, his jaw tight. "The bastard has been killing for fifteen years. We have to find a way to stop him."

Quinn looked so distraught Rowan wondered if it was really the killer or the thought of facing Miranda after all this time that had him worried. The Quinn Peterson she knew didn't back down from a professional challenge.

"You'll do what you do best, Quinn," Rowan said. "You'll investigate."

"Every year he kills and still eludes the police."

"Maybe he'll slip up."

She and Quinn stared at each other. Contrary to popular belief, most serial killers—especially the sadistic kind like the Bozeman Butcher—didn't want to be caught. His job was to stop them. Rowan had confidence that if the Butcher made even a small mistake, Quinn's steadfast doggedness would stop him.

"I'm leaving tonight for Seattle to pick up clean clothes, then I'm heading for Montana in the morning," he said. "I just wanted to come by and wish you well. You deserve a little happiness." He looked pointedly at John.

"I'm making it my number-one priority," John said, bringing her hand up to his lips. The simple, romantic gesture moved her.

"Give my best to Miranda," Rowan said as Quinn turned to open the door.

He glanced over his shoulder and she couldn't read his face. "I will." He left.

"Did I miss something?" John asked.

"No. Just Quinn being arrogant and stubborn." And Miranda, she thought.

"I figured that out working with him these last weeks." John smiled. "But he's a good guy."

"Yeah, he is. One of the best."

John leaned over and kissed her lightly on the lips, then kissed her hand again.

"I hear you have a cabin in Colorado. Believe it or not, I've never been to Colorado. Tess is taking a civilian job with the FBI in Washington, so there's no reason for me to hang around L.A. Besides, I just have this little studio with nothing but a bed and radio. What say you and I head off for a little R & R? Indefinitely."

Rowan sighed and closed her eyes.

She loved John. And for the first time since she was ten, Rowan felt like she could love someone who would be around for a long, long time.

Was it fate? Destiny? She didn't know. But she couldn't imagine waking up alone in bed anymore. She didn't want to fall asleep with her Glock as her only companion. She wanted more. A friend. A lover.

A husband.

That was down the road. Their love had been forged in a hellish world created by Bobby MacIntosh. The thought of her sick, sick brother made her stomach roll over and she stifled a sob.

But Bobby was dead. And this time, it wasn't a lie.

"Rowan? Are you okay? We don't have to rush anything—"

John sounded so defeated, as if she might turn him away.

"No, no," she said.

"That's okay. I understand."

"No!" she said more firmly. She swallowed, opened her eyes and looked at him, willing him to understand what she really meant.

"I love you John."

"I know. You're just not ready for—"

"Shh." She motioned for more water. If he was going to make this difficult, she needed more fuel.

She swallowed the cool liquid and started again. "I need you."

At first he looked skeptical, then optimistic. "I never expected to hear that from you."

"I never expected to say it. To anyone."

She squeezed his hand.

"Does that mean you don't mind me joining you in Colorado?"

"I need a lot of work," she admitted. "I still have some—problems. I don't know if the nightmares are going to go away, or if I won't snap at you or shut you out or—"

"Rowan!" he said, his voice sharp. "Do you think I care? I have baggage as well. You know about Denny. And Reginald Pomera. If I have a chance, I'm going to go after him."

"I know. You'll get your demon, John. Just like I got mine."

"But now," he said, his voice softer and full of the love she felt from him, "I have someone to come home to. If you'll have me."

"There's no one I'd rather share my home with," she said.

She could put everything behind her. And she would much rather wake up with John by her side—in good times and bad—than live the rest of her life without love.

"Then it's a deal. As soon as they spring you, we're going to Colorado. Together."

"That sounds perfect," she said quietly before drifting off to a dreamless sleep.

PROLOGUE

I don't want to die.

Her breath came in shallow gasps, her mouth gaped open as she violently pulled air in and pushed it out. In. Out. Focus. Run, Miranda, run! But be quiet. Left foot. Right foot. Left foot. Wasn't that a Dr. Seuss book? A hysterical giggle threatened to escape but she swallowed the sound. Quiet. Above all, breathe quietly.

Miranda grimaced at the thrashing behind her. A sob escaped from her friend. *Sharon, shut up!* she wanted to scream. *He'll hear you! He'll kill us!*

She ran faster even though Sharon was falling farther and farther behind. Daylight was scarce. One, two hours left at the most.

If they didn't make it to the river, he would find them.

I don't want to die. I'm too young, please God, I'm only twenty-one. I won't die! Not here, not like this.

Miranda's sight blurred as sweat dripped into her eyes. She didn't dare wipe her face for fear of losing her balance on the rocky terrain. Her bare feet ached with each step, but they were so cold only the sharper rocks cut through the numbness. *Watch where you're going! One wrong step and you'll break your leg and he'll find you . . .*

A faint, familiar echo reached her ears. She wanted to stop and listen but didn't dare slow her pace. She scurried another hundred feet before putting a name to the sound.

Water! Running water.

It had to be the river. What she'd promised Sharon would lead to freedom. She silently thanked Professor Austin and his tedious geology class. Without it, she wouldn't have known where to run, the signs indicating a river was close. After the miles she and Sharon had already covered, surely now they would make it.

From behind, a shriek.

Miranda stopped at Sharon's startled cry, whipped around, her heart gripped with dread. Sprawled on the hard ground, Sharon lay half obscured by undergrowth, sobbing in pain. Her shirt rode up, exposing bare buttocks to the cold Montana air.

She stared at Sharon's fallen body, the sound of the whip that had made those hideous marks ricocheting in her mind.

"Get up!" Miranda urged, panic clawing her.

"I can't," Sharon sobbed, her face buried in decaying leaves.

"Please," Miranda begged, not wanting to backtrack. She glanced over her shoulder, toward freedom. The water so close.

She looked back at Sharon and bit her lip. *He* was still

out there. If she stopped to help Sharon, he'd kill them both.

She took a step toward the river. Guilt tickled Miranda's spine. She *knew* she could make it.

"Go," Sharon said.

Miranda almost missed the single word. Her eyes widened at the implication. "No, not without you. Get up!"

For a moment, Miranda thought Sharon hadn't heard her, by choice or distance. Then, slowly, the blonde pushed herself up on all fours. Sharon's terrified eyes locked with Miranda's. *Please, Sharon, please,* Miranda willed. *Time is running out.*

Sharon grabbed a small sapling and braced herself. "Okay," she said. "Okay."

Miranda sighed in relief as Sharon took a shaky step forward. She began to turn toward the river, toward freedom.

Whap-whap!

The shot echoed in the forest. The flutter of wings and the squawking of startled birds seemed to move the sky. As Miranda watched, Sharon's chest opened. Deep red, darkened by shadows of dusk, spread across the filthy white shirt. In the moment between life and death, Miranda watched Sharon's stunned expression turn to bliss. Relief.

Death was better than suffering.

"Sharon!" She covered her mouth with her filthy hand, tasting and smelling rotting dirt. The coppery scent of blood hung in the air. Her chest heaved with mute sobs as she watched Sharon's body fall to the ground.

"Run."

That voice. Bloodcurdling in its dry, grave monotone. The same emotionless pulse he'd used when he fed them and whipped them; when he touched them or raped them.

She trembled even before she made out his silhouette. In camouflage pants and a thick black coat, he stood among the trees, face obscured by a cap and the darkening sky.

Three hundred feet away? Two hundred? Closer? She would never make it. She would die.

His shout echoed through the mountainside. He took one step forward, cradling a rifle. He brought the stock up to his shoulder.

Miranda ran.

CHAPTER
1

Twelve Years Later

Nick Thomas stared at the outline of the petite body under the blinding yellow tarp. He pinched the bridge of his nose, swallowing anger so bitter he could taste it. The foul stench of death surrounded him and he turned away.

He still pictured the dead, broken body of twenty-year-old Rebecca Douglas as he'd found her only an hour ago.

"Sheriff?"

Nick looked up as Deputy Lance Booker approached. He was clean cut, a good cop, though a mite wet behind the ears. Much like Nick had been twelve years ago when he'd been called out to his first murder scene. "Deputy."

"Jim said there's a guy claiming to be an FBI agent at the road, wanting to be let through. Quincy Peterson."

Quinn. Nick hadn't seen him in years, ten to be exact, but they shared an e-mail relationship since he'd been elected sheriff more than three years ago. After the Denver sisters had been found.

Now there were seven dead girls. That they knew about.

"Let him through."

"Yes, sir." Booker frowned, but relayed the orders through his walkie-talkie. In matters that would as a rule fall under their local jurisdiction, no law officer welcomed outside interference, and usually Nick was no different. Nick didn't mention that it was his call to Quinn last week that precipitated this visit.

Nick turned and walked away from the deputy, away from the bright tarp, down the path to where Rebecca Douglas's last steps were evident. He squatted next to an unusable footprint, a mess in wet, hardening mud. It might have been Rebecca's last step. Or the killer's. It had rained nearly three inches in the last two days, a heavy deluge that saturated a ground recently recovered from a cold, wet Montana winter. The clouds broke this morning, the sky such a vivid blue and the air so refreshing that Nick would have enjoyed it if he hadn't been called to a crime scene.

He closed his eyes and breathed the clean, crisp air of his Gallatin Valley. He loved Montana, the vast beauty and sheer majesty of its mountains, its swift rivers, green valleys, big sky. The people were good, too, down-to-earth. They cared about their neighbors, took care of their own. When Rebecca Douglas turned up missing, hundreds of men and women—many from the university where she'd been a student—had scoured the wilderness between Bozeman and Yellowstone looking for her.

Nick's jaw tightened in restrained fury. Good people, but for one. One who had killed Rebecca and at least six other women in the past fifteen years. And other women were still missing. Would they ever find their bodies? Had the harsh Montana weather or four-legged animals obliterated their remains? He'd never forget finding Penny Thompson's remains—nothing but a skull and scattered bones. She had been identified through her dental records.

Nick surveyed the area. Tall pines grew primarily downslope; as the mountain rose the trees thinned out. Possibly an old logging trail, the ancient, heavily overgrown road he'd driven on was unmapped. It appeared to end here, in this natural clearing, roughly thirty feet square. On the edge of this clearing, Rebecca's body lay.

They'd mark off the area in grids and search for anything that might possibly lead back to the killer. But if it was the same bastard, they'd find nothing. He was so damn perfect in his every crime that even their one surviving witness could tell them little. Defeat weighed heavy in Nick's heart, but he would not give up.

Sometimes, he hated his job.

He turned when he heard an SUV roll into the clearing, rocks and muddy clumps of leaves shooting out from the backs of all four tires. Sun reflected off the windshield and Nick shielded his eyes to watch Quinn approach.

The SUV jerked to a stop behind Nick's dark green police-issue truck. The driver's door opened and Quincy Peterson jumped out, slamming the door shut and striding toward Nick. Quinn hadn't changed much since Nick had last seen him, he still looked more like a damn cover model than a fifteen-year veteran of the FBI. Nick stood and absently brushed the dirt off his jeans.

"Rebecca Douglas?" Quinn nodded toward the covered body. His face was blank, but his dark eyes revealed the same anger and sadness that Nick felt.

"Yep. We'll need a positive ID, but—" There was no doubt it was the missing woman. He glanced at Quinn and raised an eyebrow at the bandage over his left eye. "Bar fight?" he asked, half-joking.

Quinn reached up and touched the bandage as if he'd forgotten it was there. "The last few days have been quite eventful," he said. "I'll tell you about it later." He glanced around. "When are you processing the scene?"

"I wanted you to check it out first, but I have my men waiting up on the main highway."

Nick didn't know why the Fed made him feel so inferior. Maybe it had something to do with Quinn's quiet confidence, his knack for seeing through bullshit, always getting to the heart of the matter. Or, maybe it was because Nick had puked his guts out at his first murder scene and Quincy Peterson hadn't.

Or maybe it was that the woman Nick loved was in love with Quinn.

Despite all that, there was no one Nick trusted more than Special Agent Quincy Peterson.

Quinn bent down, pulled on latex gloves, and lifted back the tarp. His square jaw clenched and a vein twitched in his neck at the sight.

Rebecca had been beautiful. Now, her long blond hair was tangled, matted and caked in mud. The happy face reproduced on thousands of flyers was gone. She was swollen, purple, grotesque in death. The recent rains had washed some of the dirt from her naked body, leaving her pale and blue.

Her neck had been cut, slashed deep with a sharp knife, though there was very little blood to see. It had been washed into the ground by the rain, along with any trace evidence. Her body showed signs of abuse. Torture. Bruises of all shapes and hues of purple covered her skin. Her breasts had been clamped into some sort of vise. The strange marks wouldn't have indicated that to most eyes, but both Nick and Quinn had read the coroner's reports for each of the six other women murdered in these woods, and had grown familiar with this killer's m.o.

Quinn removed the tarp to study the victim's legs and feet, much as Nick had done when he first arrived on scene. Her left leg was crooked, broken. Her feet were covered in raw blisters and deep cuts. From running.

She was white, so pale, lifeless. Clinically, her gaunt, thin skin told the cops that she'd bled out, her life drained from her. She died quickly; nobody could survive long with the carotid artery sliced open. Small consolation for the previous week of terror she'd lived through.

Quinn covered the body again. "Coroner been called?"

Nick nodded. "He'll be out by noon. He was in the middle of an autopsy on that hiker we found up on the north ridge the other day."

"So who found Rebecca's body?"

"Three boys—the McClain brothers and Ryan Parker.

The Parkers have a spread three, four miles west of here. The boys took a couple horses for the day, were going to shoot their .22s at rabbits and whatnot." He shrugged and added, "It's Saturday."

"Where are they now?"

"A deputy took them home. Told them to sit tight at the Parkers' until I came by."

Quinn nodded, surveying the scene that Nick had marked with yellow and black crime-scene tape. Observing the clearing, the old path, the trees.

"It looks like she came up through that underbrush over there." Nick gestured. "I checked it out, but didn't go down the trail yet."

"If you can call it a trail," Quinn said, frowning at the overgrowth.

"I'll just take a look while you call in your team. How many people do you have?"

"I have a dozen of my own men right now, more later, and a crime-scene specialist. I'll need volunteers if we're going to do this right."

"Agreed. The more eyes the better, but no hot shots. We can't have someone going off half-cocked." Quinn put his hand on Nick's shoulder. "I know you were hoping the bastard dropped dead after Ellen and Elaine Denver were found. I'm sorry I couldn't come out personally then. But Agent Thorne is good. She would have found something."

Nick agreed, but he still felt so damn helpless. The Butcher was the only bastard who had ever gotten away with murder under his watch. "It's been three frickin' years! Three years since he killed. And we had nothing then—no clues, no leads, no suspects."

"And there are other girls missing." Quinn didn't need to remind Nick. The missing girls haunted Nick in his sleep.

"It's been slow, but we're gathering evidence," Quinn continued. "We have casings, bullets, a partial from Elaine Denver's locket. We'll get him." Quinn turned and walked down the path. He sounded so confident. Why couldn't Nick feel the same?

He glanced down at the outline of Rebecca Douglas. At least she would have a proper burial. Closure for her family. But not for him.

He thought of Miranda.

He started toward his truck. He'd put in the call for all available law enforcement to head to this location. Then he heard the unique but familiar sound of a Jeep bouncing over the rough trail. He didn't need to see the vehicle to know who approached.

"Damn."

The red Jeep jerked to a stop behind Quinn's rental. Almost before the truck halted, Miranda Moore jumped out, the mud no match for her heavy boots and confident stride. Deputy Booker approached her, and she glared at him without stopping as she pulled a red down-filled vest over her black flannel shirt. In any other situation, Nick would have grinned at the way Booker backed off.

Then she focused her sharp blue eyes on him.

His heart quickened and his stomach lurched. If only he'd had more time to prepare for her inevitable arrival. If he'd been warned she was on her way, he could have steeled himself for the confrontation.

"Miranda," he said as she approached, "I—"

"Damn you, Nick!" She poked a finger at his chest. "Damn you!" Nothing intimidated Miranda. Though she was tall for a woman—at least five-foot-nine—he had six inches and a hundred pounds on her. You'd think he'd intimidate her, that any man would frighten her after what she'd gone through, but he guessed he shouldn't be surprised. She was a survivor. She didn't expose her fear.

"Miranda, I was going to call you. I didn't know for certain it was Rebecca. I didn't want you to have to go through it again."

Her darkening eyes told him she didn't believe him. "Screw that. Screw *you*! You *promised* you'd call." She brushed past him and strode over to the tarp, staring at the covered body. Her fists clenched, her shoulders reverberated in tension.

Nick wanted to stop her; to protect her from seeing another dead girl. Most of all, he wanted to protect her from herself.

And she'd always been perfectly clear that she didn't want Nick's protection.

Miranda worked to control her temper. She shouldn't have yelled at Nick, but dammit! He'd *promised*. For seven days she'd been searching for Rebecca, the nightmares destroying the few hours of sleep she allowed herself. He'd promised she'd be the first to know when they found her.

Neither she nor Nick had expected to find Rebecca alive.

She stared at the yellow tarp in the middle of the quiet earth tones of the land and inhaled sharply, her throat raw with hot anger and unwanted, ice-cold fear. Her fists squeezed into tight balls, her nails digging into her palms. She knew it was Rebecca Douglas. But she had to see for herself, force herself to look at the latest victim. For strength, for courage.

For vengeance.

She pulled latex gloves over her long fingers, knelt beside the still woman, and fingered the edge of the tarp. "Rebecca," she said, her voice a whisper, "you're not alone. I promise you I'll find him. He'll pay for what he did to you."

She swallowed, hesitated, then drew back the tarp to reveal the girl she'd been searching for, twenty hours a day for the last seven days.

At first, Miranda didn't see the swollen face, the slit throat, or the many cuts washed clean by the rain. The image of the young twenty-year-old in Miranda's mind was beautiful, as she had been when she was alive.

Rebecca had a contagious laugh, according to her best friend Candi. Rebecca cared about those less fortunate and volunteered one night a week reading to the infirm at Deaconess, according to her career counselor Ron Owens. A straight-A student, Rebecca had wanted to be a veterinarian, according to her biology teacher Greg Marsh.

Rebecca hadn't been perfect. But no one had shared the less attractive stories while she'd been missing.

No one would ever repeat them now that she was dead.

As she watched, the image of Rebecca she'd held so close to her heart during the hours and hours of searching morphed into the broken body before her.

"You're free," she told her. "Free at last."

Sharon. I'm so sorry.

"No one can hurt you anymore."

She reached over and touched her hair, brushed a matted piece to the side, cupped her cheek.

Stay in control.

She repeated her mantra. How many times would she have to go through this? How many dead girls would they bury? She'd thought it would get easier. But if she didn't keep her emotions tight and protected, she feared she'd collapse under the enormity of the Butcher's continued success—and her own failure to stop him.

She eased the tarp over Rebecca's face, hating to do it. The act of covering the body reminded Miranda of the other dead girls they'd found. Of Sharon.

The morning Miranda led them to Sharon's body was so cold she'd shivered constantly under the half dozen layers of clothing she wore. She'd wanted to return the day after she'd been rescued, but she hadn't been allowed to leave the hospital. When she'd tried walking on her own, her damaged feet had failed her.

She'd been too numb to cry, too tired to argue. She'd mapped out the location as best she could remember, but the search team couldn't find Sharon.

Miranda couldn't bear the thought of her friend's body exposed for yet another night. Leaving her to the bears and cougars and bugs. So the following morning she withstood the pain in her legs and led the search team and law enforcement back to where Sharon lay. She had to see her one last time.

She might have been in shock; that's what the doctors said. But she walked with help. She knew where Sharon had fallen, would never forget it. She brought them to the spot, and there Sharon lay. Exactly as she'd fallen when the hunter killed her.

Silence filled the air, birds and animals mourning with the humans. Even the spring wind held its breath; not one leaf rustled as everyone finally grasped exactly what had happened to Miranda and Sharon.

The sudden cry of a hawk split the stillness, and the wind gently blew.

The medic covered Sharon's body with a bright green plastic tarp while the sheriff's team started searching for evidence. Miranda couldn't stop staring at the tarp. Sharon was dead underneath it, reduced to a lump under a sheet of plastic. So wrong, so inhuman.

It was then that Miranda had first broken down and cried.

An FBI agent carried her the three miles back to the road. His name was Quincy Peterson.

On the hunt for more heart-racing suspense from ALLISON BRENNAN?

Catch the whole series!

THE PREY

Rowan Smith, hoping to leave her violent past far behind, left the FBI to pursue a career in writing. But obscured by shadows, a killer patiently waits. He plans to break her first, knowing just which nightmares will drive her into his trap.

THE HUNT

Years ago Miranda Moore survived the Bozeman Butcher, a twisted murderer who hunts women in the Montana wilderness. Now a search-and-rescue specialist, Miranda must once again face her worst nightmare when another young woman turns up missing. The hunt is on, and there can only be one victor in this ruthless butcher's game.

THE KILL

While FBI scientist Olivia St. Martin couldn't save her sister's life, she did testify to help put the killer behind bars. But now, years later, new DNA evidence has surfaced that exonerates him. And Miranda must risk everything to find the real killer . . . before he finds her.

 Ballantine Books • www.ballantinebooks.com